WAR OF THE DONS

The Guarda brothers run capo Messina's territory. Pepe, the oldest, is the muscle. Nuncio, the younger brother, is the accountant. And Marco, he's the wolf. Restless, hungry, he's through taking orders. It's his idea to get rid of Messina and take over. But to do that, the hit has got to look like an accident, or they risk the wrath of Messina's boss, Don Angelo. So Marco hires a twitchy drug addict with a penchant for danger, a guy who knows how to turn Messina's simple hospital visit into a fatality. It's all going so well, so smoothly. Then Don Angelo steps in to take control, and the Guarda brothers really go to war.

BLACK MAFIA

Cutter used to be part of the movement, but got busted for knocking over a bank. He did his time, now he's out. But things have changed. His former mentor is now a teacher, and wants nothing to do with him. It's all Cutter can do to stay one step ahead of the Man. And now some white guys are coming into the Belt to stir up trouble, busting the local action and making it look like a Perrini job. But Perrini is quite happy with the status quo. Sure he skims the Belt, but he's not looking for trouble. Trouble finds him anyway in the form of Don Santino's nephew, Angelo, who's got a hidden agenda all his own. And that's when Cutter figures it's time to make *his* move.

PETER RABE BIBLIOGRAPHY

From Here to Maternity
  (1955; non-fiction)
Stop This Man! (1955)
Benny Muscles In (1955)
A Shroud for Jesso (1955)
A House in Naples (1956)
Kill the Boss Goodbye (1956)
Agreement to Kill (1957)
Journey Into Terror (1957)
Mission for Vengeance (1958)
Blood on the Desert (1958)
Anatomy of a Killer (1960)
My Lovely Executioner (1960)
Murder Me for Nickels (1960)
The Box (1962)
His Neighbor's Wife (1962)
Tobruk (1967)
War of the Dons (1972)
Black Mafia (1974)
The Silent Wall (2011)
The Return of Marvin Palaver
  (2011)

Daniel Port series:
Dig My Grave Deep (1956)
The Out is Death (1957)
It's My Funeral (1957)
The Cut of the Whip (1958)
Bring Me Another Corpse (1959)
Time Enough to Die (1959)

Manny deWitt series:
Girl in a Big Brass Bed (1965)
The Spy Who Was Three Feet Tall
  (1966)
Code Name Gadget (1967)

As by Marco Malaponte
New Man in the House (1963)
Her High-School Lover (1963)

As by J. T. MacCargo
Mannix #2: A Fine Day for Dying
  (1975)
Mannix #4: Round Trip to
  Nowhere (1975)

Short Stories
"Hard Case Redhead"
  (*Mystery Tales*, 1959)
"A Matter of Balance"
  (*Story*, 1961)

WAR OF THE DONS

BLACK MAFIA

TWO NOVELS BY
PETER RABE

INTRODUCTION BY RICK OLLERMAN

Stark House Press • Eureka California

WAR OF THE DONS / BLACK MAFIA

Published by Stark House Press
1315 H Street
Eureka, CA 95501
griffinskye3@sbcglobal.net
www.starkhousepress.com

ISBN-13: 978-1-944520-52-6

Book design by Mark Shepard, SHEPGRAPHICS.COM
Proofreading by Bill Kelly

First Stark House Press Edition: September 2018

FIRST EDITION

The End of the Line:
Peter Rabe's Last Mafia Stories

by Rick Ollerman

Mob novels and stories are no stranger to popular fiction. Having been a mainstay of pulp magazines from the Prohibition twenties through Don Pendleton's paperback original (PBO) "Executioner" series that began in 1969 (still being written now, with a Bradley Cooper-starring movie franchise in the works), stories of the shadowy and infamous Mafia or La Cosa Nostra, Donald E. Westlake's "Outfit," David Chase's television series *The Sopranos,* and far too many works to even contemplate a bibliography, have been pouring out of the minds of writers for decades. And there's no reason to think they will stop.

What better villain than a shadowy organization with enough power and influence to corrupt officials at all levels of power, including all the way to the top? To seat a President? An organization where defiance means retribution that is swift and permanent.

When author Mario Puzo was starting his career, he worked with Martin Goodman's Magazine Management Company writing for Goodman's line of men's magazines. Most of Puzo's work had been inspired by his time in World War II and he was tasked with writing mostly fictionalized war tales. (The other part of the company was called Timely Comics—later it would change its name to Marvel. In those days it was the magazine division that brought in all the money.)

Puzo had written two novels for adults, 1955's *The Dark Arena* and a decade later, *The Fortunate Pilgrim,* but together they had earned him, an inveterate and debt-ridden gambler, a modest $6500. It wasn't until his next book, sold without an outline to Putnam, where Puzo related more or less real-life stories of New York's Five Families, that he hit it big. Putnam bought *The Godfather*, the titular character based on Puzo's own mother, and it stayed on the bestseller charts for 67 weeks after it was published in 1969. The subsequent paperback rights alone sold for $410,000. The gambling debt that Puzo had owed when he'd first spoken with Putnam were gone and a new renaissance for the Mafia novel was born.

When Don Pendleton kicked off the PBO men's adventure series genre that same year with his first Executioner title, *War Against the Mafia*, he said: "I wanted an enemy beyond redemption—an enemy that all civilized procedures had failed to put down. The Mafia was ready-made. They embodied all the evils of mankind." (from Linda Pendleton, www.donpendleton.com)

Puzo and Pendleton were right. This was decades after much of America held a nudge-nudge, wink-wink attitude toward the mob and its most public face, Al "Scarface" Capone. After all, in the age of a supposedly dry country, wasn't he the one who got them their booze, gave rise to speakeasies and private clubs, helped kick off an entire culture centered around grown-ups playing naughty? It took a terrible killing field, the St. Valentine's Day Massacre, for the public to realize the cherubic and charismatic Capone wasn't just the "give the people what they want" good-time Al. No, this was the same guy who ended up in a cage in Alcatraz, flinging his feces at other inmates while syphilis destroyed his brain before he was granted early released to die in ignominy at his home in Miami.

No, this was the time after the infamous 1957 meeting at Appalachin where police blundered into a meeting of dozens of organized crime's top figures, a time when the Genovese family was trying to consolidate power as the first of the five families, and a time when pictures of men in tailored suits where shown in black and white pictures sprawled across the dinner tables or in front entranceways of their favorite restaurants, or the seats of their automobiles, riddled with holes.

Importantly, after Appalachin, this was the first time that J. Edgar Hoover publicly admitted to what every underground creature already knew: the Sicilian Mafia was more than a myth. It was real.

The success of Puzo's book (and subsequent movies) wasn't lost on the copycat nature of the entertainment industry. The book itself is notable for what it reveals at the time it was published. It's not clear how the long-time gambler Puzo knew what he knew about the inner workings of the mob, but he certainly knew enough to make it *feel* real. The book reads less like an adventure novel and more like a memoir told in the third-person. As an exposé it's a thrilling work, much more so than as a work of fiction.

There is no humor in the book and the plot itself is fairly minimal. It gave what many took to be the closest thing to an inside look that we'd gotten yet of the Mafia itself; it was an organization, much like a business where, except that when a deal went bad, murder was often the consequence. Unlike earlier pulp story references where machine-gun fire seemed to be the point of the stories, Puzo gave us some choice dialogue and phrases, and showed us the consequences of not just men of power, but men of power and violence.

A rush of writers followed not just Puzo's path, but also Pendleton's, whose series stayed in the more outlandish and idealistic mode. Pendleton gave us a hero, Mack Bolan, to stand against the mob. There was no such character in Puzo's work.

Fawcett Gold Medal, *The Godfather's* mass market publisher, developed a logo of sorts that contained the words "From the publishers of The Godfather," where "The Godfather" was presented in the same typeface as that used on the actual book's cover. Gold Medal used this on Mafia books from several of their writers, one of whom had been one of *Black Mask* magazine's early core of hard-boiled writers, W. T. Ballard. Using his wife's initials in place of his own, "P. D. Ballard" produced two mob books with that Gold Medal logo, *Brothers in Blood* in 1972, and *The Death Brokers* in 1973.

Another writer whose work sported that logo was Peter Rabe, a huge seller for Gold Medal during a furious period in the late fifties to early sixties. Many of Rabe's best books were about the Mafia. A Jewish German émigré who came to America ahead of the Nazis in World War II, Rabe spent a lot of time in Italy, at one point moving there to seek treatment for a fatal medical condition with which he had been mistakenly diagnosed.

Known by many as a "mob writer," books like *Benny Muscles In* (1955), *A Shroud for Jesso* (1955), *Kill the Boss Good-By* (1956), his Daniel Port series, and *The Box* (1962) were horribly titled (by the publisher—except for *The Box*) but showed Rabe's unique abilities as a writer. Trained as a psychologist, Rabe claimed that this fact did not influence his writing but it's ludicrous to think that someone versed in the study of the human mind and its affects on behaviors in different contexts could separate that from the characters he would create. Indeed, it's the combination of the authenticity of Rabe's characters—their real-life mental illnesses and fears rather than the common quirks assigned to many of today's contemporary protagonists—combined with his unique writing style—nobody has ever written sentences like Rabe—that have made his books so influential over the years. Especially among other writers.

Where Puzo gave us a multi-generational story of the fortunes of a large family and organization, Rabe gave us the stories of the soldiers, the individuals on the ground. He told us about the wannabes, the betrayed, the big guys that tried to be bigger but couldn't, the big guy whose mind fails him while still on top with sharks at his heels. If Puzo showed us the macro, Rabe gives us the micro. Like Puzo, Rabe offers no heroes.

Just as *The Godfather* popularized a version of a more realistic Mafia, Rabe gave them a face on the street. Not the big fish in the country estates and the fancy restaurants uptown, he let us in on what it was like to want to get there but not quite have the stuff for it. To maybe be a bit too ambitious, or a bit heavy on the dope or the horses, or maybe they thought a little bit more of themselves than anyone else did. Whatever the case, the dream was over and it died hard but the answer at any level was the same: violence, often laced with spite and dosed with vengeance, or revenge.

The last two books published under Peter Rabe's own name before he passed away in 1990 were both post-*Godfather* books, and both coming as that particular cottage industry was winding down. This is unfortunate because both of the books are uniformly fine and deserve to be thought of more as vintage Peter Rabe works rather than grouped together with a largely forgettable faddish group of "mob lit of the '70s."

The first of these, bearing that same "From the publishers of The Godfather" emblem on the cover, was Gold Medal's *War of the Dons* from 1972. Rabe thought of the book as *The Gallo Brothers* but with the exceptions of *The Box* and *A House in Naples* (1956), Rabe's titles had all been given to him by Fawcett.

In the usual Rabe complex plotting, the book is a story within a story that ends with a twist. There are three brothers, each with their own strengths but more importantly, each with their own weaknesses. In the deft hands of Rabe, these are shown as both things used to their advantages and used against them by their opponents as the brothers attempt to rise in the organization.

The second book is 1974's *Black Mafia*, a Gold Medal that lacks the now passé cover reference to Mario Puzo's book but instead references Rabe's own *War of the Dons* as well as the blurb, "A brutally authentic novel." Which is exactly what it is.

In *Black Mafia* Rabe actually brings together two worlds, the Mafia and the black ghetto. Rabe said the *Shaft* movie with Richard Roundtree was doing well just then (from the 1971 book by Ernest Tidyman) and he felt he was being "opportunistic" by using the ghetto as a theme. In this same interview (with George Tuttle, *The Big Book of Noir*, Carroll & Graf, 1998) he also said he'd been fascinated with a particular crime family in New York at the time. From those two things he gave us *Black Mafia*.

As a book, it is a hard look at hard people doing hard things in a harder world. But it's written so well and is so elegantly plotted that, as with all of Rabe's work, the ending is as unpredictable as the location of each card after you toss a shuffled deck in the air. The fad days of the Mafia crime novel may have been over but then, as now, there is always room for well-written and exciting thrillers of the old school definition, and *Black Mafia* is a fitting if unwelcome end to Rabe's publishing career. He began teaching at a university instead of producing more books, much to the loss of the world of crime fiction.

The following year saw two novelizations of TV's *Mannix* under the house name of "J. T. MacCargo" that are credited to Peter Rabe. These are *A Fine Day for Dying* and *Round Trip to Nowhere* but unlike his other pseudonymous work, these books read as though someone has done a thorough job of de-Rabing them and little is left of Rabe's style. This is in direct contrast to the brilliant job Rabe did when he undertook what we now call the "media tie-in" version of the 1967 Rock Hudson vehicle, *Tobruk*. In that book, Rabe brought his sort of perspective to the characters and filled in the plot holes of the movie and made a literary version that was very good indeed. Even more than usual, the movie suffers the more for those who happen to read the book first.

Rabe passed away in 1990 at the age of 68, leaving two unpublished manuscripts behind. These, *The Silent Wall* and *The Return of Marvin Palaver* were published posthumously by Stark House Press in 2011. Rabe's contributions to crime fiction were influential to writers like Donald E. Westlake, Harlan Ellison™, and many others. His mob books stand out, especially his own two favorites, *The Box* and *Kill the Boss Good-By*, as some of the best the genre has ever offered. It leaves one to wonder what may have happened to Rabe's career had Puzo's book come before the years of Rabe's primary output instead of after. Markets change, most often unpredictably, though quality writing stays the same.

—Compass Lake, FL
June, 2018

WAR OF THE DONS

BY PETER RABE

CHAPTER 1

It was seven A.M., and the desert air over Palm Springs was all hard light. Roberto Messina stepped from his expensively decorated house out to his custom-landscaped garden. He checked the three men who sat all but immobile in unlikely places; by the bath house near the pool, by the gazebo where the yuccas grew, and by the boulders which were wetted by an artificial waterfall. A fourth man was watching from a high window two miles away, but Messina did not know about him. Messina nodded at the men, and patted his straight, dark business suit.

He felt that the suit made him look like a banker. It might have made a banker look like a banker, but on Messina's squat body the obvious expense of the suit made the man look cheap.

Messina stepped back into the glassy, two-level living room, stopped there, and yelled at the emptiness.

"*Andiamo, andiamo!*" He could hear someone running in the corridor. "Let's get going and outa here!"

A few minutes later Messina, with an entourage of men who kept their hands in their pockets, stepped into the empty street.

The man behind the high window two miles away was chewing gum rapidly. He could see the Messina place through his heavy binoculars. He could see the flat roof angling around a splash of green garden and the wall that squared off the estate. Below the wall, on the street, stood Messina's big limousine. A gate in the wall opened.

"Right on," said the man through his gum.

Messina and five of his men walked to the limousine and Messina got in. But then the men did not move. They were all looking toward one end of the street.

At seven o'clock that morning when the yellow air over Burbank was already fuzzy with smog, Marco Guarda stepped from the shower. He slapped his flat stomach rapidly a few times and then, with an excess of energy, did a series of knee bends. The exercise was not for body building, but rather to alleviate Marco's nervousness. When he stopped bobbing up and down he glared at himself through a tangle of nylons hanging in front of the bathroom mirror. He roughed his black, wet hair, grimaced so that his very white canines looked prominent, and shot his eyebrows up and down.

"You'll have to do," he mumbled at the image. "*Minqua*, you'd better—"

Then he made a wet trail to the kitchenette where the phone hung on the wall. He eyed the phone and then the clock on the wall. Neither the knee bends in the bathroom nor the invocation at the mirror had done much good. He had worked hard and well so that everything was as it should be. But at this point of readiness matters were out of his hand. He seethed with nerves.

He hunted around in the kitchen and found cold orange juice, cold milk, and cold coffee. He poured the cold coffee and sipped.

Across from the kitchenette, in the living room, an open daybed took most of the space. In the bed, taking hardly any space at all, lay Francine. She lay on her back, her mouth open, hair fanned over a pillow, legs spread. Marco could see her breasts rise and fall in a slow sleeper's rhythm. The rumpled sheet over her served no practical function.

"*Minqua—*" he said again and looked at the phone. He sat down on a stool by the breakfast bar and sipped some more of the cold coffee. He felt that the yellow air over the valley had crept in and was grinding its dirt into his body.

Francine woke up. She rolled over to lean on one elbow and watch Marco sit naked by the phone. He looked uncomfortable and very attractive.

Francine felt awake and refreshed. She twisted the sheet across one hip and grabbed it between her thighs. The rest of her was not covered anymore. Francine was small and lean, except for her breasts. She idled her hand around and around.

"Marc?"

He glanced at her and grinned, but not as if he were paying attention. Francine moved a little, gesturing at him to lie down with her. Her hand kept going around and around.

"*Minqua—*"

"You keep saying that," said Francine. "What's it mean?"

"You're looking at it," he said.

"And?" she kept doing the thing with her hand. "And for how much longer?"

The phone rang and Marco jumped for it. He could see Francine slowly pulling the sheet out from between her thighs.

"*Pronto!*" Marco said into the phone. The man in Palm Springs was chewing gum inside Marco's ear.

"He just got in the car," said the man. "His apes are still standing around."

Francine was sitting up on the bed now, smiling across at him. She had one leg up on the bed, knee high, arms in back of her, and was moving the knee back and forth, driving him crazy.

"Okay, okay," said Marco into the phone. "Call me when he gets on the plane."

He slammed the phone down and jumped off the stool. There would be no need for any more calls from Palm Springs because Messina was a methodical man. In fifteen minutes the old bastard would climb into his Lear jet and sit in a lounge chair while an assistant handed him his first cup of *caffè con latte* spiked with Strega. In fifteen seconds, he, Marco, would have himself and Francine in a delicious pile-up.

She watched him come across the room while sliding herself back onto the bed. She let herself fall back, keeping her knees high, and smiled at him. He stopped at the edge of the bed and leaned both hands on her knees. She felt his hands slide down the inside of her thighs. Francine closed her eyes, waited, and then sucked her breath in. But his hands kept on sliding up, over her, until abruptly they clamped her shoulders. She waited for the blunt probe and thrust, angling up for him.

The sound was like a slap in the face when the phone rang. Marco did not realize that he was hurting the girl with his hands, that the heat drained out of him in a sudden, thin sweat, but he felt his knees shaking. That ringing was now as insistent as panic. Back on the stool, touching the phone, he became a different person, face still, back curved, and his shoulders dropped slightly.

"Yes?" he said into the phone.

"He's getting out of the car," said the man in Palm Springs.

CHAPTER 2

The other car, big, black, and old-fashioned, hummed next to Messina's beige Fleetwood Cadillac. It stood there in polished preservation, with a lunging figurehead over the radiator, and a spare tire sunk into a well built in next to the hood. It now hummed a little louder, moved past the Cadillac, and came to a stop up ahead by the curb.

First the driver got out. He looked like an old pushcart vendor who moved in a sidling way, like a crab.

Messina, his man Cass next to him, and the four bodyguards by the gate and on both sides of the touring car all stood still in the quiet, cool morning, watching the crab scuttle around the black car and swing open the passenger door. Then it took another few moments before the passenger came out.

He emerged doubled over and holding his hat by the crown, as if bucking a wind. Once on the sidewalk he stood up very straight but leaned on his cane.

"That's Don Pietro?" said Cass.

"Shut up" said Messina. "And he ain't Don Pietro no more. Just an old man by the name of Vinciguerra."

Cass nodded and did not say anything else. He was shorter than his boss, which was all right with Messina, and he was not Sicilian. He was not even all Italian. Only his mother was Italian. Even that was slightly less than proper, since she came from the Po valley and was blond. Jack Cass's black hair was due to his Irish father.

"Don't stand around," said Messina. "Get inside and fix the coffee." Cass's improper heritage made him a proper servant.

Vinciguerra walked toward Messina, placing his cane with precision. His use of the cane did not suggest the infirmities of age so much as the court-liness of a boulevardier. He walked slowly, though it was hard to decide whether his slowness was due to infirmity or was simply a manner. Vinciguerra stopped, took his hat off, and bowed.

"*Benedicide*," he said.

The phrase startled Messina. It was pure Sicilian, and in his memory only the most obsequious or the most devout peasants would use it, and they would only use it when addressing a priest. In any case, the phrase meant too much self-abasement on one hand, or might be used as a derisive joke. Then again, thought Messina, the old man was known for his courtly manner, and for the ridiculous way he had of apologizing for being in your presence.

Messina looked at the oddly smooth face, which was strange in a man of Vinciguerra's age. It suggested the unformed planes of a baby's expression. But the mouth showed waste. The lips were too full and too lax, with a purplish color. The eyes showed wear, even though they were shiny. Yellow eyeballs, brown irises, black pupils, all seeming to blend from one tint into the other.

Messina had to say something. He did not know how to respond to *benedicide*, unless it were by extending his hand for a kiss, and most of all he did not know why Vinciguerra had suddenly appeared out of nowhere at seven o'clock in the morning. That puzzle alone provoked the utmost suspicion.

"Yeah," he said. "*Va bene*. Come in the house," and walked abruptly through the gate and into the garden.

Pietro Vinciguerra followed more slowly because it was his accustomed pace. Two of Messina's bodyguards moved along behind him and the other two stayed by the gate. If Vinciguerra's driver had tried to follow, they would not have let him in. They stayed by the gate and puzzled over the visit.

"That guy with a cane is a *Don?*"

"That's right. Don Pietro."

"From where? Never heard of any Vinciguerra Family."

"That's on account you ain't been around. And on account the Don is no Don no more. So *he* ain't been around."

"Some Don."

"Let me tell you, some Don. In his day, his Family made it from San Diego to Seattle in everything—waterfront, numbers, horses, vending, houses...."

"On the Coast, houses? When it's free?"

"Before the breakdown in morals it weren't free."

"Then what happened?"

"He retired."

The retired Pietro Vinciguerra clucked and nodded at all the fine things in Messina's big living room. He marveled at the see-through effect of glass doors to the garden at one end of the room and to the terrace at the other. He wanted to know what held up the suspended fireplace which hung centrally and was enameled in blue, and he wanted to know why the bar was so big, considering that this was a private house and prohibition was over. Messina became more confused with each comment. Vinciguerra, he decided, was either stupid or plain mad. Neither conclusion helped much.

"But above all, *signore*," said Vinciguerra with a courtly bow, "I am happy to see you in good health."

He smiles like an undertaker, thought Messina. He was convinced that this old man had come to do more than deliver platitudes at seven o'clock in the morning, but he did not know how to rush Vinciguerra. The ex-Don, whom Messina hardly knew, was an unknown quantity. The wish for speed and the fact of inaction made Messina irritable. He could feel his own growing tension claw itself through his chest, his neck, and into the base of his skull. His hand touched the box of pills in the pocket of his vest.

"But what is wrong with your hand, *signore* Messina?" said Vinciguerra. He sat down opposite Messina and leaned over the free-form coffee table as far as he could without falling over.

"Nothing. Nothing anymore." Then he hesitated because he did not know whether to address the old man as Vinciguerra or as Don Pietro. The problem irritated Messina even further.

"Ah," said Vinciguerra. "You have had a stroke. A little stroke of no consequence." Then came the smile again. "But a stroke," he said while closing his eyes.

Cass came in with the espresso and the bottle of Strega. One glance at Messina and he felt that his boss should not look that way.

"Put the stuff down and call the clinic," said Messina. "We'll be late."

"How late?" said Cass.

"Just tell 'em late!" yelled Messina. He grabbed the Strega bottle and poured the sticky liqueur into his empty espresso cup. Then he drank the whole portion in one toss, leaned back, and waited for the medicinal warmth to occur.

"*Signore*," said Vinciguerra quietly. "I am sorry, if I am responsible for delaying a vital appointment with your *dottore*. In fact, why do you not simply drive out to your jet airplane and fly away to the clinic in Santa Monica and forget about my thoughtless intrusion. And, why, instead, do we not simply ..."

"How did you know about my checkup?"

"Was it a secret?" asked Vinciguerra. His round mouth made a tremulous letter O.

Messina did not bother to answer. He leaned over to pour coffee into his sticky cup. While he had worried about how to address Vinciguerra, he had not bothered to call for another cup for the guest. He sipped espresso carefully and talked right through the sounds he was making.

"What did you show up for, Vinciguerra?"

The older man sighed. It was difficult to deal with a man who did not know the graces, who did not abide by the rules of proper timing, and who had no respect for his elders. Aside from that, he, Vinciguerra, would not expect anything else. A *caporegime* who held his position merely by virtue of appointment and nothing else, such a one would know nothing about true power and its child, which is a benevolent feeling for all who are in need of you.

"I made bold," said Vinciguerra, "to offer my help."

"At seven in the morning, at a place where I don't do business?"

"Like all men of importance, you are hard to reach in the ordinary ways."

"*Mu—*" said Messina and poured more coffee for himself.

For just one moment, Vinciguerra was impressed with that lout of a man opposite him. Only a native Sicilian could use that short, multimeaning expression effectively. The word had a shrug of deprecation in it, a disavowal of importance, and an unaffected acknowledgment of having been complimented.

Messina noted the approval in Vinciguerra and pressed for more. He dropped his usual manner when with has-beens and inferiors, and instead copied Vinciguerra's more stately ways of getting what he wanted.

"A man who's had his own Family, why would he bother with a small *capo* who can't make a move without getting directions from a bunch of bookkeepers, mouthpieces, and tax consultants?"

The description was far from Messina's idea of a strong *caporegime*. But this kind of peasant self-abasement should work with a type like Vinciguerra. That type ate it up. Nevertheless, the approach did not work.

"I live in Tucson now," said Vinciguerra. Messina knew that. "Retired. I don't get around much." He looked up at the ceiling.

Messina, in a fit of distraction, took three pills from his case instead of two and swallowed them. While he was still trying to swallow them dry, Vinciguerra looked at him and smiled.

"I used to know your territory very good. Long Beach and all the way into the valley, *da vero?*"

Messina just listened now. Here it came.

"Is MacAdoo still on the bench in lower circuit?"

That wasn't it. He was still building up to something.

"No," said Messina, and poured espresso.

"Hmm," said Vinciguerra and watched one of Messina's soldiers walk around and around the cactus bed. "You are in a very good way, I think, in a very good, strong way in your territory when you don't need the Mac-Adoo person. His kind of person." And then he said without any transition, "You have instead three very good, strong lieutenants. I forget their names."

Messina put down the espresso cup very carefully but missed the saucer. He thought now here it comes.

"The Guarda brothers," he said. "Three champs."

"But they were not themselves born in Sicily," said Vinciguerra. It was not a question, but a statement of no confidence.

"They were born in New Jersey. So what?"

"Nothing. Nothing." Vinciguerra shrugged. "They are good boys."

"They're not boys. Nuncio keeps the records like he was the department of Internal Revenue, Pepe keeps the button men on their toes, and Marco I keep right here," said Messina with some show of emotion. "Right here," he said again and tapped the front of his head. "He thinks like I do. *For me.*"

"Good, good. So even when you are sick, there is nothing to interrupt."

Vinciguerra stopped, as if out of politeness, because Messina had stood up quite suddenly. He stalked over to the bar, yanked the lid off a porcelain humidor, and pulled out a cigar. He held it for a moment and then looked at his wrist watch. He put the cigar down on the bar very gently. He started to talk while still turning around to face Vinciguerra again.

"*Signore,*" said Messina with insulting politeness. "You come in here at the crack of dawn. Not invited. You make me miss an appointment so you can badmouth the setup I've got. The setup I've built." He came stalking back to the coffee table where Vinciguerra sat very low in a slinky chair. "What's so goddamn important that you're here?"

Messina could not see Vinciguerra's face now because he stood over the older man, who kept his head down.

"You must know," said Vinciguerra. "Or you would not have bothered and allowed yourself to miss an appointment. The first one, the one with your doctor," Vinciguerra added. "Not the other one."

Messina hissed a string of horrible curses at the air in front of him, and under the circumstances, this was a measure of his deference to the ex-Don.

So that was it. Not the touch from a broken-down has-been; not a tip about something dangerous inside his own organization; but an offer of some kind.

"Your own Don will be there to meet with you, so I have heard," said Vinciguerra. "A fine man. A little too remote for a man at the head of a closely bound Family, but that is only my own, old-fashioned view. A strong man, I think."

Messina, drained and calmed by his curses, sat down again.

"All right, Vinciguerra. What do you want?"

"Nothing!" Vinciguerra raised his hands, then dropped them, as if he felt helpless. "Nothing in the way you are using the phrase. Only, don't you see, dear Messina, I am a lonely man with nothing to do. I hear things, but I am no longer involved. I see things, but I can no longer partake of them. And that is good. I am not here to complain, because I have no regrets about anything. My life has been good." Vinciguerra was serious now, his voice even, his face without the masks he used when he dealt with various people. "Except for this," he said. "I do not like to see waste. I do not like to see dirt on excellence. Do you understand me?"

"No," said Messina.

"Then I will show you. You have been a sick man—no, I should not say that. A sometimes sick man, so that even now, before the meeting with your Don later today, you want to run to your doctor in order to bring the proof that you are truly all right. You run a clean, strong *regime*, my good *capo*, but your Don, who is not close enough to really see for himself, wonders only about your little vacations, the needless ways in which some business things are done twice, the wondering if perhaps there are too many *regimes* in his Family ..."

"That's not it," said Messina. "Nobody's trying to reshuffle the territories."

"Of course not."

"I asked you a question," said Messina. "Why did you come here?"

"And so," said Vinciguerra, "since it cannot be your good, strong *regime* that invites question, then perhaps it is only the *capo* himself about whom the distant Don wants reassurances."

Messina felt the temper pound inside his skull, but perhaps there was something that the old *bastarde* knew, and he, Messina, did not.

The meeting with the Don was late in the afternoon. The distant Don, as Vinciguerra had called him, rarely met singly with his *caporegimes*. And since, in fact, there was nothing to criticize about the operations of the territory itself ...

"And then again," said Vinciguerra with a look of no focus in his eyes, "then again it may be the *consigliere* who is such a strong, right hand to the distant Don, perhaps it is he who wonders."

Like any man whose good points are limited to mere tactical cleverness, Messina needed to be forever suspicious of the unknown alternative. It could be Cipollo, the Don's bookkeeping shyster, who wanted the meeting. This *consigliere* was the one with the doubts about the time-honored system of button men. An army, after all, is not run by lawyers; an army, as a matter of fact, made little tangles and messes for lawyers to settle afterward. Meanwhile, Cipollo had the whole thing turned around in his deskman's brain. The better the *consigliere,* the less need for a sharp set of soldiers like Messina was running.

"Are you listening?" Vinciguerra was asking.

"Yeah. What?"

"I am saying, it would be very nice, would it not, to demonstrate to the likes of the *consigliere* that you, *capo,* have everything with which to do anything and that without need for advice from the likes of that *consigliere.*"

Messina sat down. His head did not pound anymore. His insides felt very still. *Forza!* To walk in on that meeting and show the Don some new, foolproof operation using no more and no less than his own *regime's* present equipment—like Pepe Guarda's button men, Nuncio's paper plans, or Marco's ways with juggling the influence and squeezing just ever so tenderly where it counted with the connections. Who needs Cipollo?

"It would be nice, would it not," Vinciguerra continued while looking at the bright morning sky outside, "very nice to show that you, the *caporegime,* are needed."

There came a pause that was totally unpleasant for Messina. It allowed the heaviness of the topic—which had to do with Messina's worthiness— to become very much worse. Concerning his worthiness as a man and a *caporegime,* Messina now found himself in an intolerable bind. If he asked Vinciguerra what to say and to do at the meeting with his own Don, then proof of his own incompetence was established. If he did not ask Vinciguerra, then all the worth of Messina might not be enough to battle some great, unknown plot. Caught within his own caution, Messina retrenched behind total suspiciousness.

Vinciguerra, long out of touch with real action, had not kept pace with Messina and had instead only pursued the formula of his own tried and true way of dealing with lesser men: first lull them, then expose them, and next offer help. Vinciguerra never got to the last step because Messina exploded.

"Cass!" he yelled. "Get over here!"

Besides Cass, who came charging into the room, there appeared one man each at the two glass doors leading to the outside. From where they stood they could not see much that looked like anything. Cass stood there with one hand half way up to the center button of his jacket, but then he dropped his hand, though he did it slowly. The boss was standing up, hunched over a little, his banker's suit looking like something with a barrel inside. They could see his face working and his jaw snapping back and forth. They could not hear what he said, but by the looks of him he was talking his ugliest in that hoarse, wheezing whisper. Maybe the sonofabitch was getting ready for another stroke. The old man, in contrast, seemed to be doing nothing. He sat quite still in that silly chair that jackknifed the knees up to his chin and he was holding his cane in one hand, just below the handle. The silver handle did not move. The other hand, slow like a worm, was moving toward the black hat the old man had kept on the floor next to him. Messina saw that too.

"That's right," he said. "And now get out. No more double-talking me about all the help *I* need. No more of your sucking around for favors on account of ..."

"Favors?" said Vinciguerra. The baby mouth in the old face stretched and stretched until it held in a horizontal grin. It showed his teeth for the first time. They were short, completely even and ground flat at the ends. "I need no favors, *signore*. I have all I want. *Mu—*" he said. "I do need something. I need to talk together and think together with a good man. About matters of responsibility for good, strong men. *That* I miss." His hand had found the hat and Vinciguerra tried to get up. It was too hard for him. "*Per favore*," he said and held out his arms for help.

"Cass!" said Messina very sharply. "Stay there." Then he put his hands in his pockets. "Anything else you don't need help with?"

If Messina had not left Sicily with his parents at the age of six, and if he had not left his parents in Hell's Kitchen at the age of twelve, perhaps he would have known better. It was utterly *maleducado* to mock a man because of his age.

"*Signore*," said Vinciguerra and put his hat slowly and squarely on the top of his head. "Do not cause for yourself unnecessary regret."

"Are you threatening me?!"

Vinciguerra's chest heaved once, slowly. "Not yet," he said.

"*Bastarde!* Before I die from a fit of laughing," yelled Messina in bad Sicilian. "Get out!"

It was either from rage or from sheer ignorance that Messina had cursed

Vinciguerra the way he had. Calling a man a bastard in English was one thing; however, the term *bastard* in Sicilian is a literal accusation of bad birth, worthless mother, and foul blood line, all of which is in the original spirit of a curse, since the accused can do nothing about it.

Vinciguerra now rose from the fetal posture in the modern chair, even though the blood pounded in his ears from the effort. He stood up and squared his hat.

"*Va bene*," he said evenly. "*Now* I threaten you." And then he left the house.

CHAPTER 3

Marco rolled off Francine and felt no different from the way he would have felt after doing a few push-ups. It was the first time he had been skin-close to a naked woman and had visualized a black telephone on a wall.

Francine lay on her back and looked up at Marco's face. When he looked at her she crossed her arms and covered herself with her hands. She felt awkward, so she drew her legs up a little.

"What happened?" she said.

"What happened? If you don't know what happened, what the hell can I tell you?"

"Far as I know you were drilling a hole." She sat up abruptly, swung her legs off the bed, and walked to the bathroom. "And thank you very much," she said, "I already got one."

Marco watched the hard bounce her steps produced and wished that he could appreciate it. When she slammed the bathroom door he got up and dressed. Then the phone rang again.

"The old guy from the hearse ..."

"What?" snapped Marco.

"The car I been telling you about. The guy with the cane, he's getting back in his car."

"And Messina?"

"Hasn't showed."

"*Cornuto*—" said Marco, making the man in Palm Springs wince away from the phone.

"What you want me to do now?"

"You can stop popping that gum in my ear! Are those Messina guys waiting around out there or what?"

"No. They're going back inside and closing the gate now."

Marco raked one hand through his hair, several times. The hair was not wet anymore, but even now it had the strong, metallic sheen of a black cat.

Marco checked the wall clock. A most delicate sequence of timed events all shot to hell.

"Something I can do?" asked the man in Palm Springs.

"Yeah. You can hang up. Then you can tell Rizzo at the airport to phone in to the office when Messina leaves."

"That's it?"

"Stop cracking that gum!"

Marco hung up when Francine came back out of the bathroom. She had clearly given up on any plans in the bed. Her face was set, noncommittal, and her brown and yellow striped hair was tied back so severely that her eyes seemed to be on a slant.

"Leaving?" she said.

Marco had a turtleneck on and yanked his chin around as if he were coming up for air. He did not answer her. He slipped his jacket on, and immediately looked a little too sharp.

"All you need is the black shades, Joe Hollywood."

"What was that?"

"Forget it."

"I will."

He had meant to make three calls from her phone but not now. The mood was too rotten. He put his hand in his pocket and came out with a fifty-dollar bill.

"Here," he said. "For the shower." It took care of the feeling.

Francine took the bill and then held it as if she did not know what to do with it. She did not like the way she felt. When she spoke, it came out unexpectedly mean.

"Half a C," she said. "Now I can tell them that when the great Marco Guarda balls me it's worth half a C. You know how much I used to make on one trick in Vegas?"

"Sure. I paid it, remember?"

The riposte was cheap and true. Marco went for the door.

"Marc?"

He stopped and waited for her. He himself would not have known what to say before leaving and he wondered how she might do it. She did not look hard anymore, she was not going tearful, she just looked at him straight.

"You brought me down here and I knew it wasn't for money or anything else real, like love, because you said so and so did I. You got me the job in the club, you pay my rent here where it's out of the way, and the nicest thing you ever did for me was to tell me that I didn't have to work topless. Let me finish. In some kooky way, that silly thing you said was the nicest. And when I want some money you give it to me. And sometimes you give me—

" she moved the bill between her fingers, "you give me this."

"Okay," he said. "Okay." He opened the door for himself. "That's so you'll cover for me, if the fuzz should come. I was doing a B and E while you were asleep between sets."

She did not know what a B and E was and she did not want to hear his tone or believe it. She watched him go through the door.

"Marc?"

"Yes."

"All I wanted to tell you," she said and showed him the money, "all I meant was, you don't get the best of me this way, Marc. Ever thought of that?"

He just looked at her for a moment. Francine was glad that he was not saying something harsh. He did not say anything. He looked at her and gave her a nod and then went quickly down the hall.

It was uncommonly hot on the street for that time in the morning. Marco felt the heat even under his skin.

She almost blew it, he thought. On top of everything else she started to get him involved in her hang-ups, but then, just in time, she let him go. He had neither the temperament nor the leisure to dwell on it anymore. Instead, he walked quickly to the corner. The gas station in the neighborhood was still closed, but the telephone was in a booth outside the station. Marco hated to talk in a booth but the pressure was on him now. He squeezed in, got his credit card out, and then placed a call to Messina. He was sweating in the glass incubator before Messina came on.

"Where in hell have you been?" was Messina's opener.

The voice and the manner set Marco's teeth on edge.

"Balling. Why?"

As Marco knew, that stopped Messina for a moment. The old *capo* was no longer quick, as if the doctor-fear had given him stoppage of the guts and constipation of the brain.

If I did not need that *cretino*, Messina was thinking. No, not that one. He is no *cretino*. It's that I-spit-in-your-eye attitude, like myself a hundred years ago—ah, the envy of it, the rotten weakness of envy. Messina felt suddenly weak, not in the body, but weak and flaccid in spirit. It was something that came over him more and more in the recent past. Some of it whined behind his voice when he talked again.

"Marco. You're there, Marco?"

"Yeah."

"I've been calling you. At the office, the club, at the hall ..."

"*Dunque,*" said Marco. "Something's wrong?"

"You know anything about that Vinciguerra?"

"Who?"

"Don Pietro."

"What's to know? He's comic opera, *buffo*."

As the confusion boiled up in Messina again, he reacted in his typical manner, and pulled back into total mistrust.

"Marco." His voice had changed. It was more his usual, rapping assault with the voice. "How come you happen to be calling *me?*"

"Because I've got to know why in hell you didn't show at the plane like you're supposed to."

"*You've* got to know! *I'm* supposed to!"

"Yeah, you. And I'm supposed to know what you're up to or I'm no good on the job. You're on a schedule and I'm supposed to keep track. You're due at the clinic. We got a meeting after that. You got that thing with the Don. *Che fai, Roberto, che fai?*"

Marco knew he was on solid ground. Next, he needed Messina's new schedule. But then his *capo* surprised him.

"Cancel the clinic. I'm not coming in."

"You've got to," said Marco without pause. "You've got to show the Don the record." Then he switched and took a bead on Messina's real state. "And if you're going to hole up, let me get a hold of Pepe and send you more men. Besides, Roberto, your Palm Springs place isn't the best for a hole-up."

"All right. Shut up talking." Messina's voice stayed harsh but he was warming himself in Marco's show of loyalty. "I'm coming in."

"When?"

"Never mind when. Tell the clinic I'll be there."

"If I can't tell 'em ..."

"*I'll be there!* What I pay that bone breaker, he should interrupt himself inside a woman when I ask for an aspirin and a glass of water!"

Messina was in form again. As far as Marco's own plans were concerned, this blew it.

"I'll tell 'em to stand by," he said.

"And get Pepe. I want him to throw a ring around that place so that a burp from a flea can't get through without him knowing it."

"Better tell me what I'm looking for."

"A *pazzeria*, all of it maybe. But I got to make sure. You say you haven't heard a thing about that Vinciguerra?"

"Hell no."

"All right. What about Rubenstein. Anything there?"

Messina was in shape again because he was talking business. Rubenstein and his union was the only slightly troublesome thing in Messina's *regime*.

"Don't worry about him," said Marco. "The way you've set it up, he knows he's a mark, if he gets out of line."

"Don't tell me what I know," said Messina. "Now get off the phone and do what I said. Keep the eyes open."

"*Ciao* ..."

Messina slammed the phone down in the middle of it. Cut the hardnose right off. Slam him right in the middle of his familiarities.

Messina looked at his fancy room, the expanse of glass and nobody in it except him. Messina got that feeling of weak spirits again. He thought of Pamela and had to have her. He kept her in the house for just such times as these, when he needed to feel that he was not weak and old but perfect, the way a *capo* ought to be. He found her in the kitchen, having coffee with one of the button men. He told the man to get the hell out and herded Pamela into the large bedroom. He opened her housecoat and worked his hands over her young body. The touch warmed his dry palms. Then he told her to sit bare in front of him on the bed. He himself kept his clothes on.

CHAPTER 4

Marco yanked the door of his booth open and got a lung full of dirty heat for his troubles. He could see it building against the Santa Monica ridge where the foul yellow air hung like a smear along the flank of the mountain. He leaned back into the booth and made two more calls. They came harder than the one to Messina.

Nuncio Guarda ran his day like most of his neighbors in Inglewood. He had breakfast with the kids at seven-thirty in the morning, discussed plans with his wife between the children's departure for school and the time when he drove to the office, then he sat at his desk until six in the evening. After that, as much as was possible, he was again his children's father and his wife's husband. He liked the time in the morning best, after the children had gone. Then there was only he and Rosetta.

Nuncio was a frailer version of Marco. He was the younger brother with the more thoughtful eyes, the more delicate hands, and he had a very clearly devoted manner toward those he loved.

He sat in the breakfast booth and watched Rosetta pour two cups of coffee. Like many Sicilian women, she had passed her first bloom by the time she was sixteen. Then came the children. This was the time of the brood female, the washerwoman, and the ascension to house goddess. After that, she might have become an overworked drudge, a despotic matriarch, or a wife who had entered a second bloom. Nuncio felt that Rosetta, at thirty, was the last. She could have been a coarse-haired, mustachioed crone—which she was not—and Nuncio's eyes would have seen the bloom. She sat down opposite him, bringing the coffee, and sighed.

"Aha," he said. "It's time. Next Sunday I'm going to get out the tools and move back that bench. What would you say, *bella*, ten inches, a foot?"

She was not very good at repartee. All she said was, "Listen to you, smarty," and then almost blushed.

She was neither fat nor was she pregnant again, but she now had a roundness that reminded Nuncio of fruit.

"And besides," he said, as if there had been considerable conversation, "I felt your belly last night. There is one starting, you know," which was not quite true.

"And I felt yours."

"Bah."

"And also—yours. And then yours."

They smiled at each other. He reached over and squeezed her arm, high up by the shoulder, and she slapped at him. In his head, Nuncio could see himself doing more, but they never did out of bed. It was not the way they lived. Then the phone rang.

"Watch how easy," she said and got out of the booth very smoothly. "It's Marco," she said when she brought him the phone to the table. Then, by unspoken accord, she left the kitchen.

Nuncio listened and looked down at his hand. He was a doodler and wished he had a pencil at hand.

"So it's off," he said. "I'm just as glad." As he knew, Marco would not protest. He listened to Marco explain how the traces should be carefully covered. Nuncio knew most of that, since the arrangements for Messina's removal had been largely his; the carefully timed rerouting of the car which Messina would have taken from the International Airport to the clinic; the changing of detour signs around the street excavation; the switch of crane operators where the heavy shovel by the hole in the street would come down on the car. They talked of it in a minimum way, incomprehensible to an outsider. It was more a way of sharing between the brothers than of one giving instructions to the other. Except that what had to be done next was Marco's decision.

"We better meet," he said.

"I'll be in the office in an hour."

"We'll have to talk about Rubenstein," Marco said. "That's where it's at, what we do next."

"I know you think that, Marco."

"So we'll talk. There isn't much time."

"Will Pepe be there?"

"I'll call him." Then Marco hung up.

It took several calls from the booth before Marco found Pepe. Since, in theory, the whole day's events had been arranged, Pepe was not prepared for interruptions.

The big place was high in a canyon over Sunset Boulevard and the wide open view from the bedroom looked right down the line of La Cienega. Without the white haze, the whole view could have spilled right on to the ridges to one side of the metropolitan basin and way out to the ocean on the other side. The same view opened up in the bathroom because the sunken- tub was next to an enormous window.

Pepe did not see it. He barely saw the blue tile of the miniature pool that was the tub, he hardly smelled the fruity odor of the red liquid in which he was sloshing around, but he felt the white shape of the woman float before him. Her slim body felt limp in his hands. He felt tired and what he really wanted was to go to sleep.

She did not want him to go to sleep. That was not why she had this hairy pack of muscle in her house.

"Cuddidout," he said.

Elaine laughed. It was a cultured laugh that grated on his nerves. She floated her long legs up and hooked her toes behind his back. She splashed the warm water and wine in his face. Then she moved one foot down into the depths and groped for him.

"Enough," he said. "I got enough."

"I don't, dovey. Come here. Give me your hand."

"Enough. Fact, I can't."

"Oh?" She used her foot. "Ah! You see? You're a liar, dovey. You mean I can tell more with my little toe than you can tell with *that?*"

"Ohjeesismercilesskrist—" he said. Pepe felt victimized. While his head hurt and his eyes drooped, his groin started smoldering.

"I'm too drunk," he said. "That's a fact."

"You weren't supposed to *drink* it, dovey. You're supposed to just lick it on me. Come here. Like this. Here—"

He yanked his head out of her reaching hands and pushed her away by pushing into her belly. That's where her age shows, he thought. That's the only place where her age shows, in that flabby belly. He tried to concentrate on what he liked least about her, that goddamn cultured voice and that goddamn used-up belly. The whole bath scene with that cheap wine, was not his idea of a lay. He was a simple mount-it-and-bang-it man.

"No," she said. "Dovey, wait, I'm not ready!"

"When you're not ready," he said, struggling to grab a body that was like an eel, "when that happens is when every cock artist has died from hard labor," and then he grabbed her by the inside of one thigh and around her back with his fingers dug into one breast. She gagged with the sudden pain.

Then he threw her out of the tub and climbed after her. He yanked her up and pushed her hard into the edge of the massage table. The white sheet on the padding stained pink from the water and wine.

"Dovey, please—"

He did not even answer her. He slammed her down on her back, on the table, and when she tried to sit up he hit her in the face. He yanked her to the edge of the narrow end of the table where he stood ready. He did not care whether her scream was from pleasure or pain, and his thrusts shook her body.

It always surprised him how suddenly she went limp. He stopped bouncing her right away and felt no need to finish anything else. Very often that was all he needed. The kick was to see the woman played out like that. When the phone rang, it was no interruption for him.

He listened to Marco without pleasure. His brain had a vicious coil of barbed wire around it, and his eyes were full of edges.

"When are you going to learn, you dumb son of a bitch, not to mess around with a customer?" Marco shouted.

"Why in hell not. She's asking."

Marco, encapsuled in his glass cell, groaned with frustration. Pepe refused to understand the matter of business. Elaine was a fairly prominent figure, hooked into the Messina enterprise by extortion. In that arrangement, she paid regular amounts that were fixed. Any other usage of her as a person was simply bad business.

"Did you hear what I said about today's setup?"

"Yeah, yeah. It's off. That what you said?"

"Are you drunk?"

"Hell no. I'm sick."

"Now listen, Pepe—"

"You can stop yelling, can't you?"

"I'll make it simple, Pepe."

"Don't you talk down to me!"

"It's business now, Pepe. Or we can just go down the drain. You listening?" He had Pepe's attention. "You're supposed to put a tight ring around the place. Roberto's orders."

"When?"

"Now! Get that done and then come to the office. He'll get to the clinic any time this afternoon and we got things to do before then."

"I thought you said it's a bust?"

"New things! You hear me?"

"Okay, Marco, okay! I'm with you."

"Finally. Now hang up."

Pepe hung up and tried to sort himself out for the rest of the day. Pills for the head, a shower for that smell on him. Elaine was still on the table. Pepe watched her breathe. She woke up when he moved her legs.

"I want to sleep," she said.

"Go ahead."

"Put me on the bed first, would you, dovey?"

He put her on the bed first. There were the pills for the head, the shower for the smell, but then he needed something for that awful tension She was asleep before he was done with her, but when he left the house he was still dissatisfied.

CHAPTER 5

Don Angelo del Mare—the distant Don, as Vinciguerra had called him—was never so distant that he did not know the important survival matters and the profit matters of his Family operations. He knew, for example, where Messina was that morning, and he could even guess what Messina might be doing after his visitor had left so abruptly. He knew who the visitor had been, but he did not worry about him. There was a slim file on Vinciguerra, that muttering has-been from another era.

Vinciguerra, at odd times, would emerge from his two-bedroom contractor's special and have himself driven to his bank in downtown Tucson, in order to closet himself with his safety deposit box. By all accounts, the old man counted his cash there. He had no known savings accounts. At other times, Vinciguerra would appear in the territories of his former reign and would sniff around. He of course found nothing to his liking and in his roundabout ways would say so. Sometimes he would add hints of special promise and renewed glory. Then, as now, Vinciguerra would disappear again.

The Don, on that morning, was also apprised of the fact that Messina's *regime* was in very good shape and that the Guarda brothers were running effective interference for their *capo*. Which, in a manner of speaking, was the reason for that afternoon's meeting with Messina. That is to say, if Cipollo had measured it right. It would be best to see in person.

On the other hand, Angelo del Mare was a public man. He was known as the manager of the Las Vegas hotel where he kept his quarters, and at odd times, not infrequently, he strolled through the lobbies, the casino, and along the mosaic pool. Del Mare was affable, and dressed and behaved like the traditional hotelkeeper. The cool lines of his Romanesque profile moved between affability and an air of distant concern. In public, del Mare rarely talked. His Italian was gutter language and his English turned easily into Brooklynese. But he posed well. As Don Angelo, by contrast, he did not remind one of a hotel-keeper.

He sat in his penthouse on top of the Las Vegas hotel and looked at the neon clutter that stuck up everywhere. Beyond that lay the desert, looking empty and colorless. Del Mare looked away. He scratched at his plum-colored smoking jacket where his breakfast egg had made a small, yellow glob. With the other hand he picked up the phone. When he heard the answering click from his switchboard he started to talk immediately.

"It's after ten. You got the call set up for Washington?"

"Holding. The New Jersey office isn't on the line yet."

"Tell 'em to get the lead outa their ass."

"Yessir."

"I'll talk to Washington while I'm waiting."

There was a click and some humming. Then a voice came over the Washington line.

"Hello? Hello there?" it said.

"Senator," said del Mare. "Good to hear you."

"Well—" said the voice, sounding pressured. "I'm due in committee in three hours, you know. If there's anything else to be settled before I go in ..."

"Nothing, nothing at all, sir," del Mare said, the way he might talk to a disgruntled loser in the casino downstairs. "Let's just wait for Jersey, okay?"

"Well, I don't see ..."

"I don't either. Let's just humor 'em, okay?"

Del Mare chuckled a little, to soften the edge of threat that had crept into his voice. Anyway, as far as he was concerned, the senator was in the right shape as it was, except that the New Jersey people felt it was best to add just a little bit more of the pressure. Then the Jersey line opened.

"Senator? Vegas? You there?"

They were all there. The cat-and-mouse talk started. Del Mare felt that the senator was going too soft, leaving him too small an out for his own self-respect. That was an error. That was always Jersey's error, leaning too hard on the people they used.

"*Da vero, da vero,*" he cut in on Jersey, "but you gotta remember the senator's got some brains of his own. That's why he's where he is, right? You're not talking to no bum—"

At that point, del Mare's direct line to Los Angeles blinked its signal light. There was no switchboard to hold the call for him, or to listen in. While Jersey talked to the senator in Washington, D.C., del Mare picked up the white phone.

"What?"

"Cipollo," said the voice. "Something just came up."

"Like what? No, nothing, senator, Go ahead." He listened to Cipollo.

"It's about Messina."

"Can it wait? I'm talking to ..."

"No," said del Mare's *consigliere*.

It took del Mare two minutes to disengage himself from the conference call. Let the senator sweat. Let Jersey blow it. Let another half year go by until that tax and franchise business would come up again for manipulation. That's what the holding fund was for, to take up the slack when something did not come through on schedule. And that's what conference calls were for, to get the straight dope on bums like Jersey, greedy bums, who are no good for business.

"All right, Chip," he said to Cipollo. "Stop sweating."

Cipollo always sweated. He was fat and slow moving. His face had a look of composure that sometimes suggested firmness and sometimes sleep. But somewhere on his body more or less, he was always moist. Del Mare's remark was for that reason an unkind cut. Cipollo was used to the manner.

"I think you have to decide something right away," he said. "There's a man who got to me this morning who says that somebody is going to kill Messina."

Del Mare closed his eyes and touched the bridge of his nose lightly. If Messina should go, this was not the time for it.

"Send him here."

"I have arranged it," said Cipollo, which was the measure of del Mare's *consigliere*.

Pappagallo is one of those literal names which, by its very concreteness, could be misleading. Guarda meant to watch out, Vinciguerra meant the victor in war, Cipollo meant the onion, and del Mare meant the one from the sea. Pappagallo meant parrot. But the man Pappagallo was neither colorful, nor loud, nor a fairly rare bird. He was just one of the shifty, unsuccessful, and vague little grifters who snagged an occasional, meaningless job in the network of activities that fed into the action of any *regime*. At the same time, what fed into the action of a lost, useless man like Pappagallo, was the constant dream of the main chance, then the growing certainty that he, the failure, was destined to make it, and lastly the conviction that almost any chance event was now the smile of the gods.

Pappagallo had had another one of those moments of certainty just a week ago. When his friend the barman at the Red Eye in Inglewood eighty-sixed him for the evening, Pappagallo had not been ready. He had started yelling and breaking things. His friend the barman had hammerlocked Pappagallo to the door and from there into the gutter of the street.

"Screw you!" Pappagallo had yelled.

The barman shrugged and turned away.

"I got connections!" yelled Pappagallo from his position in the gutter.

The barman kept going without having answered.

"I'm coming back in!"

This, as Pappagallo knew, would stop the barman.

"You come back in here and you're dead."

"I'm in with Messina!"

"He's dead too," and the barman went back inside.

Pappagallo's inflamed sensititivities had then taken him off into a soaring flight of brain action. Somehow, all his unused potential of persistence, of analytical faculties, and of plain, patient leg work began to hum and to move. And this now was the moment. The swift flight in the private jet from L.A. to Las Vegas, the private limousine from the airport to the hotel on the Strip, and then the private elevator to the top of the building ...

Del Mare looked reassuringly small to Pappagallo. He could not tell what the small man's expression was, because there was a big picture window glaring at the room from the back, a big view of the world shining in on Pappagallo, with just that little runt in between.

"Sit down," said del Mare.

Pappagallo sat down on a couch that felt as if he were sinking into a bed.

"*Padrone*," he said, rolling the word. It was practically all the Italian he knew. "I come here to ..."

"Shaddap."

Pappagallo felt like sinking some more. The man who had brought him followed del Mare to a desk at the other end of the room. Del Mare sat down there and the man gave the Don a brown envelope. The man left and del Mare read pages from the envelope for an eternity.

"Come here."

Pappagallo jumped up and walked quickly across the large room.

"All right," said del Mare. "Tell it." He did not ask Pappagallo to sit down.

Behind del Mare hung a framed color print of a wet boulevard in Paris. With a rush of good feeling Pappagallo recognized it as the same one he had often studied in his dentist's office.

"Well, *padrone*," he said, "it really all came to me the night I had a discussion with my friend in the Red Eye ..."

"You got no friends. Let's hear what you know."

"*Padrone*—"

"I don't wanta hear nothing about you, and about what a sharp operator you are. I just wanta hear what you *know.* Go ahead."

Del Mare had spoken in his own, matter of fact way, without any venom. Pappagallo, however, did not know this. Pappagallo gagged on a lump of fright and the wet boulevard in Paris swam out of focus. This was wrong. This was staged wrong. But before the very purpose of his action slipped out from under him, he rushed it. He lost all the prepared touches, the crescendos of emphasis, the brainy stuff where he himself clarified hidden meaning. He just rushed out the facts. They were suddenly hard to find. A few did seem to fall out, then sank away. Del Mare just sat there, elbows on the desk, fingers alongside his nose, and his black eyes still as glass. When Pappagallo was done, he wanted to rush out of the room. The fat one that morning had been bad enough, asking the same things again and again. But at least he had looked human, sweating like that. This one? Was this runt even listening?

"Why don't you sit down, Pappagallo?" asked del Mare.

The offer was another shock. Pappagallo shrunk himself into the chair by the side of the desk. Del Mare had moved his head and his eyes, and he looked human. But Pappagallo could not be taunted. He just shrugged.

"I thought it was worth something."

"To me?" When del Mare did not get an answer he went on. "Let's try it out. You say Messina don't spend the night at his place in Beverly Hills one week running. So he's hiding out?"

"I thought ..."

"He *lives* in Palm Springs! Now. You say that Messina thinks Rubenstein at the union is getting too big and with his fingers into everything, like the loans, and the numbers. So he has Pepe Guarda lean on Rubenstein, because it's a plot to take over from Messina."

"Sure. Because Rubenstein's been screwing the ..."

"Shaddap! What kinda plot? Rubenstein's been costing us money." Del Mare crossed his arms. "Next," he said. "Pepe and the other two Guarda brothers are in with Rubenstein because the Jew ain't dead. You seen him stuff himself with *knishes* or *kishkes* on Fairfax Avenue."

"I saw him."

"They weren't *supposed* to hit him, just lean on him a little. Is that all right with you, is that decision all right by your opinion?"

Pappagallo, even in his dispirited state, was aware of del Mare's cheap technique: instead of chopping the head off with one effective cut, he was teasing his way into the job by first pulling the hairs out, one by one. That was surprising for a Don with a reputation for no nonsense.

Angelo del Mare looked down at himself and saw the egg stain on his smoking jacket. Suddenly he felt revolted. The lousy monkey jacket disgusted him and so did that leech of a person on the other side of the desk. The whole game with the little man revolted him. However, it was the only way left to the Don, under the circumstances.

He had been raised in an atmosphere in which Family loyalty assured mutual trust. From that unity came true strength. It had been the secret of Mafia power in the homeland for centuries, and then here in the States, for a while. But complex expansions and many contradictory pressures had made the blood bond as the sole source of strength less and less efficient. The operational units of action were still called a Family. The thought made Don Angelo ill. He did not head a Family. More properly, he was regional head of a business combine. It worked better that way. People like Pietro Vinciguerra had not understood that, which was the reason they had had to drop out. The family bond existed in name only. The fact of this robbed Don Angelo of conviction and left him with nothing but tricks. And tricks were no substitute for the trust that came from blood loyalty. He could not trust Messina to tell him truthfully how secure he felt within his own *regime*. He could not trust the Guarda brothers to tell him how concerned they were about the safety of their *capo*. And he could not trust Cipollo to decide whether this Pappagallo was in fact on to something important, or whether this bum from the gutter was simply fishing in the mud that was everywhere. And if there was something that had entered Pappagallo's ear while close to the gutter, then how else to tease it out of the bum's murky brain?

"Well, you got any more?" said del Mare.

Pappagallo gave a start. During the Don's lengthy silence he had almost felt like going to sleep. He did not want a drink. He wanted sleep.

"I don't know. I thought—" He stopped to look up at the Don on the other side of the desk, because the Don did not want to know what Pappagallo thought but only what he knew. To his surprise, Pappagallo saw the Don nod at him.

"Go ahead."

"Go ahead?"

"The thoughts. The precious thoughts." Del Mare tapped one finger on the side of his head. If Pappagallo had been raised as a true Sicilian he would have known that the gesture questioned his intelligence. Instead, he felt encouraged to search his innermost imagination.

"The way I see it, *padrone* ..."

"Don't call me *padrone*. Mr. del Mare to you." The insult was lost on Pappagallo but del Mare felt better.

"... so the way I figure it hangs together," Pappagallo was saying, "since the Guardas been running the union end pretty much with Messina being outa most of it, well, since they been doing that but need Rubenstein for a front, naturally, when Messina smells a rat on accounta the skim-off dropping steadily, right then Messina thinks it's gotta be the Jew behind the swindle."

Del Mare listened. No matter how harebrained the tale, at this point, only hours away from the meeting with Messina, he had to listen for anything he had not known before.

"So what's to do for the Guardas except hit Rubenstein before Messina roughs him up and gets him to talking?"

"They didn't hit him," del Mare said mildly. "They sent him to Fairfax Avenue for *kishkes*."

"*Knishes*. I know why they didn't hit him. He's got friends. Friends who will talk, if Rubenstein turns up dead. And so, being in this bind now, what's to do for the Guardas except hit Messina."

Pappagallo was no longer scared. The fact was, he believed everything he was saying and del Mare was clearly listening to the whole tale.

"How?" said del Mare.

"I got this from one of the drivers Messina's got. I mean, *pa*— what I mean is, Mr. del Mare, I got this from a source close to the victim, the intended, is what I mean. Him and me ..."

"What did you get from him?"

"Yeah. This. Did you know Messina was going to that clinic today where he went for his stroke? What I mean is ..."

"I know what you mean. Give."

"And on the way there, this is what I figure, the Guardas were gonna make the hit."

"How do you figure?"

"The driver, my friend I been telling you about, he took sick. Never sick a day in his life, but yesterday he takes sick. Poison!" Pappagallo added.

"From what, rotgut?"

"Please, Mr. del Mare. I mean it, he's sick. If you want the details about the sudden sickness ..."

"No. Skip it."

"So now he's sick and *I* know who's gonna drive Messina instead. Pino Valdez is gonna drive him, and if you don't know Pino Valdez, he's like an asshole buddy to Marco Guarda and was a wheelman from way back when the Family was still running things like ..."

"*Family*, what Family?"

"I mean, I'm sorry, sir, what I meant was, when Vinciguerra was still around and heavy heists were good business. That's when Valdez was the best wheelman around."

"He's with Messina now?"

"I guess so."

"And Messina took him?"

"Messina takes anything those Guardas hand him, Mr. del Mare."

"Any more?"

"Well, I don't know. The way I see it is the way I said it." Pappagallo stopped because he was watching del Mare hit a switch on his desk and bend over to get close to some gizmo.

"Did you hear it, Taylor?"

"I got it all down."

"All right. Send for him." Del Mare let go of the switch and looked at Pappagallo. "When they come in," he said, "they'll take you up to the roof. Up there, with nothing but the big sky looking the other way, they will work on you, parrot, and slowly. All that time, Taylor will ask you to tell your story again. Keep telling it, parrot, in all the different ways you remember it. When you can't talk no more, Taylor will compare all the stories you told up there. And then—" del Mare stopped while Taylor and two other men came into the room. The two men took a hold of Pappagallo and hefted the speechless body toward the door. "And then," del Mare finished, "you're done."

While Pappagallo was getting his systematic beating on the roof above the penthouse, del Mare called his *consigliere* back.

"I got the same version he gave you," said del Mare and flicked a finger at the folder that had come with Pappagallo. "What did you check out?"

"There was little enough of factual nature. Since most of it was conclusions ..."

"I know that. Did you check out that Pino Valdez?"

"Yes," said Cipollo. "He was in fact a driver for a safe-cracking and burglary team operating under license of the former ..."

"Forget that. Is he driving for Messina today?"

"He was," said Cipollo.

"And he's a friend of Marco's?"

"Yes. In the limited sense in which Marco has friends."

"Did you say Valdez *was* driving Messina today?"

"Yes. He has canceled all arrangements of transportation and will have to make others."

"What kind?"

"He has not told anyone, as far as I can ascertain. I know he hasn't told the Guardas because while they have cancelled the L.A. connections they have not arranged for new ones."

Del Mare said nothing for a moment. Then he said, "Who picked Valdez?"

"Messina."

"Chip," said del Mare. "What's it all sound like to you?"

"The reason I sent that person to you, Angelo, is because I would not accept the responsibility of basing a decision upon his sort of a story. On the other hand, Angelo, you *have* to make a decision."

"You think there's something to it and it's the Guardas."

"I am prejudiced," said Cipollo. "As you know, I wanted today's meeting in order to point out to Messina that too much decision making in his *regime* has passed over to the brothers."

"I know what our disagreements are." Del Mare gnawed his lips and looked up at the ceiling between himself and the roof. He wished they were done up there, and he wished that his *consigliere* were not so impersonal all the time and so right most of the time.

To cut out the Guardas at this point would endanger the *regime's* operations. Messina was not that well anymore. To get rid of Messina would most likely topple things even worse. Messina had built the *regime*, and all the supportive connections in that area were very personally his. The worst danger lay there—losing Messina.

"What have you decided?" asked Cipollo over the phone.

"That this Pappagallo has got something. Have you reached Messina?"

"No. He has left and is airborne. Valdez, if that's why you're asking, has remained in the Palm Springs house."

"All right. I guess Messina knows what he's doing. I want you to put a tight tail on the Guardas."

"Have them pulled in?"

"I didn't say that. Just a tail. And keep muscle in calling distance."

"Angelo. Don't you think ..."

"I'm not thinking your way, counselor." Then he added, "Hold it."

Taylor came into the room. Del Mare waited with one hand over the phone.

"He's changed everything around a coupla times but it comes out the same."

"What didn't he change?"

"About Valdez being put in for driving and that Valdez knows the big shot."

"You mean Marco Guarda."

"I mean that Don that used to be around. Marco he just seems to know from work."

"He said they were buddies."

"He just said that. The part he never changed was the other. Valdez ran with Vinciguerra."

Del Mare held his hand so that Taylor should wait. Then he talked to the *consigliere* again.

"Chip. You got it straight nothing's to happen to Messina."

"You want the Guardas ..."

"Forget about the Guardas. Before they can move they need Rubenstein."

"That's the decision?"

"And find Vinciguerra."

Then del Mare hung up. He sighed at Taylor.

"How's the bum?"

"Not good."

"He got any family?"

"No."

"Get rid of him," said del Mare. *Porco dio*, he thought. How much easier it is when a man does not have a family.

CHAPTER 6

Some years ago Boyle Heights had been rather a stately section. The houses had tall windows and a good deal of careful gingerbread. After a while Boyle Heights had become quaint. During that time the view across the basin where Los Angeles grew toward the beach was still brilliant with light. But now the air was rotten and it was anybody's guess where the ocean was. Boyle Heights itself had all the charm of greasy dishes.

Ditch—second floor, third to the rear—lay on his bed looking up at the ceiling that he did not see. The ceiling and the sheets on his bed were the same color. Occasionally he had a sensation that told him he was awake. He lay very still because that was the way the stuff worked best for him. He had enough Seconal in him to knock out the average insomniac, but as a veteran user Ditch knew that the somber effect of the drug would disappear as soon as he moved in any purposeful way. He lay still with this knowledge when he heard the knock on the door. "Be still, my heart. You make me—" He did not finish the rhyme and did not answer the knock. One more second of the peace of the grave would nourish him. Then came the knock again and Ditch got off the bed.

"Hi, man," he said and stepped away from the door to let Marco in.

"What took you so long?"

"Long? When I heard the knock ..."

"Forget it," said Marco. He went straight across the room, around the carton with odd things in it and over the dirty laundry on the floor. He opened the window, heaving and banging it a few times, to let the dry smog waft in. It was better than the air Ditch had been using. Ditch sighed, went back to his bed, but permitted himself only to sit on it. He sat thin and straight, with a faint sheen on his scalp where the hair was thinning.

"You look awful," said Marco.

"I'm beautiful," said Ditch. "You shoulda seen me yesterday."

"Where are you?" Marco said realistically.

"Coming off a freak. I'm fine, man, I really know how to do it."

"I should think so."

Ditch looked forty. Marco knew that Ditch was twenty-eight, that in spite of his dreamy looks he was possessed of a fast mind. If only it were functioning today.

"I got a job for you," said Marco.

"I do not need a fix," said Ditch with precision.

"Then how about a stake for a rainy day?"

"Man, don't tell me the sun is shining!"

Marco looked at his watch, groped in two pockets for a cigarette, and cursed when he couldn't find one. Ditch watched him and laughed.

"That bad, huh? You poor, addicted bastard."

"Listen," said Marco. "I'm not here because you need me but because I need you." He stopped to watch Ditch react. He was gratified to see that Ditch had been listening and that he appreciated the pitch. Sometimes, Ditch looked almost his age. "It's a job," Marco added.

"I don't need a job."

"Ditch, it's a very clever job."

Somewhere behind the opaque glass of the drug, Ditch had a hectic brain. He was of the class of users who paid the price of addiction not to shut out the world, but to stretch, tear, and wrinkle it. Even after the many years he felt as experimental about things as that first time when he had tossed his mother's Midols down his throat. He smiled at Marco, appreciating the fact that the sleek bastard had touched him where he could be reached.

"Clever, you say. Don't you mean suicidal?"

"Not if you're good."

"If I'm good, man, it's suicidal and I live to tell."

"Yeah. I know," said Marco. He patted himself for a pack again, even though he remembered that he did not have one. He was worried. He believed Ditch well enough about the suicidal touch. Ditch craved it in some unstraight fashion. It was the touch that could ruin the job. It was also the only touch that made Marco's emergency scheme possible.

"What kind of job, Marco?"

"You're a male nurse," said Marco.

"I *was* a male nurse." He closed his eyes and smiled in a stilted way. "I was a male who was nursing, / I bunged patients until they were cursing. / Now I am too frail, to call myself male, / in spite of my balls which are bursting."

"Cut it out, Ditch. This is serious."

"You're embarrassed, dear."

"I'm hurting," said Marco. "I'm hurting for time."

"Where, dear? Where's it hurt?"

There was no point in losing one's temper with Ditch, and Marco knew it. There was only one thing that would get the man interested when he was like this, and that was some promise of excitement. The explanation escaped Marco, because a downer made no sense to him, except perhaps for going to sleep or for wanting to be out of it. But while Ditch did not make much sense to Marco in a number of ways, he was, in his own fashion, a predictable person. Ditch, whose real name was Jim Ditman, had been male nurse on a health ranch that was underwritten by the Messina *regime.* Aside from servicing the carrot juice and high colonic trade, the ranch was a repair shop for Family cases. Ditch did not get fired, until he mistook activities outside the law for freedom to violate Family rules. He did not steal drugs, he just used them. He did not crave profit, just highs. This did not noticeably affect his efficiency, but it undermined the confidence of the patients. Sometimes they were influential patients, and at one point Ditch was going to be dumped dead in the desert. Marco Guarda countermanded the contract, as a move of efficiency. Why remove a man who still functioned? When on uppers, Ditch was quick and clever. When on downers, he was normal. And when he freaked out he always stayed alone. Since he did not have to hustle for supplies, he was never a desperate, unpredictable junkie. But also, he was not a grateful man, which seemed to have to do with his lack of desperation.

"The job," said Marco, "is in three hours. You can appreciate my concern."

"In three hours," said Ditch, "these reds are going to be dead. In three hours I'll graduate."

"To what, for chrissakes?"

"Muscle pop."

"Listen, Ditch ..."

"Listen, hood. You're hassling me." Then Ditch giggled.

The vocabulary did not bother Marco, but the giggle did. And he was naturally concerned about the junk Ditch was proposing to shoot. Though it could be worse, the shot in the muscle was more benign than a blast in the vein. Ditch claimed that he muscled for the same reason that a gourmet ate with delicate slowness, though Marco guessed that the state of Ditch's veins put them beyond easy use. Marco suspected that the dose would be murderously heavy.

"Maybe you'll change your mind, once you gimme a chance to tell you what the job is, Ditch."

"We got three hours," said Ditch. He felt like lying down.

"I made that up! I had to make it up because I don't know when I need you. Could be two hours, could be four."

"Your operation, dear General, can hardly be described as being on a wartime footing."

But it was, except that nobody knew it. Neither Nuncio nor Pepe could know what Marco had decided after talking to them. He alone was on a wartime footing because only he seemed to have the requisite sense of time.

The Don knew nothing, Cipollo groused habitually, and his brothers went along, eventually, because of the force of his pressure. It's now, or the *regime* disappears in the large stomach of the computerized Family. It's now or the syndicate juices would melt him down into mush. Now, because Messina was weak, and now because of that Rubenstein matter.

Marco felt the laughter form itself like a bubble inside. He alone with the dauntless Ditch by his side. That's like the doped leading the stoned, he thought. He knew he was doped, in his fashion. He could no more stop himself than Ditch could, when he was freaking out. The kinship made Marco wince. But he went on.

"Ditch, are you at *all* interested?"

Ditch heard the tone and looked up.

"Dear heart," said Ditch. "Nothing short of murder would interest me."

"Yes," said Marco, and walked over to the bed so he could stand by Ditch. "That's what I need you for."

CHAPTER 7

Pepe Guarda, full of aspirin, sauerkraut juice, and a potent Bloody Mary, picked up his Lincoln Continental from the basement garage in the city of Long Beach and drove from there to Santa Monica. He did not take the San Diego Freeway directly, but meandered on and off to make a number of stops. Each time he picked up a man. He should have taken one of the vans, except the mere thought of the bounce and the racket made him feel ill. When he had picked up five men, he stayed on the freeway until he came to the Santa Monica loop which turned him back upon himself, then headed him toward the Pacific. Before the freeway sliced through Santa Monica proper he got off one more time to pick up the last man. Then he headed due west again.

Nobody talked. The last man in, who did not have the exposure of the drive from Long Beach, did not understand the silence.

"I see," he said. "It's a secret."

That did not accomplish anything either. He was not a funny man or a joker, but a funereal silence after being ordered out of bed before noon was not his speed either. He looked at Pepe Guarda next to him. The heavy, immobile face with the black, wraparound glasses did not tell him very much. Pepe was hanging onto the wheel as if he were not sure who was driving.

"You got a hangover, Pepe?"

"Please shut up, Blazer," said somebody from the rear. Pepe had not opened his mouth.

Blazer, who was a careful and expensive dresser, turned slowly in his seat.

He straightened his jacket and then he popped his cuffs.

"Straightman," he said, "that was a dumb line. Before you smell up the script, let me—" Blazer hesitated and stopped. "As a matter of fact, what *is* that smell in here?"

Nobody answered.

"Well?" Blazer sniffed. "Shaving lotion? Vinegar! You using vinegar, Straightman?"

Pepe angled the big car to the far right and rolled down an off-ramp. They were in Santa Monica. The smog was less yellow now and more like the usual coastal overcast.

"Blazer," said Pepe. "Stop rattling."

Pepe spoke so quietly that Blazer missed the point of the mood. Pepe had made sure with the others that they understood his mood but now, closing in on the clinic, he felt strangely depressed. The fact was that more than a month's preparation had been lost that morning and while Pepe was angered on one hand, he also was relieved. The contradiction was more than he could handle. He felt sullen and withdrawn.

"So that's *your* smell," Blazer was saying. "What you do, Pepe, bathe in it?"

If the business of the morning were not at hand now, Pepe would have exploded without hesitation. But now the job started. He crossed Wilshire on Twentieth and then made his first stop. He nodded at two men in the back.

"Alberto's at the wheel in that T-bird over there. He knows where you're going." The two men got out on the street. "The guns are in the car. He'll tell you the rest."

The next stop was below Twentieth where the coastal fog was for real. Blazer could see well enough but there was a white haze over everything. The man whom Pepe dropped off was sent across the street where he had to stand by a drugstore entrance. His second was already waiting there. When Pepe started to roll off, Blazer said, "Are they going to watch that Buick over there or is that Buick watching them?"

During the next fifteen minutes Pepe dropped off the other two men at two different places and at least one of the times Blazer was sure that somebody else who was not one of Pepe's team was also watching the street.

"I saw it, I saw it," said Pepe with a lot of irritation. "And I don't know what the hell to make of it."

"You made a ring around the clinic," said Blazer. "Didn't you?"

"Messina's coming in."

"I know. And who else does?"

But Pepe was not up to it on this particular morning. He only knew enough to get to the office as fast as he could and let Nuncio or Marco—

most likely Marco, he figured—hassle over this thing.

He swung into the basement garage of the Tealbaum Building on lower Wilshire where the Messina Development Company took up half of the twentieth floor. Part way down the incline Pepe had a second thought and backed out again.

"I'm going to park on the street," he told Blazer. "With that concrete down there, the car phone don't work." He pulled up near a fire hydrant, got out, and told Blazer to sit behind the wheel. "There's now eight teams around that clinic and there's three men inside the place. If any of those guys call in," and he pointed at the car phone hanging under the dash, "tell 'em to call upstairs. Give them Cino's number."

"Why's Messina that worried?"

"Because he thinks he's gonna die, what else?"

"What about those other guys out there?"

"Don't bother me with spooks," said Pepe and walked away. He felt ghastly. Let his hotshot brothers handle that. He got on the elevator, disgusted with his own smell.

Nuncio Guarda was in the office which bore his name on the door. The office was not a half-wall cubicle like most of the office space on the Messina floor, but it had solid walls and a solid door. Nuncio required privacy.

He had his desk chair swiveled away from the room and was looking out towards the Pacific. He could not see the water.

When Pepe came in the two brothers said hello to each other and then not much else.

"There's fixings on the cabinet," said Nuncio. He was looking out of the window again.

"Why? You want me to make you one?"

"You know I don't drink during the day."

Pepe sat down on the leather couch by the wall and made the pillows hiss.

"How's that juicy wife of yours?" he said.

One of the phones rang on Nuncio's desk and he picked it up quickly. He said yes a few times and listened. Then he hung up.

"Man at Orange airport checking in. Messina isn't there yet."

"Orange? He uses International."

"We don't know where he going to land, or when."

"Careful bastard." Pepe thought a moment. "So careful, maybe he's pulling something."

Nuncio became very alert. He picked a pencil up and started doodling on the cover of a trust deed copy.

"And? Finish it," he said finally.

"There's maybe more men hanging around that clinic than I put there."

"Well? Did you look into it?"

"Into what? Into the car and ask the man what in hell he's doing there or I'll call the cops?"

Nuncio sighed. He would liked to have groaned instead or maybe kicked himself for the dumb move he had made. There was never any point in discussing anything with Pepe. The door opened and Marco came in. He looked winded.

"Any word?" he said. He did not stop to listen but went to the dressing room-bath that led off from Nuncio's office. He left the door open while he changed his clothes.

"He hasn't shown at any of the airports," said Nuncio. "But he left Palm Springs an hour ago."

"He ought to be here, with that plane he's got," said Pepe.

Marco was buttoning a fresh shirt. "The way he was feeling, he might be circling the Sierras before coming in. Anyway, I've got it set up and we've got the time."

"Got what set up?"

Marco came out, stuffing the shirt in his pants. His tie was hanging around his shoulders.

"This is the time," he said with emphasis. "We just crapped out with a complicated setup. This time we'll make it with a simple one. We got the clinic sewed up. And we walk in through all that protection and make the hit."

"Just a minute," said Nuncio. He had stopped doodling. "There are a number of obvious shortcomings ..."

"Not if he dies and nobody can tell it's a hit."

"My brother the big-assed magician," Pepe said.

"Just shut up a minute, willya?" Marco was buttoning his shirt. "For this job, I got the best, the unlikeliest professional. And with us pulling the watch, all he has to do is walk in and walk out."

"Who?"

"Ditch."

"Unlikeliest!"

"You outa your gourd?" Pepe's voice made his own sore skull reverberate like an echoing vault. "That freaked-out queer is going to set us up in business? Like Custer he's gonna set us up!"

"Don't talk dead history," said Marco but then, for the moment, nobody talked. The phone rang and Nuncio listened for a long time. Having said hardly anything himself he then put the phone down. First he picked up his pencil and dropped it again.

"That was Cipollo," he said.

Marco stopped knotting his tie.

"And you and Ditch," he said to Marco, "are not just going to 'walk in and walk out.'"

"Come on, give," said Marco in a careful voice. He looked a little bit like he was going to spring across the desk.

"On the basis of information received by the Don himself," Nuncio recited, "he extends us the assistance of additional men to protect our *capo* in the clinic, because his life has been threatened."

As if nothing else mattered, "By whom?" said Marco.

"Maybe Vinciguerra."

Marco relaxed like someone whose tendons were slashed. He went quietly to the window, leaned on the sill, and looked out. His brothers left him alone.

"Blazer saw it right," said Pepe. "Who are they?"

"*Capo* Trattomajore's crew."

"That *bastarde*— And all the way from San Diego—"

Pepe went to the sideboard and fixed a drink. The ingredients were one glass plus whisky. Nunico picked up his pencil, flipped it, and let it fall to the desk. The pencil bounced once and lay still.

"Well," said Nuncio. "From where I sit, that's that. We best forget about the whole thing." He waited until Marco had turned around, looking at him. "And whatever you had in mind for Ditch to do, Marco, they've got Cipollo's special, that Doctor Drexel, right up there in the room when Messina gets there."

Marco put his fists on the desk, silently like cat's paws. "*Porco*," he whispered, "*Porco, porco dio—*"

In the background, Pepe gave a wheeze and a cough and then made the careful sound of a glass touching a table top.

All that Marco did for the moment was to straighten up and walk into the dressing room. When he came back he had his jacket on and the tie tucked in straight.

"There's just this," he said. "I'm not stopping now."

Nuncio's loyalty was greatly colored by his notion that he was the inferior brother. Therefore, he was patient. Pepe's loyalty took the form of doing what he was told to do. But Marco had given him nothing concrete, and had failed to come through with the first scheme, which they had plotted for months, and now with the second one which he had made up on the spur of the moment. The great, fat-assed magician was a confusion to him.

He came out of his corner and yelled, "*Che fai*, huh? *Che cazzo fai, cretino disgraziado mio?* You gonna come down with a helicopter so they don't see you walking in at the door? Huh? Or let down a sky hook, maybe, and lift up the whole house outa the way for those dumb Trattomajores so they can't get near? No! You're gonna climb up through the plumbing, right? And when Messina sets himself down on the pot feeling secure with the door shut, you, maestro, will grab the slob by the balls and pull him down after you, huh? Did I figure that right, *bimbo?* Huh?"

Pepe had made a lot of noise. Both brothers said nothing for a moment, but for different reasons. Marco did not seem to have heard, and Nuncio wondered whether it was his turn to say something. He wanted to make the same point Pepe had made, but do it reasonably.

"We've got nothing to lose, if we drop it now, Marco. We're covered. You saw to that," he said. "And if we go ahead, with what do we go ahead? We got nothing!"

When Marco answered he sounded reasonable to Nuncio and he sounded strong to Pepe. They both needed him in their own way. He talked with a quiet intensity.

"We got the same thing we had when we started. Us. When I think of it alone, it's me. When I think of it with you, it's us. But you come right down to it, it's just what you've got yourself. It's just the me. Me that wants, me that can either afford it or can't. Anybody's say-so or a pat on the head is not where the action comes from. That's just crap for the peasants. Look at it, how it stacks up in the *regime*. Messina lends a name. He's riding an old reputation. *We* run things. He and that whole Family crap is just a thing in the head, something to impress the peasants. We run things!"

"The Don is strong," said Nuncio.

"Sure. All the strength the *regime* is willing to give. No Messina, no *regime*. Just us. No *regime*, and the Don gets no feed and the Don's got no channels to get to us."

"There's the other *capos*. The Trattomajores are here right now."

"Pepe tells his men to sneeze hard enough and the Trattomajores just fly out to sea."

"You don't believe that," said Nuncio. "Also, there's Cipollo. He holds the strings that hold the protection we need. I mean, if Messina were dead."

"You forget," said Marco, "we got plans for that."

"I know those plans. We need Rubenstein."

This was the loose end. But it would get looser and worse the longer they waited. Marco wanted to be convincing about that.

"The way his union is tied up into everything else, if he goes, the *regime* comes apart. I know that. And the only reason he's stayed is because he's got a loyalty to Messina."

"And more money than the usual," Nuncio said mildly.

"Rubenstein wants to quit," said Pepe. "I don't get it myself, but Rubenstein wants to quit."

"Some people got a feeling for retirement," said Marco. "And Messina knows, and so do we, when Rubenstein quits, the *regime* needs a hauling over and Cipollo does *that*. End of a strong *capo*. Or, in our case, end of a strong organization; strong enough so we don't need the Don."

"I point out," said Nuncio, "that I did not get a final yes from Rubenstein. He doesn't like the way Messina is trying to cut down on his take …"

"There's that feeling for retirement," said Marco.

"But he's on the fence when it comes to staying in, if Messina should be dead."

"I don't believe it," said Marco. "When Messina cut his take, he was glad enough when we paid the difference out of our own pocket. He's lit up every time when we diddled him with handing the loan operations over to him. You know that. Besides," said Marco, "you being the desk man, Nuncio, you don't appreciate just how much he worries out there in the rugged field. Pepe scares him. And he does want to take as much as he can into retirement. You don't really get that about the man, Cino."

"It's a gamble," said Nuncio.

At that point Marco was sure that he was on his way.

"Right. Always! But right now, a winning gamble. Messina goes and there's just us. The Don isn't ready for anything like this. Rubenstein isn't ready, so he won't pull up stakes. We need him, he still needs us. We hit now!"

"You've got another way figured out already?" said Pepe. He did not make clear whether he talked from admiration or scorn.

"Even so," said Nuncio. "I need time with Rubenstein. He's not sewn up."

"Any more than a few days?"

"A few days, yes. But how can you make a hit and everybody thinks it's okay, so it's a hit, so let's just stand around til the Guardas get themselves organized after such a loss?"

The sarcasm was unusual for Nuncio, so Marco figured that instead of dragging things out, the best thing would be to give his anxious brother a shocker. Just before, at the window, he had worked most of it out. Marco patted himself, as he often did, and then took a cigarette from a box on the desk. He lit it and then he grinned.

"I make it this way," he said. "Natural causes. There's going to be no hit."

CHAPTER 8

The difference this time was that Marco could not get near the clinic without blowing the hit. The difference was that Ditch had to get in on his own which was best done by making it look legitimate. Then it would be simple. And the less Ditch had to do, except for the things for which he had a talent, the safer it was to rely on him. Marco explained little but instead gave instructions.

"I need a drunk and I need an ambulance."

"Legit?" asked Pepe.

"Legit. Cino, order one that's got a garage near the wino belt. Downtown Broadway, San Pedro, you know where."

"Now?"

"Right. And I need ten thousand cash."

"Did you say ..."

"Come on. It pays for time we haven't got. And you, Pepe, get on the street with your men, but stay by the phone in the car. I'll call you when it's time for a little distraction."

"Tangle with the Trattomajores? Right out there in Squaresville?"

"No. To tell you when to pull your men out."

"*What?*"

"Then it's Cipollo's bag, don't you see? Besides, it'll flatter him." Marco was ready to go. "One more thing. I need one of your suits and stuff."

"Anything else? I mean, ten Gees and one of my suits doesn't seem quite enough at a quick glance."

"Cino, Cino—" Marco grinned again. He felt like rumpling his brother's hair. "I'll do the rest. Stay by the phones because I've got to know when Messina comes in. Ready?" and he went to the door.

"I'm asking you," said Pepe.

"I say ready," and he left the place.

Marco took Blazer along. Downtown, they found a drunk who was a proper drunk. That man knew everything and understood nothing. When somebody took the lamp post away from him he knew that he was nevertheless not going to fall. When somebody pulled the pavement out from under him he knew nevertheless that he was moving under his own power. He knew that the ambulance was a hearse in disguise and that somebody was making a serious mistake. He started to scream. This summoned two identical attendants, both of whom he killed instantly with a vicious word. Then there was peace.

That was as much as the drunk knew. After Marco and Blazer had gotten him into the rear of the ambulance, the young driver slammed the back door shut, got behind the wheel, and sat very still with Marco's gun pressing into his liver. The traffic hustling by on San Pedro looked as unconcerned as ever and the driver did not understand a thing. Marco, without having to say a thing, pushed the young man over the seat and to the back of the ambulance where the drunk lay on the floor. Blazer came in on the driver's side, slammed the door, and slid the big unit into the traffic going to Third. Marco put the gun behind his belt and looked at the driver. He looked like a beach bum temporarily dressed in white. His big shoulders stretched the tunic.

"Tell the man in front how you call your central."

"You pick up the mike ..."

"Louder. He can't hear you."

"Pick up the mike and the girl comes on. Then you press the mike button and tell her who you are and ..."

"He'll tell her. Who are you?"

"James Harlow."

"James, who are you when you call in?"

"Oh. You say, you just say, 'This is Zephyr ten.'"

He had hesitated too long. He could tell by the way Marco's face had changed from interest to something unreadable. He never saw the hand move but felt the hot, noisy splash of it across the side of his face and in his nose mostly.

"Again, Jamie." Marco's voice had not changed.

Nobody had ever gotten away with backhanding Jamie Harlow across the face. However, what changed his mind was Marco. He was the meanest looking guy Jamie had ever seen, and for the first time in his life, Jamie was scared.

"It says number two on the door," said Marco.

"What you say is ..."

"Louder."

"You identify with 'This is number two unit. Made pick-up on ...'"

"He knows the rest. Now the next thing, Jamie. Take a look at me and give me a description."

"Uh—a neat dresser. Big knot in tie, and a color scheme ..."

"Get off the clothes. Me."

"Black hair, sharp cheekbones, biggish black eyes—"

Marco hit the driver across the side of the neck, letting his knuckles catch the edge of the Adam's apple just slightly. Jamie gagged with all the fright of suffocation.

"Again, Jamie. What do I look like?"

"You—you gotta complexion like—like a tan. You got a straight nose—"

Marco hit him again. Jamie fell back from his crouch under the low-ceiling in the compartment and licked the metallic taste of his own blood from his mouth.

"Again, Jamie."

"You—got—mean, I mean, blue eyes and brown hair. Getting thin on top. You're like fifty—"

"Good. Sit up. Come on. I don't hit as long as we understand each other and the rest I'm going to tell you is important. Vital. You know what that means, *vital?*"

"Yeah—yes."

"Good. Here's what you did for the record. You picked up a fancy drunk ..."

"Fancy?"

"Just listen. On San Pedro. The drunk gave an address somewhere in Brentwood—he was mumbling, you see—on lower Montana. You got to the neighborhood and he sounds bad, like needing more than a good night's sleep. So you bring him to the nearest place you know, the Waynefort Clinic, and deliver him as a fancy lush who got loaded down in the wino belt. That's *all* you know. Clear?"

"Yes sir."

"I'll make it even clearer," and Marco reached into his jacket.

Jamie Harlow tried to shrink away into nothing but then he saw the bundle of bills. He had never seen such a stack, except in advertisements for insurance companies.

"Five thousand," said Marco. "What's your address?"

Harlow told him and Marco wrote it down on a manila envelope which was already stamped. Then Marco put the bills inside and sealed the envelope.

"First stop we make, I'll drop it in the mail. It'll reach you in two days. Of course, knowing your address, and assuming you decide not to play, I'll reach you. Clear?"

"Very."

"And in two days, think of all the surfboards you can buy with that, and all the endless summers on Waikiki. Now get in front while I prepare the patient."

Five minutes later Marco changed seats with Harlow. He raked his hair back with both hands, tucked his tie in, and smoothed his jacket. Blazer was bucking the traffic going west on the Santa Monica.

"I could open all this up with the siren," he said.

"Sure. What we really need now is a helpful cop, running interference."

"What was the screaming?" asked Blazer.

"He woke up for a sec."

"How's he look?"

"Just right, like a disaster."

"You got the rags off him?"

"Jesus," sighed Marco and wiped his hands absently.

"What did you forget?" Which was the sort of things that made Blazer special. He thought right along with his partner and kept step with the job.

"From the skin out, money, clothes," Marco recited for himself. "Some of it soiled. The head, just for show. Contusions, abrasions. Maybe a loose tooth. I did the right ankle, so they don't walk him out of there, just in case the kidney damage doesn't show."

"You planted the stuff?"

"Wallet, alligator, empty. One torn round trip stub, Vegas. You pass La Cienega yet?"

"I'm past Robertson. Where's your head, Marco?"

"I'm nervous, I'm nervous."

"A marvel how anybody as choked up in a pinch as you are ever got this far *and*—" Blazer paused for effect and to work his way into the off ramp lane. "—and is trying for more."

"Because I haven't got anything yet," said Marco without emphasis.

Blazer took the ramp to Overland and Marco started to look for the nondescript Chevrolet as soon as they were on the street. As arranged, Ditch was parked by the curb in the second block, except that he had pulled up next to a fire plug. Marco was cursing rapidly and Blazer kept his mouth shut. The ambulance slowed, turned into the next side street, and stopped.

"Go get him," said Marco.

Blazer was still getting out of the cab when the Chevrolet came around the corner. Ditch made the tires squeal. When he came to a stop behind the ambulance the car rocked on its springs.

Marco closed his eyes for a moment. My life and everything tied in with the kicks of a dope fiend. How much do I want any of this?

Marco Guarda did not like himself very much for this kind of thinking. It was no good for his style. It did not improve his hard, final way of making it with money, with safety, and with power. The vagueness of doubt could suck the marrow out of the bones of a man. There was only one answer: push some more.

He jumped out of the ambulance. He jerked his head at Ditch to get into the front and walked back to the Chevrolet with Blazer.

"The lab is a small place on Wilshire, like two blocks from the clinic. When you go there, watch out there isn't a Trattomajore bunch near enough to see you."

"You're slicing it thin, Marco—"

"Shut up. Here," and Marco handed the remaining five thousand to Blazer. "There's just the head man and one helper. Convince the man, like I told you."

Blazer nodded, got into the Chevrolet, and took off. The speed of it all relieved Marco and for a moment he felt as if everything were done and sewed up. Then he got behind the wheel of the ambulance and braced himself for the worst. Ditch and not Marco himself would now be the lone agent of everything. He drove back to the freeway and continued west.

Ditch looked back into the ambulance and then turned front again. Ahead, where the ocean would be, hung a vague disk of burnt orange intensity. That was the sun, which he could not see. He felt the orange heat on his skin and a slight shivering under his skin. He looked at his hands. They held quite still, showing nothing.

"When you called and changed plans," he said, "you didn't tell me there was meat in the wagon. Is he dead?"

"No. He's a rich drunk that got rolled on San Pedro. The blond guy's the driver. The reason you tell him to change course for the clinic, the drunk got worse."

Then Marco explained the condition of the patient in back and went over Ditch's routine again. Half way through he stopped and snapped his head around.

"Are you smoking a joint, you dumb bastard?"

"According to research conducted ..."

"Shut up and throw that thing out! You can't go on the job turned on!"

"Marco, if you knew how silly that sounds."

Marco whispered something between his teeth.

Ditch was sure that it was vulgar and most likely insulting, but what upset him was Marco's tone of voice. It was quiet and deadly.

Contrary to medical experience, Ditch became highly sensitive to other people when he was geared up with speed. Marco was sending him bad vibrations. Looking at him from the side, Ditch thought that the other's ears had flattened along the side of his skull. That, together with Marco's sharp white teeth, reminded Ditch of a wolf. Ditch looked away, turning carefully, as if afraid that his head might roll off.

"Before you lock me into this thing," he said toward the windshield, "I want to ask you something."

"Hurry up."

"Why did you give me this contract?"

"Ditch. You sound scared."

"Yes. Of you."

"I gave you the contract because I can count on you."

"Man—don't talk like that."

"Because you didn't ask me for money."

"Beautiful. I can always do that, like now."

"I can get a professional who'll do it for money. That's what he does it for. Which isn't you. I can count on you because it's for kicks, you need that most, and this one you never had before."

"You're making me nervous, Marco."

"Then don't ask me to tell you about you."

"Then maybe I'm nervous about the job."

"Never happen. Not this one. It's your kind of setting, your kind of smell in the air, and the technique is something you can do in your sleep. I *did* hire a professional."

"Right on," mumbled Ditch. "Professional coward—"

Marco took the off ramp to Twentieth and then headed North. He pulled over in the first block and let the motor idle. Ditch had one hand in his pocket.

"Give it here," said Marco and held out his hand.

Ditch did not move. His scalp under the thinning hair glinted a little.

"I'm shaking to pieces inside. I mean it, Marco."

"Did you over-amp, you sonofabitch?"

Ditch went stiff when Marco touched him while trying to get at the hand in the pocket. Then Ditch shook his head very rapidly.

"Cut it, cut it," he said with his voice sounding flitty and shallow. "I gotta hold on for a sec—"

Marco heard the distress and moved away a little.

"I want to know what the pill is, Ditch," he asked again.

"You trying to freak me, man?"

Ditch saw how Marco was getting that look again and he pulled himself together with teeth clenched. "Meth," he said, feeling weak and powerful all at the same time.

"You were going to *add* speed on that, you crazy head?"

"I got the system, Marc, I got the system, from experience, Marc," and then Ditch was going to explain it in detail, how speed on top of speed took the wobble out of the wheels. But he was not listening.

"When'd you eat last?"

"You trying to make me throw up?"

"Ditch, I'm trying to help you stay off that bummer that's starting to show on you. You can keep that bomb you got in your hand. You hold onto it. But just *hold on* a sec, okay?"

Goddamn that crazy, thought Ditch. Now it's a wolf sending me warmth. But he accepted what he felt coming from Marco, some kind of mothering warmth and no hassle at all. With the pill in his hand, he even felt the sort of calm and certitude which a drunk can feel once he has that first drink of the morning sitting in front of him, and once it is there he can just groove on it sitting there without even touching a drop for a while.

Marco was leaning into the back and talking to the driver. Ditch was not listening but just sat there like the drunk who feels all anchored with that drink sitting there in front of him. Then Marco came around again, sitting behind the wheel as before. He had a transfusion bottle in his lap and was working the top off its neck.

"Drink it," he said to Ditch and held the bottle out. Ditch looked at the dextrose solution and how it moved behind the glass, like oil. He gagged.

"One swallow. A small one," said Marco.

Ditch looked at the face next to him, the ears looking flat again, but then he saw Marco smile a little. He felt the warmth and listened to Marco talk to him like a father.

"Let me run this trip for you, Ditch, for just ten minutes. Here," and he put the bottle in Ditch's lap. "You got snow in your survival kit?"

Ditch nodded. He had a small deck of cocaine among his rations.

"Good," said Marco, and there was no doubt in Ditch's mind that Marco was taking him seriously all the way. "What I'm after is what you're after, to keep you off that bummer that's starting to show on you, and to put you on a trip that's special ..."

Ditch nodded again.

"Here's how. First a few sips of this," and Marco nodded at the bottle. "That's basics. Then a yellow, or whatever you take to get evened out."

"Yellows are fine."

"And then, like ten minutes before you go in on the job, a snort of cocaine. I want you bright and sharp in there. No shakes, and very, very smart. Now, first the meat and potatoes."

Marco did not wait for Ditch to pick up the bottle but shifted into gear and continued towards the clinic. Ditch felt all right now. He had a feeling of faith about Marco. There was a man who could make the gears mesh in a very beautiful way. He did not smash things up and then take over the shambles but instead geared into the other person and sort of made himself into the guiding force inside your own muscles. A vast comfort came from that. Ditch nibbled at the sugar solution and then took two workaday swallows. He sighed heavily a few times in order to keep the stuff down.

Ten minutes later Marco pulled the ambulance over again. Just ahead was the big Lincoln with Pepe leaning against the side. Before Marco got out he told Jamie, the driver, to get behind the wheel and he told Ditch to get into the back and attend to his patient. Pepe was waiting for him.

"I pulled the men off, like you said. Were those Trattomajores confused."

"Let's hope it does the same for Cipollo. What's the word on Messina?"

"He did set down at Orange, like you said."

Marco had not said that, but like Ditch, Pepe had a way of giving Marco a soul-satisfying sense of superiority.

"Where's he now?" asked Marco.

"Last word on the phone, he passed the Venice off-ramp about five minutes ago."

"He's later than we figured."

"Better than early."

"I hope," said Marco and watched Ditch walking to the back of the ambulance. "Right now we're on another kind of schedule. I've got to time Ditch."

"Listen, Marc, you really think that freaked-out head should ...?"

"Yes, I do. Get back to the phone, will you?"

The tone was a little too sharp for Pepe who was up in the air with too many quick-change routines coming from Marco. He stopped turning, without knowing ahead of time what he would say or do next. The sudden anger took over for him.

"*Che cazzo fai?*"

"Cool it."

"No! I wanna know how it's gonna work this time. Your set-up crapped out twice. How do you know ...?"

"I don't. But it will."

"How'm I gonna have confidence in something I don't know? Answer me that, *bimbo!*"

Marco shrugged, but he did it gently. It did not stand for indifference or resignation but it underlined a simple truth.

"Because I am your brother," he said.

Pepe's acceptance of the answer was inevitable. He nodded and went back to his car. Marco, feeling less at ease than he looked, went to the ambulance. Jamie was behind the wheel. He looked tense like an overtrained athlete. Marco nodded at him and went to the rear where Ditch was waiting for him. Marco scanned him the way a trainer might.

"How's the downer? Take hold yet?"

There was no sweat on Ditch's face and his eyes looked slow.

"I don't know if it's that or the dextrose. Listen, after I take the snow I need about fifteen minutes for it to come full on."

"Don't rush it. We got some fine tuned timing to do now. Messina won't get there for about half an hour. They'll be ready for him with their routines when he gets there, so I figure he'll be lying down five minutes after he gets in. How soon after can you walk in with your spiel."

"They'll take blood for clogging time first thing. It takes fifteen minutes to run."

"Plus ten minutes for the trip between lab and clinic makes thirty five."

"During that time they'll strap him into the EMG, the electromyographic ..."

"I know you know what it means." Marco checked his watch and figured how soon Jamie the driver should head for the clinic after word came through that Messina's car had left the freeway. He took a deep breath and looked at Ditch.

"You take the snow when the driver takes off. I'll give him the timing. Once you're there, do your routine with the drunk for fifteen minutes. You got that clear?"

Ditch nodded, thinking about the bright and sharp blast which the cocaine would put in his brain. Marco thought of the problem, of the hole in this last-minute attack.

"You got the floor plan in mind?"

"Sure."

"For godsake don't forget it. When you leave the drunk you switch roles, Ditch."

"I know. How old is Messina?"

"Pay attention! You got to make sure nobody sees you both ways, who you are downstairs and who you are upstairs."

"I'm not some kind of a nut, Marco! I want to get out of it as clean as you."

"All right," said Marco, "all right." He did not allow himself more.

"And I do hope," said Ditch with a disturbing intensity in his voice, "that he's a puffy, foul-mouthed old bastard, all helpless and freaked out with that great, big panic—"

Marco did not interrupt the private fantasy. He had to rely on it.

CHAPTER 9

The Waynefort Clinic in Santa Monica was a small, private establishment. It occupied a tree-shaded residence three stories high which was built in the Twenties. The overdone foppery of the facade was nowhere repeated on the inside. The Waynefort Clinic was a full-fledged hospital in precise, expensive miniature, and then some. Full scale hospitals, for example, did not have muted pastel drying-out rooms fitted with soundproof walls, light-proof drapes, and neutral music piped in through the wall. But everything else was standard.

The ward clerk put the file on the Messina account away and listened to the siren coming closer. She looked at her admissions roster and then at the current message sheet but saw nothing to indicate a predicted arrival.

Nevertheless, the siren came closer and then wailed itself down to a low throated expiration point. The ambulance, she concluded, came from a reputable company. They turned their racket off within prescribed limits of the hospital environs.

Within minutes she saw the long, shiny unit slide into the back drive and up to the ambulance ramp. Zephyr Twenty-four Hour Service, she read on the driver's door. Far from home base, she thought. They service mostly downtown, and out towards Alhambra. Obviously an emergency, and an odd one.

Miss Bradley saw the young driver in white spring from his cab, run to the rear, pull open the doors, and slide the stretcher out. Next, an orderly with a black bag hopped out of the rear and took the stretcher over. The driver closed the rear door and went back to his cab. All movements were fluid and swift, and in an instant the young man with the stretcher would slam through the swinging doors. Miss Bradley prepared herself for the usual.

Ditch saw the man who leaned by the wall. The man had both hands in his pockets and kept them there when he straightened up quickly. But the man did not know what to do next. He leaned again while Ditch slid through the doors.

Ditch saw Miss Bradley as soon as he came wheeling into the corridor. Never a sister of mercy, he thought, but always the biddy with the accounting pad.

"Where's your Receiving?"

"How do you do—"

"Come on, where is it?"

"That door. Can the patient talk?"

"He can't even breathe. Move it!"

Ditch pushed into Receiving where a young man dressed like himself was cleaning his nails.

"Dr. Waynefort?" said Ditch. He did not believe it but he had to ask.

"Dr. Sims. What you got?"

Intern, thought Ditch. Goddamn, moonshining intern making a buck on his day off and *that* wasn't in the plot either.

"Picked him up downtown for delivery in Brentwood. A mugging, I think. He just got worse. You want him here?"

"Just a minute," said Miss Bradley. "I need to know whether this is an insurance or a cash patient."

"Watch it, or it's a dead patient." He wheeled the stretcher next to the padded table. "I think he's going into shock," he said to Dr. Sims. "Pulse going like crazy last I felt him."

"Are you the driver?" asked Miss Bradley.

"I'm an R.N. How about yours, you got one around here?"

"Find Crocker," said the young man to Miss Bradley.

"And shake it, sister, shake it!"

Miss Bradley left, wishing that the swinging doors would bang. Ditch and the intern unstrapped the patient and nudged him over on the table.

"Scleral ictus," said the intern. "That, taken together with his awful breath suggests the diagnosis: drunk. Hand me the cuff, will you?" He pointed to the blood pressure gadget while taking the drunk's pulse.

Crocker came running in. Ditch made way for her and helped get the drunk's jacket off.

"Quite elevated," said Dr. Sims while letting go of the pulse. "Hundred and ten. What was it when you took it?"

"Same," lied Ditch.

The nurse strapped the sleeve on the drunk while Ditch pulled shoes, socks, pants and shorts off. The intern was pumping the cuff up and getting his stethoscope set. Ditch looked at his watch.

"Who signs him in?" Ditch asked the nurse.

"Dr. Waynefort," she said. "What makes you think we'll sign this—this one in?"

"Doesn't his suit look expensive enough?" said Ditch. He felt a great rush of exhilaration and had to check himself forcefully. His strongest urge now was to make brilliant chatter with the nurse and the doctor, with the latter to talk esoteric shop, with the former to shame her with her ignorance. He clenched his teeth and forced himself to slow down. It still came out fast.

"You don't move a patient in shock. You don't walk him out on a broken ankle," he pointed, "and if I read his underpants right he got socked in the kidneys and pissed his pants."

"*What?*"

"Hematuria."

"Oh," said nurse Crocker.

"One hundred over sixty," said the intern. "You were right about shock. Crocker, I.V. kit and a bottle of D-ten-W."

Ditch moved out of the way while Crocker put the intravenous set up together. His problem now was to get Waynefort down here, and keep him here.

"Shouldn't you get the chief?" he said to the intern.

"He's busy," said Sims. "He'll sign him in later." The intern checked eyes, jaw, neck, ribs, joints, and the blue-black swelling over one kidney. Ditch needed Waynefort in the receiving room, now.

When the nurse had the needle in and the dextrose was going into the drunk, Ditch stood next to the bottle stand. He kicked his black bag between his legs and sat down on the stool by the table. Then he got his own stethoscope out. While he hooked the instrument into his ears and set the diaphragm down on the place where the heart was beating he did a swift, one-handed finger piece inside the bag. His coked-up blood shot coked-up speed into his nerves and his muscles. He had to watch his precision. He got the hypodermic into the rubber top of the loose bottle in the bag and sucked up a few ccs. Then he pulled the syringe off the needle, all inside the confines of his bag.

"I don't like that heart," he said to Sims.

Sims laid the swollen ankle down and looked nervous. "Let me hear," he said and came up to the chest, getting his own stethoscope ready.

The drip tube from the bottle hung down next to Ditch where Dr. Sims could see only part of it. The add valve near the needle juncture was under Ditch's hand. Then the syringe with the nicotine solution was adding its fakery to the ease.

Nurse Crocker, who knew a drunk when she saw one, was getting a B-12 additive ready, just in case young Sims bethought himself of the standard procedure. He should know, she thought, seeing that unpremeditated labor pains and falling-down drunks were the bulk of an intern's on-the-job experience. Then she almost dropped the bottle.

"Get Waynefort!" yelled Sims. "The heart stopped!"

Nurse Crocker dashed from the room, still holding the B-12 solution. She ran right past the house phone out of experience. At such moments Dr. Waynefort always argued on the phone.

While Sims started heart massage, Ditch left the receiving room. He hoped that the heart would not start up too soon.

In a private hospital the corridor traffic is not very heavy. Ditch had to rely on that. He saw no one. He did not see the man who was standing guard outside the swinging doors, which meant that the man could not see Ditch either. He did not see Miss Bradley behind her glass partition because his back was turned towards her. Once around the bend which led to the stairs going up, Ditch put his bag down. One minute later he was carrying a small tray with racked tubes, syringe, heavy needle, alcohol, swabs and a coiled rubber tube. Also, he was now wearing a wrinkled lab coat. This was his image when Dr. Waynefort and Nurse Crocker passed him at single-minded speed. Shortly after that, on the second floor, Ditch entered Number Twenty-one where Messina was lying on a bed.

Naturally, he was not alone. Two men jumped away from their place by the wall and Dr. Drexel turned sharply from the bed. Messina did not move. Dr. Drexel, checking deep tendon reflexes, still had his hands on him.

"Sorry," said Ditch, heading for the night table. "The lab goofed."

"Goofed?" said Dr. Drexel.

"Blew it. Sorry, Doc. One side, buddy," and he pushed one of the men by the wall out of his way. He put his tray down on the bedside table and looked down at Messina. A mother, he mumbled. Whatta mother....

"May I ask," said Dr. Drexel with precision, "what in hell is going on here?"

"Like what?"

"First, an emergency downstairs which the attending physician is too incompetent to handle, then Dr. Waynefort dashing out at the beck and call of an ordinary L.P.N., and then—uh—you!"

"I'm the lab tech, Doc. Maybe we didn't goof, but the coagulation time was too long, that is, too long if Mr. Messina has maintained his K intake, which I assume he did. I'm taking another sample. Double check."

"Just a minute."

Dr. Drexel looked short and hard, and his color was grey: the hair, the eyes, the suit. His lips had no color either. He did not know the details which had led to his assignment, but he was on a *per annum* retainer from the office of Cipollo. That meant he worked only as assigned and then he worked without question. In this case, the assignment was simply that nothing untoward, medically speaking, should occur during the routine, periodic examination of a patient who had suffered a right hemiparesis. He knew, of course, who Messina was. He did not know who this cheeky technician was. In fact, he did not know anyone in the Waynefort clinic. Most of all, he found it unusual that a lab should have doubts about their results in the matter of a simple clotting time routine. Also, this young man seemed unusual. The rush in his voice, the precision of pronunciation, the hard glitter in his eyes.

Dr. Drexel walked to the head of the bed and looked at the tray. Tourniquet, sample tubes, bottle with alcohol, swabs, empty syringe, heavy needle capped in gauze. Dr. Drexel picked up the bottle and sniffed it. Most of all he wished to take an unobstrusive look at that young man's pupils.

Ditch turned his head to look at the two men by the wall, on either side of the door. He smiled at them alternately, until one of the men got uncomfortable enough to put his head down and look at his shoes. Ditch liked that. Then he checked his watch. The excitement rose like steam inside him.

"You may proceed," said Dr. Drexel. He went back to the foot of the bed.

Ditch felt the sheen of moisture grow on his scalp. He was humming. He sat down on the stool, in line with Messina's belly, and smiled at the old man's uncomfortable face. Everybody in the room could hear Ditch humming, but they did not get to hear the words which he kept inside: proceed with speed to feed the need of ... He did not finish that thought but instead gave words to the smile he was beaming at Messina.

"Are you ready for the final trial?"

"Huh?"

"The last try. Your arm, please—my! What youthful veins, Mr. Messina. I wish I had a vein like that. Ooops! is that too tight? Please, no fist clenching. Your vein's popping as it is. What a pop! Ready?"

"You gotta talk crap like that? Just do it," said Messina. He sounded pained and uncomfortable. He had things on his mind.

Ditch held the empty syringe and pulled the plunger jack to fifteen ccs. A big, sluggish mother like that, he was thinking, and the veins all glued up with sludge inside, better give him a regular mother of a slug. He kept the syringe down so that Dr. Drexel, who was at the foot of the bed trying for a Babinski on Messina, could not see the business end of the performance.

"Well, Mr. Messina, here you go." And then Ditch added silently, good-bye. Good-bye you ugly mother, you everloving motherloving answer to my—easy now.

He turned all business, easing the tourniquet so that he would not have to cope with the pressure of the blood. He omitted the swabbing of the area, though he remembered about it. He sunk the needle with that healthy feel of pop through the epidermis and swish through the rest and into the spongy vein. He allowed to suck just a little purple sap —played with it and made pink froth, envied Messina his unmarred veins, and then—he was flashing now—pushed the plunger home.

He did not forget protocol. Ditch sucked up a fat column of blood because that's what he had announced as the purpose of his visit. He nodded a smile at Messina whose face was relaxing into putty after the needle ordeal. He gathered up his paraphernalia and breezed out while Drexel was hunting for a patellar on the right side of the patient.

Ditch was done but he wanted his due. The door, without lock, swung back imperfectly. Ditch had his shoe in the crack. He saw Messina's bulk laid out on the bed, limp and waiting. Drexel, unseen, imparted an occasional, passive motion to the body, liked pudding that shakes and comes to rest. Face turned up, Messina's eyes were probably directed at the blank ceiling. From blank ye come, to blankety-blank ... Ditch stopped and watched.

Messina, the still bulk, was shaken with clonic spasms which thrust out his jaw, jerked his arms, fluttered his hands, and jolted his chest. An obscene sound was pressed out of him and with that, he collapsed into stillness.

Ditch let the door slide shut. He was disappointed.

CHAPTER 10

At times of extremity, Cipollo did not sweat. He could see the late afternoon sun as a brown luminescence now and he had an unpleasant sensation of heat. He felt the telephone in his palm and the contact was like glass on dry paper. After a short wait in great distress he reached Angelo del Mare on the private line.

"What can't wait?" said the Don. "I'll be in Los Angeles in two hours."

"Don't come, Don Angelo. Messina is dead."

At first Cipollo only heard a hissing, then silence.

"*Maledetto*," said the Don very quietly.

In Sicilian use, the term was the opposite of a benediction and, as used by some, was meant to protect from further evil. Angelo del Mare, a thoroughly modern man, sometimes fell into ways which were even incomprehensible to himself. But then he recovered quickly.

"What else do you know?"

Cipollo reported all the stray facts which he and several telephones had been able to gather in the short time since the death. He also added what he thought, which he offered separately. Then he had to wait out the Don's silence again.

For del Mare, it was an unusual welter of probabilities, surprises, and dangers. Of course, nowadays, in the streamlined business fashion in which *cosa mafiosa* had become syndicate operation, everything was a disaster that did not spring from the nitpicking pages of shysters and bookkeepers in his employ. In that way, everything meshed nicely with the legit, was slower, and was a pussyfooting drag. *Né carne né pesce,* he thought. Who the hell am I? He calmed himself by running his eyes over the open page of a ledger that lay on his desk. He added the figures as swiftly as he scanned them with his eye and came up with the same total as the one at the bottom of the column. Then he slammed the ledger shut.

"First question, before anything else. What's the action in the territory? You didn't mention any."

"There isn't. There is no disruption. I sent a few key people but they found nothing to do. The Guardas are handling everything. It is for that reason that I have the feeling ..."

"You got no feeling, *consigliere*."

"After a sudden death, Don Angelo, after a death for which there is no preparation, there is always a shock wave, and a vacuum. There is no vacuum in the *regime*. My conclusion is obvious."

"It's a guess. I will test it later. Next, *consigliere*. Was it a hit or was it natural death? Drexel says natural causes. A massive stroke. What Drexel says don't make sense to you?"

"I am no physician. However, I have to explore other factors, other than medical ones, Don Angelo."

"Let's say you explore the fact that an old cock like Messina with a blood pressure like a fire hose does a regular job of balling on that kid, what's her name, who's sixteen years old."

"I am not qualified to ..."

"I bet you're not." Del Mare sighed. He had exercised his spleen. It was a periodic thing which had less to do with Cipollo than with all the checks and balances which the *consigliere* stood for. Then del Mare went back to business.

"By your lights, Cipollo, where's the hole?"

"I have to look at everything that is unscheduled in the proceedings, Don Angelo."

"Start with Pepe Guarda. He pulled out his men and left only the Trattomajores. Smart! Now security is your responsibility."

"The pretext, of course, is that my orders superseded his."

"Plus the flattery to your superior know-how."

Ignoring the comment, Cipollo went on, "The effect was relaxation."

"So what got through, that ambulance? You said the call was legit."

"It was. But the patient has not been able to identify himself or explain the events."

"He's a talking drunk?"

"Er—yes. But nothing makes sense."

"Have him dried out at Waynefort's place and then go at him again."

"I have arranged it. But it is my point, Don Angelo, that this takes time, and that an optimum takeover always profits by time."

Del Mare knew that this was true. The way to check out any individual takeover was to try and take over himself; replace lieutenants, reroute collections, clear every action in the territory through Cipollo's office. A lot of waste, a lot of waves, especially if all were done without cause. Del Mare's bind was as tight as ever.

"You checked out the ambulance driver?"

"He never went inside. The orderly did."

"Who's the orderly?"

"Not a regular employee of the service. They have a call list for heavy days and they don't collate the call personnel and the service rosters on a daily basis. So ..."

"It takes time. I know. What about the guy from the lab?"

"That checks. He sent out for a second blood sample."

"Same man who took the first sample took the second one?"

"No. That is, maybe. There hasn't been time."

"Time."

"I understand your distress," said Cipollo who felt under heavy pressure, "but the odd chance exists that the orderly who came in with the ambulance case and the technician who came for the second sample of blood might be the same person. If that were the case ..."

"You checking that out?"

"Yes. There is a lady, Miss Bradley, who keeps the records. She's trying to remember whether she saw the orderly leave with the ambulance or not."

"And it'll take time. Any law in on this?"

"Not unless you say so. It's 'natural causes,' as you know."

"So what have you got, counselor?"

Cipollo had nothing. He had a smart crook's intuition about opportunity and when it was ripe. That was how he knew in his bones that the Guardas had their opportunity now. Their position of strength had been in force for some time, and only a tricky state of health, an addiction to teenagers, and a blindness about blood loyalty could account for the fact that Messina had not thrown the Guardas to the wolves long ago. The wolf, of course, was Marco. There was a lust for getting his way, using everyone, and for coming out owing no one. The Family had bred a loner. Not that he would ever take it over because, built as he was, Marco would simply destroy it. So, what did Cipollo have?

"I don't know how to answer you, Don Angelo," he said into the phone.

There was a moment's pause. Del Mare had a keen ear.

"You're not satisfied," he said to Cipollo. "Go ahead and stick with it." Then del Mare said what he saw in the midst of all the vagueness. "If the Guardas made the hit, then a lot of the setup shows that they still need time. Get a straight story out of that woman."

"Miss Bradley."

"That one. If it shows that the orderly and the lab man were the same, then it was a hit."

"Why not treat it as if they'd done it?" said Cipollo.

"Because you'd have to bust up a very strong *regime*, Cipollo! You know what that means?"

Cipollo knew. It would mean that the struggle would show, that the struggle could not remain strictly Family business. And then all the connections in the legitimate world would run for cover, and the law would come in, and the newspaper zealots. Syndicate business was good only when it took place behind closed doors of *omertà*. Like the blood bond, another one of the mafia legacies which Marco Guarda could not be counted upon to respect.

"Then how do I handle the Guardas?"

"Screw the Guardas," said the Don. "Find Vinciguerra."

This astonished Cipollo. Del Mare was always a little puzzling, but at some times it was worse.

"He is not in Tucson," said Cipollo.

"You told me. Get me somebody who saw him last."

"Cass was there when Vinciguerra showed up."

"Get him."

CHAPTER 11

The evening traffic along the beach ran heavy to open convertibles and to vintage delivery vans painted wild colors, with surfboards sticking out of their ends. But Nuncio's limousine had other company too. Heavy Jaguars and overpriced Maseratis were wending their way towards their Malibu Beach nighttime slots.

Nuncio sat in back with Cass, and Marco sat up front with the driver. A flotilla of button men followed their limousine. At this late sunset hour the sky had come into its own. A red and blue cloudscape glowed overhead and arced way out to an orange horizon. The Pacific lay still under it.

"We're going to be late," said Nuncio.

"If we are, so is Rubenstein," said Marco without turning back. But he had to say something else so that Nuncio could get his mind on something. "What's the last you heard in the office?"

"Not much. That's why."

"Pepe's men are out. So don't worry."

"I haven't heard from del Mare."

"So what. You heard from Cipollo. And he didn't have any messages."

"I know that. But he hasn't pulled out the Trattomajores either."

Cass sat quietly through all this. If he had told them that he felt grief over Messina, they would not have understood.

The limousine worked its way across the Pacific Highway and into a parking lot which was a long deck built out over the beach.

"Should we send a man in first?" asked Nuncio.

"Crap. Not in this place."

The restaurant was a three-level post and beam structure that staggered down to the beach. It was all glass between the massive poles. Inside, at the bar and the tables, were mostly film industry people. They made the business look like all happiness and money.

"Did Pepe say he's coming?" asked Marco.

"I don't know." Nuncio got out of the car and hesitated when he looked at the view. "Matter of fact," he said, "I asked him to keep an eye on Inglewood. I was sure the Trattomajores would get pulled out by now."

"Oh Christ, Cino, stop worrying. Everything's arranged."

The street in Inglewood looked as it was intended, a clipped suburbia with lamp posts on lawns and leaded windows under eaves. There was also a touch of haste, as if the developer had been thinking of other things. But there was nothing anywhere to show that this was Messina territory. Regular people lived here.

Rosetta Guarda sat in the front room. The T.V. set was chattering and the dishwashing machine made a hum in the kitchen. She still had her apron on.

"In fifteen minutes," she told the two children, "you turn that off."

"But I don't *have* any homework—"

"Shush now."

She got up from the hassock because the door chime was ringing. When she opened the door she was a little startled.

"Pepe!" she said. "I thought it might be Harriet from next door."

"Naw," he said. "Look again." He grinned at her and walked in.

Sometimes his resemblance to Nuncio startled her. It startled her that so heavy a face could remind her of her husband's.

"Is anything wrong?"

She closed the door but saw that he had not heard. He was rumpling Paula's hair and was saying something. The children got up to hug their uncle because they were raised that way. Then they sat down again. Pepe went to the breakfast bar that separated the living room from the kitchen.

"Anything wrong?" she asked him.

"Course not, Rosie." He grinned again and looked her up and down. "Leave that on," he said. "You look good in an apron. Notice how that flower comes blooming out over your boob there?"

"Stop that, Pepe!"

He said "*Mu*" then dropped his hand. "Matter of fact," he said and looked around the room, "Cino asked me to drop in."

"What for? You *did* say there was nothing wrong."

"Nothing, Rosie," he let her worry for a moment, and then, "There's a different bunch in town, is all, and Cino asked me to check ..."

"Don't," she said and looked very stern. "I don't want to hear about that, Pepe. You know I don't ever want to hear about that!" She turned sharply and walked away to the nursery.

Pepe followed her and watched how she moved when she walked. She left the door to the nursery open and went to the crib where her youngest was sitting up and looking at her with large, quiet eyes. Then the baby looked past his mother towards the door, where Pepe was coming in.

"You know, Rosie," he said, "I read in a magazine once how when the mother is nervous she can give it to her kid, just like giving him a cold she's got."

Rosetta turned his way abruptly, grabbing the crib behind her just as someone might who is leaning against a railing. Pepe smiled again. He liked the tension in her body and face.

"Where is Cino?" she said. "Is Cino all right?"

"But honey, you said we shouldn't talk about it."

Rosetta felt caught and helpless with confusion, and then Pepe walked up to her and put his arm around her.

"Come on now, honey, it's all right."

She felt the warmth and the strength in his body and quite involuntarily she held on to him.

"He's fine, Rosie. I'm telling you. I can even tell you where he is, just sitting with Marco and a businessman, having dinner."

She heard him and she knew that he was saying more but then she could feel him, against her thigh. He was patting her head, but she mostly felt him moving against her thigh. She tried to twist away, but Pepe was holding her. He looked down at her face, watching her.

"Hey now," he murmured, "hey! You're not gonna scream, are you, honey? Think of the children. What are those kids gonna think, if you scream and they come running in here, huh, Rosie?" All this time he kept her pressed close but turned her away just enough so he could use his free hand. He pulled the apron strap off one shoulder but did not try to do anything to the top of her dress. He just ran his hand around and squeezed her as if testing a product.

"Hey, Rosie," he kept saying, "that's all yours, huh, Rosie, hey! Now you listen, you best hold real still, huh, Rosie? Now you just feel that, because one of these days ..."

"Mother of God," she said through the hoarseness in her throat. "Please—the baby, he's watching." And then, quite suddenly, she went limp against him.

Pepe took a deep breath, then sighed. He felt quite satisfied and even benign. He let go of Rosetta and let her lean against the crib.

"There, you see? No harm done. Like it's all in the family, huh, Rosie?" Pepe looked around again, as if he did not know what to do next, and then he went to the door. "I'll tell Cino I was here, like he wanted it. I'll tell him I found everything was all right. And when I say all right, I *mean* ..."

"Get out!"

The change in her startled him. He felt that a beast was looking at him.

"Now," she said. "Out!"

"Watch it," he said but kept going towards the door that led to the outside while she followed him. "You just watch it."

She stopped in the doorway while he turned back and looked up at her from the steps.

"Next time, Rosie, it's gonna be *tutto o niente*, and *niente* has never happened with me."

"Yes," she hissed at him. "I will kill you! *Tutto o niente!*" And then she slammed the door.

Pepe spat on the sidewalk and went to his car. He picked up the car phone and waited for his connection. The man in the parking lot with the view of the ocean reached into his car and answered the call.

"Yeah?" he said.

"Who's that? That you, Blazer?"

"No. Gino. You calling from Inglewood, Pepe?"

"Right. They still talking inside?"

"Yes. Nuncio says he wants to talk to you personal when you call."

"Tell him I don't have time. Tell him his wife didn't expect no family. I walked in and she was expecting a neighbor. You get it?"

"A neighbor? Yeah, yeah, I get it. You really want I should—" Gino stopped talking because Pepe had hung up.

In the restaurant, at a table where the windows formed a corner like the end of a flying bridge, the group looked like people who were chatting over drinks. The hum of the room covered their talk. Nuncio interrupted everything when he saw Gino walk towards the table.

"Be right back," he said and got up.

"Sit down, Cino—" But Marco did not reach his brother. He watched the man from the car talk into Nuncio's ear.

"Well," said Rubenstein, "we going to talk or we going to whisper?"

He looked around with his perpetual look of being harassed by dirty jokes and by a dirtier fate. There was a cast of suffering around his eyes but the eyes themselves were quite hard. His stocky frame looked hard, as if all the muscle and fat had turned to cement. Marco, who appeared cool and alert, was the one who felt harassed by dirty jokes and by a dirtier fate. Cass turned out a dud, behaving as if he were the bereaved retainer who wanders aimlessly through the echoing halls of the manor house. Nuncio was high-strung and had shown a tendency to get stubborn. Rubenstein, for his part, never seemed to have heard of bargaining. Every suggestion was a shock, and every compromise violated the memory of a dearly departed.

"So, would you explain again, in slow English, about the *kakamaika* with the loan company?"

"All right, Nate," said Marco. "It really amounts to just this. The longshoremen and the equipment operators, all that comes in from those unions you keep. That really means a loss of income up to a hundred fifty Gs per week to the *regime*. In return, Nate, you do work contracts like we say, like Nuncio figures out from the larger picture."

"Markele," said Rubenstein, his forehead bunched up in painful concentration. "You trying to tell me something? You trying to say to me maybe, here, Nate, you make like you got something, you just go on and pretend you got a union but me and my baby brother and that gorilla brother, we play with it, like something new from under a Christmas tree?"

"Nate, it's open and shut—we need you. More building inspectors, safety inspectors, precinct inspectors, and daylight savings inspectors are hooked in on the protection through your unions than any other place in the territory. That has got to remain without waves. *And* we got to be able to control the plain economics of all those peasants so we can hook in with the loans, the road contracts, and not to mention the trade in dope. And for all that, which is a lot, you get a lot. You get Pepe's army, you get Nuncio's City Hall-pipeline protection, and you get a quarter mil per month. Now, I don't know how to make it any plainer, or more honest."

"Hm," said Rubenstein. "You know what it means, *chutzpa?*"

"It sounds like you're going to spit up a lung. Here's Nuncio."

Nuncio sat down and said nothing.

"What was it?" asked Marco.

"Nothing. Just go on with what you were doing."

"I sure as hell don't want to go on with what I was doing."

Rubenstein laughed, sounding as if a whole quarry was having a landslide. People turned their heads to stare at them.

"He's right," said Rubenstein. "You talk to me, Nancy-o. You and I know about the feelings people got when they talk about business that's got their life blood in it."

He wants in, thought Marco. He's ready—

"The name is Nuncio."

"Huh? Why, I should apologize!" said Rubenstein. "Here. I bite my tongue. And I apologize for me such a poor immigrant boy who don't know American like you native *goyim*. *Si, si*, Signor Noonsio Gwaarrde?"

Marco was dying inside.

"Nate, for godsake, at least one of you don't lose your head. Just forget my kid brother and his lousy manners, willya, Nate? We're not talking personalities, Nate. We're talking about helping each other!"

"You mean, business."

"Right. And it's got your life blood in it, Nate. You can't call it retiring when you're abandoning something like that!"

"You talk sense, Markele."

When he uses that awful name on me, Marco thought, then he's with it again. We're on—

"Nuncio," he said. "Can you add something at this point?"

"Sure. Did you tell him about the protection that Pepe can render?"

"Sure."

"Trustworthy," said Nuncio to Rubenstein. "That's one thing. And once he's locked into his work, Mr. Rubenstein, he'll as soon smash everything in his way as give you the time of day."

"Huh? What kinda *mishigass* now?"

"Forget that," said Marco. His voice was clipped and he felt himself getting hard with anger. "My idiot brother is not even here. Let's you and I ..."

"What about that ape you got for the other brother? That time he muscled the Rizzos outa the numbers game he caused a lot of breakage."

Rubenstein shook his head, to get rid of the awful scene he remembered, something that put him in mind of newsreels and documentaries of Nazis and concentration camp torture. He wanted to get clear of all that, and clear of that greenhorn brother, because here was a fitting deal, a crowning thing to be done before leaving the business.

"Anyway," he said. "I listen to you, Markele. The fact is, you can do a lot for me. I can get out, and lose a lot. I can go to Cipollo, and get hardly nothing. I can do business with, you, Markele. Maybe not so good with Nuncio here, and maybe never mind about that ape you got for another brother. He got to have a firm hand put on him. I mean that really. The way he did those men in, and then what I heard about him and the Rizzo woman. Well, anyway, Markele ..."

"Did you know," said Nuncio with precision, "did you know, Mr. Rubenstein, that Pepe knows your granddaughter?"

"Wha—Whatsat?"

"The grown-up one. She's fifteen, I think?"

Now the ice came down all over that corner of the room. Rubenstein stood up.

"Is that *putz* trying to tell me something, Marco?"

"Nate—" Marco had to take a deep breath before he could go on. Then he said, "I'll take care of him, Nate. Forget him. Let's you and me get out of here so we can *talk*. Talk sense, Nate."

"I get out. You stay. You talk. To the *putz* brother."

"Nate!"

"Don't call me. We'll call you," and with that depressing platitude, Nate

Rubenstein walked out.

Marco sat down again. For a moment he just watched Nuncio as if through a very long telescope. The focus would not adjust. Nuncio too gave no sign of recognition. He was drinking from his warm highball until the glass was empty.

"Mr. Guarda," said Cass.

Marco looked around as if he had forgotten that Messina's sidekick had been there.

"I don't guess you need me right now," said Cass. "How about I blow?"

"Go blow," said Marco. "Everything did anyway—"

CHAPTER 12

Angelo del Mare made his last bow, gave his last nod, and then flashed his last smile for the evening. It was midnight and time for work. He had disentangled himself from the guests and their artificial fever. His large room was dark, except for the lamp on his desk, and for a while he stood by his picture window. In the daytime the view was dead. All the neon looked dead, and beyond that, of course, there was the dead desert. At night it was different. Colors of excitement were pumping through the neon veins of the view down below. He took his dinner jacket off and dropped it where he stood. He did the same thing with his tie and then went to sit down at his desk. Cipollo in Los Angeles was ready at the phone.

"No," he said. "It's not like you could say anybody took over. The Guardas are just running things like before."

"Anything on Vinciguerra?"

"Yes. But it's nothing, Angelo. He's in Tucson, in his house, watching the midnight movie."

"So what if he's right now watching television?"

"No action, Angelo. He hasn't made any withdrawals, he hasn't seen anybody he used to know. Please, Angelo, forget that for a moment. I *have* action."

"Whose?"

"As you thought," said Cipollo, distorting the facts as a matter of flattery. "Marco and his brothers."

"*Porto dio*," said del Mare and then he concentrated with force.

"There was that hole in the setup, Angelo. If it was the Guardas, then they needed time. If they needed time, then there may have been hasty covers. I found it."

"Stop scratching the ass, Cipollo. What?"

"The lab men described the technician he sent and the ambulance driver described the orderly he brought along. They both looked the same."

"Like who?"

"Like the man whom the ward clerk saw come in with the ambulance but who didn't leave with the ambulance. He went upstairs in the clinic, you remember."

"*Who?*"

"I don't know if you know of him. His name is Ditman, or Ditch."

"Friend of the Guardas?"

"Marco's. Yes."

"And you have this Ditch?"

"Not yet. Cause of death, by the way, was probably an injection of air, according to Dr. Drexel. He says ..."

"Never mind what he says. Find this Ditch. In the meantime, we're going on the assumption that the Guardas let out the contract, that they covered the way they did to gain time, and that the time was to swing Rubenstein. Have they met yet?"

"I'm not certain. Pepe didn't meet him. The other two went off together with Cass, but we lost them in traffic."

"Get Cass," said the Don.

"How about simply asking Rubenstein?"

"Cipollo, did anybody ever *simply* ask Rubenstein anything and get *simply* an answer?"

Cipollo nodded at the phone.

"Besides," the Don continued, "he's in a tricky place, if he's talked to the Guardas, and there's no point spooking the man while he's sitting where he's dug in."

"As you say, Don Angelo."

"Find Cass. He will know."

Marco knew that the time he had bought with ten-thousand dollars was fast running out and at any time now Cipollo's tricks and the Don's money would find the hole. He wondered how Blazer had made out with Ditch. The other two peasants, the lab man and the surfer kid did not matter. By the time Cipollo could piece a story together from the little they knew, the time would have been well spent or it would all be down the drain anyway.

And now? Marco sat alone in his car, in the dark, down at the gut end of Wilshire. The night sky looked like dust on velvet and the street frontage looked cheap; too many neon lights jumping around like sick nerves, too many cars glaring too much. But there was an odd calm in the air, the odd calm of not knowing. This was the bad phase—

And Nuncio? He apologized and clammed up. Then he had clammed up some more and did not bother to react to the disaster with Rubenstein. This should have been the time to work all the steps through with Nuncio. *Cazzo—*

He started the car with too much of a howl and took off. He suddenly knew exactly where he had to be.

First he stopped at the Tealbaum Building which he reached in ten minutes. He reached Pepe from there in one of his cars.

"How's your end?" was the first thing he asked.

"Nothing. Like nothing happened. And yours?"

"Like nothing happened," said Marco. "Never mind that. I've got to find Cass. You got enough men out to check this through?"

"Where do they look?"

"The old Messina place in Beverly Hills, the bar he hangs out in on Hollywood and Western, and—where else? Didn't he used to visit his mother?"

"She's dead."

"The funeral parlor!"

"Come on, *bimbo*, she wouldn't be lying there for five years."

"Where Messina is, jackass."

"Oh. Didn't think for a minute."

"I want him brought in. The house we got in West Hollywood is a good place. I don't want him to talk to anybody from Cipollo."

"Gotcha. Hold it."

Marco could hear Pepe talking to somebody about finding Cass. Then he came back on the phone.

"You got a notion where Blazer is?" Pepe wanted to know.

"No. Why?"

"He went after Ditch. He didn't bring him in and he didn't show up himself."

Marco was not worried, especially about someone competent like Blazer. But he had a question of his own.

"How about Nuncio? What happened to him?"

"I don't know. He called in through the board to say he was home, in case something came up."

"I don't mean that. I want to know what's wrong."

"With him? You name it," said Pepe.

"You called the man in the parking lot, and left a message that Rosetta was with a neighbor and you walked in and surprised them."

"Crap," said Pepe. "She was surprised to see me. She was expecting a neighbor. Ask her, *bimbo*. That's all she'll tell you." And then Pepe said, "Just a minute," and left the phone.

His tone had been nasty. There had always been some pressure of difference between the brothers, but this tone was something extra. Marco wanted to tell him to lay off, that this wasn't the time, but Pepe was not on the phone. He was making sounds in the background. When he came back it was not time for family matters either.

"Dicky and the Cat found him in the funeral parlor, but Dicky says he won't come along."

"What did they do, come at him with guns?"

"I told them like you said."

"They shouldn't harm him, tell them that. And I'll be right over."

Marco hung up and five minutes later he was threading his car through the empty streets towards Beverly Boulevard where the funeral parlor was.

And if the Don was worth his salt, thought Marco, he'll have Cipollo send the Trattomajores to all the same, likely places. On the off chance that this might be true, Marco passed the parlor at normal speed and then swung into a side street to park.

There had been a few empty cars on the street. The Cat had been leaning against one of them, looking at the funeral parlor with the thin, white columns painted on the black stucco. The decorator's shop next door had the same facade.

When Marco came back to Beverly on foot, the scene had changed. A police cruiser was pulled up to the Cat's car. One officer had Cat leaning with hands on the roof of the car and was frisking him. The other officer just stood by.

Inside the funeral parlor was Dicky with a gun and there would be Cass with a gun. There would be poor visibility and just the sound of their breathing....

"None of your big, blue lip," said the officer who was doing the frisking. He tapped Cat on his back and stepped away. "You can straighten up, feller."

"It's *Mister*," said Cat. "If that's all right with you, pig."

"You know something," said the officer. "You calling me pig is like me calling you nigger, right?"

"Right."

"So don't call me that, feller."

"Except I figure you got such a handicap on me, I got the right to a little gratis, pig."

Cat was very big and very fast, and he could have taken both policemen in a pinch. When Marco came up, he thought that Cat might try to do just that and he was sure that the officer who was standing to the back was already going for his gun.

"Excuse me," said Marco. It sounded very mild.

"Beat it," said the officer who had done the frisking. He stepped away for better freedom of action and talked to his partner without looking at him. "Call in for a wagon," he said.

"Just a minute," said Marco. The haste showed in his voice. "And while you're on the radio, ask for Captain Lattimer. That's Burglary. Downtown."

"Why?"

"So he can vouch for me. If he's in at this hour," Marco added. The touch of realism, he thought, might take the comic opera desperation out of the set. Then he went on, "My name's Marco Guarda," and held out his wallet with the driver's license showing.

The officer did not bother to look.

"Ever hear that name?" he asked his buddy.

"If it's the same one, yes," the other policeman replied. "You're the Messina boy, aren't you?"

"He was my boss," said Marco. "He died in the Waynefort Hospital this afternoon. He's in there."

The officer turned to look at the funeral parlor.

"How's that explain anything out here?" and the officer nodded at the Cat.

"He was told to drive a friend of the family down here. A friend who's mourning inside there right now. That's a fact, officer. I don't know what the gentleman here told you."

"Did you hear Messina's dead?" the policeman asked his partner.

"I heard it on the six o'clock," said the other officer.

"Okay," said the first one. "Maybe so."

He hesitated and looked around because a car was driving by. It drove rather more slowly than normal and there were four men in it. The Cat looked too and then grinned at Marco.

"San Diego plates," and then to the officer, "I make a hobby of knowing."

"Look, officer," said Marco. He made no attempt to disguise the haste in his voice. "To get all of us off the hook, I'll just go in and bring out the mourner. His name's Richard Catania and he's a blood relative of the deceased. I guess you know how ..."

"Stop wringing my heart," said the officer. "First I get a race riot from him there, now I get Sicilian ancestor worship. All I'm interested in, Mr. Guarda ..."

"Let me just get him," said Marco, who felt the pressure of trying to solve a great number of problems with one stroke. He went quickly into the building, closed the tall door behind him, and called Dicky's name.

"Here!" said Dicky.

Off the dim hall was an open doorway to a room with chairs all along the walls. To the other side was a door marked Office where Dicky was looking through the crack.

"Where is he?"

"Which one?" said Dicky.

He let the door swing open and there stood a bald man who looked hastily dressed. He had an overcoat on which showed a sport shirt without tie and casual slacks.

"This is his place," said Dicky. "Cass called him to open up for a special showing."

"*Viewing*, sir," said the funeral director.

"And where is the bereaved?" asked Marco.

"With the deceased."

"And where is that one?"

"They're both locked in there," Dicky pointed to the back. "Mr. Stonewall here is a little bereaved himself about the way Cass acted up crazy when I showed."

"All right, all right," said Marco. "Mr. Stonewall. I want to help you save the good name of your parlor here ..."

"Establishment, sir."

"And that too, so go on out there and tell the cops in your own, serious way, how the deceased is a little crazy with bereavement ..."

"The bereaved."

"Shut up. You do that and send them away, sir, and for that special service you can pad the fee for the corpse ..."

"Deceased!"

"... with this here," Marco stuck two fifties into Stonewall's hand and started shoving the man towards the door, "which will help embalm your confusion." He grabbed Stonewall by the arm and made him stop by the front door. This time he talked slowly and distinctly. "Don't be confused out there. Protect your name, Stonewall, or else it'll be on a headstone. Watch the big black man out front. He's quick. Clear?"

Stonewall nodded and clutched the front of his coat.

"And then come back in here. Now, out!" He closed the door after Stonewall and turned to Dicky. "Where is he?"

"Through there. He's got a gun, Marco."

"You got one?" Marco took the gun, told Dicky to run interference at this end of the parlor, and went through to the back.

It was an artistic arrangement of an asexual figure with wings, tiptoed on a pedestal, many palms, and the corpse. Messina lay in a satin quilted casket, wearing a banker's suit. His cosmetically treated face showed no signs of the stroke that had killed him. Mucilage on one cheek and styroid matter inside his mouth had made him smooth and young. A rose-colored light from the ceiling completed the staginess.

"Now that you're here," said Cass, "I guess I got nothing to lose."

"Where the hell are you, Cass?"

"Behind this gun that's looking at you."

Cass had not sounded fierce, or desperate, or insane. He had sounded tired as a man of his age might after a long hard day. Marco took all that in very swiftly. Even though he had not yet seen where Cass was standing, he came away from the door and into the rosy hue.

"Cass, I don't know what they said to you but I know what you think. You're wrong. Just look at me."

"I am. So hold still."

"I came to talk sense, Cass. Cipollo's got a contract out for you. I don't."

"And now you came to tell me you didn't have a contract for Messina, either."

"I'm here to level with you. I'm taking the territory, you're right. And I need you with me. Like you were with Messina."

"He was my friend."

Marco stiffened a little. He had misjudged it. Cass was not fierce, or desperate, but perhaps a little insane. To speak of friendship at a time like this made no sense. Then Marco heard the steps in the hall and next Dicky's voice.

"Marc, you okay?"

"Yes."

"The cops bought it. They left."

"Good."

"No good. A bunch of Trattomajores cruising by. The Cat says it's the second time."

Marco stood in silence for a moment, and then he thought he had it.

"Dicky? Tell Cat to be ready with the car and sit tight. You still got the undertaker with you?"

"The ghoul's right here."

"When the time comes, lay him out, that's all. And he shouldn't talk afterwards, make that clear to him." Then Marco turned back to the gloom where Cass had to be. "You stalled around, Cass, and now they're here. You heard Dicky."

"Maybe they're after you, killer."

"The word is, you set Messina up. It's not true, but that's what Cipollo thinks and that's why that carload is here. You ready to make a break for it, with me?"

There was silence, but Marco knew there was movement.

The time and the moment slipping away was so important that Marco told Cass the truth.

"If I lose you, Cass, I'm through. If you go with them and tell Cipollo how I muffed it with Rubenstein, then I'm through."

"I know that, you bastard."

"Cass, please! I can't sew it up without you siding with me. That's for the pull you have with some of the men, and that's for your silence, till I've sewed up Rubenstein."

Marco waited. Then Cass talked, a little further away.

"Maybe you don't know there's a back door here, Marco," he said. "But I don't know if you got somebody out in back."

"I do," said Marco. "Let me come to where you are and I'll call to him through the door."

"If nobody answers," said Cass, "you're dead."

"I'm coming," said Marco and started walking across. Then he threw himself to the floor. Cass, as expected, let loose with a shot.

After that, neither man talked anymore. Cass knew that Marco would never let him get to the Trattomajores, and Marco knew that Cass would never help him with his more and more uncertain gamble.

"Marco?" yelled Dicky. "You need help?"

Dicky did not have a gun. Marco was holding it, trying to guess where Cass had gone since he had fired his shot. To judge by the silence, Cass seemed to know that Marco was too close to the back door to make a break possible.

"Dicky! Kick your door open and watch it!"

When the door flew open Cass, as expected, pumped off another shot. Marco had the angle now and let Cass know it. He shot at Cass' darkness and leapt for the back door. That immobilized Cass. He thought he now had two guns on him, from two different directions. He held very still.

"Marc?"

"You know I'm here."

"I'm coming out."

"First the gun, Cass."

The gun came sailing. It arced through the rose light, nosed down, and fell with a sickening plop on Messina's belly.

At the front of the building the door opened and shut. "I'm waiting," said Marco.

He felt the back door, which was a double-hinged metal affair that could swing open to let in a casket. The bolt was pushed shut. In the middle of the room, Cass was walking into the light. He looked bent like an old man. He stopped near the casket and looked into it.

"Don't touch it," said Marco, eyeing the gun on the belly.

"You got no right calling him an 'it,'" said Cass.

Marco walked over. The closer he got the worse Cass looked. Cass had lost his hat and his bald head shone like a beacon. His face looked more like a cadaver's than Messina's putty features.

"The Cat is here," said Dicky from the dark corridor. "He says they left the car aways down and must be all around. I think— *Marc!*"

Cass, stiff as bent wood, suddenly moved. He almost made it, but not well enough. Marco's hand clamped down on Cass' wrist just as the other reached the gun on the corpse's belly. The two men jerked and tugged, bracing against the casket. Marco could feel Cass' gun under his arm. He could feel the gun sink, as the belly gave way. Messina shook. Messina's dead mouth bubbled open. Styrofoam dribbled out and a burbling grunt squeezed through.

Marco let go of the wrist and the casket. His knees felt limp. And then the casket tilted like a sinking ship, the draped underpinnings gave a squeal and a cracking sound, and then the whole stately presentation collapsed to one side.

The corpse was out of its satin cocoon. Marco could see the broad back. It was covered, down to the yellow thighs, with a thing like a hospital gown. The banker's suit was another artful disguise, covering only the front.

Cass was making no attempt to get up. He had one arm around the corpse but probably did not know it. His eyes looked just past one of Messina's ears. Marco raised his gun and Cass closed his eyes. He kept them closed while Marco changed his mind, pocketed the gun, and instead picked up the one which Cass had been using. With that he shot Cass through the right temple. When the spasm was over, Marco wiped the gun and bent Cass' dead hand around the butt and the trigger. Then he walked into the dark corridor where Dicky and the Cat were waiting for him.

"That was beautiful," said the Cat.

Marco rubbed his eyes and the sides of his head. He rubbed and tried not to think and not to hear.

"The ghoul passed out," said Dicky. "Don't worry about him."

Then they were quiet, to give Marco time and to listen to sounds from outside. But the outside was quiet too. Then the phone rang in the office.

"Answer it! They know we're in here."

Dicky ran to answer it; then he called Marco. So it was there, in the dead of night at the funeral parlor, that Marco Guarda got his first call from the Don.

"Did you kill him?" asked the Don.

Marco just sighed. He sat down in the leather chair by the desk and the chair sighed too.

"Shithead," said the Don. "I will now tell you what I know. If Cass had reached me, he would have told me that Rubenstein would not make a deal. And since you killed Cass, you must really be hurting for me not to know about it. Are you with me?"

"It's your dime, del Mare."

"Ah! Not the Don anymore, eh, shithead?" Del Mare thought of laughing, but then decided against it. "My advantage," he said, "is that you and me think alike. You and me know that you can't make it without the Rube."

"Why the song and dance, del Mare?"

"To save wear and tear. Can you afford to run Messina's *regime* into the ground?"

"Can you?"

"No. But not for the same reason. In your case, you'd be a dead man. In my case, I'd be a poor business man. So I'll tell you what. To show faith, I pulled the Trattomajores off. You can go home. Go to sleep. And tomorrow, come and see Cipollo. You can pick the place. *D'accordo?*"

"You're calling it, Don."

"Good night, *capo*."

Marco hung up and felt heavy with tiredness. It was something he could not afford, because he had to keep moving.

CHAPTER 13

If he did not find Rubenstein and sew him up, Don Angelo would do it.

But it was two o'clock in the morning and the tiredness lay like wet sand in his joints. Marco sat in his car and held his head in his hands. He was aware of tiny things, like the fact that at this angle there was less effort in keeping his eyelids open. The Cat leaned in through the driver's window.

"I sent Dicky off like you said, Marc."

Marco nodded without looking up.

"Big man," said the Cat. "Let us, like the ayrabs, fold ourselves the hell outa here, big man."

"Go on with Dicky to the office. Got to check out where the Rube is."

"You said that before. Marc, hey, you don't act like you know what you did. You fixed Cass, big man. You made it!"

"Yeah. I know. Beat it."

The Cat shrugged, opened the door on the driver's side, and got behind the wheel by pushing Marco out of the way.

"Where to?"

"Yeah. Drive around. I'll tell you in a minute."

"The West Hollywood place?"

"Drive around! I'll grab some sleep and then think of something. I gotta find Rubenstein."

"Dicky's on the board in the office. All you gotta do is call in off and on."

The Cat stopped talking because Marco was asleep. Marco was a white man, he was even a very clannish white man. In the Cat's new-found language, here was another representative from an ethnic minority group. And they were the worst. But Marco also was a man who did not belong anywhere in the world, no member of power group or minority group anywhere, and that was what made Marco bearable. It was possible to look at his tired shape and just see a flaked-out guy. So the Cat decided to take Marco to Burbank where he kept his chick.

Francine heard the men arguing outside in the hall. She had taken off her wig and her high heels, but she was still wearing the working makeup which under normal light, made her look like cheap.

"Yeah, yeah, yeah," said the Cat. "I'll be here at six in the morning."

"Or sooner, if they find Rubenstein."

"Yeah, yeah ..."

"Stop saying that!"

"Watch your tone," said the Cat, using his ethnic protest voice. Then he left.

Francine opened the door and let Marco in. He patted her hip and went straight to the bed.

"Just to crash," he mumbled.

She did not hear him. She was in the tiny bathroom, quickly washing her makeup off. When she came back with her face feeling cool and clean Marco was already in bed. He watched her undress but said nothing.

"Big day?" she said.

"Lot of action. And you?"

"Some." She got into bed and rolled herself up against him. "A lot, but in a funny way," she said. "A bunch from out of town and they were all very—well, very quiet. But just being there, they made everybody feel jumpy."

"Bunch?" he said. His hand was moving along on her back.

"Trotters or something like that."

"Trattomajores," he said but did not care to think about it. He was thinking mostly with his hand. He had found the dent where her bra strap had crossed her back and was moving along that line where it would have joined the cup. When he got there he opened his hand and his fingers. When he got that far Francine rolled over with her back on his arm.

"Gimme my arm back," he said.

"I'm glad you came over."

"I'm coming in."

He thought of what she had said about getting the best from her and for the moments while he still thought about it, he felt that this might be the sort of time when he and Francy could be a very special thing with each other.

They made love in a simple way, a curve with a start and a finish, and then he fell into sleep almost instantly.

Francine answered the phone when the morning showed light grey outside the windows. She said yes a few times, then put the receiver down. Marco had slept through the ringing, but he jumped up when she said his name.

"He says his name's Dicky and ..."

"Okay, okay."

He took the phone from the breakfast bar and Francine noticed the speed in his voice and his motions.

"We got this lead on Rubenstein," said Dicky. "He called Nuncio, making it sound like he called to give him hell ..."

"When? At five in the morning?"

"Last night."

"What in the hell's the matter with Cino? Why didn't he let anybody know?"

"Search me, Marco. You want to talk to him?"

"He's at the office? This time of the morning?"

"He slept here," said Dicky. "He's working at his desk now, I think."

"All right. What about the call?"

"It's like he gave your brother hell for the way he acted or something but then he said he wants to talk to Blazer."

"Blazer? Why in hell Blazer?"

"To negotiate. Because he trusts Blazer and you trust Blazer, but he's not so sure about you and your crazy—excuse me, and Nuncio ..."

"Let me talk to Nuncio."

"He says I should tell you he doesn't want to be disturbed. Unless it's important, of course."

"Screw him. Go on."

"That's it. So, you want to send Blazer?"

"Where to?"

"Rube said that Blazer would know. Where they used to have policy meetings when Blazer was the *regime* man for the union."

"All right," said Marco. "Get him."

"Get him? Where is he?"

"You mean to say he hasn't called in?"

"All I know he went off yesterday, doing something."

"I sent him," said Marco, and he thought of the simple job of taking Ditch out of town. "I suppose it's been checked," he added.

"I didn't, but they did through the board here at the office."

"And?"

"Nothing. No place. Pepe sent men out too."

Marco was wide awake and alert with irritation.

"All right, Dicky. Tell the board and tell Pepe to keep looking. And tell that goddamn— forget it." Then he meant to hang up.

"Another thing," said Dicky. "Rubenstein said to make it at nine in the morning, and if you don't show, that'll mean you got nothing to say and he'll get in touch with the Don instead of talking to you."

Dicky kept his ear to the phone all through the lengthy time that Marco was cursing. He understood little of it, since most of it was in Sicilian, but he could guess at the violence of Marco's mood from the tone. He only hung up when Marco hung up.

Francine stayed at one end of the room and watched Marco get into his clothes. It looked as if he were stomping and slashing something to death. The best thing would be, she thought, if he just left without saying a word.

He did not bother to shave or to wash but went straight for the door.

"Francy?"

"Yes." She came forward and wondered what he might say. He did not smile and he did not look angry anymore. His face was quite blank.

"I want you to pack up."

Why, she thought, should I feel the shock. We had a simple, straightforward, and no more

"I'm going to move you someplace else."

She asked why automatically.

"Because the party's going to get rough."

The trip from Burbank in the Valley to Boyles Heights above downtown took no more than twenty minutes that time of the morning. The Cat had slept in the car and looked fresher than Marco.

"Why Ditch's place?" he wanted to know.

"Because nobody else thought of it."

"Massah," said the Cat, "you is so profound ah is consternated."

"Cut out that crap."

The Cat appreciated his own imitation and guffawed for a while. That too was an imitation. Then he dropped it.

"You got iron?" he asked.

"I don't carry a gun." But Marco appreciated the thought. Blazer would not stay away this long under normal conditions. "Have you got?" he asked.

"Who, me? A black cat? Do you know what the establishment minions— I am here talking about the pigs— do you know what ...?"

"Lay off," said Marco. "I don't want to hear that crap."

The Cat gave one sideways look which Marco did not see.

"I know," he said. "Which is what makes your day so happy. Groove on that, big man."

Neither of them talked after that.

The rooming house looked the same and smelled the same, and Ditch's room in the back was locked as usual. When Marco knocked nobody answered.

"Want me to open it?" asked the Cat.

"How much noise you going to make?"

"It'll hiss a little," said the Cat. He took out a fountain pen and held it for demonstration. "Twitchy old ladies carry this mother. When you press the dingus here a very far-out type of Mace gets blowed out. The blow job is tinted a truly spiritual blue. The rapist sees that and it blows his mind. A torn-down freak like Ditch sees that blue come sliding outa the key hole and that's the end, the mother's other end freaking at him." He stuck the gas pen into the keyhole. "I just thought that up," he said. "Maybe it works." Then he pressed the release.

It took one irritable minute before anything else happened. Then Ditch started to scream.

"Just hear the child groove," said the Cat, but Marco had a belated thought.

"Get around to the outside! Before he'll go for the door with that blue stuff coming out of it, he'll jump out the window!"

The idea was reasonable, but Ditch was not. They could hear him clawing at the latch. He was coughing a little. When the door came open, Marco and the Cat pushed right in.

The used-up smell of the room was more prominent than the effect of the gas, but the Cat hefted the window open while Marco closed the door. Ditch had moved back to the bed, and sat down.

"Where's Blazer?" said Marco.

"Oh yes," said Ditch.

Marco was in no condition to handle delay. The Cat saw that, so when Marco went for Ditch the Cat was suddenly there holding Marco still with one hand.

"He's in deep space, big man. You gotta use different signals." Then he let go of Marco and turned to Ditch who was looking at them but seemed to be seeing something else. The Cat leaned down into that line of vision. He distorted his face in a hideous way, showing all the white of his eyes and all the white of his teeth. "Jabberookeritchit!" he said.

Ditch blinked and then he smiled.

"You see?" said the Cat. "He understands."

"Good heavens," said Ditch. "Is this man stoned or something?"

"All yours," and the Cat stepped aside.

"Ditch," said Marco, "I have got to find Blazer."

"Dig."

"Where is he? You and him were supposed to split town."

"Dig."

"*Listen* to me!"

"I am, Marco. You want me to send you there?" Ditch giggled.

In that instant Marco knew what had happened to Blazer. He did not know how and he did not know why because the only thing he cared about was to find out where Rubenstein was holed up. He, Marco, had to get there in less than three hours.

"Don't," said the Cat. "You gotta be patient, Marco."

"Get away! Ditch, is he dead? *Answer!*"

"It was awfully fast, awfully fast," said Ditch. He looked as if he were thinking about it. "Just like with the big, fat mother, that first time. You know, Marco, nothing ever really lasts?"

Ditch never knew what happened to him. Suddenly, he was flat on the bed, pressed deep into the springs, and his head would now burst because very soon Marco's fingers and palms would tie off the neck like the end of a knotted balloon. What stopped Marco short was Cat's remark.

"Here's Blazer."

There was Blazer, recognizable by the dapper clothes. They were just a little bit dusty and smudged while the pile of dirty laundry in the corner of the room disguised most of the form. The Cat was holding the blanket which had covered the pile. The face was clay and was the least recognizable feature; as if someone had pressed hard into it and wiped the shape of one side of the face. The rictus of the mouth had by now set like stone. The Cat was tossing junk aside and went over the corpse.

"Not a sign of nothing. How'd he do it?"

"However, I'm clever—" said Ditch.

"He gave him the needle," said Marco, "and now I'm dead."

Now nobody's making sense, thought the Cat.

"Little amytal in a little glass," said Ditch politely. "A little glass with one for the road while I'm packing. The slow way, was my thought, not like the first. Just a little air, lighter than a hair, altogether clever, suddenly instead, a jerk and he goes dead. Jesus," said Ditch and looked up, "what in hell's coming off?"

The Cat watched Marco for the next move, and Ditch watched Marco, as if for advice.

Something was going on inside Marco to which he could not give a name. It was not rage and it was not fright. It most certainly was not love, but instead a sinking away of whatever there had been before. He watched himself as if from a distance and saw himself throw away and give up most of the things he had counted on. Rely on a freak, and he'll foul you; rely on a brother and he'll mess you; rely on a plan and it can drive you nuts; rely on a big chance and you bank on nothing. Down the drain. Less than three hours and three thousand worries away and maybe everything would come out all right because you just trust in good will and mutual admiration or bank on simple things like making a promise—then all of a sudden, you're alone!

"Blazer was a friend of yours?" asked the Cat. He did not know what was happening with Marco.

"Crap," said Marco. "I just thought I needed him." He took a deep breath and looked around. The room looked barren and clear, the corpse in the corner was dead. Ditch had his black bag on the bed, preparing a fix.

"And now?" asked the Cat. It was hard to figure the man out, but he had to know where he stood. "You don't find the Hebe and then what? I mean, that's Endsville, Cliff City, Doomstown. What's left, big man?"

But Marco felt like yesterday's clothes on him were fresh and brand new and as if his rough jaw were clean shaven. He did not bother to answer the Cat but just gave him a smile. It was quick and was meant to tell him, don't get yourself all up tight. If I need you, I'll let you know. If I don't, just bug off. Then he watched Ditch pull the needle back out of the vein and lie back on the bed.

"You gonna leave him here?" asked the Cat.

"Sure."

The Cat had meant Blazer, but he realized that Marco had meant Ditch.

"I think you're crazy," he said. "How do you know when he comes around that he won't sing himself hoarse?"

"Because I'm going to leave him like Blazer," said Marco.

But he did not use air. He had the Cat sit on Ditch to keep the body from jerking and then he refilled the syringe, a full ten ccs. The Cat saw this and swallowed. Marco found the hole in the vein without any trouble because it had a raised rim, sore and thick from use.

The Cat got off Ditch because there was not much movement on the bed. Ditch just lay there. He saw everything but nothing fit. He saw the hypodermic and the way Marco was holding it, needle up, drop squeezed out, to eliminate deadly danger of embolism.

"Why?" said Ditch. He felt innocent of everything.

"I'll tell you," said Marco. "I was seventeen and had my first kill. That was him or me. A while back, I did my first murder. That was to tie up a plan. And this here," he said, "is something else."

Ditch tried to attend to everything, the way he had always planned it for the time when it should happen—the fear, the courage, the godless detachment from life and death. He watched the needle and felt stupid.

Marco pushed the needle in without any ceremony or without any sense of a special event. Then he jacked the plunger home till all of the heroin got washed into the blood and would now ruin the host.

"This isn't to save anything, Ditch. Not my life, not my plans. This is *per niente, poverino*. It's an execution!"

CHAPTER 14

When the Cat got out to the street, Marco was already behind the wheel. The Cat discovered that he was a little afraid.

"You can get in," said Marco.

The Cat got in and slammed the door. Marco was already moving off.

"Can I talk?"

Marco shrugged and kept driving.

"That was all out front, up there. I mean, right out front about being done with everything. Did I glom that right?"

"Why ask?"

"Well, big man, like I'm part of the family—"

Marco got on Third, a five-lane street, all going one way. He jockeyed back and forth until he was where he wanted.

"I'm done with hiding from the Don. I'm done with coddling my brothers. I'm done slinking. You dig, pussycat?"

"Dig," said the Cat. He still felt afraid.

The neons on the Strip did not get turned off that time of the morning but the rising light sucked the life out of them. Angelo del Mare was ready for bed. The girl *du jour* was new to him, except for what he had seen in the chorus line-up. He belted his paisley pajama jacket while sucking in on his gut. She came from the bathroom, gowned in something resembling ectoplasm, and then stopped by the bed.

"You already done the auditioning," he said. "Just drop it."

The ectoplasm floated off a standard center foldout body. Del Mare wished she would move instead of pose.

"Get back inna shower and wash the lousy lacquer outa your hair. I don't wanna get all scratched up."

Unaccountably, he thought of his wife—not of her pasta body, but of her heavy, healthy hair.

He started to follow the girl into the bathroom. She could not possibly pose while washing her hair; she would have to *move* in that shower. The phone rang and the button light for the line to Cipollo stared at him.

"*What?*" he yelled.

Cipollo, who had not yet been to bed either and furthermore had none of his Don's prospects of rest and relaxation, gave an irritable start.

"I'm sorry about the hour—"

"I'm sure that you called to tell me more than that."

"All right, Angelo. I am in no mood." Cipollo paused, feeling startled with his own boldness, but then he experienced again the rankling helplessness of his office in which he had all the obligations and none of the authority. So he said it again. "I'm in no mood."

Del Mare had been watching the naked girl through the open door of the bathroom. She was looking at herself in the long mirror, holding various attitudes.

"Get the goddamn lacquer outa your hair!"

Cipollo gave another start. Also, he touched his bald head.

"Chip," he could hear del Mare. "Now say something that makes sense."

"*It's not that simple!*"

Angelo del Mare had never heard his *consigliere* shout at his Don. He forgot about the girl in the bathroom and everything else that had nothing to do with business.

"I'm listening," he said simply.

"All right. It's early in the morning, Don Angelo, but it's been a long time without action. In the event of any changeover in business ..."

"Don't explain it. Just tell it, Chip."

"Lippi in traffic, Giancarlo in loans, Bianca in betting, Nuncio in protection, Nuncio in pay-offs, Rubenstein in unions—I'm just reading them off here, Angelo—all transactions and so forth, normal. *And* they are all Guarda men."

"You include Rubenstein?"

"I have to. We have not found him to verify otherwise."

Del Mare thought for a moment. He could hear her singing to herself in the bathroom but paid no attention to it.

"Did Marco Guarda get in touch?"

"No. The Cass hit is suicide, by the way."

"Anything else and I'd be disappointed in Marco."

"Angelo?"

Del Mare heard the tone and knew that this was another one of those worry moments which Cipollo kept getting like a disease.

"He has never been anything but a very competent member. I include here the basic rule, Angelo: whatever the business or the quarrel, it is Family business and a Family quarrel. He has never made any move which invited the law or the press to pay serious attention."

"Have you done anything to provoke him to do it different?"

"No. So far, there have been no replacements and—so far—the Trattomajores have been restrained. But he has not tried to reach me, as you asked him to do."

"I figure we give him till noon. Hold it a minute." Del Mare covered the phone. "Are you going to get in that goddamn shower or are you asking I should throw you out?"

The shower came on that instant.

"Chip?"

"I'm here."

"All right, listen. Before he gets desperate and starts acting wild—he's got it in him, like that clown he's got for a brother."

"Pepe? No sir, Angelo. Not like that. I can tell you everything Pepe will do and when he would do it. However, speaking as one company man to another, Angelo, this Guarda is all independent. And that means you don't know what he'll do. I basically see only one alternative—"

"Don't start that again. Nothing's tight enough right now for that kind of a play, for chrissakes. Now listen. Right now he's still out there going *forza, forza, forza*. He don't think of losing, even for a while after he has. So now's the time to cut the ground out from under. You know who gets paid off in that territory. Pay them *not* to cover for the action. All at the same time."

"But that might cost an unnecessary ..."

"All we *got* is money right now. Do it. I want shutdowns and a few arrests. You know, where it scares the peasants. *Dunque*. What else?"

"Rubenstein."

"Find him."

"I will."

But Pepe found him first.

He had wanted to let Marco know right away but first, there had been no phone in the car he was using and second, he had tried Francine's apartment but nobody had answered the phone. It was a little strange, not to be able to get in touch with the *bimbo*. It had always been possible to find him.

The way in which Pepe had learned where Rubenstein was had been innocent and simple. Blazer's girl had come to the West Hollywood house late at night. While Pepe was sleeping in the top floor apartment she had gone to the poolroom they kept in the basement garage. She asked the button men there where Blazer was keeping himself. Now that you're here, somebody had said, how about let's forget about Blazer, but that had only been a joke. Blazer was fairly big and Blazer's girl found out that she was not the only one looking for him. Which is how Pepe was called and how Pepe then learned that sometimes Blazer holed up on business out in Pacific Palisades. Somebody by name of Rubenstein with a laundry business there.

It was an unlikely place. The community lay high along the ocean, with well-kept houses along well-kept streets, with a shopping center whose shops were spelled shoppe. The Rubenstein steam laundry plant was identified as Mrs. Murphy's Linen Care. The ugly flatness of the front was cut up by geometric cyprus plantings and all the delivery vans were parked in the back where the cement yard ran up to a rise.

Rubenstein sat in an office over the plant and listened to the machinery hum underfoot. The plain casement window showed white air where the ocean would be once the sun got hotter. By looking straight down from the window, Rubenstein could see the curve of the street which came up from Sunset Boulevard. Nobody came this way, except the laundry vans and a few Cadillacs from up in the hills. Then a tan Lincoln swung into the yard with the vans.

Rubenstein scurried to the desk in the room and sat down. He pulled up his tie, pulled down his vest, buttoned his jacket, and popped his cuffs. Then he sat in a manner of concentration while holding a brochure. He re-read the first paragraph several times. When, finally, there was a knock on the door his concentration seemed to deepen. When the door opened he looked up, as if emerging from a trance of deep thought.

"What in hell you want?" he said.

"There's a gentleman wants …"

"Who?"

"Mr. something, I dunno."

"He come across the loading ramp? Go back and sweep the loading ramp like you should and tell the Mr. something to come in by the front like a *mensch* and then maybe I see him."

"He's coming already!"

"*Geh aveck, aveck!*" and then, with the sound of footsteps on the stairs coming closer, Rubenstein tried for the busy pose again. When he looked up he sat completely still and said nothing.

"You don't know me, Mr. Rubenstein," said the young man by the door. He smiled, shut the door behind him, and walked up to the desk. "In a moment you will have a visitor who, I believe, is Marco Guarda. I was not prepared for this early an arrival by the competition, so I can only suggest, what with the pressure of time, that you promise everything but do nothing."

"What's with you?"

"From Vegas, directed here through Mr. Cipollo's office."

There were footsteps on the stairs again.

"Unprepared as I am—" the young man smiled and shrugged at the door. "However, we will be in touch. You know, of course, in whose authority Mr. Cipollo is acting. If you will now simply dismiss me as you would after any ordinary business meeting—" He stepped aside as the door opened and Pepe Guarda came in.

Rubenstein said, "Yek—"

"Thank you again, Mr. Rubenstein, and let me repeat that you can count on early delivery." The young man went away, closing the door behind him.

"Who was that?" asked Pepe.

"Why you? Where's Blazer?"

"And where in hell have you been so we gotta chase around like a bunch a spies after you?" Pepe came to the desk and sat down next to it. "Who was that guy?"

Rubenstein was struggling with a lot of pressures, none of which he had sorted out. He could tell by his stomach. He thought of seltzer water.

"That was the competition," he said.

"Huh?"

"This is Mrs. Murphy's and he's from Monsieur Pierre's French Dainties. Sometimes we get together."

"You do, huh?" But Pepe had too many other worries to press the issue. "I don't know where Blazer is or for that matter, where Marco's at. Things are a little confused right now, what with the *capo* kicking off like that. So, let's go to the office and you talk things over and everything's going to be all right."

"I'm not leaving," said Rubenstein.

"Why in hell not? You wanna talk, don't you?"

But Rubenstein did not care to discuss the delicate details with Pepe. He was not even sure anymore that an alliance with the Guardas was a healthy idea altogether.

"All I said to your brothers," Rubenstein explained, "was that there may be something to work out. I'm not eager, you know."

"Not eager? Don't gimme a cramp, Nate. Without my troops your operation folds, you know that."

"I've been thinking of retiring."

"You're giving me that cramp right now, you know that, Nate?"

Rubenstein burped without finding relief. There was no point in talking to Pepe. That gorilla version of Marco had neither the skill nor the authority to do anything. And of course there was the man sent by the Don whose implicit message was clear. Don't deal with the Guardas, deal with us. But that profit angle was zero while the risk angle was acute.

"I'm gonna call in," said Pepe. "Maybe Marco showed."

While he called the office, Rubenstein looked out of the window, down to the curve that went towards Sunset. The young man who had visited him was by the curb, talking to somebody who had pulled up in an unimposing economy-class car. Rubenstein's stomach took on the action of a cement mixer.

Marco pulled the car into the lot of the Tiger's Folly. Since he had given up on the scramble to find Rubenstein by nine o'clock he had started to do first things first entirely by his own lights. Let the Don sweat it while he set his own pace.

Marco went to the trunk of the car while the Cat held the front seat back so that Francine could get out. In the trunk was room for one more suitcase.

"It's in my dressing room," Francine said to the Cat. "Would you help me?"

The Cat sucked his breath in, but did not say anything.

"You're making the minority feel like an Uncle Tom," said Marco and went towards the rear of the building.

The dining room was locked and the nightclub area looked strange with thin daylight intruding. The clean-up man had a mechanic's light on a long cord lying on the bar. The utilitarian glare made the carefully color-graded decor look repulsive. Francine sat down on a bar stool. She said, "Hi, Sam," to the clean-up man and asked him to pour her a cup of coffee.

"I'll get the suitcase," said Marco, and then told the Cat to call in to the office.

When he came back with the bag, the Cat was still on the phone. Marco sat down on a stool.

"Here's the ticket, Francy." He gave her the envelope. "When you get to New York, call this number. They'll fix you up with a place."

Francine nodded. She had been shunted around before, on the Vegas, Miami, Acapulco circuit, either with one man for the full season, or as businessman's companion in each mecca separately. But she had never been sent off alone, asked to wait. For what? Marco's quick, rapacious sex for half an hour at three in the morning; an afternoon in bed with the newspapers all over and a plate of dates and tangerines on the floor; or the utter mess of his ritual in the kitchen; the long beach days, the long intervals when she did not know where he was.

"Marco, they want to talk to you," said the Cat and held out the phone.

"This is Nuncio," said the voice in his ear. It was his brother's voice, but with a fine edge of breakable sharpness.

"*Pronto*," said Marco. "What happened?"

"Pepe found Rubenstein. He's holding him for you."

"*Dio*—" It was a low sound.

After the clearness of having chucked all manner of unnamed weights and feelings, he suddenly felt the thick, hot greed again, the driven force in him which did not allow him to look right or left. They had Rubenstein! They had the whole teeming *regime* in the palm of their hand and the Don's octopus, Cipollo, would have to ink himself out.

"Is he out there alone?" said Marco.

"Rubenstein is. Pepe brought a carload."

"*Bene, bene*. Where's it at?" And when Nuncio told him Marco thought rapidly of freeways, streets, traffic, and the hour of the morning, and decided to settle everything out there in the Palisades. "Call 'em back and say forty-five minutes. I'll be there in less than an hour."

"Shouldn't we work out some guarantees here in the office? The way things are beginning to look …"

"Later. If a word is no good, neither is the paper."

"Marco—before you hang up."

"What?"

"I think," Nuncio said, "that a few things are beginning to happen."

Marco waited. Knowing Nuncio, he knew that his brother never gave equal weight to anything but tried to gauge differences.

"Three dealers were beaten up in the Valley."

"The Trattomajores have been hanging around here. Could be just their idea of a vacation."

"Perhaps. And the big room on Pico got raided. Probably will be in the papers this morning."

"The wire service? Who gets paid off in that district?"

"And two numbers places in Downey."

"Never mind the small potatoes. Who's supposed to cover the Pico action?"

"Minelli, on the Commissioner's staff. But he's just a front, Marco. What worries me is the man who keeps him there, somebody called Quillan. State Coordinator for …"

"Strictly Messina personnel. Can you get to him?"

"Haven't been able to reach him."

"We got anything on him?"

"No. But maybe the Don has. Maybe that's why we can't reach him."

"Never mind. We lose protection and it'll hurt some. It'll never dry us up with the Rubenstein block *en tasca*."

"Have you ever heard of a man called MacAdoo?"

"Who?"

"Judge MacAdoo. Retired. He's Quillan's father-in-law. He got Quillan the post through which Messina got most of the betting protection."

"I'm in a hurry, Cino."

"He was before our time, but I think he used to be for sale."

"All right, Cino. Do your thing, I do mine. First comes Rubenstein or nothing else comes after. *Ciao.*"

He now felt as if nothing had happened to him since Blazer had died from a crazy clown's trick, and when he came back from the phone, Francine noticed the difference.

"You still want me to go, Marc?"

He grinned at her.

"Well, the difference now, Francy, it's not like I'd have to put you away someplace safe anymore. It's more like, I'll be back later, home from the office."

She smiled back at him, stuck her leg out far enough both for him to see it and to reach the suitcase with her toe. Then she kicked the suitcase over.

"See you when you get back from the office?"

He kissed her on the cheek and took off.

He drove down the Hollywood freeway to the junction where the San Diego swung him over the pass. Once on Sunset, he wound down through the hills towards the ocean. And Rubenstein would be sitting there in his laundry, waiting with Pepe.

"I think we better get the hell outa here," said Pepe and turned back from the window. "Twice the same car and that other one parked down there and every one of them clunkers."

"By you it's a clunker if the wheelbase isn't like a hearse?" said Rubenstein. But the joke was strained. Only his bind was real. Go with the Don and lose money; or go with the Guardas and maybe worry for the rest of his life.

"I mean clunkers! Five, eight years old and with a sound like a 12-cylinder Ferrari under the hood."

"Up there in the hills, maybe there's a lot of those hippies living there, *ver veyss.*"

"Sure. On fifteen thou per lot. Come on, Nate. Up!"

"Wait!"

Pepe caught the fright in Rubenstein's manner and waited for the rest of it.

"I think," said Rubenstein, "maybe that's a delegation from Cipollo. I think maybe the fat lawyer got a smell of a deal in the air."

Pepe folded his arms across his chest and cocked his head. Rubenstein saw a very alert cat, a very big cat like a mountain lion, waiting there for the deer to come just a little bit more out of its shelter. Rubenstein thought of himself as a shy little deer and sighed.

"It does mean," he said with eyes closed, "that the bargaining conditions are coming out different."

"Nate," said Pepe. "You're starting to sound like some kind of a Jew."

"It don't help for you to get anti-Semitic, wop."

Pepe did not answer. He went to the office door and opened it. There was a man leaning against the iron railing of the staircase.

"Fredo, tell the guys to wake up. I think there's guns riding around out there. The Rube and me's coming down."

Rubenstein had not moved.

"Up."

"Just a minute, Pepe. Listen to me, Pepele, I promised to make the deal, you know that already. Lemme call up ..."

"Up!" This time Pepe showed his anger.

"*Gewalt*—Pepele, I'm not used to this kinda roughness. It's no way, Pepele—"

He was stopped abruptly by the jolt of Pepe's blow. By Pepe's standards it was nothing, but it was enough to get Rubenstein to move as he was meant to move.

In the lot, where the vans were parked, Pepe's crew seemed to be ready. All four doors of the Lincoln stood open. One man sat behind the wheel, and the other three were not conspicuous. The fact that they were all in one of the laundry vans and that the driver in the Lincoln was not one of Pepe's men either, did not occur to Pepe until he heard the voice behind him and felt the gun in his kidney.

"Keep your hands by your side and follow Mr. Rubenstein into your car."

But Pepe did not scare because of a voice in his ear and a gun in his back in broad daylight. There were certain rules of thumb to the business, such as doing the minimum necessary to get what you want. Shooting a man at nine in the morning behind Mrs. Murphy's in Pacific Palisades was not in accordance with one of those rules.

"Sez who," said Pepe, feeling that was as good as any remark.

"Which Guarda are you?" said the man behind Pepe.

"This one."

It was a very fast play, unexpected from one the size of Pepe. Also, Pepe got help from Rubenstein.

There is no way of slapping a gun out of the way when the man who is holding it feels free to pull the trigger. But when the gun-in-the-back play is a sham, designed only to impress, then the one with the gun has to handle his conflict and the one with the gun in his back has all the time in the world. During this time, which by actual count is worth two or three trigger pulls as Pepe well knew, he fell to his knees, exposed the man to Rubenstein, and flung himself against the gunman's legs.

Rubenstein acted from indignation and anger. He grabbed for the gun hand, as if he knew that there would be no shot, and then he yanked at the man who lost his balance because Pepe was between his legs. The last thing the gunman knew was that he was getting slapped in the face by a stocky old man who was hurling Biblical curses at him. Pepe's hands hardly registered because once Pepe had reached up into the crotch and clamped the scrotum, the hard twist produced a flash followed by instant blackout.

But the whole play, like the gun in the back, was for nothing. When Pepe had disentangled himself and came off the cement, his rage was not so powerful yet as to keep him from seeing clearly. It was not his play. Also it was not a hit but a snatch.

He was looking at the young man from Monsieur Pierre's French Dainties or something, and Monsieur Pierre's flat little automatic was looking at him.

"This time we mean it," he said. He pushed Rubenstein to one side without looking at him. Two men led Rubenstein around the building. "My name's Salvio Trattomajore," said the young man.

"*Dunque,*" said Pepe. He pulled at his clothes. "So you're the Porco's son."

"My father does not like to be called a pig," and then Salvio lashed out.

Pepe knew it was coming and knew that it was not going to be with the fist. This Salvio was a slim, superior type with all the magic of his father's brutal name to back him. Pepe got an insulting jab with stiff fingers into the side of the neck. It hurt like hell. Then he got slapped over the cheekbone with the flat side of the automatic. Pepe felt no fear or respect for the young Trattomajore. The whole grandstand play was a cheap move, the gesture of a weak man. Pepe saw another man covering the scene, he saw his own men looking through the glass in the rear of one of the vans, he saw the next van with rear doors locked and two laundry drivers inside. Pepe let the tears run down which the pain had brought on, but that was all he allowed himself.

"Too bad you're not the other one," said Salvia. "The important one."

"It's good for you," said Pepe, "that I'm not Marco, the other one."

The simple loyalty upset Salvio Trattomajore. He thought of stupidity, pig-headed stupidity and narrow, old-fashioned ways. He felt a sharp hatred for the big man who bled without caring, whose eyes cried without pain, but he thought he'd better save the scene for some other time. First, complete the assignment.

"Herd him out with the other one," he said to his man by the ramp. "You know where to go."

Then he went quickly to the street and drove his car down the curve to Sunset. He parked and went into the telephone booth by the gas station. When he had dialed he watched an overpowered Camaro squeal through the turn and up the street. Then his own men drove down to the corner and turned west on Sunset towards the Coast highway below.

"Yeah, Cipollo? Hold it a minute."

The Camaro was back. It idled at the corner and then swung west, as the Trattomajores had done.

"Get him or not?" Cipollo was saying.

"Yeah, sure, got him. And the big Guarda was there. We got him too."

"Christ!" said Cipollo. On this leg of the strategic journey he was alone. The development was unforeseen, and a bonanza. "That's the kingpin," he said. "Be very careful with Marco. He goes by none of the rules. Bring him in!"

"The *big* one, I said. We got Pepe Guarda. The one you're talking about just drove up and is following. I'm sure it was him."

Salvio Trattomajore could hear Cipollo groan. He felt restless in his glass cage and altogether hamstrung by the Don's orders. To bring in the outsider, the Jew, was one thing. To make no waves, not to tangle with the Guardas, that was asking a lot.

Cipollo, for his part, felt completely ineffectual. "Salvio? Yes. Here is what I want you to do. I want nothing to happen to Pepe. If his brother finds out—anyway, the Don is not ready for that. If it is true that Marco is following—er, I can't imagine such a fool thing."

"I said maybe."

"Yes, so if he is, er—let me put it in a simple way. If one goes, they both have to go. Clear?"

"Sure."

"But not separately."

"Hell," said Salvia. "You sound scared of them."

CHAPTER 15

Pepe knew that he had been right about the clunker. The motor made a tight, heavy sound and pulled the car through the curves of lower Sunset as if the vehicle had been a snake. To his surprise they turned right on the Coast highway, instead of heading towards Santa Monica and then perhaps south, to San Diego.

Rubenstein, on the seat next to him, was fidgeting badly. He had been obedient and still enough while the man next to the driver had held the gun across the seat towards them, but now he was full of notions.

"Don't bother," said Pepe, looking at Rubenstein's hand. "It locks from the front. So does the window."

The man next to the driver laughed.

"You up front there, Mr. Smartypants," said Rubenstein, "you can forget about the funny jokes when you find out pretty soon what kinda connections I got."

"He knows about the connections," said Pepe. "That's why he's taking you to the Don."

"Don? *Gewalt.* And you too?"

"They didn't figure on me," said Pepe. "I don't think they know what to do yet."

"Salvio will think of something," said the man in front without turning around.

The punk's tone did not bother him, nor did the whole Trattomajore operation. He knew about this sort of thing, and when he thought of the way Salvio Trattomajore was handling his assignment, he thought that was little league stuff.

Salvio had started out with five men, plus himself, to snatch one slow-moving old man. Then something unexpected had happened, and all Salvio had known how to do was to lock the Guarda men in a laundry van, to slap Pepe across the cheek, and then to let him sit in a back seat with his arms folded. The dumbest move of all, thought Pepe. He was left alone with only two men while the son of Porco Trattomajore was not even bothering to follow them closely. Father Porco would want words with the ninny, if the ninny lived that long.

"How's your cheek?" asked Rubenstein.

"My what?" Pepe came back out of his thoughts.

"I should bite off my tongue, Mr. Masterful, but you are bleeding a little bit there and all you do is look at the view. Also, I should mention, I am worried."

"Don't," said Pepe. "Pretty soon we're going to stop for a Band-aid."

The man next to the driver turned around for a look and Pepe grinned at him.

"Aren't you glad," said Pepe, "that there's just an old man, and me weak from bleeding to death, and your driver all tied up with steering this dangerous course down highway numero uno, and of course you with the only gun in view?"

The recital had the proper, unnerving effect.

"And looking out the back window you don't see the great Salvio flying wing, do you?"

"Shut up, fat boy."

Pepe laughed. He leaned back in his seat and put his hands on his knees.

"You don't get it, do you?"

"Shut up, fat boy."

"You said that. What I mean is, in just ten seconds I could have my hands around that driver's neck in front of me and squeeze good enough so we got this corpse driving the car. Ever think of that?"

The man's revolver was resting on the back of the seat and the big .38 barrel was looking at Pepe with single-eyed intent.

"And one messy corpse in the back seat. Think of that," said the man.

"I am. You don't think I'd waste it on a clear stretch of road, do you? I mean, first I'd wait for more traffic—like when we get tangled near Zuma Beach—and then of course I'm all this time waiting for my men to come a little closer. You don't think they stayed in that laundry van, do you now?"

"Alberto," said the driver. "Do something!"

"Shut up!"

"You see?" said Pepe. "Just now you looked away. Aren't you lucky you still got that gun where I can reach it?" Then he laughed again.

Alberto sat away from the back rest and held the gun close to the side of his body. He looked uncomfortable and mean.

"We ain't going to Zuma," Alberto said.

It sounded inadequate to Alberto but it was informative to Pepe. It was either a beach house on the way, a big house on the slope of the hills, or on one of the gravel and blacktop trails that cut away from the ocean and into the Santa Monica range. These roads went nowhere, or they were a bumpy way of making the Ventura freeway on the other side of the hills. In which case, Pepe figured, they did not intend to head north, but east. And east, going this way, would be the smart though improbable way to avoid the whole Los Angeles basin and still reach Route 15 into Las Vegas. It had to be like that unless they stopped soon, because there would be no other reason to go into the hills. Rubenstein was not worth anything there. But a hill trail would be nice for him and his men who had to be following.

And then the driver did pull into a road that went off to the right and up into the country.

It took another fifteen minutes before the car had climbed away from the houses which were scattered along the rise. Then they wound their way into chaparral country. Pepe folded his arms again and closed his eyes.

"Nate," he said.

"Yes, *kindchen*, what?"

"Don't sound so anxious," said Pepe. "I just want to tell you that if the driver gets himself killed in about five or ten minutes, it's all for you, Nate." Pepe opened his eyes. "Uh-uh! Don't get modest about it. Just be grateful.

Like, very grateful later."

"My dear Pepele, I want you should know ..."

"*Shuddupthebothayou!*"

Pepe looked at the man with the gun but did not move. That one, he thought, was most certainly ripe. He was not so sure about the driver. They were going slowly enough so that a struggling driver need not precipitate too much damage. And, of course, there was no obvious sign behind them that anyone was following, be it Salvio or his own men. The road wound and dipped and the growth was as much as man-high on the sides. Some dust rising would help, but there was none.

"All I want you to get clear," said Alberto as if talking through the barrel of his gun, "is that you're dead as soon as you move, Guarda, as soon as you move."

Pepe believed the man and closed his eyes. He was very good at this. He was better in this kind of a situation than either Nuncio who would defeat himself with thought, or Marco, who might snap himself into pieces with tension. But Pepe just sat, the way any good predator learns to wait for the rare moment.

It took half an hour to make the first flank of the range. It took the same length of time to rise and fall through the ridge country on top. This was not chaparral country anymore, just occasional scrub of some kind and some twisty live oak. Pepe waited until the view of the Valley opened up, a view of yellow junk hanging like bottom murk in a still river. The Ventura freeway swung in long curves along that bottom.

It was important to Pepe that he should not destroy the growing routine of the ride. He sat as still as he could in the heat of the closed car, and concentrated on moving with the jounce, the speed-ups and slow-downs, and with the sway of the car. He squinted at the growing shimmer of heat in the air outside and avoided the closer, darker sight of the meaningless details inside the car. He had already begun to ignore the outside signs of where they were.

Pepe waited for the turn with the steep bank on one side and the rocky incline on the other. He never said a word or made a move. But suddenly, as far as Alberto was concerned, he had done something.

Rubenstein was screaming but sat stiff as a board. Pepe, arms folded, looked mildly surprised. Alberto did not know what to do with his gun because nobody was moving. Once his startled reaction was over he did the natural thing, he pushed up to the back of the seat to look closer, moving his gun hand around in a confused effort to cover everything. At that worst possible moment for Alberto, Pepe's snake like strike at the gun came across the seat with the gun blasting off into the ceiling. Alberto's trigger finger was broken inside the guard, and Pepe's big hands were mashing bone and metal into one paralyzed mass. Alberto felt a great geyser of pain, and tried to be as limp as possible so that Pepe could slip the gun from his mangled hand.

The driver was already fighting the car away from the bluff and towards the incline when Pepe's fingers circled his neck. The driver did the wrong thing. He reached for his holster. One second later the massive vise on his neck had clamped shut and his voice box was broken. He was already gagging to death when the car bounced off the road and stopped itself under a tree.

"Out!" yelled Pepe, but his door would not open. He had also forgotten for the moment how he had started all this. His feet, out of sight from the front, had suddenly clamped Rubenstein's ankle in a scissor squeeze.

"*Himmel*, don't move," Rubenstein managed to gasp.

Pepe picked the gun up off the floor and told Rubenstein to shut up. Then he turned to Alberto.

"Throw the switch for these doors."

Alberto was slow enough so that Pepe's barely balanced temper spilled over. Pepe fired Alberto's gun into his face, tearing off the nose and one side of the face. Then he flipped the switch on the dashboard himself.

The fact that nobody had a gun on him anymore did not affect Pepe right then in one way or another; nor did the two dead men in the car make any difference for the moment. What mattered was the fact that he had lost mobility. In no way could he get the car back up on the road and in no way could he get Rubenstein to walk faster than at a slow limp. Pepe had to wait for the traffic, which would either be Salvio Trattomajore with his remaining three men, or the Lincoln with a load of three of his own. So he counted on the Trattomajores.

"Up the hill, Nate. Hold my arm."

"I will lean here and hold my foot, you son of a bitch. I will stand here and wonder before God how a human being can do a thing like you do, a butcher carves up the meat, except they don't do it with human beings, they—"

Pepe was not listening. He was up on the road, where the curve started, and looked back towards the broken land that stretched away under a high, metallic sky. They were above the coastal haze and the clear air showed the plume of dust. He ran back down to the car, collected two guns from two dead men, and hefted Rubenstein in a fireman's hold over his shoulder. Rubenstein, as if bereft of reason, kept beating at Pepe's face and chest, but Pepe made it to the lip of the road anyway. He did not fall down until he was almost there and then he watched how Rubenstein rolled back down the grade. He did not go after him. He could hear the motor.

Pepe waited long enough to see the car bounce out of a dip and then disappear again. It was Salvio in the other high-powered clunker, and he would have his other three men along. One would perhaps not be much good, but sitting gingerly and hanging onto the wheel, he might give them all the muscle they needed to grab Rubenstein who could not run, and out-gun Pepe who had no car. Pepe felt that there was only one good place for him, and it was not down by the busted car and the busted ankle. He retreated behind the curve.

The man driving Salvio's car jumped on the brake, as if he had not seen the wreck until he was right over it. Then the car just stood there for a while with the dust hanging over it. They could see Rubenstein. He leaned in full view by the wreck, and had his hands up in the air.

"Go get him," said Salvio.

The man who was spoken to had an impulse to say, "Go get him yourself," but controlled himself.

"There's somebody leaning over the wheel," he said.

"That means he's dead! Now get your ass out there!"

"He's dead don't make me feel easier in the mind, Salvio."

"That Guarda had no gun, Fredo. Remember? I got it." While they were arguing, Rubenstein started to crawl up to the road. They opened the door for him, but Rubenstein sat down at the edge of the road.

Pepe was sweating. He smelled sage and dust. He held a gun and thought of a shoot-out in the days of the Western desperadoes. He did not feel anything like that and knew that he could not shoot that way, but when somebody finally came out of the car he squeezed off shots in succession. They both missed. So did the half dozen shots which answered and drove Pepe out of sight behind the curve of the road. But the main effect was that the fusillade had caused Rubenstein to leap rapidly for the shelter of Salvio's car.

"Close the door behind you, Mr. Rubenstein," said Salvio.

Rubenstein gasped for air and closed the door.

"He's behind there," he said. "Up the road."

"I know that. Alone?"

"What else? Maybe walking along with a man what's got half a face, or arm in arm with the cracked gullet that made a sound?"

"What next, Salvio?"

"He's got two bullets left. He's back there ..."

"Two bullets?" said Rubenstein. "Two guns! And not a one wasted on the dead men down there, except one in the ceiling. If I had my way ..."

"Shut up, will you? Fredo, you and Cassi get up there on the bluff looking over the curve and try shooting that son of a bitch from up there. We come around with the car when he can't hit the tires anymore."

It took them five minutes of uncertain, unaccustomed climbing and scrambling before they met Pepe. He was somewhat below and aiming up. He shot Cassi through the liver and one lung, a lucky shot at thirty feet.

"Fredo?"

But he did not answer Salvio because he was ducked down next to Cassi and could not take his eyes off the red foam boiling out of Cassi's dead mouth. Instead Salvio heard a very vulgar voice.

"*Filio di porco! Scenti!*"

"That's the Guarda animal," said Rubenstein. "Why are we sitting here while that *verkackte* animal is running around free out there?"

"Cassi, Fredo! You still up there?!" yelled Salvio.

"They're dead!" bellowed Pepe's voice. "*Bastarde di porco*, you hear me?!"

Salvio froze with rage at the insult, but had no time for an answer. Fredo showed at the rim, waving like mad.

"That Lincoln's coming this way!" he called. "You better get your ass up here, Salvio!"

"Cover me!" called the young Trattomajore and he got ready to go. He checked the impulse and grabbed Rubenstein who right now was the reason for everything. The driver who had been manhandled by Pepe in the laundry yard got out from behind the wheel, groaning painfully. Salvio did not care about the driver. One cripple on his hands was bad enough. He made it up the steep side which climbed away from the road while Fredo was above, firing a shot now and then, and the driver tried to shove Rubenstein from behind.

Pepe could see the insane procession from his place around the bend in the road. He had cascaded back down to get out of Fredo's range, which also meant he could do nothing about Salvio or Rubenstein. And if he waited much longer all the halt and the lame were going to make it into the hills. A hell of a lot of time had passed since Fredo had called the news about the Lincoln.

When he could not see the Trattomajore group above anymore he followed, but before he saw them again he had made enough height to see his own Lincoln.

The long car had bottomed once too often. The ridiculous overhang of the rear sat broadbeamed on one end of a dip while the front wheels were up on the other. The rear wheels barely touched and the tank was pouring gasoline on the road. The men and the car were so far away they could not even hear him, if he had shouted. Pepe forgot about them and went after the Trattomajores alone. From his angle he could not see the Camaro convertible parked below.

The first one he spotted was the man he had injured in the laundry yard. The man had passed out. They had taken his gun, Pepe discovered, but he did not continue until he had delivered a safety-minded crack across the unconscious man's skull.

"You hear that?" said Rubenstein.

"Shut up!"

"That animal is right ..."

"So he can hear you too!"

But they had no inkling where Pepe was until the ricochet sprayed stone splinters their way.

"Fredo, crawl on back that way and around. He'll be between us."

"Listen, Salvio, this ain't no goddamn movie, just remember that."

"And he's no Houdini in these rocks with two guns holding him!"

"He's doing pretty good, Salvio, pretty goddamn good, is the point I'm making."

Salvio Trattomajore's father was so powerful to the son, that he could feel the derisive eyes in the old man's fat face looking at him. Salvio started to tremble.

"Go," he said and pointed his gun at Fredo.

The other man reacted more to the voice than to the gun. Fredo got up but stayed low. Then he crawled away.

In a while there was nothing for Salvio to see or to hear, except that he could spot the impaled Lincoln in the far distance and he could hear the men who had left it. They were out of view, but now and then their indistinct comments carried his way. He gave a violent start when Pepe's voice sounded so close.

"*Porcorino!* Let's talk like you had sense!"

"Of course," said Salvio. "Keep talking."

Pepe laughed.

"Fredo don't need it," called Pepe. "He's found me already!" and then came the laugh again.

Rubenstein could see the young man shiver. There was now an animal loose in the wilderness and a boy to protect him. It was time to live or to die. It did not matter. But not this. Not this unseen animal and this shame of a boy.

He stood up, bearing the twinge in his ankle well enough.

"Pepe," he said. "See me, a *meshuggener alter*, yes, but not a worm that hides." He wanted to say more but saw the crazy Trattomajore leap up at him and grab him around the middle. Salvio had the gun in his other hand, close to Rubenstein's ear.

"See me too!" he screamed at the landscape. "You got to have him alive, right, Guarda?"

"That's right," said Pepe and stood up. He was far enough to make a shot problematic, but there was nothing maybe about Salvio and his gun in

Rubenstein's neck.

"So I'm going to walk right out of here, Guarda, straight and simple like that. Clear enough?"

"Yuh," said Pepe. "And then I think I'm gonna kill you, *piccolo porco.*"

It was a very bad jab to give to a jumpy man, but Pepe did not know it. He had a hangover feeling from all the mayhem that had happened, and a hangoverish feeling of doubt and disgust. It was not so clear anymore why all this was so important but meanwhile the mess of the action kept piling up. So he started to walk towards Salvio with a stubborn look on his face.

"I said I'll kill this man!" yelled Salvio.

"Yeah," said Pepe.

"You don't believe me? You better believe me!" screamed Salvio. There was a tantrum quality in his voice. "*In pieces, I'll kill him!*"

This time Pepe stopped out of sheer amazement, but it did not stop Salvio.

"Drop the gun and let me through or I'll do it!"

But Pepe just stood there.

"Like this!"

Salvio's gun, the small automatic, bounced at Rubenstein's side. The old man gasped.

"That was the bone in the hip!" yelled Salvio. "Now you believe me?"

"*Pazzo—*" said Pepe with disbelief and stood there.

And Salvio could not stop. The old man was heavy in his arm but Salvio felt as strong as Goliath.

"*Solamente per dimostrazione!*" he screamed. "*Ecco! Ecco!*" and each time he fired a shot into Rubenstein's body.

Pepe dropped his gun. For no apparent reason, he just dropped his gun. Salvio saw this clearly and felt the vast surge of strength in himself. He saw how stupid Pepe looked and that his mouth hung limp. For that reason the sharp voice tore at him with frightful surprise.

"Salvio! Here!"

Salvio snapped around and saw a hard, compressed version of Pepe come towards him from the top of the rise.

"Drop it," said Marco.

Salvio did not drop the gun but he let go of Rubenstein. The old man fell like a sack.

Marco leapt around shrubs and over boulders and on the way stuck the gun under his coat. By the time he got to Salvio, Pepe was getting up. He looked down at the dead face and wiped his hands on his sides.

But Rubenstein was not dead. He looked up at Marco and moved his head so that Marco would know that he should come closer. Rubenstein's face looked so tired that all his worry lines had become soft.

"*Markele*, you can hear me?"

"Yes, Nate."

"You know what it means *chutzpa*?"

"No. Don't talk, Nate."

"It means like me to think all my life I'm doing right. Me thinking that is *chutzpa*." Rubenstein sighed and lowered his eyes. "Think, Markele. Think." Then he died.

CHAPTER 16

The electric view from the window which always lifted Don Angelo's spirits seemed especially bright to him. He stood and watched it a little bit longer than usual, and with a little more leisure. He walked over to the bar cart and gave it a push. It rolled on the parquet until it hit the rug. Don Angelo went back to the window. He undid his tie and took off his jacket, but this time he did not drop anything on the floor. He held them as if he had forgotten them, and then dropped them to the couch. The room looked big with darkness, except for the small space of light on his desk. He went there and sat down, doing so with an obvious sense of leisure. Then he called his *consigliere*.

"How's the mood?" he started.

"Holding steady."

"You're not talking about the stock market, *consigliere*. In the territory."

"Except for the Trattomajores, fine. They want something to do."

"There is nothing to do. You told them?"

"Of course. I spoke with Raphael Trattomajore. He says the Guardas sent the body of Salvio to him."

"They know the manners," said the Don. "He took it like a Family member?"

"Uh, I guess. What can he do."

"He can keep his pack of mongrels in check, that's what he can do!" Don Angelo sighed, and changed the tone of his voice back to leisure. "Did they clean up that mountain top, or wherever it happened?"

"Of course."

"Now tell me about the state of the union." Don Angelo laughed. When he stopped he noticed that Cipollo was not laughing with him.

"As you said, Don. Everybody is running scared and the organization is useless for business purposes, for the Guardas' purposes, is what I mean." Cipollo coughed. "I took the liberty to go one step further."

"Like what?"

Cipollo had some sense of accomplishment on that night, like a deserved pause at any rate, in the unending, natural striving and straining which goes into anyone's appointed work. So he took a cigar from its humidor and put it in his mouth. He never smoked one anymore. He just put it in his mouth and took it out again.

"As you recall," he said to his Don in Las Vegas, "you urged me to watch my timing. The Guardas, with organization, would be fiercely protective of each other, and therefore a disruption to our overall organization."

"Is there something you can say with the words shorter?" del Mare said. When finished with the customary put-down he sat back and listened.

"I am rephrasing your own idea. About rocking the boat, was the way you put it."

"You're trying to say something, *consigliere*. Get the lead out, willya?"

"I think we can afford the final touch now, Don Angelo. I'm in touch with Mr. Sturgeon. He's standing by."

Mr. Sturgeon was a cover and his price was ten thousand. It was exceptionally high because he worked completely alone and left no trace.

"I don't know," said Don Angelo. "Do we need it?"

"Granted, there is not much left. The attrition is getting terrible. The whole ..."

"The what?"

"To put the screws on, in your words, Don Angelo. It seems effective."

"So why Mr. Sturgeon?"

Cipollo sighed. "Because there is always that unpredictable element, as I have pointed out. I am speaking of Marco, of course."

"Not yet," said del Mare. "Could be, he's even salvageable."

Cipollo winced at the thought but got nowhere in further conversation. The Don hung up and turned to other business.

An exceedingly clear moon gave cleanliness to the city view and made the black sky look deep. Nuncio paid no attention. He had dropped the pencil, pushed the paper cups and the thermos aside, and his head was down on the littered desk. He was asleep.

Marco came back from the dressing room into the office and wrinkled his nose at the smoke in the air. He had taken a shower and had changed his clothes. He was conscious of the soft feel of cloth on him and the coolness of his skin but not much else had changed. The bone weariness was still there, and the unvarying feeling of pressure under his skull.

He hefted the thermos and put it down again. He went to the sideboard, took out bourbon, and fixed a drink with water and ice in a tall glass. Then he sat down and sipped his drink while watching the moon stand still in the black sky. He did not really see it. All he saw was that it was still nighttime.

His brother moved on the desk and made a sound. Nuncio moved like a man trying to stand up in a vat of glue. Then he woke with a start.

"You still here?" he said to Marco.

"*Mu.*"

"Yes," said Nuncio and stretched. "Where's there to go."

Marco moved the glass back and forth in his palms.

"Why don't you go home?"

"Why?"

"That's someplace to go."

Nuncio got up without answering and went to the dressing room. He went into the bath from there and washed his face. Marco looked at the moon. When Nuncio came back he asked what time it was but Marco did not answer the question.

"Why don't you tell me what's going on?" he asked.

"Like what?" Nuncio's voice showed the sharp irritation again, the same tone which had made the conference with Rubenstein a session of bickering and backbiting instead of a business session. He had upset the men and he had alienated the frightened contacts and go-betweens that handled protection. Something had happened, thought Marco. This had been going on much longer than tonight.

"I think there's something wrong," said Marco. "I'm talking about us, the real family. There's something wrong with you and Rosetta, perhaps?"

"Nothing. And not your business."

"*Capisco.* But it is my business when you bring it here."

"There is nothing wrong with Rosetta!"

"I know that, Cino. I know that." But the innuendo made no dent. Then Marco became more direct. "Why don't you lay off Pepe? He's no match for you."

Nuncio straightened up and smoothed the front of his clothes. He gave his brother a very cold look, the way only Nuncio could look cold.

"Because the idiot is doing a lousy job with the men. Right now he has to guide them, not drive them. Right now they have nothing to go on or work for but loyalty and in the face of that Pepe offers them ..."

"I'm not going to get sucked in on that, Cino. You're right, but it's off the subject. You think he's after Rosetta."

It was out. And for the moment it produced nothing but silence as if he, Marco, had been off the subject himself.

Nuncio walked around the desk and sat down. It was a strange performance in control, done with precision of movement, except that the eyes moved too much.

"You are right," said Nuncio, as cold as before. "He is no match. And he knows this. Except for his monkey gymnastics with his women."

"Did Rosetta say he went after her?"

"No. Quite the opposite."

"Then why don't you lay off? Or do you envy him his monkey stuff, maybe?"

It had been the wrong thing to say and Nuncio handled it typically enough.

"I have my ways and he has his." Nuncio started to sort papers with great intent. "As he will discover."

After that he refused to be diverted. He changed the mood in the room by making a phone call to Long Beach and another one to San Francisco. They were both necessary but not at that time of the night.

Long Beach said that he could not get in touch with the City Hall contact until nine in the morning and San Francisco said that the loan information might take as long as two days.

Marco knew all that. He put his unfinished drink on the sideboard and went to the desk.

"None of it matters," he said. "What matters is the room."

Nuncio was all sensible business now.

"Granted. They closed the wire service. They made arrests and they made all of them stick. And that alone shows where we lost the protection. Up there! Where it counts! Without that money we have *no* money, and without money we can't buy the protection we need in order to make money!"

"Don't talk to me like to an idiot, Cino."

"Then don't act like one!"

"Shut up a minute, will you?"

Nuncio shrugged and started to doodle. He also glanced at his watch. Then he talked more quietly.

"That's why the loan," he said. "And that's why the territory contraction, which you won't understand. None of the old contacts are our contacts anymore. Cipollo paid them more to do no business than they'd make by doing business with us. So we pull in. New contacts, less spread in commitments. Chuck everything from before."

"We will," said Marco. "But not because we're running."

This time he looked at his watch. Nuncio saw it and smiled for the first time in a long time.

"You too, eh?"

"It's all we got left," he said, and thought of the new wire room and the reshuffled bookie system which might save their position.

"It won't open til six A.M.—if then," said Nuncio.

Marco went to the corner window which looked out towards the west. A sliding streak of white showed in the blackness beyond the roofs of the city, a rare glimpse of the Pacific from this distance. But Marco did not really see it. His muscles pulled inside him, as if they were trying to pull him to finish a motion, an act, anything.

"Gimme that sheet with the lineups again."

He came back to the desk and picked it up himself. Nuncio did not look up. He was clicking the adding machine.

The sheet displayed something that looked like a genealogical tree. The boxes contained names and they sent out lines which went in various directions. Most of them were connected. Marco concentrated on just a few.

Minelli, Commissioner's office, ten thousand a month, of which six was for distribution.

Corby, City Board, three thousand. This was Minelli's back-up man with option money coming when he had something to do.

Quillan, State Coordinator, participation percentage in Messina Construction, disguised as real estate investments. The payments were complicated but the net was high.

Above Quillan was a box with a question mark. Both the box and the question mark had just been penciled in. They had never used MacAdoo, as long as Quillan had been in their pocket. They did not even know MacAdoo, except for the rumor of his one-time connections.

The problem was Quillan. If he had accepted their bait—all the operating money they could still command—then, at six in the morning, they would be in business again for at least long enough to maintain an eight percent operation. For a month, anyway—a month's time in which to calm all the nervous small fry on which most of their operations depended, a time to get at least the low-level protection in line again, so that the bottom did not fall out of everything. He looked at his watch again.

"Heatherton was supposed to call."

Heatherton was the manservant in Quillan's house. He was no steady connection, but for five thousand in gambling credit—to help with his only vice—he was to check on the phone calls that Quillan might make from his private phone during the night.

"He would call if he could," said Nuncio. "And if he calls and says that Quillan talked to Minelli, that still doesn't mean Minelli is going to let the Room open up."

"The hell it doesn't," said Marco.

He pulled the desk phone his way and dialed a number in Beverly Hills. While it rang he looked at his watch again.

"Leone? This is Marco."

"Hell," said Leone. "I thought it was going to be Heatherton."

"He didn't call yet?"

"Marc baby, wouldn't I let you know? It's only three plus in the morning and Quillan didn't come in till two. So get off the phone and don't block the action." Leone hung up without waiting for Marco to say anything else.

"That creep, the *cazzo*," said Marco to himself.

"Who?"

"All of them!"

Then he paced. It was true, even an affirmative Heatherton call need not mean a thing. But that was true for everything Marco could think of at the moment. A call from Heatherton, a little straw spinning out of sight in the undertow of a brown and green monster wave, that little straw right now would be something!

The phone rang. Nuncio picked it up but Marco snatched it out of his hand.

"Yes!"

"He called," said Leone. "He says Quillan called Steve, that he used the name Steve which is Minelli's first name ..."

"Get to it!"

"I am! And he said to him, he used the phrase, 'business as usual.'"

"Business as usual. What else did he say?"

"That's what Heatherton said. Quillan told Minelli 'business as usual.'"

"*Nothing* else?"

"What more do you want from a crooked politician, a contract?"

"Now listen to me, Leone, I can do without your goddamn lip at a time like this. I want to know ..."

"What you want and what I give ain't the same thing, Marco. Fathom that!" and once again, Leone hung up.

"The help," said Marco to the wall, "is getting restive." Then he lowered the phone very gently and cradled it.

"It shows," said Nuncio. "But, your nerves aside for a moment, was it positive?"

Marco wondered how Nuncio kept so calm. He tried for the same facade, the same absence of feeling. He faked it well enough with his voice.

"Positive," he said. "Quillan passed the word."

He did not add, we made it, though it was on the tip of his tongue. The fakery went as far as that but did not control the hope. For an instant he fed on it.

"And if the room doesn't open," he said, "can we hold it a few days?"

"Forget it. Except for the loan there's nothing else. Long Beach and dope are locked in and will close down as soon as the word is out—if the room doesn't open."

"I see," said Marco, as if he had not known this before. "I'm going out. If it works, we're in. I got plans for that."

"You were going to say something else."

"And if it doesn't work," said Marco, "I'm taking the leash off Pepe and I'm canceling everything."

He grabbed his jacket and went to the door. Nuncio looked uncomfortable behind his desk, uncomfortable with the hope that Marco had not lost his reason.

"*Omertà* is going to be a dirty word," Marco said from the door. "Call Cipollo so he can tell the Don. I'm going to tear them and theirs into screaming pieces!"

He drove around for two hours. He turned the heater on in Pasadena and turned it off again when he got back towards the coast. In Laguna Beach he watched the cops bust a hippie who had been sleeping on the beach, and in Venice he watched them pick a senior citizen out of the gutter who was either dead drunk or dead from a heart attack. In Culver City he watched the lunch pail crews and the fancy car crews make the early call at the studio, and then it was just past six o'clock.

He had planned it that way. He wanted to be just slightly late. He drove down the empty street, through the yellow lights blinking, and across the railroad tracks where the freights moved by only once at night. Then he rolled to a stop, one block from the building.

He could not have gotten any closer, if he had wanted to do it.

There was a van in front and four cars all around without any markings. They were loading switchboard equipment and office files into the van. The paddy wagon, it seemed, had already left.

Marco held very still and curled his hands around the wheel tightly. It was a small thing to do in the face of having lost everything.

At seven in the morning he let himself into Francine's apartment. He did not wake her up. He sat on a stool in the kitchen and sipped a glass of milk.

CHAPTER 17

By the middle of the morning the word was out. There was a good deal of confusion in the territory where the Messina *regime* used to be.

The crew from the wire room was let out on bail to the tune of one hundred thousand total. Minelli came to work as he did every morning and went out to lunch at his usual time. But he did not come back at his usual time. A connection in Burbank saw ten of his customers and told them he would promise nothing until he was told what to do. Three bookies left on a noon flight for Miami. Three freighters in Long Beach paid dock fees with no prospect of getting unloaded. Two Trattomajores were booked for drunken driving. One lawyer for the Messina Development Company was asked to account for an unclear bid.

Pepe Guarda, very unsure of the situation, walked into the Long Beach Union Hall at the head of fifteen men. Usually, he walked with no more than one. He felt even more unsure when he got to the offices in the back. It was true that only half the staff seemed to be there, but those who were there were working. The manager, who was Rubenstein's brother-in-law, came running up very fast.

"Don't get sore about the staff," he said to Pepe. "They got all confused. I called everybody up and tomorrow it'll be like usual." He was a small man with long, serious lines in his face. When he winked at Pepe, it looked out of place.

Nuncio Guarda was on the phone in his office while half a dozen calls were stacked up for him at the board.

"What about the bid you didn't send in?" said the caller. "Do you want it or not? We got to start breaking ground at least a month before the tourist season."

Marco Guarda was in Burbank. He slept.

Consigliere Cipollo had three men in his office, a Frenchman who handled the Marseilles end of the line, a New Yorker from Brooklyn who was a small business organizer, and a man who was a management expert for loan operations. They had a briefing session which was constantly interrupted by telephone calls. At one point Cipollo told them to go out to lunch. They had settled nothing.

Angelo del Mare was in Las Vegas. He slept.

Marco Guarda woke up in the afternoon. He could tell the approximate time by the view through the window where he could see the long backline of the Hollywood Hills. The hills looked dim and had the color of nicotine, which was the smog color on a warm afternoon. The air conditioner hummed, filtering the Valley air.

He had woken up once before, when the phone had been ringing. He had come awake enough and aware enough to know what day this was and what the change was in him. There had been no point in answering the phone.

He got up and went to the bathroom. On the breakfast bar was a slip of paper which said, "You sleep like a husband. Will be back soon. Francy."

He took a shower and shaved, taking his time, because he felt that he had the time and that he needed it. Then he got dressed and sat at the breakfast bar with a cup of coffee. The electric pot was full and hot, making a morning-time aroma. Then Francine came back. She put down a grocery bag and blinked her eyes.

"Christ, that air bites out there," she said.

He smiled and thought of smoking a cigarette. He did not ask her about the phone call.

"Pepe called," she said. "I didn't want to wake you and he said it was all right."

"It's all right, Francy."

"He said it was. You should call him back though. At the West Hollywood place."

"You want coffee?"

"Yes, please." She dropped a pack of bacon on the counter by the stove and put a small bag of mushrooms next to it. The milk and the juice she put in the refrigerator. Then she sat down on the kitchen side of the bar and pulled the coffee cup over so that it sat between her elbows. "He sounded confused."

"What?"

"Pepe. He sounded confused."

"That's Pepe. I think I'll have one of your cigarettes."

She gave him a cigarette and watched him for a while.

"Marc?"

"Hm?"

"What happened?"

He exhaled smoke and watched it drift away.

"We're through," he said.

Francine gave a start and slowly balled one hand into a fist in front of her mouth. Marco saw it and smiled.

"Not that, Francy. I mean the business. Everything. The Guardas are through."

It was a relief to hear him explain, even as little as he did, because nothing had happened between them to change things. To have no change at all was better than to have the tenuous thing between them disappear altogether. She sighed and smiled back at him.

"How about some breakfast?" she asked. "I got mushrooms. I know that if it hasn't got tomatoes in it somewhere it's not really food, but I can make you ..."

"Fine, Francy." He drank coffee and looked at the nicotine cast over the Hollywood Hills. Francine made an omelet with mushrooms and little pieces of bacon and parsley in it. She was humming to herself. When she turned to look at Marco she stopped humming with surprise because she saw him making the bed and folding it back into the couch. Then she turned back to the stove and hummed to herself.

"How long are you staying?" she said in a while.

She could not see his shrug, but then he said, "How'd you like to go to the beach?"

She almost turned around very rapidly to ask, how long, but she stopped herself and kept looking down at the omelet she was building slowly. Then she nodded.

"I'd like that," she said. And then she wondered about the difference between what he had said and the way he sounded. It is true that he had told her before that he was through, that all that business was over. But he did not act as if he were through or as if everything old was over for him. When the phone rang she picked it up because he had not made a move.

"It's Pepe. He says this time it is important."

"Tell him I don't think so. I'll call back."

Francine talked into the phone and then she listened for a while. Marco could hear Pepe's voice getting louder.

"Let me have the phone," he said to Francine, and when he had it he said to Pepe, "You can stop yelling. What in hell's the matter with you?"

"What in hell's the matter with *me?* What in hell's the matter with you, is why I'm calling!"

"You haven't said anything yet," said Marco. "Take a breath."

Then he waited while Pepe did just that. When Pepe talked again he no longer sounded so violent, but Marco could hear the confusion. Pepe, it seemed, was out of his depth and perhaps, Marco thought, he was the only one honest about it.

"I tell you something," said Pepe in a while. "I feel lost. I don't think I ever felt like this before, Marco."

Marco did not ignore the touch of pleading in the voice. "I hear you," he said. "What do you want to tell me?"

"I want to know what the hell I'm doing and why?!" He had his usual attitude back. "Listen. I'm in Long Beach. Kominski at the Hall tells me not to worry. The action's going to pick up again tomorrow. I call Cino and he don't sound like himself either and tells me not to believe anything, and as far as he's concerned I should just fade out. I come back from the phone and there's two squad cars piling my men in the back and the guy in civvies is that jerk from the D.A.'s office, that nothing punk we put in there, and he's acting like Napoleon. I split. I call the house in West Hollywood and ask for the Cat, and *he's* split! You know something, Marco? I can't find my own men anymore!"

Marco did not want to upset his brother but he also did not want to get back into the useless shuffle and dance which the Don was calling so well. He wanted to tell Pepe to let go and get out, to stop dreaming and do something on his own for a change. But then he held it down to a tone of advice.

"It's over," he said. "Just fade right now, Pepe, and I'll be in touch tomorrow."

"Tomorrow? The action's today, *cretino!* They're taking everything!"

"Pepe, right now it's no good even trying to figure it. Go and work out on Elaine. There's no point bucking it now."

Pepe heard that and waited a moment. Then he said, "You mean you're giving up, *bimbo?*"

"I didn't say that! Now get off my back!"

"You know something, *bimbo?* You're starting to sound like Cino, you know that?"

"No, I don't know that."

"That *cornuto* he said why in hell didn't I use my head just once in my life and just give up trying. And the second time I called him, like just now I did, he wouldn't even answer the phone! Francisco answered and said, 'Nuncio's getting smashed in the office. He's sitting in a corner there, like a kid, and drinking *hard* liquor!'"

"*Meno male*, Pepe. What's the difference? Go work it off on Elaine."

"And to hell with you too, *bimbo!* I think I got a better idea!" and Pepe hung up.

Marco put the phone down and controlled himself. Once or twice there had been a time when Pepe was something that ought to be wearing a leash; a loyal creature when linked to a master but a violent menace without the chain on him.

"What's wrong?" asked Francine.

"Forget it. How about that thing you're making?"

She served him the omelet and put two scallions on the plate with it. He picked up one of them and handed it to her.

"You better have one too," and then he started to eat.

She watched him and was not sure whether she should feel good about him. His silences did not give her much peace.

"Marc?"

"Hm?"

"You know what time it is?"

"Yeah."

"Did you still want to go to the beach?"

"Sure," he said. "I like you on the beach. I'm crazy about scallions wearing bikinis."

She watched him eat and smiled.

"I like you home," she said. "Feels just like it, doesn't it? Me in the kitchen here and you having your meal in the living room."

"And nothing between us but the bar."

"Stop looking at me like that."

"What else? You got 'em piled up on the bar top like the desert coming up."

She stood up straight immediately. He laughed and kept eating. She came to his side of the bar and brought her coffee cup. She sat down on the stool next to him so that she felt the touch of his arm.

"Let's stay home, Marc."

He looked at her and then turned back to his plate.

"So it's just scallions and no bikini. *Mu*. But you do cook pretty good, considering there were no tomatoes, oregano, and parmesan cheese." He was finished with his plate, wiped his mouth, and turned her way. "And now I will tell you a thing, *bambola*, which no man living, no woman living, has ever known. I hate parmesan."

"And oregano?"

"Keeps the moths out of clothes."

"Tomatoes?"

"Mush. I got nothing against them when they're firm."

She did not move away when he put his hands on her but leaned towards him with her face next to his. She put her teeth on his ear and held on.

"Marc—"

"You're hissing in my ear."

"You're wrinkling me."

"You don't wrinkle. I can tell."

"Let's go back to bed, Marc."

"A bar stool isn't good enough for you?"

They got off the stools and looked at the living room which no longer had a bed in it but just the tricky couch with the low table in front of it. Then they looked at each other.

"In the ads," he said, "they never make clear that you have to redo the whole living room each time you want to make love."

"There's the bar stool."

"Don't be shameless like that, Francy. Let's go sit on the couch and think about rearranging the living room."

They sat down on the couch, next to each other, and looked at the Hollywood Hills which were turning mustard color.

"I would like to sit like this with you and see a hill that's green, or even a sky that's blue," he said suddenly. "And have a room that doesn't have to be collapsed after making love and uncollapsed before making love?"

"Right."

"Why don't we, Marc?"

"Yuh," he said and kept looking out at the mustard air.

"Couldn't we leave, Marc?"

He touched himself for a cigarette and did not answer.

"Didn't you say you were through here?"

She was immediately sorry that she had said it. The change in him was not entirely clear, but the ease had gone out of him, the fun was gone, and he was invisible inside his silence. When he talked he sounded very cool and controlled, so much so that Francine felt apprehensive.

"I'm through with the games," he said. "That's all I meant. I'm through reaching, the way I'm supposed to, and not making it, the way I'm supposed to. That's what I meant."

She did not move away from him but she felt that she might as well sit behind a sheet of glass.

"What is it, Marc? What's driving you?"

He looked at her and seemed to be thinking about it.

"I'll think of something," he said. "When I've got the time. Right now, all I can tell you, I'm just reminded of something. I used to get to wear my older cousin's clothes, because Pepe's were too big for me and Nuncio was younger and smaller. But the cousin was just my size. Except he wasn't. And I'd wear those clothes, they'd look fine, except in some way that nobody knew or could tell, they'd pull me this way and pinch me that way, and would creep around on me like something that was no part of me and just didn't belong." He got up and walked away from her, looking out of the window. "That's what's driving me." His voice all but sank away. "And I can't stand that!"

Francine got up too. She understood him, which also meant that he would not understand her. So she said nothing else about their leaving together and getting a room that could just stay the way it was, a place that did not have to be collapsed and made to disappear each time it had been used.

When the phone rang she answered it and then laid it on the bar.

"It's Nuncio," she said. "And you better talk to him. He sounds bad."

Marco listened at the phone for a while. He kept his hand over his mouth and nothing about him seemed to move. Then he held his hand out to Francine, snapping his fingers.

"Gimme a cigarette," he said.

She gave him one and watched him turn away.

"You're drunk!" he said to the phone sharply. But he kept listening.

She was holding the match for him which he did not see and then she blew it out. He never looked up when she walked out nor did he hear it when she closed the door.

"Now shut up a minute! Then start over."

"I have not yet begun," said Nuncio. His tongue, he felt, was a large, humped-up worm in his mouth and it had a life of its own. He struggled with it, trying to push the thing out of the way so that he could talk. His head, in contrast, was entirely his and seemed very clear. "*Minqua mia,*" he said, except that the worm interfered.

"Cino. Nuncio! Who else is there with you?"

"Just us worms. *Scusi*, Marco; for Gossake, don't hang up. This is important. Just the goddamn tongue is all," he said clearly.

"Let me talk to Francesco. Is Francesco there, Cino?" Francesco took the phone. He sounded a little frightened, but he was blessedly sober.

"You there, Marco? Listen, he's trying to make sense, I mean really he does, except what he wants to say doesn't make sense. You get what I mean?"

"No. What's he doing now?"

"Lying down on the couch."

"Don't let him! I got to know what he's talking about. If he goes to sleep now ..."

"He's talking about the union thing, the whole Long Beach scene, actually. It's running."

"Christ, you too. What's running?"

"Everything! Like Cipollo never happened!"

"Francesco, I'll be right over. Just keep him awake!"

Marco dropped the unlit cigarette on the bar, slammed the phone down, grabbed his jacket, and left. On the freeway he joined the outbound traffic which was a nerve-racking, dangerous trip even at the possible twenty miles an hour. The joining maneuver which sluiced him onto the San Diego Freeway going over the pass from the Valley and into the basin was like an exercise in futility. Every so often the progress stopped altogether.

The trip took more than an hour. If Marco could have paid attention he would have seen that the evening had started, and the air was still with a touch of dusk.

But all Marco knew was that he was raging and that he did not know why. What if it was true and nothing had changed at all since the morning? Then what was he to do with the banked inferno in him? What if he were no longer fit for the delicate work of balancing his strains and tensions, of making a greedy grifter mesh with a violent punk, and to get an intelligent man to cooperate with one who was stupid?

When Marco got to the office in the Tealbaum Building, Nuncio was not there. Francesco was there, looking thin and out of place behind the desk. When Marco came in, Francesco got up immediately. The desk held an assortment of drinkables: an electric coffee pot, an open can of tomato juice, Worcestershire in a bottle, half a bottle of beer, a salt shaker, a jar of clam juice, a glass of hangover seltzer with the fizz all gone. The original bottle that had sent the demon into Nuncio was nowhere in evidence. Nuncio's clothes were all over the floor.

"He's in the shower," said Francesco.

"And you're out here? He can go to sleep in the shower too!"

"The Cat is with him."

"I thought he'd split."

"He had. He came back because there's this rumor, he said, that Cipollo gave up and you're in."

"And you? You've been on the board most of the day, what have you heard?"

"I don't listen in," said Francesco.

"Yes. But you heard the rumor too."

"Yes. Nuncio told me, except he says it isn't a rumor."

"He's been on the phone all the time?"

"A few hours. He quit out that one time, when he got too drunk, and then I got him back on because Quillan kept calling. So then he started to work the phones again, but more like a crazy man, aside from being so drunk."

"Okay, Francesco. Go back to the board."

"Quillan's called back since, but Nuncio never returned the call. You want me to make the connection?"

"Later."

Marco opened the dressing room door and felt the warm steam. Nuncio was on the floor, moist and pink, while the Cat sat hunkered down over him working his hands into Nuncio's shoulders. Nuncio groaned with pain.

"If the hangover don't kill him, this will," said the Cat.

Marco went back to the desk and told Francesco to get him Quillan. Then he watched Nuncio get up off the floor and pick clothes from the wardrobe in the dressing room. The Cat came in to look at the stuff on the desk and then went to the cabinet with the liquor. He poured scotch in a glass with nothing else and drank it down.

"I'm back," he said. "You want me?"

Marco nodded. He did not know what he wanted right then but the Cat was all right, as far as he was concerned.

"Who else is back?" he asked.

"All the guys at the house, except five of them. Except for those five, the others never left. Like I did."

"They didn't know any better," said Marco.

"You might put it that way." The Cat went back to the scotch bottle and poured another drink. Nuncio stood in the door of the dressing room and shivered. He was dressed, except for the tie he was holding in his hand.

"Okay," said Marco. "Can you talk?"

Nuncio nodded.

"It sounds simple," he said. "Kominski pretty much has the trust of the operators in the union and he called to say he's in. For a token, he sent the week's receipts."

"This happened?"

"*Da vero*. First Pepe tried to tell me something like that, I don't remember just when, and later Kominski. And then the receipts." Nuncio touched the back of his head. "Let me finish," he said. "There's more. Then Giancarlo sent a man with the books, all the loan records for the current month, I should keep them here in the safe, he said, instead of in Long Beach like we always did—well, you know how we did it when Messina—Cat," he said with a sudden sharpness in his voice. "Would you mind not sloshing that stuff around with your glass?"

The Cat drank it down and put the glass on the cabinet. Marco just sat and waited.

"And then Quillan called. I talked— I mean, I tried to talk to you right after that. He called to say it's all right to open the room. Anytime. Same place even. The only thing, he said he was sorry we couldn't get the equipment back. It wouldn't be the proper thing to do, he said. You know how he talks."

"Right now," said Marco, "I wouldn't trust myself to know anything."

The phone rang and he picked it up. He said yes a few times and then he hung up.

"Quillan. An address in Pasadena," said Marco. "Let's get out there, now."

"Quillan doesn't live in Pasadena."

"Just shut up and let's go there. It's the thing to do."

It was dark when they got to Pasadena and except for the smog bite in the air it was a cloying night. The two cars circled the block a few times, each street containing very few houses. The grounds and their landscaping lent a touch of theatrical menace.

One car distributed five men and the other car drove through the gates of the place that took up the length of one block. The Cat was driving, feeling peevish about it. Marco and Nuncio sat in the back. They had not been able to locate Pepe.

The Cat missed the porte cochere which he had mistaken for a porch. He stopped before the car nosed into the grounds of the swimming pool and all three got out and walked back to the house. A manservant opened a full double door and then led them through a second set of etched glass doors. Next came the hall, done in parquet, marble, and pastoral tapestries. A converted gas chandelier hung like an extinct insect of monster proportions from the arch of the ceiling. A very small man, shrunken with age, so it seemed, entered from a door in the rear. His voice had a surprising booming quality.

"I'm MacAdoo," he said. "You don't know me and I don't know you. Matter of fact, I didn't realize that one of the Guarda brothers was black." He held a hand up and went on, "Don't bother to explain. We'll have enough to do with each other later. For the present, just follow me."

Both his tone and his manner were curt and had very much the disinterested touch of coming from on high. He turned away and obviously expected to be followed.

"We came this far," said Marco. "Now it's your turn."

MacAdoo stopped and eyed them from the dark near the tall door for which he had been heading.

"The Don is waiting," he said.

The Cat made a quick move which MacAdoo interrupted by simply shaking his head.

"Don't be an idiot," he said. "Pietro Vinciguerra is waiting."

He sat by a great, curved fireplace with a sandstone facade, whose black maw was empty. The room was a library with all the books behind glass and instead of studious comfort the room seemed cold with cleanliness. MacAdoo sat down in a high-backed chair that did not creak. Pietro Vinciguerra was the only other one in the room who was sitting down.

His chair was bigger than he but that did not distract from the solid, paternal sureness of the man. He had his hands folded on top of the cane between his legs and his black hat lay within reach on the floor. His disturbingly smooth face smiled with no show of emotion.

"*Fratelli mie*," he said. The nod of his head extended tolerance to everyone.

Nuncio suppressed an involuntary shiver and Marco put his hands in his pockets. He looked for a handy chair but did not find one. The Cat felt like he had walked into a bad movie.

"You know my name," said Vinciguerra. "You are here to know me as friend. Which one are you?"

"Marco Guarda."

"Then you there are Nuncio. But you are ill?"

"It's nothing."

"Then perhaps you will ask your man to fetch you a proper tonic. He will find the other servant beyond that door."

The Cat froze, including his brain. The bad movie had jerked to a stop and he could not get his eyes off it.

"This man is my lieutenant," said Marco. "When Pepe Guarda is not here, the Cat takes his place."

Vinciguerra stopped smiling and looked as if he had a problem about dismissing his error. He closed his eyes for a moment and then looked up again. His yellow eyeballs moved back and forth.

"Ah yes, Pepe Guarda is not here. And you don't know where he is." The remark was not a question and he was looking at Nuncio now.

"This whole bit," said Marco, "happened kind of suddenly. The point is, why are we here?"

Vinciguerra started to smile slowly and then held it without ever showing his teeth. He nodded his head and then winked at MacAdoo in his chair.

"*Veramente, detto con forza!*" he said and there was life in his eyes for the first time. "You are the strong one, and so I was told." He relayered his hands on the top of his cane. "And now, why don't you ask your—why don't you find the chairs by the wall there and bring them over."

They found the chairs and brought them over. When they sat down the distance between the old man and the young was still there.

"To the point," said Vinciguerra.

"Yes," said Marco. "Why don't you?"

Vinciguerra closed his eyes once again, as if reviewing his inner state. When he opened his eyes again he talked as straight as he ever did.

"You are here, and your *regime* is safe, as a matter of demonstration. I have—to use a phrase—outbid your own Don. It is my money which is holding your territory together."

"As a matter of demonstration," said Marco.

"It goes without saying. I cannot pay this much for your protection for long." Vinciguerra saw Marco waiting and he saw Nuncio come alert. He ignored the Cat, "It is oil on water, you understand. And once the waters are calm again, there will be no need for so much oil."

"You're saving our skin," said Marco.

"Yes, yes!" Nuncio seemed to breathe it.

"Why?"

Vinciguerra smiled again, showing his appreciation.

"Because I admire you. I have watched from afar how a weakening man let control slip from his hands, I have watched from afar how you and your brothers did *not* snatch and steal like a bandit might, like a wild dog might snap at the dying bull." He stopped, apparently to gather the thread of his message. Then he went on in the same tone of relating an epic. "I have seen how you have shown at all times the respect for a beautiful design, the respect for immaculate workings together." He took a deep breath, as if gasping with admiration. "For a *regime* can be man's work of art, even as a Family is God's creation!"

For a moment, Marco thought he was not hearing right, even though he felt pretty well tuned in on the former Don. Here was the *paterfamilias* with a mission. The mission was unity from which flowed strength—and the strength was used by the Don through God's will.

Marco rubbed his face, as if he were trying to wake up.

"Did you follow me?" asked Vinciguerra.

"Yes. I'm glad you admired the way we did it."

"*Ecco!* And then the sacrifice of a good man who had lost his strength." The old Don leaned forward. "How *did* you kill Messina?"

Marco smiled.

"How *do* you know so much?"

Vinciguerra smiled back, but more quickly.

"A Don, due to circumstances, may quit. But he does not cease to be a Don. My feeling of responsibility, Marco Guarda, cannot abdicate. You know that all this," and he waved his hand vaguely, "used to be mine."

"Yes. Now I know why you're here. You admire our work, and you hate to see it go down the drain. What you called your feeling of responsibility." Marco watched the old man closely to see if he were talking the right language. It seemed he was.

"*Ecco!*" said Vinciguerra and refolded his hands. "And you approve?"

It was not a question, and Marco knew it. It was a demand for a pledge of allegiance. Refusal would be treachery. The very least that would happen to the traitor was that the *regime* would instantly collapse from the lack of funds.

"Sure," he said. "And I'll add this," he went on. He made the pause and the look he gave the old man as significant as he could. "We need you, Don Pietro."

Judge MacAdoo had been fidgeting for some time and the heady talk reminded him of nothing so much as the ten pages of self-justification before the one sentence verdict that killed the victim.

"I gather they want in," he said to Vinciguerra as if nobody else was in the room. "Now what about the arrangements?"

"Only strangers and enemies must have arrangements ahead of time. Among brothers, there is understanding."

Nuncio looked at his brother, as if in despair, because this part of the meeting would properly be his department. However, he felt like he was in a swamp, and the hangover did not help any.

"And in fact," said Marco to Vinciguerra, "I do understand. The important part has been settled. How about Nuncio and Judge MacAdoo getting together on, uh, familiarizing each other?"

Marco took it as an answer when Vinciguerra reached down to the floor and picked up his hat. The old man put the hat squarely on his head.

"*Ecco,*" he said and got up. He added an afterthought. "But for our full accord, should not your big brother Pepe be here?" and he addressed the question straight at Nuncio. "Or perhaps you know best. Perhaps he is not important."

"Not for this part," said Nuncio.

"*D'accordo*. Though absence in itself is important. *Mu*, perhaps not this time," and the Don walked to the door.

And if the old bastard had known about Pepe and Nuncio, he could not have done it better to make the split worse, thought Marco.

Someone opened the door from the hall and Marco saw that it was Pino Valdez, the wheelman from Vinciguerra's time.

And if the old bastard had wanted to widen the split, where would he have gotten his inside information?

"As far as anybody knows," MacAdoo was saying, "Don Pietro isn't even here."

"Fine with me," said Nuncio. "So when do you and I get together?"

"We don't. Someone will be sent with instructions. As far as anybody knows ..." He waved a hand to indicate they were done.

CHAPTER 18

Because of the complexity of the *regime's* situation, the *consigliere* Cipollo—who was no longer in a position of direct knowledge—could not make a clear conclusion until more than a week had gone by. But when he knew, he knew, so he called his Don at the forbidden hour of twelve o'-clock noon.

Del Mare jerked up in bed and the first thing he saw was the girl who was supposed to be lying next to him. She was standing in front of the full-length mirror, wearing his dinner jacket from the night before. The con-strictions of the jacket made her beautiful body look obscene. She was six feet and two inches tall. She looked at herself and giggled. The sleeves were half way up to her elbows.

"Hey look, dovey," she said when she saw del Mare sitting up in bed.

He leapt up without a word, looking white and frail, and as soon as he was close enough he slammed his fist into her belly. There was a knock on the door. Del Mare hit the girl again and stepped aside so that she would not touch him while she doubled over. Then he went to the door.

"Who in hell—" he started but the man at the door interrupted him.

"You better take it," he said, and pointed at the phone.

Del Mare was panting. He tightened the belt on his robe and went quickly to the phone.

"*Pronto!*" he barked.

"Er—you are all right, Angelo?" Cipollo started.

"What else?"

"The Guarda matter."

Del Mare sat down and felt himself go very still. The control and the urgency of his interest showed in his voice.

"Are they in or are they out?"

"In," said Cipollo.

Del Mare looked towards the open bedroom door, wishing that the naked girl would show there. She would look pleading and in pain. He wished she would show so that he could throw something at her. Then he looked away.

"Let me hear it," he said to the phone.

"They didn't run out of money," said Cipollo. "And there is no trace of a loan. The San Francisco money was never picked up and there's no word about any other backing."

"What about Messina money, private stuff he left?"

"The Swiss account hasn't been touched. And he didn't have *that* kind of cash."

Del Mare accepted it. Next, he thought of the countermove.

"*Dunque,*" he said. "So we get down to old-style."

But Cipollo was ahead of him.

"I sent two specialists," he said. "The Messina office is on the twentieth floor, two stories below the roof. One came down from there, the other one came by the door. The one from the roof was going to go for the safe where the records must be. So ..."

"Get to it!"

"They left him lying where he smashed on the street and they left the tools for good measure. The one by the door disappeared."

"What about the men who covered him?"

"Same thing. And the wheelman disappeared too. Marco called this office to say where we should pick up the car."

Cipollo sweated through the awful curses.

"All right," said del Mare in a while. His voice was relaxed now. "Anyway, they're still playing by the rules. Now we switch."

"The reason I called at this particular time, Don Angelo, in spite of the hour, they switched. I had sent two cars of Trattomajores to Long Beach—loan places, pick-up rooms—anyway. Word came in half an hour ago. They got shot up. Right near MacArthur Park in broad daylight! Three dead, two dying, and the rest, on account of a shot-up car, arrested by two simple daytime police!"

"And none of them were Guardas," said del Mare quietly.

Cipollo, who was out of breath, did not bother to answer, and del Mare, without asking, knew that the Guardas had bought into some heavy protection.

"I have nothing to add," said Cipollo after a moment. "Unless it needs to be said that they have stopped forwarding all revenues."

Angelo del Mare, the businessman, was writing off the loss. Don Angelo, responsible to a wider commitment, was thinking of the next phase. In this respect, it was not a matter of money but a serious question of avoiding a precedent, because no *regime* ever split off from the organization.

"Chip," he said. "Get rid of the San Diego bums and lay low on everything else. I'll call you back later." While del Mare hung up he swiveled his chair to the bedroom door.

"Kate!"

She came quickly, a tall, very beautiful girl with a worried face. She could not tell by del Mare's expression what he might do next, and she held on to the negligee she was now wearing as if the gauzy thing could protect her from winter weather.

"Open it up," he said when she stopped in front of him. "Not the top! The bottom."

She spread the gown apart with two hands. Del Mare leaned forward and looked at the healthy smoothness of her skin. Then he nodded and sat back again. Her flat belly showed no bruising. There was just a faint redness where his fist had landed.

"With your kinda action," he said, "I shouldn't have worried. Those muscles are in top condition. You can close it up now."

She let the gown fall shut and stood waiting. At three hundred a trick, she could afford a lot of patience.

"You smoke, don't you? Sit down." While she pulled up a chair he nodded at the cigarette box on the desk. He waited while she lit up. "I got a job for you," he said.

"What kind?"

"What kind, I don't mean laying bricks. You know who Pepe Guarda is?"

"I've heard of him. He's been around town a few days."

"Then you know what I want you to lay. Now, here's what's special."

"He is?"

"If you don't know what he's after, he'll wear you out in twenty-four hours. Stop smirking and listen."

She composed her face instantly and leaned over to stub out her cigarette. The posture showed del Mare her improbable breasts, but he looked away. There were hours of the day when del Mare was easily revolted.

"He's got a thing about the woman going dead under him. Like with the strain or something. So the way you work him, you give him a lot of struggle—if you can remember how that goes—and then sort of get overpowered by the goddamn passion."

He looked uncomfortable and she nodded at him so that he would notice her serious attention.

"And then you collapse or faint or something. That's when he comes."

"I should wear him out," she said.

"You guessed that good. So, time it for him to get weakened for the message. I want him out of here with the message in his brain by night. You think you can handle that or maybe it's not your style?"

"Done quick suits me fine," she said and looked away.

"So when he's had enough, you start feeding this line to him, but not before. He's not that bright, but he can be suspicious. So wait till he doesn't care enough to be suspicious."

"What message?"

"I first give it to you in a nutshell and then we go over it. I want him to head back for L. A. thinking his brothers are trying to push him out of the racket they're in. You got that?"

"First, I should wear him out."

"Shut up and listen."

CHAPTER 19

Pepe Guarda got off the plane at the airport in the Valley. It was ten at night and the inversion layer was at eight thousand feet. That meant nothing to him, except that the smog had thinned out enough to make the night clear and the moon sharp in an onyx sky. For that reason Pepe could see the Santa Monica range with exceptional clarity. As soon as he had driven the rented car within sight of the Mulholland ridge he could see and imagine the plateau where he had held off the Trattomajores alone. He had risked his life there.

He pushed the car up and through the pass towards the basin. His back hurt, his head hurt, and his mouth was a sandpaper cave which was partly painted with glue.

He had risked his life up there and then the two *bastardes*—but the thought was impossible, since they were his brothers. And then the two fink brothers, he continued his thought, had pushed him out in such a clever way that he had never spotted just what they had been doing.

He left the freeway at Wilshire and drove west, though not as far as the Tealbaum Building. There was a telephone booth in the empty parking lot of a supermarket. He could not see the Tealbaum from the booth, which was fine with him.

He called a man about laying a bet and was told to call the twenty-four hour number. That meant the wire room was open.

He called a man about a quick loan and was told who the party was with whom he should get in touch. It was the same one who was skipping out when everything was supposed to have gone to pieces.

He called a connection and was told where to wait for a pick-up. They even gave him the price for a deck of smack on the phone, and the price was normal.

Then he called the West Hollywood house and asked for the Cat. He kept a handkerchief over the mouthpiece.

"Who wants to know?" said the man at the house.

"I'm Santino's brother and Santino wants to know."

"The Cat's out."

"We just come in from New York. The Cat knows about the trip. We just come back and everything's different. Where do we find the Cat?"

"Right now he's took Pepe's place, sort of, so I don't know where he's at this minute."

Pepe hung up. That broad in Vegas had known what she had been talking about!

Marco had started to smoke again. He carried a pack of his own and lit cigarettes frequently. He usually did not smoke them very far down but sometimes he sucked them right down to the quick so that he burned himself when he stubbed the butt out. He did not put this one out but just dropped it into the tray on Nuncio's desk and let it smolder. Then he went back to the window and looked at the onyx sky.

"The take," said Nuncio, "is up. Up!" He gave the smoldering stub a hostile look.

"Up yours," said Marco without turning around. "With all the complicated crap you and MacAdoo are into, did it ever come clear to you who gets taken?"

"Essentially yes. Here are the free and clear deposits. To start with an example, thirty-five thousand your account alone, a per diem take of ..."

"And also up your per diem!" Marco came away from the window but by the time he got to the desk his mood had changed. There was no point to it. Nuncio was talking about money and he, Marco, was talking about who was being taken. But he did not try to bring it up again.

"Any word on Pepe while I was out?"

"Why?"

"He's your brother! You and he and me—*escusi*, and MacAdoo and Vinciguerra—there's supposed to be more going on between us than that goddamn adding machine can tell you!"

Marco got a look from his brother which went right down to his bones. He patted himself for a cigarette and found one. Then he sat down on the couch and lit up. The time, he noted, was ten. They should leave.

"I'm sorry," he said. "I don't know what's the matter with me."

"I understand," said Nuncio without looking up. But he felt that he had sounded too cold. "How's Francy?" he added.

"I don't know. Haven't called her."

"When did you sleep last, Marco?"

"Last night. While the Cat was driving."

"That's what I mean," said Nuncio. "Take a nap on the couch."

"We got to go!"

"There's time."

"Right. You're right." It was too curt, thought Marco. "And how's Rosetta?" he asked.

"I don't know."

"You don't *know?*"

"I sent her to San Francisco."

"Oh? Haven't you called her or something?"

"You can't tell very much by telephone, can you?" said Nuncio.

It was getting thick again and Marco got off the couch. Nuncio gathered some folders and left some others on the desk. They went down to the garage and then drove up on Montana towards Brentwood.

Pino Valdez opened the heavy door which led into the hall. There was a table in the middle of the hall with Vinciguerra's black hat lying on top of it.

Vinciguerra did not keep the hat next to his chair when in his own house but he sat, as usual, with the cane between his legs and his hands folded on top. He smiled, and clicked off the television remote control.

"*Sera, sera,*" he said. "And still there is no Pepe Guarda?"

"I brought the folders," said Nuncio, "and Marco has some questions."

"He could be anywhere," said Vinciguerra. "Las Vegas—"

"He was there, at least some of the time," said Marco. "Then we lost track of him for a while."

"Or San Francisco," said Vinciguerra. "But let us begin."

Marco took the conversation away from Vinciguerra and Nuncio very quickly. He waved at Nuncio to put his folders on the window bench where he was standing and he moved to a library table. Also, his position required that Vinciguerra crane his neck around.

"Before Nuncio comes up with the figures and charts ..."

"He should do that with the Judge, anyway," said Vinciguerra.

"Before that, I want to talk policy to you."

"Between friends ..."

"I know." Marco swallowed his annoyance and tried to find another tone. "I'm banking on that friendship feeling, Don Pietro, or else I'd be afraid to come to you with my problem."

"Marco, Marco! *Ti voglio bene!*"

In Sicilian, the phrase means much more than to wish someone well. It is what one man can say to another in the same spirit in which he would say to a woman that he loved her very much.

The phrase startled Marco, and then he was filled with disgust. The old man's emotions, if he had any, were as definable as slime.

"My brothers and I thank you," he said. "We thank you for saving our place, and even our lives. One's life, of course, is each man's own responsibility, but the way in which we conduct it has a lot to do with our friends."

Marco felt the strain of the fake language he was using, but for a while longer he wanted to play Vinciguerra's game.

"But the special way in which things are shaping up now, Don Pietro, they just don't seem good. Let me have that folder, the one on the bottom," he said to Nuncio.

He ignored Nuncio's look when he took the folder from him, though he could almost hear his brother hissing cautions at him. Marco opened the folder and talked in a dry voice.

"I'll check out what I want to say through five of our operations. Union: control, our crew; collection, through Nuncio's office; work assignments, by della Rocca. Next, numbers and horses: collecting, Pepe's crew; accounting, Nuncio's office; size of lay-offs and cash on hand, Catania. And the loans: collection, Valdez and his men; risk margin policy, Nuncio with Marino. Now dope: traffic and distribution, my job; accounting, Nuncio's office; import quota comes through Valdez. And last, legitimate investments: through Nuncio's team; percentage level, Lippi's accounting office."

Marco let the folder fall shut and waited till it was closed. Then he looked up and came around towards Vinciguerra so that the old man had to look straight up at him.

"That's how it checks out," he said. "And the way it checks out, once you stop looking at all the leg work we're doing, every single operating decision comes from you."

Vinciguerra did not say anything for a while. He wanted to look away in order to gather himself, to find the good, ringing words of the Don speaking, but he could not look away from Marco's eyes. And the longer he looked at the younger man's face the more he discovered the unmentionable quality of his own feeling.

After he had rearranged his hands on his cane and had swallowed surreptitiously inside his stiff collar, he did look away for a moment. The act tore the spell of strength which he had felt coming from this Guarda.

When Vinciguerra looked up again, there was the smile. Marco knew that he had reached the old man, and that he had reached him in the worst possible way. Now the old bastard was back in shape. He was lying again.

"Marco *mio*," said Vinciguerra. "Before, you called me Don Pietro. I appreciate your respect. It is proper, but never let it be said that I came to you as your Don! And instead, let it be said that I could not be here, that I could not try once again, in my old age, to unite in work and in strength, if it were not for you!"

"Just a minute," said Nuncio and came out of the window seat. The other two looked at him, each with his own variety of surprise. "I'm here to say, I'd like to see this talk to come back down to some kind of level that's real. Like this one," and he slapped the folders in his hand. "And this shows that we're doing better with the Don, and this shows that we're doing best with the Don, and this shows from top to bottom that we wouldn't even exist without the Don!"

It had been quite a speech for Nuncio. For Marco, there had been entirely too much of a Vinciguerra quality in it.

"Look," he said to his brother. "Without the crap now, I'm not talking about the figures, Cino. I'm talking about whose work you're doing and who sends you the paycheck every week."

And then Nuncio blew up.

"When it comes down to that, brother, I've got more faith in the Don than in the way you've been running us ragged!"

It was clearly Vinciguerra's turn and he took it. First, there was the smile, though very cautiously now, and then the warmed-over tone of voice.

"*Fratelli, fratelli*, you were never meant to fight! Go home together! And when the strain is gone, I promise that I will be here. I will be here for you when you are brothers again. And meanwhile, do not worry about having opened your feelings. That is what a family is for."

They left, feeling dismissed. Nuncio felt dismissed with assurance of help and comfort. Marco felt dismissed in a very final way.

They drove in silence for a while.

"If you blew it," said Nuncio with unusual venom, "I think I know whose brains I'm going to depend on from then on."

"If I blew it, brother of mine, I'll tell you right now what I'm going to do next." Marco swung the car very violently around a car when they crossed Sunset. Nuncio felt a touch of fright. It was not clear to him whether it was the erratic driving or perhaps something else that had affected him. "Are you listening?" said Marco.

"Sure."

"Listen good. I'm going to bust loose, if I blew it. Before the antique came along, I was almost in the same place I'm at now. I wasn't going to have an old man in Palm Springs running my life and I wasn't going to have an old man in a penthouse running it for me. And no ghost from some other century is going to come along now, and here, and do that to me either.

Basta, Cino, *basta!*"

"I hear the speech," said Nuncio. "Now, what about the money?"

"Just watch me."

Nuncio had to wait a few miles before he got the rest of it.

"Pepe is gone," said Marco, "and the Cat is just filling in. I'm taking the button men over."

When they got to their floor in the Tealbaum Building it looked as if no one was in. Then they walked into Nuncio's office and saw the big man in the chair.

He sat awkwardly and very still. When Marco touched him, he fell over. The Cat now showed the side of his face where the .45 slug had taken off almost everything.

CHAPTER 20

It was very quiet in the room until Nuncio retched. He doubled over slowly and threw up all over one side of his desk. Then there was the laugh.

Nuncio whirled around, but Marco did not bother to look.

"You can put it away," said Marco. "You know I don't carry a gun."

Pepe came out of the dressing room but kept the .45 leveled out. He needed it. He needed it against the tone Marco had used, the tone that told him he had been a fool.

"To show you!" he said. "To show you what I think of all that— that office work you been doing with me out of the way, and to show you what I'm going to do about it! Because as long as I got the men ..."

"You crazy, stupid jackass!" Nuncio screamed at him and then he leapt with all the wiry strength in his tight body and landed with his hands around Pepe's throat. Pepe dropped the gun.

They grunted and rolled on the floor until Pepe found his wits again and slammed Nuncio's head against the wall. He was going strong now, and was fairly blind with his anger. Even though he spotted his own automatic in Marco's hand he launched himself at his brother in a low tackle. He crashed to the floor, grabbing air, and then got a swift kick in the side of his head. Something came apart behind his eyes and he had to stay hunched over.

Next came the roaring, a terrible sound which he could not place for the moment, not until his head cleared enough.

It was not damage inside his own skull. Marco was roaring. He belabored his brothers with his own confusion, ranting about having wasted his time and his feelings, and about being sick to death. He smashed on like that, beating them with his voice. Then he seemed spent, but at that point he got very specific with them.

Nuncio stood by the wall and Pepe sat up on the floor.

"I'm going out to talk to the button men," he said. "Pepe?"

"Yes."

"You coming along?"

"You want me along?"

"Yes. What about you?" and he nodded at Nuncio.

"What about me, Marco?"

"I'm lining up the men and then I'm going after Vinciguerra."

"What?"

"Right. Him and his opera style is over. After that, MacAdoo falls in line. Are you?"

"Marco—please. Just let me show you some facts!"

"Screw those facts. The new fact is that Vinciguerra lines up, or he's out."

"But he's got the money!"

"And I got the muscle. Yes or no, Cino."

Nuncio was cool again and his eyes started to move around.

"You and Pepe?" he said.

"You heard."

"He was gone while you and I built this up with Vinciguerra!" Then he looked at Pepe. "Where've you been for over a week?"

Pepe got up from the floor and looked back and forth between his two brothers.

"What in hell's he talking about?"

"Where've you been, besides Las Vegas?" Nuncio asked.

"Save that crap," said Marco and went to the door. "You staying or not?"

"I'm staying right here," said Nuncio. His voice had turned stubborn.

He watched Marco push the .45 under his belt and watched him walk out of the office. He did not watch when Pepe followed and disappeared down the hall.

Nuncio felt the pain in his body, except that he knew that it was not a physical pain. He could not sit down at his desk because the black corpse was still hanging in his chair. Nuncio went down the hall to the accountant's empty office and sat down at the desk. He sat with his face in his hands and went through a slow agony of indecision. Then he made the call.

Valdez answered the phone.

"He's gone," said Valdez, "and you can't reach him."

"Pino, I've got to! They've gone for the men. I want Vinciguerra to call me and get me in on this before he lets them talk him into any harebrained decisions!"

"Don Pietro will know what to do."

"They're flipped on this thing right now, Pino, and he's got to be patient. Have him call me. I've got to be in on this thing!"

"You will be," said Valdez. "Stay there and be patient."

The patience of Pietro Vinciguerra stood for a lot of careful thought. He did not really wait for another man's decision, but rather he always prepared for the ripening of time.

This had been true for his move in the case of Messina, though he had misjudged the ripeness of that meeting just a little. It had been true for the careful timing with the Guardas, and that had been all right. It was now once again the ripe time, and while Vinciguerra merely decided upon the move, others would have to jump quickly. Others such as Cipollo, who had to cancel the routine of his desk time that night, and Angelo del Mare, who had to dash for the airport and jet to Los Angeles at a moment's notice.

As a convenience to del Mare, the meeting was held in the closed grocery store of a friend of Vinciguerra's. The store was fifteen minutes from the airport in the Valley.

There was not much room in the messy office behind the store and it smelled strongly of green vegetables and soft salami. A refrigerator unit made a distant drone and added clammy moisture to the air.

Del Mare stood, because he was fidgety. Cipollo sat, because he was fat. Pietro Vinciguerra presided from a crate by the cooler, hands on his cane, and hat on the floor by his side.

"And so I bring you a *regime*, fully operating, which you had lost," said Vinciguerra.

"Mr. Vinciguerra," said Cipollo, wheezing a little, "we could at almost any time ..."

"Shut up and don't be an ass," said del Mare.

Vinciguerra looked at the fat *consigliere* with forgiveness.

"You forget," he said, "that it is my money, not Mafia money, which welds the *regime* together. And I commanded the *forza di Guarda*, not you."

"Sounds to me," said Cipollo, "that you don't need us at all."

"*Consigliere*, how can you think in this way? Do you take me for an upstart who imagines—as the Guardas have done—that a man does not need his fellow man?" He turned his face to del Mare. "Don Angelo, I bring you this gift as a man who is lonely. I ask only that you do not cast me from your Family."

Del Mare gagged a little, but reminded himself that the old fool only sounded like a fool. Vinciguerra was a company man from before the time when the word was invented. He brought a big entrance fee and maybe even a little class that could dazzle the employees. It would certainly make fewer waves than the Guardas had managed to kick up.

"We'll do it your way," del Mare said.

This, in turn, irritated Cipollo because it left out all the complicated details attendant to such a move.

Vinciguerra nodded his head. He did not grin and he did not fawn because he was now someone official. His real sense of ascension he did not share with anyone.

"And so," he said, "I ask for my first instructions. May I have the use of the man known as Mr. Sturgeon?"

Some instructions, thought del Mare. He's *giving* them.

"When?"

"The time is ripe."

"Just a moment," said Cipollo. "I have no details, I am not at all clear about the priorities, what I mean to say, there are three Guardas involved here, not one, though the one who in my estimation is by far the most objectionable to the spirit in which we are accustomed to do business ..."

It relieved Cipollo that the telephone rang at that moment. He had been on the point of losing the thread of his sentence.

Vinciguerra, without having risen from his crate, held his hand out for the phone. Cipollo, seated by the desk, passed the instrument over.

"Yes, Pino Valdez," said Vinciguerra, and then he listened. After a while he handed the instrument back to Cipollo and waited until it had been cradled.

"The time is ripe," he said again.

"Who? What? When?" snapped del Mare.

"All of them," said Vinciguerra.

CHAPTER 21

The feeling between the two brothers was not comfortable. Pepe drove the Lincoln and Marco sat in silence near his door. They were two blocks away from the Tealbaum Building before Marco remembered something.

"Go on back," he said. "We left the Cat up there."

"Let Nuncio take care of it."

"Cino isn't cut out to do that so easy. Head on back!"

"It's time that ninny shaped up. And it's time you stopped talking to me like I was the chauffeur."

Marco kept silent while they made a number of stops around town.

"Listen," he said after a while, "you've been had. There was nothing going on here like you've been thinking. You were gone, that's all. You can't be thinking seriously that we were leaving you out, for chrissakes."

"I'm seeing to it that I ain't."

And with that in mind Pepe drove into the basement garage of the West Hollywood house where he yelled at the first man he saw to go on up and wake anybody who was asleep.

The men all came to the big room with the couches and the card tables, and they gathered around Pepe and Marco. Pepe laid it right into them.

"The Cat's dead," he said. He sounded a little like a football coach before that game. "And I killed him! The Cat was a good man till he got out of line, and I want you guys to remember who took care of it."

He looked around without expecting anything but silence. He got silence.

"Me and Marco here are going to run this whole operation different from now on. In a short while when I'm through talking I'll let him tell you about the details. But right now—" He paused to look around at every man eyeball to eyeball but then, when he was done making the rounds, he suddenly changed his delivery.

"Where in hell is Ticci and his brother and Bruno?"

Somebody cleared his throat.

"Piro called. He said for them to come on down to Brentwood on account of something, I don't know what it was."

"All right," said Pepe. "Never mind that now."

"Hold it!" Marco had spoken for the first time. "When did that call come in?"

"About a half an hour or so ago."

"What in hell's the difference," Pepe started to say, when Marco cut him off.

"The difference is that four hours ago, up in Brentwood, we kissed Vinciguerra off. He isn't going to take that lying down. But I didn't know he could move this fast."

"Move? What move?" Pepe was starting to bellow.

"I don't know yet what move. That's why we got to stop grandstanding around here and start action." He turned away from his brother and became very clipped. "Charley and Rolando, you get on those phones and call the numbers in Long Beach and in the Valley. I want guns out. And Pepe, you best give out the contracts: one on Valdez, who can wait, and one on Vinciguerra, who can't wait."

"I'm gonna do ..." Pepe was interrupted almost immediately.

There was a heavy, bouncing crash in the basement garage.

All the men froze for that instant and then most of them ran to the stairs. Pepe clawed his way through and got to the basement ahead of the others.

A car had rolled down the incline for the street and had buried its nose into the sprung trunk of the new Lincoln. Pepe, in a fury, yanked the door of the runaway open and a dead man fell out.

There were two more in there. There was Ticci and his brother, and Bruno was the one on the floor.

Bruno had a message. A piece of paper stuck out of his mouth and when Pepe read it he figured he knew what it meant: *Welcome to Brentwood,* it said.

"Get that wreck outa the way and I want four guns along!"

There was a lot of milling around while the wide open basement entrance gave an illuminated view from the street.

"Don't!" Marco called across. "It's a bum setup, Pepe!"

Pepe stopped at the stall where he had picked his car. Marco came close up to him.

"Not Brentwood," he said. The haste showed in his eyes and in his voice. "They're setting us up, you, and me, and Cino. We got to get Cino!"

"Outa my way."

"Pepe—"

But Pepe drove the word right back into Marco's mouth and when his fist connected, Marco fell down bleeding.

The car lurched back, just missing his legs, and then howled up the incline to the street.

He's letting them set the pace, thought Marco. The old bastard is setting the pace, faster than we can, and we're tripping like idiots all over ourselves trying to keep in time with Vinciguerra ...

"*Pepe!*" he roared after the car.

The car had slowed to handle the hump on top and now it yanked to a stop. One door flew open.

For godsake, thought Marco, he's coming out for another grandstand play.

"Somebody! The lights!" Marco shouted.

But the lights were on long enough. There was a high velocity crack from the alley across the street, and Pepe jerked unnaturally before he fell down with the top of his head partly gone.

There was nothing Marco could do that worked or that felt right. Nobody turned the lights off. Nobody seemed to hear what he shouted about the phones, the weapons room, or about the useless scramble after the car that took off down the alley. So he forgot about everyone else and ran back inside. He called Nuncio's number directly but there was no answer. He did not call the board. The sirens came down the street when he took the box of .45 shells and the Weatherby with the clip of longs. Then he went out the back way, where they had an arrangement which led through the building on the other block.

Three of their cars were left in the lot on the other side. He took the one with an eight-year-old body and a new Stingray engine.

That had been fast, though he was late again.

In spite of the very early hour in the morning there was a crowd of ten people by the side of the Tealbaum Building, not counting the two police cruisers with their tops swirling around.

Marco no longer felt haste. He parked down the block and walked back. He recognized Nuncio by the visible, delicate hand which reached out toward nothing.

Marco drove away slowly and found that he had the time to wonder about having made the stop to look at his brother. He had known before looking that Nuncio was lying dead on the street.

He had not gone to look in order to say good-bye. Instead, the look had given him something. Marco felt the loss and then, inside that aloneness, he felt himself strangely free and he felt a weird power.

He kept driving and lit a cigarette. He viewed the image of Pepe falling and the same thing happened again. This time there was also a touch of tradition to the feeling he had. He, Marco, the last of the Guardas.

Two weeks later, by way of a growing presentiment, the same thought contracted Pietro Vinciguerra's old heart.

The first time he had disappeared from the Brentwood house, after Pino Valdez was found shot to death, lying on the front lawn. The bullet hole in his neck had been made by a high velocity long shot.

He had next disappeared from the rooms over the grocery store, after Mr. Sturgeon was found shot to death behind the wheel of his car which was parked behind the same grocery store. There was no bullet hole in the conventional sense of the word. The near-contact explosion of the .45 had just about severed the neck.

Pietro Vinciguerra tried not to think of all this. He sat behind the locked door of the toilet stall near Gate 46 in the airport in Inglewood. He looked at his pocket watch, checked flight time, when his heart contracted again. By flight time he was dead and had fallen off the toilet seat.

Cipollo did not hear about this for some time; and Angelo del Mare saw no reason to change any routine, because that's what an organization was for: take up the slack, protect the values, keep up the progress, take care of its own. He stood by the picture window and watched the desert take shape in the thin morning light. The neon veins on the street below were pumping away in a lively fashion but they did not look so exciting anymore.

The same morning light made the Burbank street look very empty. Marco Guarda turned the key and went into the apartment.

The couch looked immaculate, the coffee was pitch black in the cup. And he remembered the cigarette with the chewed filter when he saw it lying on the countertop.

He saw that he was alone, but he only discovered what had really been true all the time.

He decided to sit down for a rest, moving the .45 to one side for comfort. He leaned his head back and waited for someone.

THE END

BLACK MAFIA
BY PETER RABE

CHAPTER 1

At nine o'clock in the morning, Angelo Forza walked into the railroad station to take the two-hour trip from Buffalo to Bethelport on Lake Erie. Buffalo was gray with rain, and the big hall of the station was dank. Forza went to the overhead board and saw that his local would be two hours late. He cursed in violent Sicilian. The trip was meant to be short, the business was meant to be simple. He carried no suitcase, expecting to be back in the city that evening. He looked around the hall where the commuter traffic was thinning out. Then a gaggle of suburbanite women came clattering over the tiles. Angelo Forza touched his too glossy black hair, plucked at his very white trench coat, and then took his sunglasses out. They were his 15,000 lire, gold-rimmed, nonprescription, blue-tinted glasses. With some variation in color and shape, such glasses were the young male's standard equipment in his kind of world. He wished to add the severity of the blue unknown to his face but felt suddenly too exposed and alone in the clammy hall.

The women seemed young and hard, and their own standard equipment was a studied look of indifference. One of them glanced at Angelo Forza in the manner of a headlight sliding by. She may or she may not have seen his rather unremarkable face, but Forza was sure that she was really reacting to the powerful quality of his eyes. They were actually small and quite unimportant, except for the fact that they seemed to finger the body of the person he viewed. The women clattered away. Forza moved his shoulder blades back and forth, a most ineffectual gesture in view of the chill in the air and the chill inside him.

At the same time, in Attica, it was snowing. Constable Cutter, a black man who did not like his first name, walked with caution and haste into the nervous gusts of wind that came down the streets. He crunched over the ice ruts and squashed through the slush, feeling all the while as if the bottom of his feet were half round. There was an unpleasant tension in his calves, in the narrow part of his back, and in the big muscles of his neck and shoulders. When Cutter reached the bus station, he was panting.

The low hall of the station was full of thick heat, and he felt the sweat moving out of him before he reached the ticket window. He learned there that the express to Bethelport had left fifteen minutes ago.

Cutter bought a one-way ticket on the local from Attica to Bethelport. But he missed the thrill he had been thinking about for five years. It had been spoiled for him by that mother of a warden's long speech about going out into society and justifying the trust by proving worthiness and not being ashamed for having paid a debt to the big mother society. And a whole lot more shit and blah. This long speech was the warden's offering to the first-timers who nevertheless had the hard-core look about them. It was the speech of which mother warden would remind them when they came back.

Cutter put the one-way ticket into his pocket, picked up his canvas grip, and went back out to the street. He swung the grip and shook it up and down so that something rattled inside. The wind plucked at him in a nasty way, and Cutter shivered a little. It was either the cold, he thought, or the craziness that had started to jump around inside his body. Snowdots made a frosting on his short hair and melted on the skin of his face.

His color was something between cinnamon and light coffee, and he liked that color even less than he liked his first name. His sharp cheekbones shone, his broad lips worked in a meaningless rhythm, and his long eyes showed a lot of white. Suddenly Cutter got the sign, the sudden omen, and he felt the excitement after all. A garbage truck rumbled by, back lid open, the dump hole sticking out like an undershot jaw. Cutter swung his bag, let it sail, and laughed when it plunked into the pile of wet garbage in back. But that did not seem enough, so he yanked his overcoat off, ran after the truck where it slowed at the corner, and tossed the balled-up coat into the garbage too.

Cutter stood by the curb and took a few noisy breaths. He was still smiling, and he liked himself now. When he saw the man and the woman look at him and walk faster where they had to pass by, he dropped the smile and showed them a very harsh mask, a stereotype of dull brain, animal blood, and lusting eyes. His voice came out pure vaudeville: "Caint yo tell no crazy nigga when yo sees one, boss?" Then he went into the station again and waited for the bus.

When the train slowed outside of Bethelport to wind its way slowly through the freight cars, Angelo Forza woke up in the tiny compartment he had taken for the two-hour trip. He had fallen asleep with his glasses on, and he had not taken his trench coat off while curled up on his seat. The compartment was full of dry heat, and the view from the window was dismal shades of black, brown, and off-white. The patches of dirty snow, the immobile freight cars, and the flat fields were like something left behind by a disaster of nature. Forza's mouth felt like glue. Then the compartment door opened, and the porter stuck his head through the crack.

"Five minutes, suh. Maybe a drink from the bar, to put body and soul together?" The porter held his face in a black-and-white grin.

Forza only shook his head. He felt as if he must have had one, five, ten drinks already.

"You can wash your face in the lavatory over there," and the porter left.

He could have said, why don't you stick your head in the crapper, sir, which would have sounded exactly the same to Forza. But Forza did not trust his command of the idiom enough to pursue the matter. He did look at himself in the bathroom mirror and saw how wrinkled his trench coat was and that his hair stood up on one side in a feathery bunch. There was no time to do anything about that either. He left the train in a rush when it stopped in the station and did not tip the porter. He walked quickly along the platform and then across the slippery hall of the station. When he reached the outside he hung around until the passengers had thinned out and the taxis had moved away. There was nobody waiting for him. The sky looked like lead, and a few cars sat in the station parking lot. Three of the cars wore big humps of snow. Beyond, the stony skyline of Bethelport was a lower jaw with black gums and jagged teeth. After waiting half an hour for the limousine that was supposed to have come for him, Forza took a taxi to the north end of town, where the Tri-State Trucking Company was.

When Constable Cutter got off the bus at the downtown depot he looked around for a moment, as if someone might be waiting for him. No one was. He made a secret joke out of it by deciding he sure as hell was glad that no hookers, honkies, or other type bums were about to lay anything on him. He walked to the street, stood by the curb, and looked up at the narrow sky overhead, a strip of gray meat that was getting the shit squeezed out of it by the buildings. Home, he thought. But at least his feet did not feel like half-round balls anymore. He walked all the way across town, toward the north end, past the docking areas and the trucking firms, and into the failing light.

Francisco Perrini, who owned Tri-State, had an office on the second floor of the long complex of buildings that held the loading ramps, warehouse space, and repair sheds of the trucking company. Where the big view of Lake Erie would be, Perrini's office had a cinderblock wall painted green. The windows of his office looked down on the loading yard and at the acre of parking space where the big rigs and the vans were kept.

Perrini had a desk of polished walnut with ornamental frills and turned wood at the corners. The desk matched nothing else in the room. He himself did not seem to match anything either. His sporty windbreaker might have looked right on one of his drivers. In Perrini's case, it produced all kinds of conflict with his inelegant barrel shape and with the pearl-gray tie on the white shirt he wore. But the most striking aspect of Perrini's appearance was his priestly face with the tonsure of white hair around the skull. Amid the commonness of his office, Perrini's expression was full of grace.

There was a knock on the door, and the expression became a little bit shifty.

"*Avanti, avanti!*"

A man built like a jockey came into the office. He wore a gray chauffeur's uniform but did not act accordingly.

"Hi, Preacher."

"Shut that door and don't call me that!"

"*Si, padrone*," said the driver and shut the door. He considered his size a deformity, and he felt that the uniform insulted his knowledge that he, Campi, could survive as a runt in a land of giants.

Perrini knew that tone when Campi called him *padrone*, but he let it go by. Why knock loyalty over an issue of manners. Perrini watched the small man walk up to the desk and envied the spring in his gait.

"You didn't bring Forza," said Perrini.

"He didn't show. Train was late. So I thought ..."

"You *thought!*" Perrini sounded angry, but his priestly face—for just one instant—seemed to show fear instead of anger.

"It's all right, Preach, honest. He ain't the Don in person."

"Remind me, by all means. Remind me he is only the nephew. He is a *cretino*, by all means, but the *nephew!*" Perrini half rose from his chair, then lowered himself again. Also, at moments like this, he did not simply speak. He intoned.

But Campi was not fooled by the theatrics when Perrini looked, in fact, like a preacher. The real Perrini, the one Campi knew for sure, was no joke in any respect.

"What I meant," said Campi, "what I was going to do was to go back there when the train is due. Maybe you had something else that needs doing. I got two hours."

Perrini sighed and hunched himself into his chair. He gave Campi the briefest of looks, very straight, with a small nod added, then looked away. Campi understood that too. He and Perrini had a silent knowledge of one another that they did not have with anyone else. Those messages always went across without words, and this one meant: Do it your way, I can trust you, and don't bother me unless the fix is bad.

"I thought," said Campi, "I'd run down to the Black Belt and ask Asikari ..."

"His name's Jackson."

"He likes it Asikari."

"By all means. You thought what?"

"Ask about the runners getting jumped on. If he knows anything."

"He didn't know anything two days ago when you asked."

"This is another time. Last night, in the back of the Jewel Bar."

Perrini blinked. He mumbled something obscene but felt no relief.

"I didn't know about that one," he said.

"I just found out and that's what you got me for," said Campi. He said it without any emphasis but simply as the straight fact it was. "So. You want me to go?"

Perrini looked at his watch, which he carried in the vest under the odd-looking windbreaker.

"Go," he said. "Then come back here."

He snapped his fingers while pointing to the closet at one end of the office. Campi went there and came back with the jacket that belonged with the pants and vest Perrini was wearing. Perrini dropped the windbreaker and put on the jacket. He buttoned all three buttons in front.

The change transformed him. Perhaps he was an elderly florist. Or, for sure, he was somebody's well-to-do grandfather. Campi admired the change and knew that this also was a deceptive front.

"Go to the Black Belt," said Perrini again, "and then come back here. Let the *cretino* find his own way."

CHAPTER 2

Francisco Perrini, in his many-layered ways, did not for a moment underestimate the advent of the *cretino*. He had never met Angelo Forza, but he knew the man who was sending him. He knew Santino Forza, a relic, a man in his seventies, a recluse with one hundred hirelings for his eyes, an octopus with one dozen telephones for his tentacles, an old man with a legendary past.

It was said that the young Santino had killed his first man at age ten. That had been in Sicily, in the interior where nothing had changed in a hundred years, not the giant estates owned by the *principes*, not the poverty of the peasants who worked there, nothing had changed there to make survival a promising thing. Only the communion of the Mafia gave any muscle to living. Santino had killed the overseer of the local estate because that hireling had raped his mother. Rape was the wrong word. Requisitioned? The overseer had kept her for just a few days. It had been, in a manner of speaking, almost proper. Just a few days, nothing greedy, and the Forza clan was allowed to continue to work the land of the absentee *principe*. But Santino's father was dead and the first-born, young Santino, did not have the tolerance of maturity. After his mother came back, hollow-eyed and silent, Santino had not been able to look at her with love or admiration. He had shrunk from her touch. For him her face was a hag's face, a spoiled face, and the worst part was that she asked nothing of him but simply endured her fate of sacrifice.

What went on for Santino was not made clear in the story but the results of his agony were a fact. He consulted no one. One morning the overseer was dead. He was found hanging from the limb of a tree by his feet, trussed up like a pig, and there was no face left on the head. There was a grindstone under the tree, the rough wheel clogged with matter, and the water in the trough was a polluted pink.

Officially, the incident went no further. Trust the Mafia. Santino Forza, one year later, surfaced in Brooklyn, New York. Trust the Mafia....

In Sicily, even the very young Santino Forza had simply been the *mafioso* who survives because he has none of the civilized fears, who is strong because he is never the only *mafioso*. But once Santino emerged in the States, he was an enigma.

Santino was nobody's protégé, and he did none of the button-man chores that can move a man up the ladder of influence and authority. But in time, he was more or less known to be a force in the protection rackets of Buffalo.

At a later point, he showed his hand in the land manipulations that put Miami beach-front properties where there used to be swamp. When syndicate money moved into Las Vegas, he turned up as percentage owner in more than a dozen operations. He was always surprised by his unexpected alliances, and he profited by a number of unexplained deaths.

In the syndicate shuffles that portioned out regional territories, Santino decided upon Buffalo, a choice that had no headline qualities. The choice fit his style. It fit his unfathomable slyness, and it kept intact his ominous net of strength.

A harsh and silent man who now lived on a street block in Buffalo owned on both sides by something called the Forceful Realty Corporation, he was, at seventy-five, a vanishing type among the Sicilian immigrants who had made good in the United States.

Francisco Perrini stopped pacing around his desk, pulled one drawer open, and looked at the bottle of cognac that stood between files F and G. Then he slapped the drawer shut again.

That breed, he thought, might be vanishing, but here was Don Santino, hungry at birth, hungry in his old age, a dinosaur that would not die, would not change, Santino who had become an old man at the age of ten and had found that his way was the best.

Perrini understood some of the Don. They had both been born in the same medieval seclusion of the Sicilian interior. Perrini had left at age five. Santino Forza had left—why go over it. *Possibilimente*, he had never left there at all.

And what in hell did the old bastard want? *Calma, calma,* mumbled Perrini and rubbed himself over the place where his heart would be. It was clearly not a question of money. Perrini's *regime,* which was the northwest territory of Don Santino's prosperity sphere, provided well....

Perrini's intercom buzzed. His face, which had been working itself back and forth between expressions of gray worry and greenish miserliness, flipped on the smoother lines that gave him the priestly nickname. Now the dominant aura was benign pink.

"Yes, dear," he said to his secretary.

"Your wife's on the line. You want her?"

Perrini sat down behind his desk. One hand reached for the phone and the other began to fish for the bottle between files F and G.

"Of course, dear," said Perrini. Then he said, "Hold that a minute. Hear anything from that young man I'm expecting?"

"The switchboard hasn't said, Mister Perrini. They did say that the union man called up again and ..."

"Silverman is handling that, isn't he?"

"Which is what I conveyed also."

"Good, Becky," said Perrini. He was unscrewing the bottle top with one hand.

"And of course the freight and rebate contract thing. The Erie Packing people called and were anxious."

"That's only two hundred thou per. Let 'em stay anxious."

"I conveyed that, Mister Perrini."

"Good, Becky. Now plug in the wife."

He switched the intercom off with one hand and poured cognac into a paper cup with the other. He watched one button light up on his telephone while he tossed the cognac into the back of his mouth. First he gargled, then he swallowed the fumy liquor.

"*Bella,*" he said into the phone. "What is it?"

"Are you busy, Francisco?" His wife's voice, as usual, was hesitant. Perrini knew the tone. He knew that it did not necessarily mean that his wife felt hesitant.

"No, I'm not busy, Magdalena."

"Oh, good. I just wanted to ask you one question."

It was the same goddamn ritual always: are you busy, oh good, one question. Perrini stuck out his lower lip and breathed out and upward toward his nose. He smelled the cognac with pleasure.

"On your way home, Francisco, will you stop at Mister Rosetti's and bring home a quart of ricotta?"

"I'll be late. The store may be closed."

"It's fresh today and it would be good to have a quart when it's fresh."

"I'll be late, *bella*. Get Rosie to drive you."

"Rosanna is not here and she took the other car."

"Where in hell is she?"

"Perhaps," said Perrini's wife, "you might speak to her, Francisco. Speak to her—father to daughter—about everything. And please don't swear, Francisco."

"I haven't even talked to her yet!"

"You swore just a moment ago, Francisco."

Perrini said nothing. He had a hold of the bottle and tapped it up and down on the desk, carefully. Then he said,

"You still want me to get the ricotta?"

"No, *caro*. I think you're too busy."

"Yes. My intercom is blinking."

"Thank you just the same, Francisco. I will see you tonight?"

"*Of course* you'll see me tonight...."

She had already hung up. Then the intercom did blink.

"What is it, Becky?"

"Campi called while you were on the line. He'll be delayed."

Perrini said *porco* under his breath and started to worry.

"He said it had to do with the errand he was running," she went on. From her end of the line she could hear Perrini's breathing. "Mister Perrini?"

"Yeah. Yes."

"If it has to do with the union matter, I had occasion to call Mister Silverman about a small detail, and he said ..."

"I don't want to hear about Silverman. Did Campi say anything else?"

"No, sir. He merely conveyed that he would take care of the matter. Yes. And that he had gotten in touch with Menotti, though he did not say who Menotti was, and ..."

"Shit!" said Perrini and punched the intercom out of action.

In the privacy of his barren office, Perrini cursed at length and with satisfying vulgarity. He glared at the bottle of cognac but hardly saw it. As with many who are raised in a wine-drinking tradition, hard liquor did not mean peace, protest, or oblivion to him. He stuck to Sicilian a while longer.

Of course, the worst of it was that Campi had called for Menotti. Nobody just called Menotti.

Perrini had every confidence that his man would not call for such assistance in a lighthearted manner. Why not use the button men? Or, when in special need, why not a specialist like José Guzman? But all of that kind of help amounted to no more than simple muscle. Instead, Menotti, which meant something delicate and probably tricky....

The intercom blinked again, and for one instant Perrini thought that the good Becky, with that touch of Magdalena about her, was calling back to say something about his secret cursing.

"Yes," he said to the machine.

"I was about to tell you, Mister Perrini, that a young man is here. He won't state his business but says his name is Angelo Forza. What shall I tell him?"

"Ah—" said Perrini and rubbed the place over his heart.

"Yes?"

"No. Tell the young man I'm not here."

"You're not here."

"He's late, and I'm no longer here."

"He said his train was delayed and he hasn't much time because he wants to go back in the evening."

Perrini had walked away from his desk and was getting his overcoat out of his closet. He shouted at the intercom from across the room.

"He said that? Mister Angelo Forza is a guest in my house tonight. Convey that to him!" Perrini shook the heavy coat so that the fur on the inside gave a shining ripple. Then he slung the coat over his shoulders. "Now call Menotti. *Subito!*"

Becky, on the other end of the line, did not understand Italian, but she understood the tone. Perrini gathered up the rest of his winter paraphernalia. Then he went back to the desk with heavy force in his steps.

"The Menotti office said he left a short while ago."

Perrini was pouring from the fourteen-dollar bottle into the three-cent paper cup. Then he tossed the stuff down, as if the cup were hot and his fingers were burning.

"Call the garage!" He was still shouting. "The big Mercedes, up front, for Mister Forza, and my own car, with the crew, in the back."

He cut off the intercom, crushed the paper cup in his fist, and tossed it on the floor while walking quickly to his private exit.

CHAPTER 3

Black Belt was a part of Bethelport that snaked along the contour of Lake Erie without ever getting within sight of the water. The trucking depots intervened, then the shipping docks, and next the heavy mudflats, which shimmered with chemical scum. This stretch of slime, junk, and silt was piling into the shallows of the lake with the slow push of the Bethel River. Much of the factory district of the town followed along the concrete banks of the river and confined the southern side of the Black Belt district. That part of the city had started as a sparse shantytown between the junk of the factories and the rock and the clay of Lake Erie. When the factories grew, the Black Belt shrank. But while the spread of the industry reduced the area of what used to be shantytown, it swelled its population. The blacks worked in the smelting plants, foundries, railroad assembly yards, and the body works of three major automobile companies. Black Belt real estate grew tall and narrow, while the eight-mile-long worm of an area had nowhere else to go. It had never quite exploded, but it bloated on its own pollution.

Perrini's pearl-gray Eldorado pushed its long nose down the main gut of Black Belt. The street had the improbable name of Buckingham Boulevard. The preferred local version was Buckingballs or—depending on the mood of the company—either Bucks or plain Balls.

A light blowing of snow had started that did none of the things snow can do for a street, lend it charm, peace, or quiet. From the long view, the sides of the street were a tangle of neon nerves: Discount Furniture, Jewelry, Savit, Washit, Discount Boutique, Soul Food, Motown, Discount, More-foryour, Pix, Snatch, Savings. There was a lot of traffic, and Perrini's was not the only Cadillac on the road. Most of the others glittered more.

"Garbage," said one of the men in Perrini's car.

"Just shut up," said Perrini.

A police car came the other way, crawling with the five-miles-per-hour traffic. Both uniformed men were black, and both of them looked away when they passed the pearl-gray Eldorado.

"You seen that?" said the man next to Perrini.

"Shut up, Benno."

"You seen how they waved at that shine in the white teddybear coat at the corner? And then when they seen you ..."

"Don't say shine around here, Benno. Don't say another word around here, Benno. *Capito? Basta!*" The last word sounded like a cross between a hiss and a spit. Then he said to the driver, "Turn on Fifteenth, *cretino*. You just missed the easy way while you were watching that hooker out there."

"But the Jewel Bar ..."

"*Not* the Jewel Bar. Go to the school."

Neither the driver nor the other two men in the car said anything else. The car took the Fifteenth Street turn with all the majesty of a hearse, then squeegeed its way in the direction of the lake. No neon prosperity now, but a lot of wet snow on asphalt, fire escapes crawling up to the skyline, and parked cars that looked as if they would never move again. On Dock Street, the Eldorado swung right and immediately hugged up to the curb.

The street looked condemned. The buildings were turn-of-the-century brownstones. At one time, the view of the sound from their tall bay windows had been magnificent. Now some of the windows were bare holes, some were boarded. Most of them showed brown shades or remnant curtains. They looked across the street at the blank backs of the warehouse installations, which faced the other way, toward the railroad spurs and the piers. The narrow street was not long. It ended by the gray river.

Perrini stepped out of his car and stood straddle-legged in the murk of the day. He had planned his appearance. He was working one mocha glove over his hand but kept the other bare. A one-carat blue diamond sat on the little finger of the bare hand. The enormous clarity of the rock was befuddled with a corona of fifty-eight baguettes. He did not have his arms in the sleeves of his overcoat but kept it draped over his shoulder. The coat hung big and heavy on him, with the fur lining exposed and the Persian-lamb collar spread wide. His scarf was white silk and his homburg was black with a bluish band. From a fair distance, and by ignoring his priestly face, Perrini looked like someone very potent, like a field marshal viewing victory. The background ruins helped.

But there were very few people. When all the car doors had been slammed, Perrini and his four men stood on the street for a moment. They looked up and down the street and at the storefront where they had parked. The light was failing. The store windows were blank, except for a hand-lettered legend that said "School of 3 R's," and, under that, "Rights, Reverence, Righteousness."

Perrini said, "Open the goddamn door, Benno."

Then he worked his arms into the sleeves of the coat, and by the time he was inside the storefront school, he had taken the diamond ring off and stuck it back into his vest pocket.

"Stay outside with the others," he said to Benno.

"Don't you think it'll look better ..."

"Stay out. Watch the hubcaps or something," and Perrini shut the glass-pane door.

It was almost as cold in the dim room as it had been outside. He could see the small tables with their low chairs, the loom at one end of the room, the chipped blackboard at the other, and the homemade shelves with an unusual number of books. At the end of the passage to the back was a curtain and a light showed behind it.

"Asikari?"

Perrini called again, louder, but nothing came from the back. He could smell kitchen odors. Perrini went to the back and lifted the curtain.

"Missus Jackson!" he said and took his homburg off.

The old Negro woman looked like a pancake ad. She turned away from the stove and walked painfully to the kitchen table with the lightbulb overhead. Then she sat down and sighed. Perrini smiled but the old woman did not.

"You remember who I am, Missus Jackson?"

"I knows. What you want, Mister Perrini?"

Such a comfortable grandmother type, thought Perrini, and such a cold voice. He kept smiling.

"What's that *nice* smell on the stove, Missus Jackson? What a good smell."

"Fatback. You wouldn't like it." She clamped her jaws so that her cheeks firmed up and pushed her eyes almost shut. Perrini could see her teeth lying in a cup on the sideboard. He looked away and stroked the place over his heart.

"I came by," he said, "to say hello to your son, Missus Jackson. Is he around?"

"No," she said. "Ain't around."

"Ah. Yes. What I mean is, would you know ..." But Perrini knew ahead of time that the old woman would say no again, that she did not know where her son might be. He smiled and nodded at the ugly kitchen. He was very glad that he had taken the diamond ring off.

"A little earlier," Perrini said, "a friend of mine came over to see your son. Did they maybe leave together?"

"Yessuh," said the old woman. "They left together."

"Ah. Good. And then they're coming back here?"

"Wouldn't know 'bout that." She folded her hands in her big lap and looked up at Perrini. He was sure she would volunteer something now and nodded at her for encouragement. "Why don't you leave my Rafer be?" she said.

"Leave, be?" Perrini did not know how to answer that and laughed a little instead.

"He ain't done nothin to you and he ain't gon do nothin for you. He a schoolteacher now, Mister Perrini."

Perrini was sensitive to the touch of a threat in her statement, but she did not develop it.

"Can't you leave him be?" she said, and there was a first touch of emotion in her voice, though Perrini could not name it. "My Rafer's jest doin his schoolin' now."

That was a laugh. The old woman sounded as if her son needed protecting. But Perrini was saved the trouble to answer her because the back door to the kitchen opened with a blast of cold air.

He was a magnificent-looking man. If the color black can glow, then Rafer Jackson's face had something shine out of it. He was built thin and hard and wore a multicolored dashiki that hung loose over his trousers. The sleeves flared like a cape and showed part of his forearms. There was a strong gold wire around one of his wrists. He stopped in the door and let the kitchen warmth seep away. Then he touched his glasses. They were round, gold-rimmed, and held heavy prescription lenses.

"Hello, Ma," he said. He was looking at Perrini but did not address him at all. Perrini, unaware of the movement of his hand, touched the hard lump of diamond in his vest pocket.

"Gowan, you," said Asikari's mother. "Close that kitchen door, Rafe."

Instead, Asikari stepped aside and let another man walk into the kitchen. When the old woman saw him, her hands came out of her lap and her old face started beaming.

"Constable!" and her voice went up to a very young lilt. "You come here, boy, and give us a big hug!"

Cutter did not mind her using his first name. He crouched like a wrestler, laughed, and then grabbed the old woman with a lot of power and warmth.

Asikari closed the kitchen door, walked past Perrini, and stood by the corridor curtain. He flicked his finger at Perrini and turned into the corridor. Perrini followed without a word. He went into the converted store, where Asikari held a chair back for him. Perrini sat down without giving it a thought. The chair was child-size, cramping his back and lumping his belly together between ribcage and thighs. Asikari remained standing. Perrini could hear the laughter and bustle from the warm kitchen.

"Why are you here, Mister Perrini?" Asikari talked through smoke, lighting a cigarette. He exhaled and put the dead match in his pocket.

"Yes. I'm looking for Campi." It was more complicated than that, but for starters, this would have to do. Perrini tried to move in his chair but noticed that his legs, at this angle, gave him no leverage.

"Come now, Mister Perrini." Asikari looked through the glass of the storefront where Perrini's crew stood around the Cadillac. "If that were all," Asikari went on, "you might have used the phone."

Perrini was getting irritated with his own confinement. Also, Asikari's affected precision of English started to grate on his nerves.

"Gimme a hand," said Perrini.

"With what, exactly?" said Asikari.

"Outa this chair!"

Asikari immediately held out his hand, took Perrini's, and gave an unpleasant jerk. Perrini got up with a groan, huffed a deep breath, and then sat down on a low table. He slapped his homburg on his head, toward the back and at a slight angle. Then he put his hands on his thighs and leaned forward a little.

"All right, Jackson. All I want …"

"Asikari, Mister Perrini."

"Forgot." Perrini closed his eyes and then opened them with a sigh. "I'll start all over."

"If you wish, Mister Perrini."

"Just shut up a minute, will you?" It was said mildly enough, and Asikari listened. "I got the message," said Perrini, "that Campi's in some kind of trouble and that he was here. Can you help me?"

"*Me*, help *you?*"

The tone was so complex with insult and disdain that Perrini held his breath for a second.

"Goddamnit," he said with a rush of air, "stop acting like a bastard *all* the time. I ever do anything to you that you gotta get it off your chest all the time?" He did not expect an answer, but he got one, nevertheless, like a slow knife that kept going in, going in.

"It's not really anything you have done, Mister Perrini, but rather an issue of who you are." Though Asikari was speaking again with that irritating touch of precision, the clear emotion had not yet come through. Then he said, "You are a crook, an exploiter, you are false, and you are white." He waited for a reaction and got a stare from Perrini. So he continued. "In view of those facts, I repeat with astonishment—you come to *me* to help *you?*"

"*Porco*," said Perrini.

He felt the chill of the room and the vagueness of the winter light. There were kitchen noises from the back and loving sounds of two people talking to each other. Perrini, to his own surprise, felt that he was suffering. Then he got up from the table and walked back and forth, keeping his legs stiff and making a noise with his heels.

"I thought you were reformed," he said at the blackboard. He turned and walked the other way. "I thought when the cops busted up your—what in hell—"

"Political organization."

"Whatever." He was saying it to the loom in the other corner. "I thought, after that, you got some sense and could talk like a, like a person."

"Stop jiving me, man." The switch to the jargon startled Perrini. Asikari gave an unfriendly laugh. "You got problems in Black Belt, right? You don't want to give and you don't want to let go. And maybe a cat like me, who's got his fingers burnt but must have some brains, on account of his record, maybe an educated nigger like that, after some correction, maybe hungry like he is, maybe he's the right mark to help the old Preach with the troubles he's got in the Black Belt rackets. I *know* your angle, Preach. You're the Man in this town, Preach, except here. You got a burr up your ass, Preach, and you think I'm the doctor." Asikari exhaled, as if he meant to cough. "No way, man," he said. "In no way whatsoever, Mister Perrini."

Perrini's sphincter had contracted in an involuntary way. He held it for a moment, and then, with a monumental effort at self control, he chuckled in a warmish manner.

"Asikari," he said. "Forget about all that." He looked around the barren room. "You're a schoolteacher now, and I did make that mistake about you, thinking you had pull in the Belt."

Asikari smiled and waited.

"But forget it." Perrini went to the door, then turned back as if he had forgotten something. "You know what I'll do for you? No strings." He reached into his pocket, looked all around the room, then pulled a wad of rolled bills out.

Asikari took the cigarette out of his mouth and ground it very slowly around the rim of one palm. Then he put the dead stub into his pocket.

"Yes?" he said.

Perrini put the bills away.

"How can anybody be such a hater," he said with genuine puzzlement.

Asikari shrugged and opened the door for Perrini. Not until then did Perrini remember the simple part of his visit.

"You know where Campi is now?"

"At the precinct station, Mister Perrini."

"You've got to be—No. Guess you're not."

"Right. Kid you not."

"You know why? You know that too?"

"It seems," said Asikari with his former precision, "that a gang of your own men beat up a black man involved in the numbers racket."

"Impossible!"

"Good-bye, Mister Perrini."

"That *couldn't* be!"

"Skat, Preach," said Asikari and closed the door on Perrini.

CHAPTER 4

The pearl-gray Eldorado angled deliberately across Buckingham, slowed, and jammed traffic. Everybody on that block of the street saw it and then heard it: the headlights flashing, the horns blaring, and the catcalls. Perrini sat in the soft leather of the back seat and chewed his lower lip.

"Now go down the middle of the street," he said to the driver.

"They're getting ugly," said the driver. "At this speed, maybe you better lock your door."

"I'm getting ugly," mumbled Perrini. There was not one touch of the preacher about him now.

The Eldorado pushed along toward the river, then turned on Twenty-fifth, and stopped in the first block off Buckingham. The precinct station was flanked by a topless bar on one side and a laundromat on the other. All four doors of the Eldorado swung open, and Perrini got out last. He had his overcoat draped like a field marshal's mantle again. The glove in one hand was slapping the palm of the other hand, and the diamond on the little finger flashed blue and white. When he walked toward the station steps, his three men grouped around him in a pattern.

"Hea come de Man, hea come de Man," somebody said from the sidewalk. Then three voices screeched with an attack of laughter.

Perrini did not mind. The point was, he had *flash*. He had learned that much about the local mythology, the necessary impact and recognition depended on flash. Perrini, at his age and station, would not wear sunglasses, yellow suede, purple silk, white velour, or shiny black leather, but he would properly wear a gigantic rock, a marshal's mantle, and three silent men around him. Only when he walked into the station did the theatrics lose some of their punch.

Campi was sitting on a bench, reading a copy of *Jet*. Menotti was shaking hands with the precinct captain. Then he turned his head towards the door where Perrini had made his entrance.

"Hello," said Menotti. "How are you, Mister Perrini?", which was one way of ignoring all the stage setting and costuming Perrini had planned.

"I'm fine," said Perrini, who was now quite out of touch with his original power-plot.

"As a matter of fact," Menotti continued, "we are quite finished here and, I'm glad to say, there are really no further problems."

It was to the credit of Perrini that he did not take his theatrics so seriously as not to drop a role at a moment's notice.

"Pleased to hear it," and he nodded at the captain. "On the other hand, young man," he said to the officer, "if there's anything else that needs doing, you know where to reach either me or our good Mister Menotti. You gave him your card, Alberto?"

Menotti bowed and smiled. He had the kind of pale, balding head that seemed to call for pince-nez and a high celluloid collar. His expression was always a little bit worried, as if he had perhaps misplaced something or other and could not decide what to do next. Sometimes, as in this case, a hesitant smile invited understanding and patience from the world. These expressions were not designed as a mask. Menotti felt the way he looked. What his expression did not convey was the powerful facility of his brain to take care of the worries over the misplaced or hidden things lawyers in matters of marginal legality had to discover.

The precinct captain, who was, owing to the cryptic wisdom of the P.D., a white officer at the head of an all-black force, spread his face with an un-derstanding smile, and larded the whole message with a conspirator's wink.

"Nothing to worry about, Mister Peneery. We got ..."

"Mister Francisco Perrini," said Menotti in the mildest way.

"Sure. Sorry. Anyways, we're all squared away, Mister—uh, Perrini. Nat-urally, I know all about you, except the name sort of got away from me. Hah, hah. Get a little rattled here sometimes with the pressure of the work. Lotta pressure."

Perrini did not pick up on any of that. When Menotti takes care, it's done. Next, time to find out what in hell was going on here.

"In that case," said Perrini, "I won't keep you any longer. Berto? Why don't you ride with me." It was not a question. To Campi he said that he did not need him anymore that evening and marched out of the station with no further look at anyone.

Outside, he waved his men into the car, except for Benno whom he told to drive Menotti's car into town. Then he ushered Menotti into the back seat, spat on the sidewalk, and got in himself. He pressed the button that raised the glass pane between the front seat and the rear.

"Explain," he said to Menotti and took the diamond ring off his finger again.

Angelo Forza did not like being told that he had to wait, but when he reached the Perrini place, he forgot about the slight to his dignity. The very lack of modesty in the layout of grounds and house appealed to the de-prived in him. Angelo Forza felt something like kinship.

Perrini's place was in Erie Strand, a self-consciously private, restricted, and highly manicured suburb of Bethelport, in which each house could see the lake and no house could be seen by its neighbor.

Forza's chauffeured Mercedes went through an iron-grill gate that opened and closed automatically, wound around strategic clumps of im-ported evergreens, and came upon the house with a suddenness that added to the breathless wonder of the place. Under the insistent supervi-sion of Perrini himself, something like five architectural styles had been pil-fered to create the facade. Forza knew nothing about the ancestry behind the effect but simply felt stimulated by the choking ornamentation. The lim-ousine stopped by the cathedral door, which was sheltered by a Ro-manesque arch of stone.

"Go on up and find the bell," said the driver. "They know you're com-ing."

While the Mercedes disappeared down the drive, Angelo Forza stood in the gray wind from the lake and could not find the bell. Somebody opened the portal anyway. The old man in the black silk coat took Angelo into the innards of the house, where the heat, the thick, dry air made him aware of his breathing. He passed through two very large rooms. In the third room, which held a lot of books behind glass, the detail and the very mass of couches, easy chairs, little tables, long tables, candlesticks, porcelain jars, porcelain vases and meaningless inlaid boxes with lids like high-steepled roofs, all these obliterated the actual size of the room. There was also a fireplace that reminded him of the cathedral entrance to the house.

Angelo thought he would stand there, with his back to the hole, and await developments. After a while, he went to one of the couches and sank into it.

"Yoohoo, where are you?"

Angelo tried to jump up.

"*Mi dispiace*—Uh—*Aspetta*—" he mumbled, then he wormed his way out of the couch. "I am sorry," he said. "I did not hear you come in."

He liked the woman immediately. She wore the constant black of the Sicilian woman, who after a certain age is bound to be in mourning for someone clan-related. She had large, soft eyes, a dark-skinned and wrinkled face, and in an over-all sense was built like a brood mare.

"I am Missus Perrini," she said and held out her hand while wending her way toward the guest.

She liked Angelo Forza immediately. He kept his feet together when he bowed, and he did not keep his eyes on her face too long when he gave his greeting. This was rare in a young man nowadays, particularly in this foreign country.

"But you spoke Italian before," she said and smiled up at him. "Perhaps you are not from here?"

He answered her in Italian, the Sicilian intonation quite broad. "Three years now," he said. "I came to work for my uncle."

"Ah. It is good for families to help each other. But please speak English. Mister Perrini always says we should speak English now that we are here."

"*Da vero*," he said and bowed again. "How long have you been here, *signora?*"

"Forty years." She smiled. "And you, with three years, speak English better than I."

He did not protest but explained it. "I learned English in school and then at the university. My uncle sent me to the University of Milan, to study business and language."

"What a nice uncle," she said. "Who is your uncle?"

"My father's brother, Don Santino Forza."

"Ah. A friend of my husband's! I have heard of him," she said naïvely.

It is proper, thought Angelo Forza. The women know nothing, and why should they?

She had forgotten to sit down, which meant that Angelo did not sit down either. When she recognized her omission she instantly made amends by ushering Angelo across the big house and into the kitchen. There, she sent the maid and the old man in the black silk coat away and fed Angelo.

Though the eating was involved and absorbing, when Angelo could not go on with pasta, peas, prosciutto, breads, cheeses, greens, onions, tomatoes, and olive oil, the man he had come to see had still not come home. It was then discussed and decided that Angelo would stay for the night, and Missus Perrini showed him the upstairs room he would use. Then, until eleven o'clock at night, Angelo sat with his hostess in digestive torpor. She did needlepoint, he sat. Shortly after eleven o'clock, a white Fiat Spyder slewed up to the front steps of the house. The motor stopped, then gave a few burps of after-firing. Angelo felt offended by the evident neglect of machinery. A woman got out of the coupe. She slammed the door shut but without the satisfying sound of *chunk*, which said that the door was in the latch. She also left the headlights on. Sounds of the front door, heels on hall tile, and then—before the footsteps faded—a shocking metallic sound from Missus Perrini.

"Rosanna! Come here!"

Sound of a mother, thought Angelo. He suddenly bunched his lips together because he felt a sudden impulse to yell back at the old woman. The feeling surprised him. He liked Missus Perrini, he honored a woman like that and such a feeling required no explanation. He might as well question the memory of his own mother, who had been an exceptional beauty, adored by all, by his father, and by Uncle Santino, he had been told.

Angelo did not remember his mother. She had died in Rome while he had been an infant in Palermo. Influenza epidemic. *Mena male*, God's inscrutable will. He had never gotten it clear just when the epidemic had swept through the city of Rome—he had also heard that it had been in Genoa—while his father had taken care of him in Palermo and Uncle Santino, while on one of his visits from the United States, had taken care of his mother in Rome. A great loss, not to have known his own mother. Angelo knew his father but did not especially like him.

"*Cattiva!* Where have you been?!" The voice yelled again.

The girl in the open library door looked all around the lumping of furniture in the room until she found her mother.

"Good evening," she said. "You have a guest, Mother?"

The mother changed her voice and her face and introduced Rosanna Perrini to Angelo Forza, who was waiting for the arrival of Rosanna's father.

"He wants to talk to you," added the mother. "I spoke to your father about bringing ricotta, and he said he wished to talk to you."

"How do you do, Mister Forza," said Rosanna.

"Fine. You left the lights on in your car, Miss."

"Is there anything to eat, Mother?"

Rosanna walked into the room and around furniture while Angelo watched her with automatic thoroughness. *Minquia*, what flesh ...

"There is always to eat. Do not touch the ham and the roast."

This *bambola*, considered Angelo, is not candy. She is something solid and full of juice. He watched her stop by her mother's chair and shift from one foot to the other. This made her thighs move together under her skirt. Angelo thought of her juice.

"... or the soup which is left. Mister Forza thought it was very good."

Angelo looked up from his point of concentration and saw that the young woman was looking at him in turn. The mother was peering at her needlepoint. When his eyes and Rosanna's eyes met, each of them saw a little bit more of the other. Rosanna had no difficulty understanding this overdone young man. He had never looked at her face but had already had her body. He was Italian or Sicilian. There was that selection of clothes and the hairdo with stuff in it. There was his selecting eye. Angelo, for his part, recognized with untrained accuracy the ready woman who had been made to wait too long. After all, consider that mother. And then consider that face with the full mouth pushing out—always a good sign about the receiving end of a woman—and the big, stupid eyes that understood nothing, except what was spelled out in the simplest way. The nose was too big to make a beautiful face but here again—straight folk knowledge among the *cognoscenti*— a good sign about the receiving end of a woman. Because of the bulk of the lamb-lined coat, Angelo could only guess at the total story of her body. That was all right. He was an active guesser, a *cognoscenti* guesser.

Rosanna dropped the subject by shifting her eyes. She as not good at guessing and forethought. It confused her.

"I'll have the soup," she said—and, while alone in the kitchen, also the ham, the roast, the cheese that was for her father only. Rosanna was not bright by United States college standards, and she was not strong by her mother's moral standards, but for one lack she made up with a measure of secret cunning, and with simple stubbornness for the other.

When Rosanna had left, Angelo felt alone with a room full of furniture and a lot of books behind glass. Donna Perrini, with her nose pointing down at the needlepoint in her lap, had changed from a soft-eyed mother to an iron-jawed chaperon. After a while of silence, Angelo jumped up and slapped his hands on his legs.

"Look! She has left the headlights on. I think I will turn them off."

He dashed out without noticing that he had awakened the old woman.

He ran out into the cold wind and turned the headlights off. Then he came back inside and hunted around for the kitchen.

It was a large, uncluttered room with a long island of work platform down the middle. The kitchen smelled faintly of oregano. Rosanna sat at the end of the island, which had a chopping-block top. There were several plates plus a pot ranged around, and her mouth was full.

"I turned off your headlights."

She was not able to say anything.

"You are hungry?" He had his hands in his pockets and his smile on his face.

She watched him come closer and then she lowered her head. The change in angle helped her to swallow what had been in her mouth. Angelo misunderstood that.

"Now that we are alone," he said, smiling with intensity, "we can meet better." In European fashion, he now held out his hand for her.

She shrugged and shook his hand. Angelo did not hold on for very long. It had been a very greasy hand.

"Ah," he said, "it is a pleasure to see your appetite."

"You want some?"

He laughed, thinking that she had made a sexual joke. Those American women, they can be brutes.

"Later. After you are done eating?"

She was pushing cheese into her mouth and could not answer.

"What I mean is, I like pleasure. And I can tell by your appetite—heh, heh," he said and pulled back a little from his close approach. *Disgraziado*, how that magnificent mouth was smeared with grease. "May I give you a napkin?"

"No."

"Heh, heh." Angelo felt that he was going too fast. Better say something interesting and neutral. "How is school, Rosanna? You like it?"

"I don't like to be called Rosanna. Rosanne is fine."

"Good, good. The Anna is rosy, eh?" He watched for a sign but got none. This incredible girl had her mouth full again. "Tell me, Rosanne, where are you most rosy?" He was running out of ways to fill pauses. "Want me to guess?"

She swallowed, wiped her mouth with a handkerchief from her overcoat pocket, and then she wiped her hands.

"I think you better make that kinda jokes with somebody else, Mister Fa—, Fo—, what was that name?"

"Angelo. Please call me Angelo."

"Maybe you can make that kind of joke with my father. He likes that kinda talk."

"I apologize, Rosanne. Please apologize me. Ah! Incorrect! I am *sorry*."

When at the end of his rope, Angelo played up his accent and broken

English. Rosanna thought he was kind of cute.

"Okay," she said. "You can help me off with my overcoat."

He got behind her and slowly pulled the fleece-lined leather coat off her shoulders. This time, Angelo had no problem filling the pause. He pulled slowly, thinking of clothes falling away, and looked down at her front, over her shoulder. Rosanna felt a sort of compliment to his greed, which was to display herself with a hint of an offer. She heard him drop the coat on the kitchen floor and knew exactly what he would now do with his two, free hands. She moved forward, crossed her arms under her meaty breasts, and leaned on the chopping block.

"Angelo? Where'd you leave my mother?"

American women could be real beasts. He picked the coat up and walked around to sit on a stool by the other edge of the chopping block.

"In the furniture. In the room back there. A very fine lady. Rosanne, I have an idea to ..."

"She's a lady the way my father is a gentleman."

"Huh?"

"Nothing. How do you like this country?"

"What country?"

"You got an accent. Aren't you from Italy or something?"

"No. Sicily. But I went to university in Italy. I learned ..."

"I quit."

"You quit? What?"

"School. I used to go to Barnard."

"That is a school?"

"College."

"You? I mean, you should not quit. After all, in this country an education is even good ..."

"That's true. My parents made me quit."

"*Disgraziado!* Why should they keep a smart person like you ..."

"I guess they don't know any better. It's because something happened, and they're kinda uptight."

Angelo felt rattled. His lust rattled him, the sight of her cupping herself with both hands right there on the chopping block rattled him, and her language was hard to follow. He looked away from her hands, which were still greasy, and sensed out the drift of her talk. She wanted to tell him something about herself.

"You got in trouble."

"Well, not that kinda trouble. It's just that a bunch of us went down to Fort Lauderdale—Did you know that we have a place there?"

"A place? No. A big place?"

"Sort of. Anyway, it was nothing. The place was closed, of course, but two of the guys stood on top of each other and forced a window and then ..."

"Guys?"

"Fellows. You didn't think I went there alone, silly. Three of my girlfriends and three guys. Anyway. It wasn't anything." She watched him to see whether her calculated downplaying got his wheels going again. She thought they were in fact going with a hum and a whine. "They're so uptight," she told him, "they didn't like it that I used our *own* place with my *own* friends without *their* permission is how uptight they are. You want some coffee?"

She got up to fix instant coffee, just to be doing something. It had been important to talk about the Lauderdale thing and just as important to leave out its real significance. The Lauderdale thing was Rosanna's single, assertive, and very frightening crash into the world that should be closed to her; after twenty years with her parents; after twelve years of parochial school; after two years of envy and self-discipline in the dormitory of that college

None of them had known what it had taken for her to go along on that crazy trip for a weekend in Florida, or what colossal courage she had mustered to suggest her parents' place in Fort Lauderdale. And then the pairing off in the cold, empty house.

"Rosanne," said Angelo from the chopping block. "I don't really want coffee. What I really want, *bella mia*, that needs very little preparation. I can tell. I can see from over here without really touching you ..."

"Later, baby. Just cool it."

The change in her voice was so startling to Angelo that he could think of no further invitation. In fact, at that moment, he needed a great deal of preparation to get back to the level of confidence that went with his perpetual rutting season. She was *una bestia. Senza dubbio.* That fresh body was a rotten sump. Those waiting eyes were just buttons. She was a whore who was too tired to lift her legs—

Rosanna watched the water which would not come to a boil. Her own tone had disgusted her so much that she now felt as tired as if she had in fact retched herself empty. But not empty enough. Something like a lump of sadness lay balled up inside. It was the lump she had discovered in the damp, empty house just that short time ago, in Lauderdale. They had known nothing about her courage or about that brief flash of freedom with which she had turned her whole world upside down.

After two drinks and with the sight of Suzy naked on the rug and big Harold with the very white ass thumping and thumping on top of her, with these as props and with Caroline bending her sweet head forward and holding her lovely hair so that Louis could unzip her in the back ...

"I better tell you," she had said to Jimmy, "I'm a virgin."

The thumping stopped and the zipper stopped. The laughter was like chains beating on the bone of her head.

That flash of freedom she had felt had really been like a rage. It was a reckless hitting back that, by the commentary in the drafty house, seemed to have looked like accomplished lust. After that, she had kept waiting for the pleasure. They had stayed two nights and a day and she had become sore fairly soon. Her recollection was specialized. There had been the one who drooled on her hairline, the one who thought a jackhammer meant ecstasy, and the one who always kept his knuckles between her shoulder blades.

When Rosanna turned from the stove, Angelo watched her face critically. He saw nothing there that reminded him of that voice she had used. More confusion. Maybe she was sad because she regretted having spoken to him like that.

"All right, *bella mia*, of course I shall wait. Perhaps you thought I was not a gentleman? Sit down. Here is how we will do it. Did you know I am staying the night in this house? Very good, eh?"

"*Rosanna?!*" Like a sharp knife thrown from the length of the house, but with accuracy. "*Your father wants to see you!*"

Angelo turned away. He stroked the sides of his head with the gesture of soothing a horse. Then he put his blue sunglasses on. It was twelve o'-clock midnight, and the object of his visit had to commence at the lowest point of his day.

CHAPTER 5

"Missus Jackson," said Cutter. "I got no way of telling you what this fine meal means to me," and then he leaned over the little kitchen table and gave the old woman a kiss on the side of the face.

She shook him off and then she grinned so that her wrinkles went away. Her cheeks squeezed up under her eyes. The hardness that made the eyes so steady went away, too, for that moment.

"Goin bed now," she said and groaned out of her chair. "You two stain to chat most the night?" She looked at her son who was resting one arm on the icebox. Her face showed the wear again, and her cold eyes looked as always.

"We'll keep our voices down."

"The soap water's good for one more time," she said. "Get the slick off them dishes good. Night, Constabee."

"Night, Ma Jackson."

She opened the door to the little hall where the toilet was behind the curtain and where her bedroom came off.

"And dry 'em with a clean towel," she said.

"Of course, Mother," said Asikari.

"Of course, son."

Even though the old woman was mumbling, she had aped the diction with sharp accuracy. Then the door slammed shut.

It struck Cutter that a noise can make a terrible silence. He looked at Asikari but nothing came back to him. The other looked blank with stillness. Cutter rubbed his hand over the short nap on his skull and made a sound in his throat, a little bit like a grunt, a little bit like a giggle. Then he said,

"Shit, man, that's better than the screws yelling at you. Compared, this is music!"

For a quick moment, the expression on Asikari's face seemed to be pained, but Cutter could not be sure. So he did the same thing he had done at the bus station when he had not been sure of his place or its meaning, he rammed the meaning he wanted right into his act.

"No screws kickassing all over the place, hey, Kari? I'm out! Lookee here—I can open the door, I can flicker the light on and off, I can walk from this here room to that room over there—man, you know what that means? That means I'm out, I mean *out*, man!"

He jumped out of his chair, rubbed his skull again, squeezed his own chest while bobbing up and down, then did a shuffle step back and forth in the kitchen, which was an embarrassment to Asikari's eyes. Cutter hee-hawed a few times while he kept up the shuffling and hugging. Then he collapsed in the chair, panting as if he had run a mile.

"Sheeyat," he sighed. "I am o-u-t out!"

Asikari had picked up the coffee pot and was drawing water to make a fresh brew. Then he put the pot on the stove and turned back to the table.

"I'm glad you came here first, Cutter." He smiled something like a welcome.

"You know it!"

"And you're quite cheerful."

"Glad. So fuckin glad, man—" There was a touch of a moan in Cutter's voice.

"We'll make more coffee and then we'll talk." He turned away to shovel the fresh grounds into the basket of the pot.

"Talk," said Cutter. "I mean, we rap all night and that's another thing. No kickass for rapping all night and never you mind if you get enough sleep before six in the morning and just go on all night, man, all night. Nobody moaning in the next cell, no crazy man jacking off all the time, all the time with the springs squeaking and sawing away at your skull, I mean, shit, I'm just getting the feel of it, being out—"

Asikari came to the table and put his hands into the large holes of his sleeves. He sat down that way.

"I think," he said, "you got something on your mind."

Cutter looked as if he were slowing down. Only something invisible kept plugging along in his brain.

"Mind? What mind?"

But it did not work. Asikari remained untouched in his seriousness.

"I think it has to do with my never visiting you, Cutter."

"That? Oh, that! Shit, man, I know you couldn't visit up there. I know that."

"And also, about getting sent up, which was largely because you got no help with your defense. We did not help you."

The thing in Cutter's brain kept plugging along and then started to kick the inside of his cranium like a bucking horse. This is my friend, Cutter said to himself. Asikari is damn well my only friend and there's no more five years alone and some of that in the hole so all alone—He took a deep breath and smiled at Asikari.

"I know why, Kari. I know the rules, and the reasons. I went into this thing with you eyes open, mind clear."

The street talk and even the intonation had started to drop away. There was just that slight movement of the tones, that mollifying rhythm in the way Cutter talked, which never went away or became the glass evenness of Asikari's speech.

"I knocked that bank over for the movement. I fucked up and got busted. That's my dues in the movement. Just that. I didn't sing to the Man and I didn't come crying to you. That's for the movement." Cutter looked at his hands on the table and rubbed them together. When he talked again he did not recognize his own voice, it was so hoarse. "That's all I got, man. You know that."

To his own utter confusion, Cutter thought he could feel the heat of tears move into his eyes. Mercifully, Asikari was getting up from the table and went to the coffee on the stove. Mercifully, Cutter had time to flash back over the bones of his past, just a quick flash of a look at the worst of it....

The moldy backseat of a car in the junkyard. He remembered that because his mother had said he had been born in the thing. He also knew it because he had apparently been old enough to remember the sight of the Capitol dome from one of the gray car windows.

Next came the picture of moving North and living in a gigantic room of luxury but he should not play with the cats on short legs, because those were rats.

The next dead bone in his past was the thing about school, getting paid for being good on the track, with a basketball, with a bat. Now he could never screw up again in his life. Letter-man, college man, scholar, and superfly—except, the way you screw up in life is to buck the Man. You don't get a scholarship to go political and badmouth the System.

Those three bones in his past and perhaps in his craw—the moldy backseat, the room with the rats, and the scholarship bust—to think about them dried the mush up inside him and turned him cool, which is why he thought about those times, when he thought about them at all. Asikari came back to the table and brought the coffee.

Cutter tried it slowly at first, then he smiled again.

"Let's rap. You tell me where it's at, Kari, and I'll just ease back in."

"Where what's at?"

"You, man. Everything!"

"I'm teaching little children."

"Fuck that. Thanks, half a cup. I mean us. The movement."

"There is no movement," said Asikari.

Cutter laughed. Then he sipped from his cup and burned his mouth.

"Where's the Drummer?"

"Hiding. I think in L.A."

"And Zappy?"

"He caught one, right after you got sent up."

"Caught one—you mean dead?"

"Of course."

"Of course. Man—sometimes the way you jive—What about Little Benjamin? Don't you tell me ..."

"Benjamin is in Cuba. And that," said Asikari, "is just about the lot of it, isn't it?"

Cutter still did not get it. He shook his head back and forth slowly, and the smile on his face was turning stupid.

"You jamming me up good, Kari." Something moved in his throat and would not come out. When he talked, the voice started quietly but already with the rush of a punch thrown wild and fast. "Listen," he said a few times before his voice became louder, then, "You listen to me, you crazy nigger. I went to the slammer for this boss thing we built here! I sat in the hole, man, in the *hole*—God—I sat in that motherfucker counting my toes and coming up with eleven, over and over. Shit on that. But I'm sitting there and counting away, coming up with eleven, but that's okay, man, that's boss, because I'm a political prisoner!" He laughed with a touch of a screech in it. "I didn't make that up, Kari, they did. Called me a political prisoner. Not some jug heavy what busts down banks. Hey, nigger, you know what we do with you wool-head politicos in here? Wammo-slammo!

Inma hole, spade! Strip, bend over, spread those cheeks and lemme see if you ain't got some nailfile stashed up your black asshole, you shine politico bastid." Cutter got up but then he did not want to move. He felt limp and dull. But he had to keep talking. "You realize, don't you, Kari, that us shines in the politico game, we always carry nailfiles up the asshole so as to clean the fingernails to a superfly condition whilst in the solitary hole, hey?"

"Cut it out, man," said Asikari quietly.

"You realize that."

"Sure."

"Sure you say?" Cutter's voice went up again, but not with the wild screaming but straight at Asikari, intending to connect. "Don't say to me there's nothing, Rafer Jackson! Don't you jam me with that shit about nothing! I'm back, Kari! We build it up, man! I'm back for *that!*"

Asikari had gone to the sink. He fished around in the soapy water and found the dishrag down there. He kept both hands under water and squeezed on the rag hard and held on that way. The telephone rang. Asikari, for the moment, did not move.

"Under the table," he said to the kitchen wall.

Cutter reached down to the floor, found the phone, and put it on the table top. Then he put the receiver to his ear.

"Yeah?" He listened for a while. "No. This ain't he. You want him, this hour of the morning?—Who are you, fucker?—Don't you jam me on the telephone, White Thing!", and then Cutter held the phone out to Asikari. "Some kinda honk trying to kickass me right here on the phone this time of night."

"Please keep your voice down," said Asikari and took the receiver.

What followed was not much of a conversation, a few times yes, a few times no. Asikari's expression was no more or no less distant than it always was. Then he handed the receiver back and turned to the sink for a moment. He looked at the murk of the soapy water but did not put his hands back in. Cutter saw him raise his shoulders with deliberation. When the body relaxed again, Asikari seemed to be broader than he had been before. Cutter had seen this before. Not much else ever happened when Asikari became upset, just the thing with the shoulders, or sometimes, rarely, his face would change in a silent and awful way. But Cutter could not see the face.

Then Asikari came back to the table, sat down, and picked up a cigarette.

"To finish more quietly," he said. "And to finish it, now that the topic is out."

"Who was that on the phone?"

"Never mind. To finish, and to repeat, Cutter. There is no organization.

We got smashed good and stayed that way. Which is when you went to jail. Now you're back. And now, even if I wanted to build something again, of what possible safe, productive, and unobtrusive use could you possibly be?"

"Cool that, cool that a sec. What I am ..."

"A man with a criminal record. A loser to the brothers, and a marked man to the pigs."

"Since when is a stretch in the slammer some kind of freaking disgrace to—"

"Just shut up, Cutter."

The tone made Cutter hold still.

"That phone call," said Asikari, "that White Thing with which you were playing games on the phone, that was Kominski."

"I'm shook. Who the fuck is Kominski?"

"The precinct captain."

"You know the precinct captain," said Cutter.

"He knows you. He knows you're out, that you're in town, and that you probably headed straight for me. He called to harass me with the reminder that you're a marked man, and to harass you with the churlish warning not to forget your appointment with the parole officer at eight o'clock in the morning—Cutter. Are you listening?"

"Yeah! But I don't believe it! Since when does the great motherfucker Asikari get shook by some pig making a midnight call to Ma Jackson's kitchen, hey?"

"Lower your voice."

"Or maybe that's not why you're shook. Maybe you're shook because I heard that honk voice and you don't want me to think you maybe got something going with the Man who's got to call at the midnight hour. Hey?"

Asikari did not interrupt. He did not recognize this Cutter who now had a red edge of madness to the things he was saying. He let Cutter talk.

"Or that other Charley, the one who drives up in a fat, bulletproof hog and a squad of button men on the sidewalk, maybe there's the action? That was Perrini, wasn't it? Now, I'm asking myself, why the private visit to Ma Jackson's kitchen so that the Man in the rackets can talk to the Man in the Belt where the rackets, the Perrini rackets, haven't been worth a shit since Asikari came into the scene?"

Asikari showed a rare expression. He was shocked. Then the telephone rang again, and Cutter, as if expecting it, snapped up the receiver.

"Now you listen here. How'd you like, I mean right now this cool morning, how'd you like me to bust you right ina mouth?—Huh? Don't you try your imitation jive talk on me, you honk motherfucker, because any—"

Cutter moved the receiver so he could look at it. Then he spat on the mouthpiece.

"He hung up."

Asikari did not seem to hear. He watched Cutter put the receiver back on the cradle and, when Cutter looked up, Asikari said,

"We've moved far apart."

Cutter did not know what to answer.

"I did something wrong," Asikari said. The cold was gone from the voice, and only the precision was left. "I forgot about your five years, which must have been like five years holding still, holding and hoping that nothing would change while time passes. And then I rushed all this in on you."

"Nothing's changed?" said Cutter like a stupid man.

It seemed to jerk Asikari back into his customary way, with an added touch of severity.

"Some things don't, Cutter. I don't deal with Perrini, which is what you implied, and I don't deal with Kominski, which was your other lunatic assumption."

"Kari. Don't hassle me no more—"

"Of course. You wanted to hear shiny things about the movement."

"And then those two honks came calling—"

"And infect *me?* You ignorant field nigger, they're *white!*"

The window pane had fogged over and the heater in the wall made a comforting sound. Ma Jackson's kitchen was small and chipped, but it was like a nest. Cutter's hands lay still on the table and then he rubbed them together, slowly, because he was cold.

Perrini said nothing to Menotti while the limousine was still moving with the traffic in Black Belt. Buckingham Boulevard at twelve o'clock midnight had the wakefulness of an insomniac, bright, brittle, and harsh. Perrini looked at the scene from his window and saw a lot of loose money and a lot of waste. That was part of the problem but unfortunately not all of it. Menotti, from his corner in the big, sighing seat, saw all the hustler motion which puts a lot of excitement into a scene but does not go anywhere. The pimp hustles to keep up with his wardrobe requirements. The hooker turns her trick to keep up with the pimp demands. The shark collects his the hard way just to set an example. And the suckers play the numbers to make up for yesterday's loss. They all keep up, which means that they all stand still. Menotti knew about that kind of hustling because he had come from that kind of neighborhood. Make a buck to pay off on the two you owed because of the deal that didn't quite make it. But then there was always the one rare one to whom everybody owed and who owed almost nothing. That was Perrini—almost. Menotti the lawyer sighed, wishing it were that simple.

"*Dunque*," said Perrini. "From the beginning."

"Campi called ..."

"I know that."

"... because he did not know how to handle what turned out to be a sticky situation."

"Menotti. Without the grandstand thing. You're not in court."

Menotti was used to the manner, and he felt that he was in part getting paid to endure it. But he continued with a little more haste.

"When Campi went to the Belt today it was because of the welcher ..."

"What welcher?"

"Just some bettor who'd placed on a race and then didn't want to pay off. He claimed he knew you, hoping that would impress. It didn't. What with the strain between your operations and that Black Belt—uh—"

"Mess. That Black Belt mess."

"Very well. What with all that, Campi, as unofficial liaison ..."

"Stop using those goddamn words, Menotti."

"Campi went in there today to play things down. Instead, he walks into worse."

Both men waited while the limousine now swung away from the ware-house district and without entering Bethelport proper took an on-ramp to the lakefront freeway. From then on the car swung along the empty nightview of the lake toward the Erie Strand section.

"I'm not nervous," said Perrini with a touch of venom. "But could you give me the rest?"

The more he pays a man, thought Menotti, the worse he treats him. I am top echelon.

"Campi went to the Jewel Bar where those runners hang out. While there, a fight starts in the alley."

"Which is nothing, considering."

"Except this one involves a policeman."

"They come in pairs down there."

"The other one was having a beer right next to Campi. At any rate, once again it's a conflict between two runners who work for your man Tiffany ..."

"Nobody is *my* man in that goddamn district!" Perrini cursed for a while. Then he sighed. "Now. About the, the conflict, please."

"Two whites beating up the two black runners, and then, the way it was reported, the policeman intervened and now he is getting the beating."

"What did he expect?"

"Gets the beating from the two whites ..."

"*Porco*—"

"... who once again claimed to be part of your organization and no black bastard—or some such language—be he a runner or policeman, was going to cheat them on their bets."

"Did you see them?"

"They got away and only the blacks were arrested. They explained it the way I just reported the incident."

"You checked them out?"

"Campi did, after going along to the station, and then I did, after Campi called me. They were not your men."

Perrini said nothing. He sat inside his fur with his head pulled down. Menotti did not want to look straight at his *caporegime* and could not tell just what was going on inside Perrini.

"At any rate," Menotti continued, "Campi called me because the precinct captain, rather a typical man ..."

"I know him."

"Was booking the blacks for the beating in the usual fashion. And that, in view of the feeling about you in the Belt, would have made your position much worse, no matter who those white attackers might have been. I arranged the release of the black runners."

"*Grazie a Dio—*"

Menotti resented the remark. Quite properly, Perrini might have thanked him, Menotti, for the adroit handling of that police idiocy. "You understand," he said very calmly, "that it is premature to thank God."

"I know."

"Excuse me, *padrone*, I think you know nothing."

When that son of a bitch starts to flip me his secondhand Italian, thought Perrini, then I must have offended his delicate bookkeeper's soul. It is all the same with those experts. They have so little, they are such little men that to insist on their specialty is to insist that they have an existence.

Perrini straightened up inside his fur, smiled briefly, and patted his *consigliere* on the thigh. It made the other man shrink a little.

"I think," said Perrini, "in matters of great delicacy I can count on you more than on God. We will have to put our heads together."

The limousine had left the freeway and was winding its way through the spaced curves of Erie Strand. At the entrance to Perrini's place, the wrought-iron gates opened when the chauffeur pressed a button on the dash and produced a beeping sound.

"Speaking of delicate matters," Perrini went on, "Don Santino has sent his nephew."

"Today?"

"The young businessman is waiting."

CHAPTER 6

After Magdalena Perrini's disruption of Angelo's kitchen maneuvers, there had been a further letdown. Perrini had in fact not yet arrived. Missus Perrini had simply executed a maneuver of her own. The maneuver had revealed the whereabouts of her daughter and that young man from New York. Also, it had undoubtedly undone the young man's sex plot and had stopped Rosanna from eating any more. As a consequence, Angelo sat once again in the library watching the woman of the house jerk her head up every time she started to fall asleep. As for Rosanna, he could watch her sit in the couch with the flower print, her arms along the top of the lean, a posture to stretch her dress across her body and to show the deep motion every time she breathed. All this he could see half-way across the room. Rosanna kept looking at him most of the time without moving a muscle in her face, except that she yawned at him every so often. Angelo knew for sure that none of this posturing was invitation or promise. She was not doing this for him, but to him. By the time the front door slammed, he was in an impossible fury. Angelo put his blue glasses on.

When the two men came into the library, there was no problem of recognizing the *caporegime*, even though the image was mixed.

Angelo had seen the priestly manner many times, the humility with the slyness behind it, and the calm that had nevertheless an edge of irritation around it. What mottled the image of Perrini the Preach was the blatant hunger in the man. He could probably eat anything, like his daughter, but unlike his daughter, no one could forbid him.

"Magdalena!" said Perrini and threw his hat at a piece of furniture. "How nice of you to wait up." His wife jerked up but did not have a chance to say anything. "Rosanna? You look ready for bed. Maybe a little something to eat, before the dreams?" Perrini did not wait for her to say anything either. "And you must be Santino's important nephew?"

While the women left the room without any further exchange, Perrini shook hands with Angelo Forza, then embraced him with the usual gesture of a kiss at each side of the face.

"But perhaps, my dear Angelo, you would rather go to bed and we have our visit together tomorrow."

"Oh no. I don't think this will take long. One short visit. No more is needed. And I have been visiting with your wife and daughter for a long time. Your hospitality is—how to say it—undeserved. I arrived at four in the afternoon," Angelo added.

Menotti turned away and smiled to himself. This overdressed punk from

Sicily showed his style in one short delivery. First of all, he had ignored the inferior. Not one look or comment to Menotti. Then he had warned Perrini that his, Angelo's, power was such that one visit was all it would take. And in the end, that impolite use of the irrefutable, the fact that Angelo Forza had been waiting an inordinate length of time. *Maleducato*, thought Menotti, which was a most devastating critique when applied to a guest.

Perrini had his own way of dealing with the offense against etiquette. He smiled and nodded, but made no reply. Instead he took his heavy coat off, gestured to Menotti to give him his, and then walked out of the room to hang up his own and the coat of the inferior. When he came back he carried a bottle of Asti Spumanti and three glasses. He poured the red wine, offered a glass to Menotti, and then gave one to Angelo. When the Sicilian sat down again Perrini walked the length of the room, gestured at the seat in a large bay window, and waited until Menotti and Angelo Forza had come across and had found their seats. Then Perrini took a small nip of wine and smiled at his guest.

"I am sorry about the trouble with your eyes," he said to Angelo. "You got pinkeye?"

Angelo did not know what pinkeye was.

"It's a disease," supplied Menotti.

"So," and Perrini sat down himself. "Now tell me about your problem."

"There is nothing wrong with my eyes."

"*Dunque*, I am pleased. Of course I know many people who wear dark glasses in the nighttime for other reasons."

"Yes, yes," said Menotti, nodding at his wine. "I just noticed it when we were in the Negro section of town. Many of the very well-dressed blacks wear dark glasses all the time."

They were a good team. Perrini sat back and watched Angelo reorient him. He noticed that the younger man was doing something with his shoulder blades. It reminded Perrini of a chicken trying to fly.

"How long have you been in this country?" asked Menotti. "Your Italian accent hardly shows."

Another insult, since Angelo Forza was a Sicilian.

"By the way," said Perrini without any transition, "when I asked you about your problem I did not mean the pinkeye. I was asking about the reason for your visit."

"Yes," said Angelo. It was as artless as if he did not know why he was here. "Don Santino sent me."

"Don't you call him uncle?"

"Uh, yes. He sent me. He wants to know what is going on with the Negro town thing."

"We don't call them Negroes," said Perrini. "They like it when you say blacks. Try to remember. It's good for relations."

Angelo could not afford to be distracted anymore. His temper was shredding the thoughts into pieces inside his brain.

"It's this relations thing," he said. "My—Don Santino has spoken to you about it."

"Has he?" and Perrini looked at Menotti.

"Don Santino has raised the question of proprieties," said Menotti. "You remember?"

"Of course!" First, the blessing smile, then a very cold, distant look. "I explained that to him. Maybe he didn't tell you."

Angelo did not catch the nature of the switch clearly, but Perrini had a different manner now. The explanation was simple. Perrini was no longer affecting the stately tones of Italian translated into English. "So what's the message?"

"It is simple. Don Santino not only wants you to stop using black Negroes for organization business, but he wishes to make clear that he is a little disturbed—just a little, you understand—by your ignoring his wishes."

Now it was serious. Now it was no longer games with a *cretino* relative from Sicily but a negotiation with the old Don himself.

"Menotti," said Perrini. "Explain it." Then he looked at Angelo and added, "You are going to listen to my *consigliere*. You know what that means. He doesn't only know everything, but he knows what it'll mean a week from now. *I* listen to him," and Perrini nodded at his lawyer.

"There are five operations of interest in Black Belt: prostitution, loans, dope, books, and numbers. The first is of no interest to us, and ..."

"Why?" said Angelo.

"Perhaps you are not acquainted with their style of the notch business," said Menotti. He chose the slang deliberately, even though he found it personally offensive. However, it would puzzle the foreigner. When he saw Angelo lean forward like a deaf man, he went on. "The prostitute works for a pimp. In effect, that makes the business a very personal operation. Based on that fact alone, prostitution in Black Belt and in similar areas, as you undoubtedly know, is not accessible to large-scale methods. The only alternative—a white pimp running black hookers in an all-black neighborhood—is too ridiculous to deserve consideration."

"You got that clear?" asked Perrini. Without waiting for an answer, he told Menotti to go on.

"Dope, in contrast, is of interest to us," said Menotti. "However, for reasons of local peculiarity, it is an area of business that is so far totally inaccessible to us."

"You mean you got no hand in it?"

"The source of supply is ultimately New York. I'm sure your uncle could explain it to you."

"I guess he didn't," said Perrini. "I don't run dope in my own territory," said Perrini with, emphasis, "because Santino runs that operation himself. All right, Menotti. Tell the kid the rest."

"The rest," said Menotti, "is loan sharking, the numbers, and book-making. Those three activities have always been a part of Mister Perrini's enterprises."

"He knows that," said Perrini.

"Perhaps there is something the young man does not know," Menotti went on. "While the demand for the services has increased, the market conditions have changed."

"He doesn't know what in hell you're talking about," mumbled Perrini. "What the lawyer means, Angelo, the blacks have a lot more money. And they have a lot more—*orgoglio.*"

"*Cosa?*" said Angelo with surprise. "You mean pride? Like a Sicilian?" Then he laughed.

"Not because of the money," Menotti added, "but because of, shall we say, a change in temperament."

"You ever hear of a man called Asikari?" asked Perrini, but he knew ahead of time that Angelo had neither heard nor would he care. "Menotti. Give him the figures."

"These are Black Belt figures," said Menotti, "and I cite them now only because you may not be familiar with their meaning. As such, Don Santino Forza has them on file. Part of the routine financial statements from district to head office. You may know that."

"I know that," lied Angelo. This part bored him, because it had nothing to do with his mission. Of course, the Preacher and his shyster did not know that yet. The thought gave Angelo a slight lift which he needed badly after insults and interruptions at one o'clock in the morning. He smiled a studied smile, like Angelo the schoolboy on Meatless Friday and there was a salami stuffed inside his shirt.

Menotti began to intone the facts. "Average income in Black Belt has risen 40 per cent during the past ten years. Ditto purchasing power 20 per cent. The combined take on bookmaking, numbers, and loans—for the moment's purpose I'll combine the figures—went up at the same rate as income. That is to say, for the first four years of that ten-year period. By the fourth year, while gross income was up 30 per cent, our take was up 60 per cent. Then Asikari happened."

"What happened?"

"It's a who, not a what," said Perrini. "Black Power thing. His version was Power to the Third Power. He wrote it P3. That's mathematics and is something like super-power. It also means Power-Pride-Peace. A real learned bastard."

"It means our take went down," said Menotti. "With income up, our take went from 60 per cent down to 20 per cent of the base figure of ten years ago."

"And he raked off 40 per cent?" asked Angelo.

"No. He made nothing. He didn't want the brothers to give it to us, is all," said Perrini. "Tell him the rest, Menotti."

"That's before I came to this country," said Angelo. "Did you wipe him out?"

"Well, the police did," said Perrini and looked at the blank window where the view of Lake Erie would be. "Tell him the rest, Menotti."

"Asikari has no movement anymore. Not for five years now. And since that time our take has not gone up again. Instead, we have continued to lose."

"*Disgraziato!*" said Angelo with surprising heat. "Who's making the money?"

"The blacks," said Perrini.

"However," said Menotti, "with revolting inefficiency. To continue, our take dipped to a level below, I repeat, below the base figure from years ago and that, of course, in the light of a 40 per cent increase in gross income. However, one year ago Mister Perrini devised a new stratagem."

"I took in the blacks," said Perrini.

Angelo almost said *disgraziato* again which means, in Sicilian usage, that something is absolutely revolting and beneath contempt.

"Our take from the three sources mentioned," Menotti went on, "moved up a cautious 10 per cent, a ridiculous figure of waste and inefficiency."

"Because you used the black Negroes." Angelo made it a pronouncement. He felt on safe ground now. Uncle Santino had said the same thing.

"Bullshit," said Perrini.

Angelo, who did not know the full power of that word, looked only slightly interested. He neither questioned Perrini's analysis nor did he object to it. He went straight to the point of his mission, as memorized from the sayings of Uncle Santino.

"They are inferior stock and they are made worse by trying to ape this very complicated but inferior culture. For example, look at the way they dress."

Perrini looked at Menotti and Menotti looked at Perrini. For the moment they did not know what to say. Angelo went on.

"They have no rights to the enterprises of a Family of which they are not a part. They are not of the blood, they do not know the loyalties, and they do not have the skills."

"*Per l'amor di Dio—*" breathed Perrini and looked at the distant ceiling.

Then he very suddenly changed. The tones of a supplicant were gone, and Perrini sounded like a barking dog. "I'm talking money! I'm talking how to run it smooth like a beautiful machine! Your uncle sits there in his block of old houses, at the end of a long career, sits there behind the window and looks at all the rooftops and the sky, maybe dreaming about the way he made it, and about the old blood brotherhood which helped him to make a new life, he sits there on top of everything and forgets that this *is* a new life! You don't drink the blood anymore and make oaths anymore, *cretino!* You watch the adding machine and you listen to what it says. And if it tells you to change the pattern and organize in a new way, then you listen and *do* it! *Porco!* This is not the dumb peasants in some cave of a house with a pile of manure in front, this is Black Belt I'm talking about. This is sharpies and hustlers with Eldorado headlights in each eyeball and a shiv up their pants. They snort coke for breakfast and shoot scag for lunch. They use dirty language for a howdoyoudo, and if you're white, *cretino*, they don't buy nothing from you. What they will do, you stupid punk, they'll *sell* you!"

When Perrini was done he jumped up and went to the library table where he had left the bottle of wine. He splashed some into his glass and some on the table and drank the glass empty. He did not offer anything to Angelo or to Menotti. Then he stomped out of the room. It was one-thirty in the morning and he was late for his pill.

Menotti watched the Don's nephew but could not tell how the young Sicilian was taking all this. It had been a rare speech for Perrini and it had all been true. Maybe Angelo Forza was too stupid or perhaps too limited in his messenger function to appreciate any of this.

"So Mister Perrini is taking in the Negroes," said Angelo.

Menotti groaned. The messenger had not heard a word.

"No," said Menotti. "He would like to, but they won't let him."

"Ah. He has tried."

"Forgive me, Mister Forza, but I just said so."

"Why must he try?"

Menotti forgot himself and said, "Goddamn it, young man, I have already answered that by quoting the income figures to you."

"Ah yes," Angelo said again. "I am sorry that you cannot function without the help of those Negroes."

"Explain something to me now," said Menotti. "Two things. Why does the Don insist that the blacks should not be a functioning part of the work? And my other point—"

Menotti stopped when he saw the expression on Angelo's face. Anger? No. It was more like impatience with the ignorance of the world. Angelo's voice had the arrogance of an overseer.

"How to tell you that a Sicilian is better than a Negro, when you do not

already know it in your bones! How to tell you that the strength of the
Mafia is the vigor of the common blood? Why don't you ask as well why
the sun does not shed moonlight? Why—"

"Excuse me once again. We are hardly dealing with what you call Mafia
matters. The family business has changed to a corporate enterprise. We
have remained vital, Mister Forza, precisely because we have adapted to
modern business ways."

"Are you insulting Don Santino?"

"If I did, my apologies." Menotti felt tired. "Perhaps I might just as well
ask you another question."

Angelo seemed to grant audience by remaining silent.

"My other point: How, by excluding the blacks, are we to do business
in the Black Belt where nobody wants to do business except with a
brother?"

"I am not the *capo* in this territory," said Angelo. "But if I were the one
to be concerned and I found that the *capo* of a territory does not know how
to run it, then there is always the method of reorganizing everything, from
the bottom up."

Angelo folded his arms and for the first time looked Menotti straight in
the eye. Angelo felt pleased. He felt it had been a successful sentence composed in an unfamiliar language. He also felt that an underling like
Menotti, a hired talent only, would surely take hope and pleasure in the
suggestion of a power shuffle. Angelo added a smile to his stare.

"Ridiculous," said Menotti. Angelo's smile dropped away.

"Recognize, please, that I am speaking for the Don!" It was another good
sentence. Angelo regretted only that the *caporegime* himself had not heard
it. But he would hear it later, and more. The real threat had not been mentioned yet.

The library door banged open and Perrini came in. He slowed down noticeably and took time to arrange his face.

"Sorry I took so long," he said. "Had a phone call." He looked at
Menotti but he noticed that Angelo acted as if he were part of the conversation. Menotti noticed the same thing.

"Mister Forza was just beginning to clarify the meaning of his presence."

"Fine," said Perrini. His face and voice were reaching for the good
preacher's quality. "Maybe we better go to bed. We started out pretty good,
why push it. Tomorrow, with a good breakfast—" He noticed that the
other two were just waiting for him to be done with the speech. "I want
a word with Mister Menotti," he said to Angelo. "You know how to find
your room?"

Angelo stood up and put his hands in his pockets. He smiled a little.

"Trouble?" he said. "I do not wish to interfere."

"Always trouble. Nothing new."

"In the Black Belt?"

"Tiffany called," Perrini said to his lawyer. "But he's handling it."

The Sicilian, Perrini noticed, had made no move to go to bed as instructed. He kept standing there with his hands in his pockets and bobbed his head up and down, as if considering everything with great concentration.

"Who is Tiffany?" he asked.

"He's mostly in numbers," said Menotti with an obvious effort to close the conversation. Perrini, on the other hand, picked up on the topic. Whatever he said to Angelo Forza, the ears of Santino Forza would hear it.

"I got only one arrangement in the Belt, and that's with Tiffany. The suckers put down their dimes and nickels and hope that their number comes up. You know." Perrini stopped, hearing a sound in the hall. It would not be his wife. His wife would be lying in bed, splayed out on her back, snoring with the force of her powerful lungs. Perhaps Rosanna coming back from the kitchen. Or going to the kitchen. Angelo was listening too. "I was saying," and Perrini looked at the Sicilian. "With nickels and dimes, that means you got to have a great deal of action and that, you know, puts it out in the open. I paid the juice and got a little cut."

"There's nothing you could call a profit," said Menotti. "Just good will."

"To keep a hand in," said Perrini.

"Then how come his people got beat up?" Angelo sounded mild, like an obedient student.

Since Perrini did not know the answer to that one, he got angry.

"I don't worry about some runners get beat up in an alley. I worry about this new thing."

"*Cosa?*"

"They knocked over his place and took records!"

"*Maledetto*—" said Menotti, who only lapsed into Italian when he was upset.

"Ah," said Angelo. "Somebody is in competition. Did they catch the black Negroes?"

"Who in hell knows if they were black or green Negroes or what in hell hit that place!" Perrini, harassed in the extreme, felt like spitting on his own rug. He most certainly did not feel like talking to Don Santino's wonder boy anymore because there was serious business at hand, it was two o'clock in the morning, and he had to talk to Menotti in private.

"Go to bed," he said to Angelo. "Tomorrow we discuss whatever in hell there is to discuss. Early!"

"No need," said Angelo. "I can stay longer."

"What's that?"

"You have your difficulties. I can wait. And later I will tell Don Santino how you handled them." He smiled, bowed like a well-trained European, and said "*Buona notte.*"

Menotti got up in time to put a hand on Perrini's arm and give it a firm yank. The motion stopped Perrini from saying something useless and violent.

Angelo closed the door behind him and felt the agitation in the pit of his stomach. He did not feel like sleeping. When he walked across the big hall he took hard little steps and grinned to himself, hating Perrini very much. But he felt well about things. When he came to the kitchen door, he heard the chunk of the refrigerator closing.

"May I come in?" he said, feeling like a polite intruder. Then he went into the kitchen without waiting for an answer.

Rosanna turned his way and wiped her hands together. The young people looked at each other across the large room and said nothing. There was really nothing to say. They had established their topic the first time they had been in the kitchen together. Angelo fingered her body with his eyes, and Rosanna accepted the touch in some unspoken fashion, because being touched was better than being alone in a shiny kitchen and in a house full of furniture. Angelo was no longer grinning. He just jerked his head at her and turned to go. At the top of the stairs to the second floor he waited briefly until she caught up.

"My room is that way," he said, and took her arm. His fingers moved on the soft flesh of the inner arm, high near the armpit.

"I know. Next to my mother's room."

She started to walk down the other way. Angelo kept his hand where it was. Then they went into her room.

"Where's the light?" he said.

"I don't need it," she said. "Let go my arm, will you?"

He let go immediately and followed her shape which he could see against the large window. She stopped by the window and looked down at the curving drive and the carriage lamp that stayed on all night. The heater under the window blew warm air at her legs. Now what, she thought. I already told him I don't want to be alone.

"Rosanne?"

"Huh?"

"I want you to know ..."

"Save it," she said, hearing the ugliness in her voice. But it was all right. The tone had killed off the quavering in her throat.

"*Ecco,*" he said. "I'll tell you without talk," and he moved up close.

First he cupped her face in his hands and stroked her hair. She noticed how light the touch was, or perhaps it was haste. When his hands moved down and along the sides of her body the quality of his touch changed immediately.

"Listen," she said without moving, "I want you to know," but then she stopped talking and almost said, what the hell. She helped him get her clothes off.

He had started to talk in Sicilian, which sounded like chattering to her. While sitting on the bed naked, she watched how he took off his clothes and how he folded them on the window seat, chattering all the time and grabbing himself with one hand.

"*Guarda*," he said and came back to the bed. "All for you." Then he giggled.

He should really shut up now, she thought. Maybe it could be heard down the hall. No. If it could be heard down the hall, then her mother's snoring could have been heard here on this bed. She lay back, sending thoughts down the length of the corridor and hating her mother very much. Meanwhile, he was very busy with her body. He felt she might move a little more in appreciation, but aside from that she was *molto pneumatica*, which he liked, even though she also smelled of salami.

CHAPTER 7

The wind had stopped rattling the fence in the yard. Inside the kitchen, the two men sat in the quiet heat that came out of the grill in the wall. They did not know what to pick up, after breaking everything into pieces.

Cutter said, "First night out and I'm sitting in Ma Jackson's kitchen. Cutter's Last Stand." The joke fell flat.

"You have anyplace to go?" Asikari did not allow any touch of concern to show, but he added, "Or you can sleep in the schoolroom."

A beat of silence and Cutter said to his hands, "Or I can find an empty car."

"Cutter. If you want to say something else—"

"What's to say. I got stopped."

The problem with Cutter, thought Asikari, is the fact that he has more push than direction. But how to say that to a man who comes on with a great roar of excitement and who has now bottled it up so that it did not even show to Cutter himself.

"You seen Lillie around?" Cutter's remark seemed to come out of nowhere, except that the name had something to do with bed.

"Of course not."

"Of—course—not. You still making it with that white chick who's got all the money?"

At that moment, somebody rapped on the door to the yard. Then it rapped again, like a code. Asikari opened the door a crack, then all the way.

"Man, you hear what just blew up at Tiffany's—"

The black in the door saw Cutter behind the kitchen table and stopped.

"You the fucker what answered the phone a while back?"

"I don't answer the phone, mother. I *tell* it," said Cutter without raising his voice. He did not have to raise his voice. He just gave off ice.

"Cool now," said Asikari. The others paid no attention to him.

"Count your balls, nigger," said the one in the door. "I mean, if you can count up to one, because in just a sec from now ..."

"I'm telling you to shut the fuck up," said Asikari. They both looked at him because his street talk was always a shock. Then he resumed his usual vocabulary. "My mother's asleep," he said. "Close the door, Willie. The kitchen's getting cold."

The one he had called Willie did not simply walk into the kitchen. He made an entrance. He looked young and he moved young. He had the elaborate gait of the hustler who wants to show at all times that his life is a dance and that his flash can illuminate the beholder. His shoulders moved with the roll of a swimmer doing an elegant Australian crawl while his legs did the lower-clef syncopation, a reaching out with the foot, a body bounce that was just short of a leap, and the knees never quite straightening through, so that the whole swing-reach-leap was a syrup motion.

Cutter had seen street clothes before, but this one was boulevard instead of street. Maybe he was wearing all of his wardrobe.

There was the white velour hat, à la Capone, with a black crepe band and a dipping feather hanging back for a foot and a half. The face was very black and had a lot of nostrils showing. That short nose, more than the mouth with the harsh smile glued on, gave a predatory look to the young face. The teeth were very small, very even, and too white. Willie wore a greatcoat of black leather, which was so long that the plum-colored flares of his pants barely showed. The shoes were brown alligator and the heels were white. Willie stopped near the stove. He pulled his green silk scarf from his neck with a motion that made the cloth move like a snake. The Nehru collar of his shirt showed in blushing pink. Except for the silver buttons, it looked a little like a pyjama top.

"And where'd you cop that sheeny serge suit, fucker, in the joint or off'n a corpse?"

"Joint," said Cutter with the same voice as before.

"He just got out," Asikari added. "This is Cutter."

The name transformed Willie. He hit the crown of his hat, slapped his hands, and his face lit up with real appreciation.

"Sheeyat! *The* Cutter! Sheeyat, I heard about you when I was yay, I mean yay high the most! Man, what you sitting around Ma Jackson's kitchen for the first night outa the tombs? Hey?" And then he grabbed Cutter's hand and shook it up and down.

But then he dropped the subject of adoring Cutter as suddenly as he had picked up on it.

"So, now the shit hit the fan, Kari, swing your cape or something over your shoulders and we *go!*"

"What are you talking about?"

"Tiffany! The *action!*"

Asikari lost interest visibly. He went over to shake the empty coffee pot and then he sat down on the other chair by the kitchen table.

"I'm gratified that you found something to do," he said to Willie. "But illegality has no thrill for me."

"Asikari, you don't *dig!* He got knocked over, the whole fuckin' joint torn up."

"Gang rumbles are like dirty politics: Brothers tearing each other's guts out for nickels and dimes."

"Brothers—*Brothers!* Sheeyat, man, wasn't no brothers tore the shit outa that place. White cats! And they's still in the Belt!"

Asikari took his lower lip in his teeth and held it for a while. He might also have been holding his breath. "No," he said. "I've got nothing to add to that situation. Tiffany is a crook. Worse, he's a Tom."

"Kari, here's our chance! You ..."

"Shut up."

Somehow, Asikari gave the common words the invective power of a prophet's curse.

Cutter remembered the manner. He had felt that the prophet thing was a lot of public theatrics, but Asikari had meant it. Even the Swahili name was theatrical, but Asikari had lived it; Asikari the Watchman, and Asikari the Warrior. All that had transformed the Belt until every shufflin joe and ofay nigger had come to think he was strong and beautiful. Five years gone. Maybe some of it was still in the people, but not enough for the Watchman. He had been beaten good and had turned away, not watching anymore—

Willie looked puzzled.

"What you all jammed up about, Kari? You mean you ain't going to pick up on this?"

"That's what I mean."

"But you said ..."

"He said shit on you field niggers." Cutter got out of his chair. "Rafer Jackson's a schoolteacher now, ain't that so, teach?"

Asikari looked at the kitchen sink and the unwashed dishes. Three or four hours later, at about five in the morning, his mother would get up. He would have the dishes done and the kitchen cleaned up. He thought all that through with a terrible concentration and so kept his feelings out of the way.

"Let's you and me split," said Cutter. "This place is dead."

He walked out the back door, fingering his awful print tie and slapping his suit which was prison issue. If there was any interplay between Asikari and Willie, he did not see it. He saw a cold night and a new guide who wore a feather in his hat, and he had no idea where he was going.

The bars were closed, which meant that the clubs were open. The Jewel Bar had become the Jewel Club, the White Spade had become the White Spade Social Association. Instead of walking in and ordering a drink at the bar, it was necessary to walk in and show a membership card. On the other hand, that was not necessary. An initiation fee cost five dollars.

While the names of the places showed some imagination, the insides did not: all darkness and glitter, with the luxury look of a dime-store counter.

They went through six places and stayed just long enough for Willie to learn where he should look next. On this night, Tiffany was a hard man to find.

They left the last place, blocks away from the main drag of the Belt, and watched a trash can roll to a dead stop against a telephone post.

"You look this way, I look thataway," said Willie.

"Street's empty."

"Let's go."

They crossed the street. The only traffic was wind. They went down an alley. A few times they crossed somebody's yard.

"You got plans?" asked Willie.

"Don't know. Gotta see the Man tomorrow. Parole shit."

Willie laughed.

"Gonna do the nine-to-five and 'work within the system'?"

"I got no offers," said Cutter. "Just a lot of disappointments."

"The man at parole, he'll kickass you for sure."

"I gotta start cool," said Cutter. They came back into a street near the factory district. "I gotta watch it about 'associating with known criminal elements.' That's the scene."

Willie had more room for movement on the street and started to dip and weave back and forth.

"Knowncriminalelement—" He started to wheeze and strangle with laughter. "You seen a motherfuckin dude this night that weren't of the knowncriminalelement? Man, you can't draw breath here and you ain't inhaling some knowncriminalcrap like you said. In a grocery, discount place, the employment agency, cut-rate drug, in a bank—ooh, man, you best shut your mouth and don't breathe none at all, if you don't wanna suck in some that sho' nuff crimashitelement, brother." Willie took a deep breath, did one of his switches in mood and delivery. "And when you breathe, 'cause you ain't dead yet, you done wrong. So anytime the Man has a mind to, brother, it goes back in a slammer, you known black-assed criminal element you. And in that slammer, brother, you sho' nuff find some known criminal elementaries. They got uniforms on, brother. I mean, right on, brother, right?"

Neither of them were laughing anymore. They just walked a while.

"I know," said Cutter. "How come you know that line?"

"Huh?"

"You been hanging around Kari?"

Willie had dropped all the flourishes now. Even his English was almost standard.

"I tried the movement," he said. "Gung-ho. Right after your trial. And then gung-ho turned to shit. You know about that."

"Karl's been making that plain."

"Even took your name," said Willie. His smile was surprisingly shy. "Remember what the dude in the Pussyfoot called me?"

"Shit head."

"Not that one. The one calling me Kisser. Willie the Kisser. That's all what's left of your name I took."

Cutter did not make the connection. He was tired and the booze in his blood felt like silt moving around.

"You had the name Kisu," said Willie. "And when you checked out, I took it on. Then I checked out and it turned to Kisser."

Kisu was Swahili for knife. Cutter did not want to think about it. He'd been checked out. First by the Man, and now by Asikari himself. There was nothing left but the jealous isolation in Ma Jackson's kitchen, and this clown who had stolen the knife and made an obscenity out of it.

"Let's get another drink," said Cutter.

"Later."

They kept walking in the night wind and Cutter was cold without an overcoat.

"I'm getting bad vibes," said Cutter after a while.

"Bad what?"

"There's two cars that don't fit the neighborhood." They passed the first one by the curb and kept walking toward a second one.

"Hey, nigger!"

They turned around and saw two men get out of the car they had passed.

The men wore the street clothes but they lacked the flash. There was no confidence.

"Who you calling nigger?" said Willie. He made a turn so that his great-coat swirled in a spectacular way. It slapped Cutter around the legs, because Willie was close enough. "You clean?" he said in a con's whisper and watched Cutter nod. "Take it," said Willie, and next Cutter felt the brass knuckles in his palm.

Known criminal elements, he thought. How about the unknown ones—

"Two more dudes from the other car," he said.

"So we gotta work faster—"

"Or run—"

In the middle of his doubt, Cutter felt the envy for Willie's way, the punk who had wanted to take the name Kisu and would then be like Cutter had been. Cutter knew that he was not like that anymore and, knowing that, something drained out of his bones and his legs felt tired.

At that point Willie hopped sideways, which looked slightly silly, but then his leg shot out like a flexible pole, and the nearest punk from the first car had to pull his head back or get it whipped off. Cutter knew the same trick, except he could not do it anymore. Asikari had brought in the small Japanese at great expense and that small man had beat them up for hours until the swagger had been drilled out of them and instead there had been the concentrated precision to kill. Cutter had forgotten and now he could not reinvent it. So he got ready to run.

All this, and Cutter's own decline, lasted no more than two minutes, and then somebody with a powerful whiskey breath said,

"Hey now, that's the Kisser!"

Everybody stopped stalking and tensing. Only the wind seemed to move anymore.

"Doing what? Why you here, Kisser?"

"And with what? Who's the dude from the funeral parlor?"

"You say dud or dude?"

There was some laughing and kidding, but not much.

"I just thought," said Willie, "that Tiffany could use a hand."

"With that along?"

"That," said Willie, "is Cutter."

It produced silence. Cutter felt that it meant, this is what's left of him, this was Cutter at one time—

"Sheez—I hear they had you in the hole for the longest."

Where the good Cutter had finally gone to pieces—

"He's all right," said Willie. "Why you cats hid out in those cars?"

"Tiffany wants to know what's coming and going. He's got two of the charleys inside."

"You jiving me?"

And that, thought Cutter, is in fact a sign of the times: two white hoods knock over a black joint and a fat house-nigger like Tiffany holds these charleys as cool as can be. The Asikari effect. Black is proud and strong, though the new way had turned out ugly....

The four lookouts went back into their cars, and Willie, with Cutter in tow, turned off into an alley, past another man who made a hand-sign from the shadows, and then down the basement steps into the backside of a brick building.

There was a cold furnace in the first enclosure and two more sentries in the way. The Kisser, it seemed, had a lot of weight. The two sentries, thought Cutter, seemed much too nervous.

Tiffany sat in a basement room with the windows boarded and one light bulb hanging down. He was fat and Buddha-bald. He wore a pin-striped business suit, a white shirt, and a black tie with a diamond pin in it. In younger days, he had also worn spats. He sat back in a creaking chair, so as to accommodate the heavy belly that sat on his thighs. His pants were so tight that they made a packed bulge of his genitals along the inside of one leg. Four of his men were standing around. They were the young ones who look tough, careless, and consciously mean, but they were not comfortable. The business at hand was being finished in silence.

Two more blacks were carrying a chair through another door. A white man was held up by the ropes that tied him into his seat, but he was hanging forward, and his head was swinging. When the door was kicked shut, Tiffany said,

"You're next, pinky."

The other one was still alive. He dangled slowly back and forth by one arm with a rope around the wrist. The rope was tied to an open rafter. The hand was bulbous and blue. The free arm, by the looks of the angle, was broken.

"Hi, Kisser," said Tiffany, and then looked back up at the dangling man. He had barely glanced at Cutter. "Best take his pants off now," said Tiffany to one of the men.

While that was going on, Tiffany lit a cigarette. Then he gave it to the man next to him who held it without smoking it down.

"Bless me," said Tiffany. "Ain't you young Cutter?"

Cutter almost said, yes sir, but then he only nodded. Tiffany smiled at him like an uncle.

"Nice to see you back." He seemed to be looking at Cutter's clothes most of the time. "Got a little problem here. You hear about it?"

"He one of them that knocked you over?"

"He is."

The dangling man jerked his beaten head around a few times and said something nobody understood.

"Problem is," said Tiffany, "he don't speak good English."

"He called you a bastard pretty good," said one of the men by the wall.

"Didn't," said Tiffany. "He didn't call me 'bastid,' he called it 'boss-tardy.' Now that, by my knowledge, is I-talian."

"That all you got out of him?" asked Cutter.

"So far."

Cutter thought it was a bad scene. Two obvious cars in a street that seemed obviously cleared. One entrance and one exit, maybe. Two white hoods who had been mauled in such an obvious way that they could not talk even if they wished to talk. Tiffany and his men were playing cops and robbers. Or they were playing underground games, the theatrics of liberation. Asikari used to say—Fuck what Asikari used to say.

The black who was trying to get the pants off the dangling man was having some trouble. The limp man swung too much and the shoes were too big. Once the man retched and something greenish oozed down his front.

"What's it like being out?" asked Tiffany and smiled his Buddha-smile at Cutter.

"Like wow," said the Kisser and giggled.

"A little strange," said Cutter.

"Got plans?" said Tiffany.

Cutter shrugged. No plans anymore.

"Get a job, I guess. Something nine-to-five."

"Good thinking. Keep your nose clean for a while," said Tiffany. He glanced at the swinging man and then back at Cutter. "If I can help—"

"That's all right."

"They're hiring freight-handlers. They ain't union."

"Maybe. I was thinking Tri-State Trucking, maybe—"

Cutter stopped when he saw Tiffany's mouth become thin.

"Shit-for-brains Perrini!" said Willie the Kisser. There was a lot of venom behind it. When Tiffany finally said something, it sounded as thin and mean as his mouth had started to look.

"After tonight," he said, "Perrini is trouble."

He looked at the swinging man, who had started to groan. The man's shoes were off now and the pants too. Tiffany did not explain any further. He hitched around in his chair and nodded at the man who was holding the cigarette.

"First show it to him," said Tiffany. "And then cool and easy, Bo. This ain't for fun. This is business."

The dangling man stared ahead of him, but there was no way of telling if he saw anything. When it was clear that he did not see the cigarette that

Bo was moving back and forth in front of his face, Bo stuck it up the man's nose. The man's head snapped back and his legs started thrashing.

"Take it out," said Tiffany.

"The coal came off in there," said Bo.

"You black-ass bastid, I told you—"

Tiffany did not get any further. The door in back of Tiffany flung open and the man from the alley came in.

"Fuzz!" he said. "Got all four cats in a car and is heading this way—"

Tiffany was very good and did it all without talking. He jerked his head at the dangling man, who was hacked down with a spring knife. While they dragged him out of the other door Tiffany snapped his fingers, and two men helped him out of the chair. When he stood free he reached into his pocket and dropped a pair of dice on the floor. Three men got to their knees and strewed paper money around.

Cutter saw all that, understood all that, but could do nothing with it. He only knew that he was leaning against a cement wall with rough bumps digging into his back, that he could hardly see, because something like mustard fog moved over his eyes. He knew he might faint. He knew that he was all hollowed out with nothing but black air wafting and waving around his insides. An intense shame came over him. He lowered his head into the fog and covered his face with his hands.

"—and what's that crap on the floor?"

"That's the name of the game, officer sir."

"I don't mean that. That green crap is what I mean."

"That ain't crap, that's puke, sir."

It was a proper raid. Nobody got brutalized on account of resisting arrest, and nobody got away. Maybe the two who had moved the corpse in the chair and the one who had dragged the broken man out of that other door, maybe they had gotten away. Cutter could not be sure. At any rate, there was no talk about corpses or broken men and the ride to the station was short and took place in a proper paddy wagon. Cutter did not really feel clear and alert in the head until he sat in the station tank.

Willie the Kisser was there and some of the other men. Tiffany was not there.

"Smoke?" said Willie. He held out his pack.

Cutter shook his head. His head was clear and his body was cold. It was an inside coldness which always came together with a deeper and more ghastly feeling.

It was as if he were not only surrounded by a bleak, empty desert, but as if such a forbidding expanse was also inside of him. This hostile land was now inside and out. And since it stretched in all those ways, where was he? At that point came the terror.

"Hey—Cutter baby—" Willie was next to him now. "Easy, man. You're not back in the hole."

Cutter heard the voice and that was better than to be nothing at all in an unchanging wasteland. Now there was a voice in it.

"I know it's a bitch," whispered Willie. "Fresh from the slammer, I'd be strung out, too."

Before the fine tremor in his flesh could settle in and become the shakes, Cutter gave Willie a slap on the leg and got up. He went to the tank door and stuck his face between the bars.

"Turnkey! Officer?" He called with a steady tone, careful not to raise his voice.

He heard a chair scrape, out of sight, and then the footsteps. The policeman had his shirtsleeves rolled up and wore glasses.

"I didn't get to make my call," said Cutter. "Can I make my call?"

There was no problem. Cutter had to give his name, wait a short while, and then was let out of the tank. He was given a dime out of the envelope that held his pocket possessions, and then he was shown to the phone. When he stood in the niche where the pay phone hung on the wall, he had to breathe slowly a few times to keep the small tremor small and not let it turn into the shakes. Then he put in his dime and dialed the number.

It rang ten times, while Cutter rubbed the palm of one hand over the cement of the wall. It produced a deliberate pain that kept him concentrated on pain. That was better than attending to the feeling that his insides were floating away again. He almost hung up when the precise voice came into his ear.

"Yes?"

"Gawdamighty—" said Cutter. "You're there. Thanks, Kari, you're there."

"Is that you, Cutter?"

"Asikari, listen. I got busted. I got busted for nothing. You gotta come down. Two Cee notes bail money, Kari, you hear?"

"Where are you?"

"Precinct. Two Cee ..."

"You and Willie went to see Tiffany?"

"Jeesis, Kari, I'm freaking out! Let's talk later!"

There was a pause at the other end while Cutter looked at the palm of his hand. He looked very calm, seen from a distance. He looked at the raw spots and the small ooze of blood, but felt very distant about the view. He stood there looking at a hand, not his hand necessarily, a hand that might be lying on the floor in front of him and that view might not have made him feel any different about it. The thought barely touched him with any meaning. The desert feeling came back; he himself thinned out while the desert spread and grew.

"Kari?"

There was no answer, though Cutter could hear the voice of his friend talking distantly. "Nothing, Mother. I'm all right.—Yes, I'll bring it to you—"

"Kari? Kari!"

When the officer heard Cutter shouting he came over to the niche and tapped the prisoner on the shoulder. "Okay. Time's up."

"Ina sec, man, gimme a chance—"

"Snap it up."

"Yessir—Kari?!"

"I'm here."

"Please, man. Get me out!"

"Cutter, we've gone through this before. If there is ever going to be a future for us as a movement, we must start clean. How can you, I mean, how can you, in your present situation, ask me ..."

"For godsake, man, don't jive me now with that shit. I'm asking you, Rafer Jackson, *you*, to gimme a hand!"

"I have got to stay clear of you and you have got to stay clear of me."

"Please—"

The phone clicked.

With that click the change started, though it did not show immediately on the outside. Cutter looked the same and he still said yessir when the police officer took him back to the tank. But he no longer felt like a paper divide between the empty space inside and the wasteland without. He did not even think about it. He felt himself move when he walked and he felt himself sit when he sat on the cot. His heart pumped quietly. He could feel that.

Two hours later, Cutter walked out and down the bare street. Tiffany had paid the bail.

CHAPTER 8

Magdalena Perrini was always the first one up in the morning. She rose in the winter darkness of six a.m., went to the bathroom wishing devoutly that the evening's laxative potion might perform as the label said, and would then sit there for a while. Next, she went back to her room, prayed twice around her rosary, and changed from nightdress to daytime apparel. Then she stripped the bed to throw the used linen in a pile near the door. The underwear of the previous day was added to the linen heap. She went back to the bathroom and washed her face and hands with cold water. After taking her dentures from a glass and sucking them into place, she started to brush her hair. It was magnificent hair and the combing took by far the longest time of all the morning ablutions. Feeling clean and organized, she then made the rounds of the house. It was like a necessary act of repossession.

Magdalena Perrini looked into her daughter's room and noted first that the window was closed. There was an unpleasant odor of night sleep in the air. The musk repelled her. Her daughter lay indistinguishable in the lumped bedding. Her pillow was on the floor. A nightmare? She would have to speak to Rosanna about order again.

She walked back to the other end of the house and looked into her husband's room. He slept on his back, making as always those revolting noises. She went quietly to the dresser, where the cognac bottle and the glass were resting. The glass was sticky. She lifted the bottle up and looked for her secret mark. It was there, much higher above the level of cognac than it ought to be. She carried the bottle to the bathroom, ran a thin stream of water into the neck, wiped spillage, corked opening, and put the bottle back.

Having certain rights in her own house, she then went back to the other wing and stopped at the door of her guest. Just as she was about to push down on the handle, she heard his voice inside. Her sense of the proper and her instincts of a mother produced chaos for a moment, while she struggled to decide whether to burst through the door or to rush back to her daughter's room and see if that spineless girl was still there. But then she heard the tones of a man who was unmistakably talking on the telephone. The dear young man, up so early and attending to business. She went quickly back down the hall to the little stand where the upstairs telephone stood. And yet a guest has a right to his privacy, she decided, and so walked past the phone and downstairs for the rest of her rounds.

Angelo sat on the bed and finished his call. He had talked to Buffalo. The next phone call was to be a Bethelport number. Then he put on yesterday's clothes, went to the bathroom, looked at his teeth. He spat into the sink and then he combed his hair. It took by far the longest time of his morning ablutions. On his way downstairs, he passed Rosanna's door and grinned at it. His nights were taken care of for the rest of the Bethelport matter. Now he would start a busy day.

It took Perrini the longest to get started. He was the oldest in the house, and the shadow of problems moving through his mind kept him bogged in half-sleep for an unhealthy length of time. When he came down to the hall, the old houseman was ready for him with the pot of espresso.

Perrini was in the habit of taking his coffee at a small table by a potted palm in the large, central hall. He could sit there with the sense of comfort and impersonality that one found in a sidewalk cafe.

There was no such place in Bethelport, but Perrini knew the feeling. What he did not know about his coffee habit was the faint sense of escape it gave him, the sense of having a front door nearby and not being captured by the custom of breakfast room, kitchen table, gentleman's den, or any of those usual ways of starting a morning in the clutches of one's own family. The idea was so odd that he could not really let himself know about it. He sat down while the houseman poured the coffee. There were also two telephone messages.

One was from Becky in the Tri-State office. The other was from Menotti.

"Call Becky and tell her to handle everything and write down, if she wants me to know something special," he said to the houseman. "Use the phone in the den."

"*Subito*," said the old man.

"And plug the hall phone in over here."

Perrini sat sipping espresso and imagined a view across a *piazza* with people walking in a leisurely way. It would be siesta, let us say, two in the afternoon, and he, Perrini, would have a small tobacco shop across the way, where he sold cigarettes, bulk tobacco, postage stamps, and perhaps lottery tickets. The store, at the time, would be closed. It would not open again until the cool of the evening, at five or six, let us say—

"Menotti? Don't you sleep? You didn't leave here until—"

"There was no time. Anyway, if you're calling about Tiffany, I can't reach him."

"He's got three phones!"

"He isn't at any of them. The reason I left word, it seems Tiffany got into a mess of trouble."

"Payoff. Whatever it was."

"Let me finish. An anonymous call to the precinct sent the bulls straight to Tiffany in some basement. The call said he was holding two whites in order to question them about that raiding party."

"*Cazzo!*"

"Please. The whites were not there, which is unfortunate. Their apprehension could have established their identity and their absence could mean that they are dead."

"Get Tiffany!"

"*Padrone*, I told you already."

"You know what that means if they're dead? On top of that fat man not coming to the phone? He killed 'em and thinks *I* sent them!"

"Er, yes. In addition, the ramifications in the total picture, I'm afraid, what I mean is, in view of the Buffalo visitor ..."

"Fine, Menotti, very good. Thank you again," and Perrini hung up.

He leaned back in his chair and smiled at Angelo Forza. Angelo Forza smiled back at him.

"What a nice idea," he said. "I am reminded of a cafe on a *piazza*. Good morning, *signore*."

"Yeah. Fine. You want coffee?"

"Thank you. I already ate in the kitchen. Your lovely wife."

"Yeah. Sit down, sit down."

"Ah! You have considered everything, I can tell. And you have come to the same conclusion as the Don, my Uncle Santino."

"As the Don, your Uncle Santino." The repetition gave Perrini the pause he needed in order to control himself. All that time he maintained his smile. "On the other hand, there are a few things you do not understand."

"Really?" Angelo was smiling too.

Perrini would not have become the *caporegime* he was if he had not known how to handle an underling. He would now handle this underling and that other one, that fat toad, he would handle him too.

"Get your coat," he said. "I will show you about conclusions."

This time Perrini took two cars. There was himself and the underling Angelo in the Eldorado, not counting the driver, and there was a nondescript Ford, full of serious men. He himself neither wore the big-carat ring nor the fur-lined marshal's mantle. Angelo, partway down to Buckingham Boulevard, put his blue glasses on.

The Belt started with peeling frame houses and gradually changed to old red brick or new cinderblock. The stories increased from one to four.

"This is where you have the trouble?" said Angelo. "This is like the block Uncle Santino has."

Perrini did not have to hold his smile for very long. The car entered Buckingham Boulevard and there was a problem immediately.

The Boulevard, at ten o'clock in the morning, was not its typical self. There were housewives going to grocery stores or to laundromats, and they had their small children hanging close by. The boulevard was not ready for much more business. Except for the silent hangover trade in the bars, the men were either at work in the factory section or asleep because their day did not start until later. There was a thin winter sun and a kind of suburban desolation to everything. And then Perrini lost his escort, which was his muscle.

The operation was crude. A stake truck pulled away from the curb and squeezed into the side of the Ford. Next, it crippled the Ford by hauling around and presenting its broadside. The truck allowed the passenger car to squeeze its low hood under the high bed of the truck. That took care of auto mobility. Next, something to take care of the five button men inside the car. Before these men could open the doors and get out, the near side panel of the rickety truck gave way in some fashion, which released the old iron and other junk from the truck, so that the noisy avalanche jumped, bounced, and clanked all over the Ford. For a reasonable length of time, nobody was going to get out of that passenger car.

What Perrini knew first was the racket, maybe old-fashioned machine-gun fire. One look back, and he knew that his escort was gone without a shot having been fired.

"Get the hell outa here," he yelled at his driver.

It was an odd time for demonstrations with lecture, but Perrini relieved himself partially by explaining to Angelo that this was the Black Belt he had been talking about, and that this was the kind of trouble he had mentioned before.

"I can't," said the driver.

"Can't what?!"

"Get outa here."

"I think," said Angelo, "they are saying something to you."

The car in front of Perrini's Cadillac would not get out of the way. The car next to Perrini's Cadillac seemed to be full of black faces, smiling faces, and the man in the nearest window was waving his yellow applejack cap.

"Come along now, Preach. We's the new escort!"

In a moment, Perrini nodded his head, told his driver to follow, and sat back in his seat. Ten minutes later, they arrived at the Recreation Palace and Fun Arcade, which was Tiffany's place and precisely the destination they had been heading for anyway.

The man with the yellow applejack opened the door for Perrini.

"You can come out now, Preach." Perrini started to say something but the black at the car door was nonchalant about it. "Yeah, yeah. Bring the kid with the cheaters too." He grinned at Angelo and clucked his tongue. "Two shiners! Man! Musta been some pussycat. You grease-balls sure got your way with the ladies." Then he laughed hard.

Angelo understood enough of the slang and the laugh to have his dominant reaction. He was insulted. He got out of the car and started to curse in rapid Sicilian until Perrini grabbed him by the arm and yanked him to the double doors of Tiffany's place.

"*Cretino*," he said very quietly. "Learn something. Leave the grandstand play to the suckers. Understand, sucker?"

The place was like a barn inside, bare wood on the walls, and no ornamentation. The arcade part was partitioned off, so that the underaged could play the pinball machines within the law. There was a good deal of clicking and bouncing noise, in spite of the fact that it was still school time. The other sound was the whisper and scrape of a broom. The old man who was sweeping between the rows of pool tables kept up a stubborn rhythm.

A man leaned by one baize table, his cue stick in front of him, like a bored sentry supporting himself by his lance.

"You can go right up the upstairs."

"I know where it is," said Perrini.

Upstairs had the look of a loft, but there were card tables with dead lamps overhead and a row of crap tables. The air held the cold stink of yesterday's tobacco smoke. One gray window pane in the roof, one immobile shaft of gray light.

"I'm this way," said Tiffany.

He sat on a chair which was only good enough for half of his bulk. He leaned sideways, one arm lying along the rim of a crap table. The shaft of light from the roof touched only his hand. It lay palm up and held two dice. Tiffany's finger motions rolled the dice around in the palm, producing a soft little clicking sound.

"Who else is here?" said Perrini, who could feel that they were not alone in the room but could not see very clearly.

"No-counts," said Tiffany. "Who's the kid?"

"He's not my kid. An associate."

Angelo bumped into a chair.

"Maybe if you take the glasses off, boy, maybe you'll see the furniture," said Tiffany.

His Buddha-face did not change. His little eyes kept moving about like mice in a secret corner, but they said nothing to Perrini, they certainly said nothing as clearly as the tone of Tiffany's voice. No con-man seductions, no hustler pressures, no touch of the Uncle Tom sucking for favors. Tiffany had summoned. He sat squeezed by his fat and pinched by his clothes, but he sat enthroned.

"No mouthpiece?" he said to Perrini.

"Menotti is busy with something important."

The remark made no dent.

"Now look, boy," said Tiffany, "you near put your foot in my spittoon."

Angelo took his glasses off just in time to see something wet and brown go *splat* in the brass spittoon at his feet.

"Why, that was nimble," said Tiffany. "And you got no shiner at all. What is it, boy, pinkeye?"

"All right," said Perrini. "You can cut out the horseplay, Tiffany."

"Hum?"

"First you don't answer my calls, then that crap with the cars like some kind of a gangster movie, and now the grandstand business with your goddamn spittoon. Come on, Tiffany, we done business before. Let's get to it."

"Go ahead," said Tiffany. "You're the one what's anxious."

Perrini could see better now. He could see two men at one end of the dark card tables, and he could see another who was wearing some kind of dark suit that did not fit him too well. He sat on the other side of Tiffany's crap-shooting table and had his chin in one hand. The card-players were not playing cards, and the one in the dark suit was not doing anything either. Then the one with the applejack came up from downstairs. He went over to Tiffany and whispered something in his ear. Tiffany listened and then he just grunted. He waved the man aside and spat again. This time the brown thing hit Angelo squarely on one pointy, three-toned Sicilian shoe.

"Ain't you gonna say something, boy?"

But Angelo had only jerked back. Perrini thought that the *cretino* displayed either the most judicious self-control or was simply afraid. For a moment, Tiffany made only that soft sound with the dice in his hand.

"Well," he said in a while, "it don't matter none. Beany here tells me what you sound like anyways." Tiffany, without noticeably changing the cast of his face, looked suddenly vicious. He looked at Perrini now. "Your boy here," he said, "does talk exactly like them white cats that's been troubling us here in the Belt. Now ain't that something, Preach?"

Instead of cursing, Perrini exhaled with a sound, as if the lungs might come up. He wiped his face with one hand for a while. When he was done, he seemed to have gained a good deal of composure. Then he talked.

"Somebody's been muscling in on you ..."

"Tried, Preach. You tried."

"... and it wasn't me."

"Won't be you, Preach."

"Just shut up a minute, Tiffany. Because the reason I'm here is to tell you this. If you want any backing from me, I gotta know whom we're bucking up against. Where are the two punks you had in a basement last night?"

"At the Lake Smelting Company, Inc., Preach. In a furnace."

"—*Cazzo*—"

"Izzatso?"

The two men at the card table and the one with the applejack on his head laughed.

"Shet your mouths and git!" yelled Tiffany. The one at the crap table got up too. "You stay, Cutter," said Tiffany.

Perrini waited while Tiffany's hired hands clomped down the stairs and while his protégé sat down at the table again. Perrini had his problem of telling one abstract black from another, but he did recognize well enough the handful with whom he had dealings. He wondered if he had seen this one before, but could not be sure. Not with Tiffany, anyway, nor in any other way of business. Then why did this one hang around? Quiet, intelligent, not so quiet inside, perhaps. That godawful suit—*Ecco!* Prison issue!

Perrini smiled and hid it. This con was fresh out of prison, and Tiffany had picked up on the punk. Not punk. This one was a street black for sure, but not punk. Had picked up on something fresh, someone with something special—*Caporegime* Perrini knew the skills of picking up talent. This one either had brains, or Tiffany simply had something on this man. *Dunque*, a parole-breaker, perhaps, and of a special talent. Desperation plus talent, an enviable find, thought Perrini.

"Who's your special?" asked Perrini and gave a friendly nod in Cutter's direction.

"That's …"

"I'm his cousin," said Cutter.

Perrini smiled openly now. Quick as a whip, that one, and already correcting his benefactor. Perrini decided to move right in.

"Well, now, between the two of you, and me begging you to give it a new look, what in hell do you think is in it for me to send a bunch of clumsy clowns into your territory so that you and I get so shook up we're almost a little bit at each other's throats over this?"

Tiffany tossed one of the dice up in the air and caught it again. He smiled briefly.

"Sweet sounds. Menotti would be proud of you. Now try again."

"Sure. And what in hell is in it for you to try and push me around?"

This time Tiffany did not smile. He said,

"Watch your mouth, Preach. I don't want nothing from you. It's you wants something from me."

Perrini closed his eyes and hoped that his face held the emergency ration of beatitude.

"You push me," he said quietly, "so hard." Then he snapped his eyes open quickly because the next voice was Cutter's.

"Mister Perrini, even with all the strain and all, I think Mister Tiffany wants to negotiate. It hasn't been easy."

"No way!" said Tiffany. He dropped one of the dice.

It was clear to Perrini that this was not a maneuver, that the cousin and Tiffany had their signals crossed. Perrini jumped in.

"Go and push me," he said, "and I'll just move out."

"Now you're hearing it, Preach, now you got the message."

"Black Belt's penny ante stuff, Tiffany. You know the figures!"

"I ain't greedy, Preach. I'll pick up the leavings."

It had all been normal negotiation and now came the pivot point. After that, Perrini thought, they would start talking money.

"What leavings, Tiffany? What you and me have been picking up, even that penny ante stuff, it's taken grease! And what do you think you'll be picking up, fat man, if I stop paying grease?"

"With you outa the Belt, Preach, and with most cops on the beat being brothers, I don't *need* no grease!"

Perrini noticed that the cousin looked startled.

"I don't care what color the fuzz is wearing," Perrini shouted for the proper drama, "because every cop in this kinda neighborhood is a take-off cop, and you know it! Right, cousin?" he added in Cutter's direction.

Cutter said nothing, but he slowly took his arms off the table and let his shoulders hang. He looked once at Tiffany and then dropped his eyes.

Cutter's silence gave Tiffany no support, and none of the day's insults and indignities to a big-shot like the Preacher had weakened that man. There still was no deal a black businessman could be proud of. And what if the Preacher pulled out? Tiffany, by some mischance of the hand, dropped the other dice.

"Preach," he said, "I ain't alone in this business. I can't just up and kiss off my losses, my men what got mauled, my place what got wrecked, my records missing, my good rep with the customers." Tiffany sighed, not needing the extra air. "Preach," he said. "The way it looks to the brothers, you got me in bad."

Perrini relaxed. A close shave, but the worst was over. Menotti would in fact be proud of him. Perrini was also mindful of the fact that the other man, the strange cousin, had quite subtly helped turn the tide for him. And now the good old preacher smile so the fox-brain could work without interference. But the calculated mood had not quite taken hold yet. Angelo opened his mouth for the first time.

"*Signore*," he said to Perrini, and there was an intense sound of concern in his voice. "Do not forget yourself! This fat liar has killed two of your men! This fat liar has hidden his own records in order to cheat you of—"

"*Cornuto disgraziato*, will you shut the asshole in your face which you use like a mouth!" Perrini screamed in his most fundamental Sicilian.

Cutter did not move, except to put one fist into the palm of the other hand, slowly. But Tiffany did not see this act of control. He jumped up from his chair, as if he had no weight at all. His dark face looked mottled.

"Get out!" he said to Perrini, and as he talked his voice became higher and louder. "And take your sweet-talk and your grease and my friend that little bigmouth right outa my place and right outa my Belt. *My* Belt, Perrini, and don't you *never* come back! Beany!" he yelled at the stairs where all kinds of shoes were already clattering up. "Take this ofay bigshot outa the Belt and right past the Lake Smelting Company! The look-see at them dirty smoking stacks might freshen the Preacher's brains back to his senses!"

In a while there was silence again, except for Tiffany's chair, which was creaking. Cutter came around the table and picked the two dice off the floor. He cupped them and, without the conventional shake, tossed them down the table. They came up eleven.

"What they say?" asked Tiffany without turning his head.

"Never mind." Cutter walked into the gloom of the loft and then came back slowly. "That was a bad scene, Tiffany."

"Cheeze. I near blew it."

"You don't get it, Tiffany. You in fact blew it."

Tiffany answered with just that brief, vicious look he could always muster when at the end of his rope. Cutter ignored it and went on.

"No more juice, no more lay-off money. Every take-off artist on the street with his hand out, palm up. And in a while, when you can't give service anymore, there's gonna be, what we call in political science, that power vacuum, if you get what I mean."

"Now you hear me good, you college nigger. Maybe the hole's got your brains turned to cement, but by luck you didn't forget it all: We got muscle here in the Belt. And the pride. You and that Swahili swami of yours, you did talk up a storm, case you don't remember."

Cutter turned away and put his hands in his pockets. He had hooked up with a windbag, a fat man with the Charley fever. Preach Tiffany, instead of Preach Perrini.

"And while I'm on the subject, boy, I did stick my neck out for you last night or this morning, in case you disremember. And put you in here because you had a way once, talking it up with those honks that came up against you and that movement."

"That was different," said Cutter to the dark end of the loft.

"Sheeyat."

"They were afraid. Perrini isn't."

"Nigger, you got shit for brains?"

"Perrini doesn't care if you're red, white, black, or blue. No fear coming from there, like with that sly bastard he had along. Perrini doesn't care how he looks when he cops that long dough. That's all, no flash, just money."

"Now he ain't got neither," said Tiffany and got up. By the sound of it, he had just declared that he had both. "Get some sleep," he said to Cutter. "Be back here in the evening."

"You know where Lillie is?"

Tiffany groaned. It was not clear whether his feet had produced the sound or whether it had been Cutter's question.

"Whyn't you ask that pimp Willie. Besides, baby, don't you know she's bound to be five years older?"

Cutter knew that. He also felt that there ought to be something that had been there before, something he could come back to.

CHAPTER 9

"And you know what else that son of a bitch said? He said he called Buffalo from my house this morning—from *my* house—and got permission from Uncle Santino to stay a while and give me a hand with my problems!"

Perrini moved the mouthpiece aside so that he could use the paper cup with the cognac in it. He stared out at the dirty snow in the trucking yard below his office but did not see a thing. He was in shirt sleeves. The windbreaker he wore in his office still hung in the closet. He had forgotten about it.

"That's what he said. And he's staying in *my* house, like I'm sleeping with a snake at my bosom."

"I appreciate that," said Menotti. "Let me check on that call. Just hold on, Francisco."

Perrini put the paper cup down and riffled the chits which Becky had left on his spindle. His wife had called, Campi had called, Silverstein—

"I'm back, Francisco."

"Find out something already?"

"Of course not. I'm having the office get in touch with the contact at the central right now."

"Okay. Then, before that son of a bitch takes off in a taxi—he's gotta buy a change of clothes, you understand, *pyjamas* and—"

"Francisco, I fully appreciate how you feel, but would you give me a chance to get a few things clear. What seems to—"

"Sure, let's talk. That's why I called you."

"What seems to look like a really boneheaded interruption, Francisco, seems possibly just a little too boneheaded, even for an ass like Angelo Forza."

For a second, the mention of that name refreshed the full flower of Perrini's agitation, but then it collapsed as suddenly. Perrini the *capo* said,

"*Consigliere*, I am listening."

"Would you recall what went on before Forza made his remark."

"Lemme think, lemme get this now—Tiffany changed his tone, I got it in my ear, he dropped the hard sell and I could hear the whine—"

"He's coming around?"

"And right! Christ, Menotti, I knew it then but I forget when I get excited."

Which is why I get paid, thought Menotti.

"Changed his tune," Perrini went on, "when I said something about pulling out my protection. Next, we're of course ready to deal."

"And next."

"*Ecco*. Now the son of a bitch nephew from Buffalo tells Tiffany my men have been drawing blood down there. Imagine!"

"I am also imagining that with that assumption in mind, Tiffany is going to worry about your doing something about the two men he killed. You follow, Francisco? The Belt's going to tighten up."

"Yes. We don't need to discuss it. Santino sends me a boy to wreck me in Black Belt. And it worked."

"One moment, Francisco."

He waited in a mood of respectful gloom. That dinosaur with the antique ideas about blood-bonds and the family had shown his mettle. If Perrini wants to work in close touch with the blacks, then he sees to it that no black will touch Perrini. *Basta*.

"Francisco?"

"Here."

"The data from the telephone company came in."

Perrini was not as interested in verifications as his lawyer was. He was already thinking about something else, something to do with dinosaurs sinking into the slime of their grave, and what would be in store for those who stayed behind—"The call to Buffalo went to one of the family members. *Garment and Linen Supply*. That's the one they use when a confidential report ..."

"I know, I know."

"He talked for thirty-nine minutes."

"So what?"

"It seems long. Anyway. Did Angelo tell you he made two calls this morning?"

"Menotti. Just tell it."

"The second call, after the clearly conference-length discussion with Buffalo, was to a Bethelport number."

During the next silence they thought by themselves, separately and severally. Menotti picked up the thread. "I did not know that Angelo Forza came here knowing anyone at all."

"I follow," said Perrini.

"That is to say, he came with some manner of foreknowledge."

"Maybe he didn't," said Perrini. "Maybe something broke while he was here. Lemme think, lemme think—"

"Go on, Francisco."

"*Ecco*." Perrini paused to look at the bottle of cognac but did nothing about it. He said, "I opened my big mouth and told you, in front of him, that Tiffany's place had been knocked over. Remember? At my house?"

"Yes. Apparently, the news was unexpected to all of us."

"That's when he decided to stay. How's it sound, Menotti?"

"I agree, it makes sense."

"And the number he called, the one here in town?"

"That," said Menotti, "makes no sense at all. It's a telephone booth."

Angelo Forza's problems were the sort with which he would cheerfully fill his days. He now had the time—a few hours, at any rate—to indulge in the solving of problems he created himself. The beige-and-brown double knit, or the gray suit with vest? (Perrini wore pearl-gray ties. That color was out of the question.) The peach-colored shirts and the blue-and-white stripes? (Or all of them peach! Another trademark might be in order.) Shoes? Of course, shoes. The Sicilian treats the selection of shoes the way an American chooses a car. The choice has recognition value and establishes status. ("I'm sorry, sir," said the clerk with ice in his voice. "Perhaps you might try one of the stores on Buckingham Boulevard.") Now the pyjamas. *Quanto ben di Dio!* What gorgeous profusion. And finally the car. Buy or rent? He rented a Stingray Corvette, because buying involved too much paperwork. The disadvantage of renting was the limited color-choice. He had to take a pearl-gray model.

But Angelo Forza was in his Saturday-afternoon mood. This is the mood of the end of the day as well as the end of the week, and next would come Sunday. In Sicily, one washed and got dressed in the once-a-week clothes, because in the late summer light of the day one went for the promenade, round and round on the *piazza.*

The winter light of midday seemed dark already, the lake wind gnawed through the clothes. It was neither Saturday, nor was there a place for a promenade in Bethelport on Lake Erie. However, Angelo felt his Saturday-afternoon feeling.

With the help of a city map, he negotiated from downtown back toward the Black Belt. Where the factory section separated the Belt from the city, he turned toward the river and parked in a city area that had retained the cramped, red-brick quality of an industrial city at the turn of the century. The street facades seemed webbed with fire escapes. Some streets still had telegraph poles, so that the canyon view of the sky was cut up by black wires. There were no supermarkets but instead butchers, groceries, and old-style delicatessens. Because of Bethelport's cramped geography, the names on the storefronts were variously Polish, Italian, and Czech.

Angelo parked in the lot of a filling station. Next to the office of the station was a telephone booth. Angelo searched his pocket, looked at the booth, then went into the office, where an electric heater made one shaft of heat.

"Can you change a fifty?" he asked the attendant.

"I'll call the boss."

The boss did not change the fifty either. He told Angelo to walk around the parked cars and into the building where the storefront sign said Polish Neighborhood Social Club.

The storefront was full of card tables. The silent men with their gnarled hands who sat at those tables all wore hats. They were peasants in city disguise. In the back room, the plaster was peeling and the only outdoor light came from a window that looked into an airshaft. But there was a bright print of a very pink Jesus child on the wall. The heavens behind the fat child were intensely blue, and the radiant heart in the middle of the baby's belly was intensely red. It was a manner of peasant art that had been adapted to the calendar medium. The print advertised Motta, an ice-cream firm.

Angelo stood in this gloom with the marzipan print on the wall and felt at home. He sat down at the single round table and snapped on the bulb that hung naked from its wire.

Angelo sat and smiled. The man who came in smiled too. He seemed related to every peasant who sat in the front, except that he was younger. But he had the same classic traits that seemed breed-determined: basically, a head, face, and body that looked made of bone, covered with thick, lumpy skin. But there was life in the little black eyes. They were separated by a high bridge of nose and seemed to wish to get a glimpse of each other. The hair of the head grew as dense as the nap on a rug, and the smile was traditional. Once established on the face, it did not move. Angelo saw all this and felt at home.

"*Benvenuto,*" said the man.

"*Grazie. Mi chiamo Angelo.*"

"*Conosco. Mi chiamo Pepe.*"

After the introductory exchange there was a brief silence, fixed with smiles. Pepe rubbed his hands up and down the sides of his suit. This dark suit was durably made, perhaps by his mother, because it seemed unlikely to Angelo that there would be another one like it anywhere in Bethelport. Even in Sicily he had rarely seen anything like it. When they talked again it was in their version of Italian.

"What a beautiful shirt," said Pepe. "Is it pink?"

"No. Peach. You have a fine suit there."

"Very. It has lasted all through my father. My grandmother made it. But your shoes! All those different leathers!"

"You can get them here in the United States. Different suits too. I will arrange it. Now that we begin to work in earnest, we must disguise, I mean blend ourselves."

"Like you?"

"Of course. But you have a beautiful place here. Why does the sign say

Polish?"

"It does?"

"Yes."

"Ask Tratto. He bought it from the ones who moved out. With all the furniture."

"Excellent. Where is this Tratto?"

"Ah, my slowness! I will bring him, and the wine too," and Pepe left.

If Pepe were to be called the basic model, then Tratto would be the luxury line. He showed this difference as soon as he came into the room. He was swifter, more finely boned, and his eyes were able to hold one steady focus much longer. He wore American clothes and spoke English. The three men sat down together at the table, with three glasses and a bottle of red wine between them.

"I had no idea you would show yourself here, or so soon," said Tratto.

"I didn't either," said Angelo. "I came for one day, to take a look, to check the *capo's* mood, to ask you how things were going. But then, you did not follow the plan."

Tratto shrugged and poured wine before he responded.

"When on the hunt," he said, "you don't know the details ahead of time. You move as the game moves. You shoot when you must."

"Good illustration, Tratto." Angelo sipped the cheap wine. "What do you mean?"

"Why? Is Don Santino angry?"

"Of course not. But I'm here to coordinate."

"And we are grateful, very grateful. To have this opportunity, in this land, to build a career in the benevolent family of Don Santino."

"And free passage to come here," said Pepe.

Tratto shut him up with a look and Angelo shut up Tratto with a look of his own.

"You did fine," he said. "You got settled in the right neighborhood, and you did all the little things to make Perrini look bad in the Belt. You just moved a little fast. I didn't know you had planned to knock over that Tiffany place already."

"Opportunity!" said Tratto. "It was not planned. Like on a hunt, you don't know."

"Forget that."

"Why? Is something wrong?"

"There was, but I fixed it. The problem was not a simple one, but I fixed it."

"But there is something wrong, Angelo?"

"You lost two men. We only imported fifteen of you, and already two are lost."

"Rudolfo and Como? They're not back, but what do you mean lost?"

"I mean dead. The fat bastard killed them."

Pepe rose slowly from his chair, then lowered himself just as slowly.

"Rudolfo—" he said. "My sweet brother Rudolfo—" and then, with a colossal eruption of the voice, "That black swine killed my brother?!"

The other two took it in their stride. They sat back in their chairs to watch Pepe rave for a moment, and then they leaned on the table again. Pepe had folded over, head on his arms, and was crying bitterly. Tratto patted him on the back of the head and then turned to Angelo.

"Don't worry. He does what I say. He is very good with his hands, you know. But I am sorry about the rest."

"Meanwhile, you have the fat man's records?"

"Yes!"

"Good. But no more of your moving around like you're on that hunt you keep mentioning. I'm staying and will let you know. In fact, I'm staying at Perrini's house."

Tratto, as was expected of him, gleamed with admiration. The gleam included envy as well, but that, too, was expected.

"Have you met his daughter?" asked Tratto. "This is the one problem we have here, being new ..."

"Have I *met* his daughter?" Angelo laughed like a conqueror. Even Pepe, his eyes welling with tears, looked around for a moment. "I have moved into a room con *riscaldamento!*" and he laughed again.

The expression was Sicilian, with the usual double meaning. On one hand, it was the phrase used to rent a hotel room that was heated. When requested out of the other side of the mouth, it meant that the room clerk should send up a woman.

It was nice to sit there at the table and talk to someone who understood the niceties of the mother tongue. But it was best not to become too familiar. Here was the nephew of Don Santino. Here was Angelo, grooming, soaring, reshaping a territory. None of this would stop with a slum called the Black Belt. This better stop now, thought Angelo. The time will come. When on the hunt— He put his wine glass down, empty.

"*Basta*," he said and got up. "I'll call in the arranged manner, at that station. The money is on its way. And then we will move to the next stage."

He cut the good-byes short and left. He did not like the greed in Tratto, and he was disturbed by the faith in Pepe. But, when on the hunt, you work with what presents itself. Angelo grinned, thinking about his room *con riscaldamento*.

CHAPTER 10

Cutter walked to the house on Twenty-second Street where Tiffany had told him he could get some sleep. Cutter remembered the address from the time when the old widow Armstrong had owned the white clapboard bungalow with the gingerbread porch and the hanging ferns in the window. Cutter had been one of her boarders and Ma Jackson had been her lady friend. Now the old woman was dead and Tiffany owned her house.

It was not white anymore, and there were no ferns in the windows, but there was no sign of neglect. The front stoop had been replaced by cement steps, there was a new, solid door with a little window, and the tumbler lock was impressive. All the windows were curtained.

The woman who opened the door for him wore a suit and no expression at all.

"You're kinda early, lover. We're just having breakfast."

"I'm Cutter. Tiffany said ..."

"Why, sure, honey, sure." She smiled now and looked like a different person. "He says give you a room and we give you a room."

She let him in and caught a lot in one glance; he walked like somebody who was very cold, his shirt was two days dirty, his suit was something you might put on a corpse.

"Come and eat first," she said, without asking him whether he were hungry.

There were three girls at the kitchen table and one old man at the stove. One girl wore a sweater and slacks, one had a bathrobe on, and the other was dressed for the street. They were eating eggs, sausages, ham, potatoes—Cutter did not focus well enough to tell who ate what—and there was also a dish of steamed mustard greens. One of the girls smiled at him.

"Tiffany sent him," said the woman in the suit. "Just to sleep." She told Cutter to eat and that the house would be peaceful till about eight at night.

He ate fried eggs and a lot of ham.

"The Kisser told me about you," said the one in the bathrobe.

Cutter wondered if they were all Willie's stable. The one in the bathrobe was still in her teens and the one dressed for the street looked blossomy and would be in her thirties. A pimp tended to specialize. Maybe Kisser was not a pimp at all.

"Tiffany also said, if you want one of them, it's on his tab."

"I'm going out," said the one in her thirties. "I plain got to show at visiting time or I just can't face that kid."

"I just want to sleep," said Cutter.

Then they sat in peace and had coffee. They asked none of the things they might ask if they wanted to know who he was. When Cutter asked if any of them might know Lillie, they were not sure.

"Did you ask at the Texas Range? There's this Lillie waiting tables."

The one in the slacks remembered Cutter from the time with Asikari. She pointed out that the Lillie who worked tables at the Texas Range would have been maybe twelve years old in Cutter's time.

"You're not *that* kind, are you, Cutter?"

She drew on her cigarette till the tip glowed red, an event she somehow handled as if she were sending a signal.

"You're not hustling the street now," said the woman in the suit. "There's no business done here in the kitchen."

It would not have worked anyway, thought Cutter. He could tell her lean shape by the sweater, her long flanks by the slacks, and the Egyptian cast of the face did not seem marked by anything yet. Her little green-apple breasts wouldn't do it, or the rich mother breasts of the one who was leaving, or the naïve youngness of the one in the terrycloth robe, all that was just something sitting around after breakfast in the middle of the day. He got up and was shown to his room—one clean bed, one empty dresser, and a door to a bathroom.

"Throw your clothes out the door," said the woman in the suit. "Tom will do 'em with the rest of the wash." Then he slept.

At three in the afternoon, the young one who was wearing the bathrobe at breakfast brought Cutter's laundry into his room. She watched him sleep for a while. She considered with some astonishment that this must be the first time she had ever seen a man in a bed and he was asleep. The rare thought made her feel shy and self-conscious. She put the laundry on the dresser and, since it was getting dark outside, put the bedside lamp on. Cutter slept and then she left.

At five in the afternoon, the girl with the slacks came into the room and brought his dry-cleaned suit. Cutter lay on his back, dreaming. The girl watched him for a while and saw how he ground his teeth.

"Hey, beau. Wake up. Hey, cool it."

Cutter woke up. Since he had been dreaming about a green cement wall that was leaning toward him, collapsing over him at any moment, he did not understand where he was when he saw the girl.

"Got a cigarette?" she said.

Cutter sighed and closed his eyes for a moment. "Got a cigarette," coming from the girl with the Egyptian face and the off-handed voice, was the kindest thing that had happened to him in a while. He relaxed and knew where he was.

"I don't smoke," he said.

Without a cigarette the girl was without a prop. She did not think she would need one. She did not dislike Cutter any more or less than anyone else. In fact, she did not give a damn about anyone because nobody—so went her formula—gave a damn about her. The attitude offered freedom and gave her a feeling of being invulnerable. Actually, it made her feel nothing at all.

"You always wake up like that, beau?"

"Huh?"

"With that tent there."

"Woosh," said Cutter, and raised his knees.

She laughed with a hoarseness in her voice that made Cutter shiver inside.

"I don't just wake up like that," he said. "I mostly been staying awake like that."

"You been up five years, I been told."

"Yeah, it's been up five years." He put his legs down again.

She raised her arms and arched her back to get at the zipper in the back of her turtleneck. "Guess I'm it," she said. "It's on Tiffany."

"You don't need to talk like that, kid."

"My name's Jerutha."

She pulled the sweater over her head, threw it on the floor, and gave her breasts a short, circular rub. Cutter had expected a bra. Little hard apples, he thought, makes me pucker just looking at 'em. He sucked his breath audibly.

"Five years," she mused at the ceiling. "I'd have no idea what that's like." She started to unzip the back of her slacks. "What you guys do, bugger each other?"

"It ain't the same thing. Come here."

"That's the damndest invite I ever had," she said and worked the slacks down over her hips.

Cutter had only thought of her as lean, very elastic in the joints, and with a motion which probably howled like a sports car. He had not expected the roundness of hips and the full curve of her thighs. He started to kick the covers down with his feet.

"Wait, lover," she said. "Don't you want to see the goods first?"

"You don't have to talk like that, kid."

"My name's Jerutha."

"Fine, fine—"

She rolled her nothing panties down her thighs and then kicked them off. She stepped back because Cutter was getting off the bed.

"Gawd," she said. "That's no tent pole. That's iron."

What came next was a total destruction of her routine. She had not known how much she relied on it. There was no chance to go wash herself with the solution in the bathroom, no time for the lube job, and none of the studied choreography of letting the man look, letting herself get into the receiving position with those everloving gasps of longing, and onward to the startled choke, the surprise that such a thing, such an overpowering thing could ever happen to her, which then led to the ever more uncontrollable arching and pumping and the pitiful moans for deliverance.... None of that.

Cutter took the girl around the back, where his palms slid around and then down for a handhold. For a confused moment, he did not know if this were still a five-year-long dream or the real thing.

The experience was different for Jerutha. She felt mainly that she was being rammed with a walking stick right in the belly button. She let out an unrehearsed grunt. To keep her balance, she made a panicky grab for Cutter's neck, which he took for eagerness. So he hoisted her by the narrow waist with one arm down and through the spread of her legs so that she ended up flat on the bed. The edge of the bed caught her smartly in the spine. Another unrehearsed sound. Jerutha yelped, which Cutter took for passion.

After that, the girl just gave up on the routine. Cutter took it for total acceptance. She flopped back her arms and gaped wide with her legs, but no amount of professional detachment gave her peace. She was dry as sand inside without the jelly. When Cutter was lined up and went in, she tensed rigid and said, "Ye gawds—", a sound she exploded right into Cutter's nearby ear. He heard correctly that this was unrehearsed, spontaneous emotion. He only mistook what emotion it was. "Wait for me—wait up, baby—" He was gasping like a runner.

While there was a lot of bounce under Cutter, he soon noticed that this was all mattress recoil, and when Jerutha finally started to lubricate, Cutter discovered that he no longer felt a thing. He started to smell his own sweat, and he saw how Jerutha was studying something on the ceiling. Perhaps he had simply not known the power of his effect. She was clearly long done, while he had not even started to climb that hill. Or he had and then had fallen off on the other side with such meteoric speed that he had missed the effect. It did not ring right.

Cutter pulled himself out of her and fell on his back. He felt athletically bushed. Jerutha felt skewered.

"Oh, lover," she said to the ceiling. "That proves it. Five years does make a difference."

Cutter did not say anything right away. He could pick up on that remark in a number of ways. Then he played it straight with himself.

"All it proves is that I can get a hard-on."

Jerutha sat up and looked down at him.

"Ye gawds, it's still there!"

"That's neat," he said. "That's neat, if you're queer for broom handles."

"Did I do something wrong, lover? Want to try something else?"

"Like what, pole-vaulting?"

For a moment it was a conflict for Jerutha between professional pride and professional doubts. What does one do with a broom handle? Cutter tried to help her with it. He used his college-day voice.

"Not now, my dear. I have every confidence that you and I have committed some type of error, and am equally confident that we are equipped to correct it at some point in time."

At first she thought that he was being cruel with her, but then she saw his face. She thought that perhaps she was seeing his face for the first time, that he was not trying to prove one damn thing to her but had tried to invite her to share his puzzlement. When he started to smile, she smiled, and then they both laughed. Not until then did the touch they felt while they held each other mean anything to them. They rocked and laughed and then they just rocked, hearing each other's breathing.

"Hey—Jerutha."

"Let's do."

They lay down to look at each other and felt each other's heat through the skin. The door opened quite casually and the woman in the suit was there.

"You know how long you been up here, Jerrie? Tiffany says he'll pay for one trick, that don't give you no call to up and make love to the joe. Excuse me, Mister Cutter, but there are certain rules of the house...."

"Why don't you shut your fat mouth, Marge, so's you can swallow your teeth an' bite your throat, you flabby dike!"

"Jerutha!"

"And don't you count on going down on me for nothing anymore either, leather-tongue!"

Cutter rolled off the bed and went into the bathroom. He tried not to think about sex-after-five-years-of-wishing, but it was difficult. He heard a sharp slap and a scream, but saw to it that the shower noise shut out whatever else was going on in the room.

When he shut off the water and came out through the shower curtain, it was almost quiet behind the door. He thought there was a sound, the kind someone might make just short of talking. He was sure that he heard a sharp laugh.

Cutter dried himself and used the shaving stuff that lay on the sink. When he came back into the room, only Marge was there. The bed was a mess and one curtain was torn. Marge looked proper in her suit.

"I want to apologize."

"Forget it. I want to get dressed, you mind?"

"Go right ahead. What I came up to tell you, there's somebody wants to see you."

"Here?"

"I first thought he's a joe, I mean a customer who—"

"Stop talking down to me. I know what a joe is. A joe is any lousy chump that thinks a trick is better than a pound of liver. Now why don't you get the hell outa here before I start charging you for looking."

She smiled and turned Cutter's stomach.

"Better hear me out, chump. Your friend's a honky and he works for the Man. He's got parole board writ all over his horn-rimmed eagerness."

"You shittin' me?"

"He's in the parlor. You get him outa here before the good people start coming."

CHAPTER 11

When Cutter was dressed, he felt clean and cold. He could feel the green cement wall leaning his way slowly. There was a back way out of the house, somewhere. This sho' nuff hideout of Tiffany's was just another one of those slipshod Tiffany ways, like the dumb play in the loft where Tiffany got himself ripped off and didn't even know it. No point to all this now, no point taking the back way out. Best to psych out the Man first.

When Cutter walked into the parlor the young man got up from the big purple couch and smiled.

"Mister Cutter? My name's Jerry Gottlieb. I'm your parole officer. I hate the term, but once you and I start working together, really encounter one another, I think we'll both forget about it."

"Sure, Mister Gottlieb."

"Call me Jerry. Or Jer is all right. May I call you Constable?"

"All right."

The sullenness of the culturally deprived. It was a thought with a sigh in it and Gottlieb issued a supportive smile while it happened. The last bastion of the will to get well, the strength of the brutalized, that stubbornness. Naturally, it comes out sullen.

"I first of all want you to know, Constable, really understand, that we in the office are sort of a new breed. We're not minor cops, we're major counselors. Can you understand me, Constable?"

"Sure."

"Constable—er, have you got another name people call you?"

"Cutter."

"Haha, of course." Sense of humor there. Valuable coping quality.

Cutter saw that the young man was working hard. He saw where he came from and where he wanted to be. This cat was liberated, and meant all of it. The liberated renaissance hairdo, the corduroy with the leather elbows, the perma-press shirt of workman's blue, and the freaky lineman's boots. Also, the chump had a face like an intellectual baby, very eager to relate. Cutter was bored and worried about other things.

"How'd you know I was here?"

"Well, first the correctional authorities supply the release date, of course, but then I spoke to the captain of your precinct. Kominski. Very nice, I mean as those things go. You see, Constable, we are all affected by what we do, we are all shaped by what I shall call the social demands of our situation. We'll be relating about that some more later, but right now I just wanted to illustrate a principle of human interaction—the only action that counts, I might add—by pointing out that a man like Kominski may well get brutalized by the interface of his job, but that says nothing about the essential goodness of man, that core phenomenon of wanting to draw together. We'll be communicating about this in depth, of course. Did you follow me, by the way?"

"I said, how'd you know I was here in this house?"

"Oh, that! Well, we got our little ways." Gottlieb laughed, inviting comradeship. When he did not see anything move on Cutter's face, he stopped laughing and said, "You didn't show up for your eight o'clock reporting schedule. So I came to see you instead. That way, I feel, I can stretch a point in your behalf and enter 'Reported' in your file."

Cutter still did not display any of the signs that would indicate that the case was experiencing trust or was moving into the encounter situation. Gottlieb shook off his gloom with another laugh.

"And besides, this way I get to see what kind of home environment you have selected for yourself." He patted the purple couch, looked at the room and the entrance hall beyond. "Very nice. Certain inviting warmth here. Too bad the old-fashioned rooming house with its communal support factor is becoming such a rarity nowadays. How'd you find this place?"

"Used to room here before I went up."

"Ah! Constable, let me share this with you. I'm going to make a note of that positive action in your file: Went back to the old rooming house. Denotes positive adjustment by seeking—"

Gottlieb stopped talking while he watched somebody in the hall. Cutter recognized the girl who had been wearing the bathrobe. She was now wearing two pigtails with red ribbons, a short jumper suit with a white blouse underneath, white knee stockings, and loafers. The little schoolgirl effect seemed deliberate, the way Cutter saw it, because this little girl had the roundest ass and the biggest tits for her size that he had seen in this house. She passed through the hall and was gone.

"Constable," said Gottlieb and slapped his case on the knee. "Now this is heartening! Let me just share this with you. That youngster out there, Constable, is one of those—well, rewards, I might call it, when you work with people. Three years ago I took that youngster on as a case in Juvenile Hall. I wasn't in probation then and little Dottie there, well, to call a spade a spade—haha, no offense—she was dysocial—you know what I mean, she was a hooker! Eleven years old and a hooker!"

"Izzatso."

"Now look at her! Dressed neat, nice house, back in school. Well, back to school for us too, Constable. Just mention it as another example. Now, as for you. Let me just bring up the counterindications in your case at the end of our first session. Yesterday, on your first day out of prison, you were arrested in the company of known criminal elements. Now, hold on a minute. I know this is serious and you know this is serious. But aside from the forthcoming official consequences, there is a lot you and I can do to change the mere conditioning effect into a growth experience. Now, I know you're out on bail, and you and I know you're up for a hearing and to look the facts in the face, really encounter the reality of this thing, you may have to go up again. But the way I justify my work, Constable, is to really work with you in depth. You understand what I'm saying?"

"Yessir." Cutter got up. He was through.

"Well, I guess you have to go somewhere." Gottlieb worked himself out of the purple couch. Then he grabbed Cutter's hand and shook it. "Good talking to you, man. I mean it. And for whatever time we may have together, I want it to be a gut-level experience. Just like today. Come to my office at eight tomorrow morning."

Gottlieb went to the front door, Cutter following. They stopped close to each other while Cutter held the door shut.

"How'd you find me, Jer?"

"Oh, that? I told you—"

"You told me nothing, man."

Gottlieb felt a crazy fluttering in his stomach, something unresolved by psychotherapy. He saw Cutter's face from very close up, the muscles in the forehead, the large eyes almost ornate in their stillness, and word snatches from the file jumped through Gottlieb's mind: activist, educated, anti-establishment, organizer, considered dangerous.

"Friend of yours—in a genuine effort to keep you out of trouble."

"Is that what he said?"

"Yes. In view of your long association."

"Asikari?"

"Yes."

Cutter opened the door and gave a curt jerk with his head. It seemed to propel Gottlieb out of the door. "Wait up one sec—Jer."

"Yes, Constable?"

Cutter turned back toward the hall and yelled, "Dottie? Will you come here a sec, sugar?"

She came from the kitchen, running a little, her front bouncing. She stopped next to Cutter who put one hand on her shoulder.

"Remember that nice gentleman, sugar? That's Mister Jer Gottlieb."

"Sure do," she said and held out her hand.

For one moment, Gottlieb could not move. His stomach was doing that thing again and his eyes were frozen on the girl and that hand. Cutter's hand had slipped around to her front and was working one breast like a lump of dough. Gottlieb fled, hearing the man's hard laugh and the girl's sweeter giggle.

Cutter went to the corner and bought himself a dozen bennies. Feeling unrefreshed by his brief daytime sleep and by the two events after sleeping, he took two of them right away. Next he went to a bar and had a beer. Mostly he brooded.

Campi looked at the storefront Polish Neighborhood Social Club. Then he made a phone call from the booth at the filling station.

Angelo Forza tried to reach his Bethelport number but found that the line was busy over a period of twenty-five minutes. He gave up and went down the corridor and past his own door.

Rosanna, awkward with all her clothes on while Angelo lay on top of her, was suddenly awed with the realization that she was feeling something, an experience like a sudden echo, or like ripples traveling outward on water. She kept the same clothes on when she went down to dinner, and walked pensively.

Magdalena Perrini felt twittery and somehow girlish at dinner. She could not quite express herself to the full measure of her gratitude. It would have been unseemly. But that thoughtful young man from Buffalo had touched her deeply with his unexpected gift of a quart of ricotta. She also worried about Rosanna. Her big girl was eating like a bird.

Perrini in his Tri-State office put the phone down and took a pill two hours ahead of time.

Asikari, all alone, stood wrapped in his cape in the back of a city bus. He was going from the Black Belt to the far side of the factory district. When he got off the bus he walked a distance which took him half an hour, and then he took another bus.

Tratto and Pepe sat in the conference room of the Polish Neighborhood Social Club behind plates of tomatoes and onions in olive oil. Pepe's plate had not been touched. He looked at the print of the Jesus child, and sometimes he went into the next room from which he could see the filling station.

"The system is no good," he said. "What if he wants to call? All this time there is a man in the booth."

"He's not ready to call."

"He's not ready. I am ready."

"Eat."

"Those *Saracenos* killed my brother!"

"He knows what he is doing. He is the brain of the Don himself."

"I don't like him. He told me my grandfather's suit is no good. He laughed in his lungs when I said I didn't know what the sign said over the store. He talked business while I was *crying!*"

"So did I, Pepe."

"That's different. We are cousins."

"In business, like on the hunt ..."

"You can shut up with that."

"Pepe—wait. Where are you going?"

"To hunt."

Tiffany had a bottle of Tokay to calm the nerves, eight hotdogs to ease the flutteriness, three beers to digest the hotdogs, and ten ounces of licorice to change the taste in his mouth. He wondered whether he should send someone to the house on Twenty-second Street, when Cutter walked in.

"Where you been? It's ten in the evening!"

Cutter looked around the small office, something a grocer might have behind the store. Then he sat down on a secondhand couch that was hard as a board and seemed to squeeze the space out of the small room.

"Looking for Kari. You know where he is?"

"Why in hell should I worry 'bout that do-nothin' nigger?"

"I didn't ask you that. I asked you where he was."

Cutter's tone introduced a dimension that Tiffany had neither planned nor expected. He had hired the down-and-out-black man who had shivered and cried in the night tank at the station. He had hired a head-shy ex-con who had nowhere to go.

"You gonna work for me," said Tiffany, "you watch your mouth. This ain't the revolution no more. This is business." When Cutter said nothing, Tiffany looked up from the mess on his desk and turned to the other man. "What you on?"

"Nothing. I asked—"

"Look at your eyes. You coked up?"

"I don't take hard stuff. I asked about Asikari because the son of a bitch knew where I was. I'm wondering what else he knows?"

"He don't mean nothing around here no more. I don't care what he knows. Like what's to know?"

"What's to know, Tiffany, is what in hell's going on here. Perrini's doing nothing, you aren't getting protection ..."

"You know something I don't know?"

"All I know is what I hear, cruising Buckingballs and the little holes in the wall to the sides. And I know those honkies you killed weren't Perrini's, and I know there's no action anywhere."

"I told the runners and everybody to lay low. Till I figure this out." Tiffany, his body uncomfortable and his mind not at ease, had to try absolutely to reestablish the proper relationship. "And I say those dudes were Perrini's. Now shut up about it."

"Perrini's button men talk English. And they don't wear clothes like from a bargain basement."

"Look who's talking."

"And he's too smart to cut himself out of a territory by showing the wrong kind of muscle."

"That's his worry. Now, reason you're here ..."

"I'm worried," said Cutter.

"I said—"

"Tiffany, just lay off a sec. I know why you hired me, so let me do my thing. You took me in because you're just not used to this kind of action. You think I can swing things big, because of the way I moved when the Asikari thing was in action. And you're used to just running the drug-store corner and maybe a floating game here and there."

"You calling me small-time, you two-bit hustler?"

"Shit, Tiffany, you don't need to prove one goddamn thing to me. You're not talking it up with one of your punks. Because I'm not."

"And never will be!"

Cutter smiled but did not say the obvious, that he never intended to be anybody's punk or anybody's chump ever again. He took a few breaths to put a rein on the speed he had in his blood.

"I was going to tell you why I'm worried," he said more quietly.

Tiffany felt around under his desk and brought up a warm bottle of Coke. He knocked the cap off on the edge of his desk and stuck the foamy neck into his mouth. While he sucked on that, he nodded at Cutter to go ahead.

"The no action worries me. It's like waiting for somebody to move in."

"That's right. Me."

"You're not doing a thing, man. You just told me."

Tiffany's discomfort increased because Cutter was talking precisely about the thing which Tiffany lacked most: the push for big action. He was in fact comfortable running his corner and a floating game here and there, which was the way that lousy street nigger had put it. Until Perrini had come along, putting a bug in his ear, until Perrini had pulled out, leaving Tiffany standing there with his pants around his ankles.

"You say to hold it till the air clears," said Cutter, "and I say, move in now."

"I am in."

It sounded so miserable, Cutter almost felt sorry for the man.

"Sure," he said. "Anyway. You wanna talk business and what to do next, or what?"

But Tiffany was not smart enough for strategy, he only knew tactics, and the tactic now was to put that street nigger in his proper and forever place.

"While you ain't got a pot to shit in, Cutter, and while I'm holding the Man off with paying your bail and all, you work like I say. You go out there ona street and talk to those fuckin' lay-off cops and how it's gonna be me paying the fare, hear? And to wait till I starts with all my operations."

Cutter had lost interest. Tiffany was too stupid for any talk that made sense—just the kind of greedy small-timer a smart bastard like Perrini would pick—and too weak to give Cutter what he needed most. Bail money was not going to save him.

He either had to go into hiding, or he had to find the kind of long dough that could wipe his parole record clean.

"You hear me, Cutter?"

"Yeah. Sure."

"So go on out there, tag up with Beany, and learn how we run things now that the Belt is wide open. And get yourself some vines so you look like something, Cutter. Can't take that funeral suit much more."

For a few days, Cutter did what Tiffany had told him to do, except he did not buy himself any new clothes. He ran circles for Tiffany, which is how Cutter thought of the job, but nobody knew who was running what and nobody seemed to care to get it together.

And then two of Tiffany's floating games got busted. At the same time,

Tiffany's numbers collections fell off.

Cutter spent less time on the street, and more time thinking. Also, before the house on Twenty-second Street got raided, he had moved out and into Jerutha's place. She had a one-room place with kitchenette at the windy end of Dock Street. Cutter could see the river below by turning one way. Sometimes he leaned out of the window so that he could see the far corner where Asikari had his storefront school. Asikari, it seemed, used the kitchen exit most of the time. Cutter saw his figure walking on the street just ever so often....

Time was slow and depressing. Once a patrol car came and made a turn by the ramp at the river, but Cutter was not sure if they were looking for him, now that he had jumped bail and violated probation. He was not sure of anything much. It was fine with him and Jerutha, but that too did not mean much. She spent more time with the woman in the suit, and Cutter liked her apartment mostly because of the three different ways he could get out of it.

The cops finally came and Cutter spent a long time on the roof until the foot noises in the hall went away. He had already gotten set up to jump for it, across the slit between buildings, but they only hassled Jerutha and then went away.

Times changed, not because Tiffany started making sense, not because Angelo made a big move, not because Perrini made a decision, but because of some stupid murder. That night, Cutter met his first Sidgie.

CHAPTER 12

Beany was wearing a pink applejack on his Afro and a shirt with the color effect of a pigeon breast. Cutter was wearing his usual, except for the different tie.

Jerutha had presented him with a polka-dot number. The gift had not been sentimental. For one thing, the tie had been in her closet; for another, the old one had a flower pattern that reminded her too much of the wallpaper in the room she used on Twenty-second Street.

Beany, who liked wine, drank expensive scotch, on account of the flash. Cutter, who liked scotch, was drinking beer. He had noticed that hard liquor got him drunk too fast. Something wrong with his liver! Maybe the scientific garbage for five years had turned his chemistry upside down. Or the beatings—maybe that one most awful working over, after which he had lain in the hole with his piss full of slimy red lumps and his shit turning black like tar.

"Lookit that nigger flash that roll," said Beany. Cutter moved his face back from the whiskey breath and turned it away from the bar so that he could look at the booths.

"He didn't make that on no numbers," Beany added.

"We know there's action," said Cutter. "Somebody's running a book."

"You hear that or you guess that?"

"Both. I hear some dudes talking. There's a horse parlor somewhere, except nobody knows where."

"Let's ask that cat with the roll."

"He won't know. If there's a parlor, it's moving. The dudes I heard talking made the bet on the street."

"Now ain't that superfly! How come Tiffany hadn't thought of that one? Keep the parlor moving and lay the bets on the street."

"Because, you stupid bastard, he hasn't got the kinda bread that buys a wire service and he doesn't have the kinda connection that gets him lay-off money!"

Beany, who was taller than Cutter, got up from his stool. He moved close up to Cutter and looked down on the other one's head. Cutter could smell deodorant.

"You just call me a stupid bastard?"

Cutter put his feet under him and thought about straightening up very fast and hitting Beany's chin with the back of his skull. He decided against it.

"Don't get shook up," he said. "We got to figure a way to find that parlor."

"I'm talkin' to you, fucker."

"Don't get jammed over nothing," said Cutter. "You been this way ever since Tom-Tom went."

The remark changed the direction of Beany's thought. But he kept standing and used the same voice.

"And what've you got on it, man? How come you don't get shook up when I—when Tiffany loses a hand?"

"He was your friend, not mine. Sit down, man. Drink your drink."

"I *am* shook," said Beany. "And I'm standing here asking you how come you ain't shook? One day Tiffany takes you in, and right after, Tom-Tom gets croaked."

"Beany, I apologize for what I said. You never was and never will be a stupid bastard, okay? Now put it down, man, please."

But Cutter was too late and Beany was too drunk. He was not used to hard liquor either.

"That's all you got to say? You badmouth Tom-Tom and that's equal to badmouthing me, nigger. What else you know about Tom-Tom? I already got it you don't like Tom-Tom."

"Beany, lay off, huh?"

"Like maybe you laid off Tom-Tom?"

Tiffany sure collected himself a bunch of crazies, thought Cutter, and the longer I hang out with those crazies—Then he made one more try.

"Tom-Tom's dead and it don't make sense. And that was no nigger killing, we both know that. Who do you know in Black Belt uses his hands, huh? Who you know that's got the strength and breaks the neck after choking his mark to death? Let's see your hands, nigger."

Cutter felt disgusted. He did not want a fight. He did not want the least little part of the jealousies or the pains of all the losers who thought that Tiffany would lead them to riches. He wanted out but did not know how. For starters, he got up from his stool and walked quickly out of the bar. Beany was just slow enough with the liquor in his brain to give Cutter a head start, and when Cutter reached the street he started to walk very fast. He cut into the first alley just as Beany came bolting out of the bar.

"Hey, pussycat! Hey, Cutter-Cutter-kitty!"

When Cutter heard the taunt he stiffened just for a moment and then, to hell with it, ran down the alley.

There was a dark lot, full of rubble and pieces of wall where the building had been leveled by the housing commission but for reasons of economy most of the debris had been left where it was. Cutter could hear the big steps coming after him and hid in the ruins.

"Hey, Cutter-cat, hey, kitty-cut—"

Cutter crouched down and just watched. He heard a good deal of silly drunk talk and a lot of sliding and stumbling in the rubble. Now and then, against the light from the distant street, he saw the silhouette. Beany would move his long, angular bones like a puppet coming apart. Then he was gone. Beany showed again from a different angle, looking big as a bear and moving like a cat. How come the bastard showed so far over?

There was a lot of rubble sound and next an impact like a fall. "Kitty-caa—" and then nothing.

For a while, Cutter only heard his own breathing, much too loud but always getting too little air, until the footsteps started leaping along. The thing with the bulk that looked nothing at all like Beany got into the alley and walked away.

Cutter found Beany very quickly. The body was warm and dead. The head rolled around like something on ball bearings.

Tom-Tom got his after Cutter joined Tiffany and he, Cutter, joined Tiffany when Perrini pulled out. Vacuum. Who's coming into the vacuum—who's walking down the alley, big as a bear and soft like a cat?

In the active days, before everything went to pieces, there had been a lot of study, among other things. It covered the spectrum from Spengler,

Mao, Engels, to operational things like survival in the jungle and police academy pamphlets on shadowing techniques.

Cutter did not run after this man. He stood where he could see the other mouth of the alley and he did not move until he saw the outline of the man again. When that was gone, he ran along one wall.

In a short while, it became apparent that the man thought he was not being followed. Also, he did not know his way around. As soon as Cutter knew that the man used the streets only according to their right-angle geometry, it became predictable where he wanted to go. Cutter, knowing the Belt, got there first.

He stood at the head of the bridge that crossed the Bethel River, and for a silly moment he felt like something in an ominous English movie. Then he attended to business again. Either the bear would now head for his car, or he would cross to the bus stop and wait for public transportation. The man was not black and he was leaving the Belt.

He walked past the cars and he did not cross to the transit stop. At this point Cutter made his mistake. He should now have led his target and simply walked ahead of him over the bridge. Instead, he first looked at the man, which is all it took. The bear angled off and ran the darkest route he could find.

Of course, he would never get clear. He had bolted away from the last bridge out of Black Belt and once the riverbank had guided him past Dock Street and the warehouse sheds, there were only the railway spurs before the riverbank turned to slime and gradually became the flats of Lake Erie.

He never got that far before Cutter caught up with him. Or rather, like something at bay, the man decided to turn, stop, and wait.

"Now ease up, man, I mean, just try cooling it—Right, see? No iron, no shiv, not even an overcoat."

"You want?"

"Clean, man. I—am—clean."

Cutter did not understand what the man said next. He understood that he was not afraid but that he was giving warning.

"Yeah. Right. Like I always say, you son of a bitch. Sure, right on—So I got a line on you and yours and all you do is lead me down river—Easy!— All I'm after is talk, and now you do and I don't get a word of—" which was when the bear turned into a cat.

When Cutter saw those hands coming at him he almost panicked and reached for them to divert their grasp and protect his throat. But the ice saved him. Cutter slipped just enough to remind him where opportunity lay and technique began. He fell backward, his back round and his feet coming up.

There was too much overcoat on the other one and all the kick did was make the man grunt. Cutter thought he had hit a brick wall. He rolled as best he could, and in the process caught the man on the shin. The other doubled over and Cutter was up. Now! From twenty-four inches up, in a hard, flat curve down with the edge of the hand—and the mother won't talk anymore, even in his own private gibberish!

When Cutter stepped back the big man swung around and ran toward the river.

"Hey—it's a drop! Hold it, no bank there, you can't—"

After the splash, and after Cutter's eyes were adjusted to the darkness below, there was a man floating inside his overcoat, looking up, looking as if he might be crying, and not caring if he sunk. He said something very clearly, in a calm voice, and sunk.

Cutter, who knew about the river, had to wait two hours before the corpse showed up. He grabbed him from the ladder where the seawall slowed the river and just before the dirty water moved into the dirty flats. He did not pull him out and he did not go through all the pockets. He found the rosary, which he dropped into the water, and he found the envelope, which he put between his teeth. He left the corpse bumping along where it would soon float into the mud.

When Cutter had a chance to look he found that there was nothing in or on the envelope, except a local telephone number.

CHAPTER 13

Perrini had a telephone in his bedroom whose number was different from the other phones in his house. None of the other instruments in the house could pick up the calls on this number. In addition, this line was not bugged by the man in the basement, which was one of those little niceties of caution Perrini had arranged since Angelo had taken to using the house phones for his business calls.

In spite of the fact that it was three o'clock in the morning, Perrini was awake in his bed when the phone rang on his nightstand. The cognac did not seem to work as well as it might. On the other hand, Perrini was worried about increasing his intake. Who knew what changes in body chemistry were taking place which had left him insomniac, in spite of an almost double dose from the bottle. Also, his bedtime fantasies came to him with an edge of worry. Perrini had nothing against the sex in them. What else to expect, when a healthy man was so goddamn busy that he could not find the time to go out and unwind himself in the natural way. What concerned him about his imaginings was that the broads were getting so indecently young.

"*Pronto*," he said into the phone.

"This is Campi, Preach."

"What is it?"

"I got a guy here wants to see you. Reason I'm calling this time of night, I think he's got something for you."

"What do I need?"

"Help. He's outa Black Belt."

Perrini did not say anything right away. He looked down the length of himself, lying there under the covers, and did not like the image that came to him, stretched out as he was. He kicked the covers back and sat up.

"What's his angle?" he said.

"Don't know, Preach. He comes into my place, wet up to the ass from being in the river—he's sitting here right now making a puddle under the furniture."

"Come on, Campi, you've got to have more than that."

"Right. Sorry. He says he's got a line on the outsiders, he called 'em, which checks out to be the Sidgies what's holed up in that Polish club."

"*He* knows about that?"

"Sort of. What he took off the corpse ..."

"The what?"

"It's a long story, Preach. What he took offen him is that telephone number, the one your boy Angelo has been using when he gets in touch."

Perrini ran over everything in his head and then he sighed.

"Campi, you call me on this line at three in the morning there's got to be more to it than all the crap we already know. About Angelo and his Sidgies and these bums trying to muscle into the works. What *is* it that's on your mind?"

"Us sitting around and we can't touch the bums, the way they're covered from Buffalo, and the way they done nothing that's got a handle. Did you know they opened a parlor?"

"No. But it was bound to happen. That's no handle."

"And two corpses. Now, the way he tells it ..."

"Maybe I better come over," said Perrini and got off the bed.

"Preach. Lemme meet you. The wife and the kids upstairs ..."

"All right."

"If she comes down and sees that puddle ..."

"All right!"

They met in the toolshed at the far end of the Tri-State complex. A bank of fluorescents was on high near the ceiling. It made a cold, flat light that seemed to increase the size of the building. The air was dank, smelling of grit and grease.

Perrini recognized the black right away, the quiet cousin who had sat at the other side of Tiffany's gaming table. The man now sat on a packing crate, feet together, hands between knees, and his lips were quivering.

"Here's the envelope he took," said Campi and handed it over.

"So what?" said Perrini. He stopped near the packing crate. "So? Say something, cousin."

Cutter did not answer right away. His teeth clicked and a tremor ran through his body.

"That son of a bitch needs a fix," Perrini said to Campi. Then he turned toward Cutter again. "What are you on?"

"I'm cold," said Cutter.

Perrini, feeling a little chilly himself, thought about moving the conference to his office or maybe just to the back of his car. He decided against it. The cousin's value was by no means established. Besides, Perrini could tell more about a man by watching all of him, clearly, from a distance. Cutter took a breath and stopped shaking. His voice was soft, showing no effort, and held no hint of nigger talk.

"You call them Sidgies, I just learned. One of them just killed a Tiffany man. I can deliver both their bodies."

Perrini looked at Campi and got a nod. Campi, as a measure of his worth, had already sent details out on corpse collection.

"The black man was strangled and the drowned killer has his fingerprints all over that neck."

"So now I got two stiffs."

"I am suggesting that you have your handle. You can flush them by putting the cops on the killing, while you and your own people keep out of it."'

If Perrini was not impressed yet, he got another example of Cutter's grasp.

"Or you can hold that over their heads and bargain for the records they took. I know from Tiffany, who isn't very bright, that his notations have you all hog-tied into his Black Belt action."

Cutter had another fit of the shivers. Perrini, his feet uncomfortable on the cement, paced around a little. He asked Cutter for the first time what his name was, and he wanted to know what Cutter had been doing for the past few years. In addition, he wanted to know why Cutter thought that any of this might be important or worth anything.

It impressed Perrini how Cutter had put it all together and had come up with the same picture that Perrini and Menotti had been sweating about. There was no question at all that Cutter knew why all this was important and why it was worth a lot.

"*Dunque*, cousin. Now you tell me why you're telling me all this?"

"I need help."

Perrini stopped pacing and started to laugh.

"Smart ass!" He interrupted to finish laughing. "You trying to be tricky with me, smart ass? Here you come and bring me something that can save my business and you tell me *you* need help?"

Cutter wanted to stand up while making his point but he did not trust his legs. The fine tremor did not show but it weakened him. He stayed on the packing crate and raised his head.

"You got nothing, Mister Perrini, nothing at all that'll save your neck. You haven't even got your foot in the door. Tell me this: Who's got the kind of long dough that'll buy a wire service and lay-off money to put those Sidgies on their feet in your territory?"

"I wouldn't know."

"Don't con *me*, Mister Perrini. It's got to be the next biggest thing around here. Like, that *old* Sidgie in Buffalo, whatsisname, the one that's *your* boss, Mister Perrini."

"Listen here, cousin—"

"My name's Cutter." This time he did get up and Perrini did not interrupt again. "And you're not about to go up against him, not in the open, you ain't."

Perrini was smart enough not to pull any grandstand play on a man who knew as much and thought as clearly and was as cool with the *caporegime* as this shivering black man with the wrinkled pants and the dirty shirt. All Perrini did was nod his head and say, "Now I get it."

"I think you did a long time ago, Mister Perrini. Except you didn't know how to do it safe."

Perrini, having admitted his need, made the next, conventional conference move. He took the hard line, so the man at the other end of the table would not get a swelled head about his bargaining position.

"And for doing a janitor's job of cleaning out the Sidgies—a job for which I can hire professionals who ask no questions and don't hang around afterward—for that, *cousin*, you want what?"

Cutter did not know whether it was his own weakness after the running, the waiting, the hiding while ice-coldness sucked the spirit out of him, or whether it was the hard enemy sound which Perrini was using with him. For a moment, Cutter could not see clearly in the barren metal shed, and he had to sit down on the crate again. That gave his heart a chance to pump his head clear again. "... maybe a seat on the board of directors of a horse parlor? Or Tiffany's job? A part of the action? What *is* the bargain here, *cousin?*"

He heard Perrini's bark and all the nonsense he was saying, but all he wanted right then was to sleep. Where? In the Belt, where Beany's friends would be looking for him? In the bus station, where the Man might by now be sniffing around for Cutter who had broken parole?

"I need help," he said to his knees.

"That's right. First thing you said was you needed help, before you started smart-assing me. What is it, a new suit? Fancy car, maybe?"

In a way, Perrini regretted pushing this hard, because the man was obviously down already. There was a point, a fine point of wisdom, where stomping on a man who was down and out did not pay off in any profit. Beat a man limp, then what can he do for you?

"The Man's looking for me," said Cutter. "And if he finds me—" he paused and said something harsh that Perrini did not understand—"when he finds me, I'm dead. I mean, I can't go back up again. Just can't—"

"You trying to tell me something, Cutter?"

"I'll do the Sidgie job for you, and you get my name off the books. You can do it, I think. The arrest with that Tiffany crowd—and violating probation—make me look clean with the Man, Mister Perrini. I need that right now—I really need that right now!"

That was all Cutter had wanted to say, though he had not thought it would come out like a plea. Bad. He had thought that Perrini would be so much in need—all that preacher face did was smile a little, and one polished shoe went tap-tap on the concrete.

"I can do it," said Perrini.

He waited for Cutter to say something, but all he got was a stare he could not read.

"I'll clean you up," he went on, "if I need you."

"Mister Perrini—"

"You stay put. You got a place to go? Course not. You told me. I'll look this thing over while you stay put with my friend Campi here. And I'll give you the word, one way or the other, sometime in the morning. That sounds fair enough, right?"

Cutter did not answer again but only nodded. They led him to a small place that was partitioned off at one end of the big shed, and when Cutter was in there they closed the door behind him and turned the lock.

It was a forgotten place, left over from a time when the cubicle had been used for a file case and desk. There was now an oil drum, a dented truck wheel, and coveralls that lay on the floor.

Cutter heard the lock click and had an insane moment of figuring out very quickly that the oil drum could be rammed into the door when placed on the wheel which was made noiseless by wrapping the coveralls around the rims—Cool now, cool! Take another benny and think!

"... won't be a problem," said the preacher voice. Cutter heard the dialogue drift in and out: *The watchman will keep this off limits—Gonna be*

long?—Company plane back by noon—Call the wife for me—You car-
rying iron, just in case?

By then, Cutter was attending again and heard more clearly.

"You mean all that crap about a piece of the action? Because all he ever said ..."

"I know what he said," Perrini answered. "So I cut him down by saying it first. Technique, Campi!" and with the laugh at the end there came nothing else, except the footsteps of the polished shoes leaving across the cement.

Cutter sat down on the floor. He started to think about what he had heard but he could not manage it. He looked at the walls, one sheet metal, one cement, and plywood for the others. Then they all turned to cement and the cement became green—

"*Campi!*"

"Stop yelling."

"Campi, you there? Listen, man, you gotta keep talking to me!"

"I'm telling you to shut up."

"Please—I'm not well, man. I mean it."

"Yeah. I'm not well either, sitting around here in a draft in the middle of the night."

Maybe if I laugh, thought Cutter, and tell him about the thing with the oil drum with the wheel wrapped in coveralls—

"Very important I talk and you talk back. Can you hear me, Campi?" There was no answer and Cutter felt the walls moving in. And there he was yelling and trying to look out the window—"I'll tell you about it, I'll show you," he started to chatter. "You see, you're snug in the back of the car, you dig? And outa one window—when you stretch up a ways—you can see the Capitol dome. That's the window on the left. Out the window on the right there's this whole field of junk and stuff, like a dump. Now wait a minute, maybe it was the other way around."

Campi was listening and started to get worried. "Maybe it don't matter which window," he said. "Capitol or dump, who cares?"

"Only the door to the dump works!"

"Sure."

"Campi, let me out!"

"Not on your life, sweetheart."

"*Please!*"

"Forget it and stop saying please like that, you goddamn spade!"

Now Cutter was back in the leftover space with the drum, the wheel, and the coveralls. He put the coveralls on the drum and sat down on top. One goddamn tired spade cat who couldn't take hard liquor or handle a benny anymore. Forget it and stop saying please. Cutter pulled his legs up close to himself and wrapped his arms around himself. He felt some comfort.

That was the last time he would ever say please, and he was not about to forget a thing.

Piece of the action, Perrini had said, as if that had been a joke—

No more please. And no joke.

In spite of the early hour, the drive from the airport to the street of brownstones took longer than the flight from Bethelport to Buffalo. Then came the street, and the brownstone that looked like all the others, and the walk from the entrance hall to the basement, through a door, up the stairs, through a room, down to a basement again, and so forth. When Perrini was led to the second floor, he had no idea in which house on the block he might be. He was allowed to go into the room with the walnut door by himself.

The drapes were drawn and a lamp was lit, but most of the space was in darkness. The old man rolled himself toward the light. He sat in a wheelchair and wore dark glasses. Only the mane of white hair looked attractive. The room smelled like an unmade bed.

"Don Santino."

"How is Angelo?"

"If he continues with your blessing, I will lose face."

"You have no face, Francisco. Does a row of figures have an expression?"

"You know something, Santino? When you add them up, sometimes they smile."

"I don't like the way you add."

"Santino. I'm here to ask you man to man. What in hell are you trying to do to me?"

"Your deals make me sick, Francisco. I can't afford sickness. Nor can the Family. I don't want deals, I want loyalty."

"Listen," said Perrini. "Are we talking business or history?"

Santino Forza coughed, then he swallowed it.

"The Sicilians stay," he said. "Work with them, if you can. Or lose face."

"To hell with the face, I'll lose the territory!"

Santino Forza turned his head away.

"We have been friends for a long time. And now you tell me that you can lose."

"For God's sake, Santino, will you stop talking like some goddamn sage that gets visits from the villagers up there in his cave over the vineyards? Talk straight!"

The old man turned his head back and, as far as Perrini could tell, he was looking at him from behind his black glasses. Santino laughed abruptly and stopped just as suddenly.

"Pretty good," he said. "And if you crap out, you're wasting my time, *and* my territory. Good night."

"With all due respect, Don Santino, it's morning."

"You talk like the village idiot. Good-bye."

It had not registered right away, not until Perrini was back in his plane. The Don in his cave over the village had oracled it all out for him. Angelo Forza, the import, was the new man, unless Perrini knew how to hold his own.

He watched from his window how the plane entered the landing pattern. There was the crosshatch of wet cement, and to one side there was a lot of Bethelport. Most of the snow was gone. It was starting to thaw.

CHAPTER 14

Rosanna woke up because of the hand between her legs. What shocked her was not the hand but the realization that she was accommodating it. She instantly snapped her thighs together and tried to sit up.

"What are you *doing?!*"

"Pay attention," said Angelo, "and you won't have to ask."

"Now stop that! What time is it?"

"Nine o'clock in the morning."

"Do you realize—"

"They're both gone, your father to work, your mother to the beauty place."

"Well, all right," said Rosanna.

She sat up, worked her behind around, and pulled the nightgown over her head. Then she flopped on her back and watched Angelo get undressed.

"You staying home all day?"

"Don't be greedy, *amorosa.*"

She was greedy. She knew that there must be much more to this, she could feel it some of the time, and she was greedy for it. Angelo did not act like a jackhammer, he did not drool on her hair, and he did not put his knuckles under her spine. He was also a bastard, but she did not mind. She only minded that he was a little too quick.

"You going to stay till noon? She's like clockwork. When she goes to the beauty parlor, she comes home one o'clock."

"Very nice. Move over."

"She should stay all day. Maybe that would show some results. You gonna stay till noon?"

"Quiet now. I first make a phone call."

He picked up the bedside phone and dialed his number. When his dialing hand was free, he put it on Rosanna's near breast and listened into the phone. His right ear and his left hand did not seem to know each other. Rosanna did not like that, but did nothing about it. She felt his hand and how it upset her body, and she heard his voice and how it clanked away at a distance. She did not understand what he said because he was talking Sicilian. Then he stopped talking and turned to her.

"Have to wait a few minutes. They have to call somebody. Okay?"

"Not so hard," she said. "I got feelings."

"Aha! Where, here? Here?"

She turned for him, now that he was attending, and tried to feel the whole thing through. And if he gave her enough time, maybe today, since they would have three hours....

"*Pronto!*" he said.

Rosanna felt immediately that his hand had forgotten her. It just kept moving around while Angelo turned away.

"Tratto! Called to tell you I'll be there after ... What?"

"Yes. Your uncle called. That is, his man called."

"Bad?"

"Good! He said to go ahead! Did you know that the Preacher came to see him this morning?"

"That's why he left so early."

"And begged on bended knee that the Don should call you off?"

Tratto, who had invented the mood of the meeting between Perrini and Don Santino, laughed with appreciation, until he noticed that Angelo was not saying anything. Then Angelo said,

"How did Perrini know it's me who's moving in?"

"Oh. I don't know. Is it important?"

Angelo called his lieutenant a *cretino*, which summed up his anger over losing close touch with Perrini, over losing the use of Perrini's daughter, and for having to move out of an altogether comfortable house.

"There is more," said Tratto, who did not like to feel unimportant. "Also, Buffalo is sending the money."

"What money?"

"*The* money, so we can open operations full-scale. It comes by car. He said, at about ten this morning. And that means you will have to come here."

"*Cazzo,*" said Angelo, who did not like to be rushed.

"And another thing for your attention. Pepe didn't come back."

"He went again?"

"The same thing. It's not up to me to control him."

"You mean that dumb ape went in there alone after I told him, commanded him?"

"My dear Angelo, the death of Pepe's brother—Excuse me, I understand that after having been in this country for three years, perhaps you do not remember that such a thing happening in a family is of the first importance."

"I know it is of the first importance! I told him myself!"

"Excuse me, you told him it was of the first importance that the business is properly organized. You made him think—"

"Shut up! I'm coming over!"

Rosanna knew that nothing spectacular would happen that day. All manner of preparation and willingness was shot to hell while the Sicilian jumped out of bed and left her aching with anger.

"I don't like this," she said.

"I don't either. Go back to bed."

"You think you can do anything you please, don't you?"

"I am very busy!" He was getting dressed again, doing a clumsy job of it in his haste. "Don't stare. And why don't you cover yourself."

"Cover myself!"

"Yes! What do you suppose a man thinks of a woman who sits around like that and does not think enough of herself to put on something decent."

In a moment Rosanna recovered herself.

"Why, you lousy hypocrite bastard!"

Not knowing the special weight the term has in Sicilian, she was completely surprised when Angelo took a step toward her and slapped her across the face. She was so stunned that she gave him the time to do it again. The second impact raised a vicious welt very quickly. Then he yelled at her.

"I'm leaving! I'm moving out! I'm sick of you and your ways like a rutting sow!"

She watched from the window while he threw his clothes into the car. She had not put on any clothes. She fingered her cheek, disliking her feelings, because she knew that she hated to see him go.

While Angelo Forza moved into the penthouse suite of a downtown hotel, Cutter was moved into a single frame house near the edge of the Belt.

While Angelo Forza sat in the Polish Club, counting two hundred thousand dollars cash money, Cutter watched Perrini make the telephone calls that would clean his recent violations from existing records.

And while Angelo and Tratto plotted their coming expansions, Cutter described to Perrini by what stages he would squeeze the Sidgies out of shape.

Rosanna went for an aimless drive and somehow ended up at her father's Tri-State office. But her father was not there. She drove away again.

CHAPTER 15

It was a bad day for Angelo Forza from the start. Never having been much of a drinker, he would wake up with unmanageable hangovers. By steps, the new habit was scotch, disguised with Coca-Cola. This morning's malaise was dissolving his bones, and his tongue seemed to be covered with a growth of mold. Next, of course, there was no espresso to be had in his fancy hotel, a hotel so self-conscious that they had already spoken to him about night visits by women.

On his way to the Polish Club, he lost control of his Stingray in the street slush and broadsided a parked car. Instead of being allowed to take off in a rage, he was stopped by a policeman who told him about moving violations and, worse, about leaving the site of an accident. The paperwork alone took twenty minutes right there on the street. And finally, at the Polish Club, they had no coffee either.

Tratto sat at the desk they had put into the room with the Jesus child on the wall and was looking at the slit envelopes he had scattered over the blotter. All the envelopes contained money.

"More of the same," he said to the pile on his desk. "Just shut up and wait till the man comes back from the store with the coffee."

"You should try a swallow of anisette. In this country they call it the fur of the dog."

The word fur reminded Angelo of his tongue. He said a number of violent things to Tratto, but then he decided to try the anisette prescription. When he came back from the little kitchen with the bottle and a glass, Tratto tried again.

"Can you talk now?"

"I can always talk. The question was, do I want to listen."

Tratto sighed. The boss was becoming a sensitive man, a drunkard. Soon, there would have to be a word about this to the Don.

"All right. We have tried it your way, Angelo. We have upped the percentage, and we have lowered the rate. As you predicted, the customers made more money and the money made more customers who bet. And now this," he waved at the envelopes with the money. "For two weeks the winners get beaten up and then robbed. The winnings are sent back, minus the price of the bet."

Angelo had another shot of the sticky liqueur.

"So few bets are placed now," said Tratto, "it does not even pay the rent on the office."

"Increase the outlet men again," said Angelo. "What about collecting?"

"First, about outlets. We are using six bartenders to phone in the bets? Three have been fired, two have called in to say they don't want to work with us anymore. Second, about collecting? Alberto is in the hospital, as you already know, and ..."

"I mean the blacks we hired for enforcing. What about them?"

"They collect nothing. They say they cannot find those who owe money. Could I have that bottle for a moment, please?"

Tratto drank from the bottle. He paid attention, with eyes closed, as the liquid turned from perfume to fire. But that miracle of sensations and aftereffects held no promise for him. The situation was much too bad. The very scheme of asking those Negroes to let themselves be robbed by Sicilian late-comers in the profit game was ridiculous. It could only be conceived by an antique in a wheelchair who lived in a room with the curtains drawn.

It was Tratto's curse that he was intelligent and also greedy. The two qualities, more often than not, produced nothing but conflict. Or else he would never have left the assured position of a hereditary *caporegime* in Palermo, he would never have listened to the siren song of the legendary Don Santino in Buffalo, he would never have agreed to supervise the imported peasants under the title head of a fop like Angelo Forza—Ah, but it would be good to be the bastard son of a Don. And then again, maybe it was not that easy.

"Maybe," said Angelo, "the Don was wrong. Maybe we should not have started with bookmaking."

"What else, numbers? They all go to Tiffany and we, as you know by now, cannot get to him."

"Tiffany. Perhaps he has organized all of this!"

Tratto just laughed.

"Give me back the bottle," said Angelo. "And if it is not Tiffany, who is doing this thing to us?"

Tratto surprised himself with the fury he suddenly felt.

"All I know about these American blacks is what I have been told before coming here: They are ignorant, lazy, and they have no spirit. They are like children, inasmuch as they want only fun. This is all I know." He breathed noisily a few times. "And now I know something additional: All of that is wrong!"

"Are you trying to tell me you want out?" Angelo talked quietly, attempting menace. He wished he had his blue glasses on.

"No," said Tratto. "But I want you to do more." His fury had now turned to viciousness, and it wanted out. "Every time one of those sayings, expressed by the Don, comes into your head—at that point I want you to add a thought of your own. Such as, will this work? And if not, why not? And I want you to stop using the men like a rag to blow your nose. Ever since you returned the Tiffany records for Pepe's corpse."

"That was the best way. The Don said, if you cannot pay off the police, do not invite their attention."

"You destroyed the corpse, you *cornuto disgraziato!* You cut off the hands and burned them up in the furnace!"

"That was the point of getting it back!"

They had both gotten up from their chairs, glaring at each other across the table, shouting so that the saliva was flying. Tratto sat down first. He slumped down, sighed, and found that he could talk more quietly again.

"What I am trying to say, Angelo, we must think up something new. We are going to pieces. The men don't like you anymore, the take is going down to zero, we are trying to do business with enemies. This must be changed."

Angelo took the change in tone for submission. He felt safe again and more certain of his position. Also, the liqueur had changed his hangover to the inner calm of marginal drunkenness.

"Here is what we will do," he said, and sat down again. "Something to pull the men together, to engage the customer, to save face, and to make money."

Tratto lent a cautious ear.

"We will move the parlor into the Belt. Boldly. That way, we need no outlets, no runners, maybe not even much telephone service. We move the supply into the middle of the demand. We open the parlor right there in the Belt, we eat there and we fraternize, in the place of business, a tight band of brothers, boldly, and here is what else we do."

Tratto sat, suffering the dramatic pause.

"Mobile units."

"What, *mater dolorosa*, is that?"

"With walkie-talkies for reporting to each other. Two men in a car, moving around, watching for the robberies which scare our customers. Also, temporarily, we increase protection money. Every time a cop helps stop one of those beatings, he makes a hundred bucks! Also, we pay for information. Canaries all over the place. That's what we do. A tight, single operation. From there, later, we expand. That's what we'll do!"

"They're doing it!" said Willie.

Cutter turned away from the window and went to his desk. He waited till Willie had closed the door, and then he grinned at his new lieutenant.

"Give 'em a week, I figure. Then we close in, right?"

"You been calling it. You called it right so far."

"Sit down. We got to talk angles." Cutter sat down at the desk he had moved into the front room of his house and looked up at Willie. "Where's

Shimmy? Aren't you breaking him in?"

"Lost him," said Willie. He took off his big leather coat and sat down. "Didn't like the way he was anyways. Cat had no cool. Never got any info straight, never could pass by a cop without shaking. He's gone, that's boss by me."

It was not all right with Cutter. After five years of absence and barely a month of action he had a recruiting problem. Not any street black would do. Many, like Shimmy, were too young and unsteady. Many others were too unsteady because they just moved with the wind. It had been different in the days of the movement.

"I don't pick up drifters," said Cutter. "But not counting Shimmy, we lost three cats in one week."

"Gotta recruiting problem. You got anything in the house?"

"Just beer. Lemme ask you, Willie. Mean anything to you if I tell you that two of those cats that split used to go to that school Asikari is running on Dock Street?"

"Where's the beer?"

"I asked you a question."

"No," said Willie. "And I wouldn't get all jammed up about it 'cause that's the only good school around and it don't cost a cent. Where's the beer?"

"Forget the beer. Put your coat on and come on with me."

"Like where, man? I hardly come in off the street."

"Shimmy's house."

"Cutter, you gonna fuck up your mind with every jive punk that don't live up to your goddamn standards? We got work here! Perrini wants to know when it's gonna be, Perrini wants to know what happened to the ten grand for juice, Perrini wants—" Willie stopped because of the way Cutter was looking at him.

"You got any *good* reason for trying to keep me from going to Shimmy's house?"

"Oh my black ass," said Willie. "You gonna go psycho on me?"

"You drive," said Cutter. "I don't know where he lives."

By street standards, it was not much of a car. It was a wide GTO that hugged a curve very well but was light enough to deliver a lot of acceleration. When Cutter had arranged for his job with Perrini, Willie had said, "And now you get you a hog that sits by the curb and glitters, day and night, and some vines, like mine, that says 'here I come'!"

"Not yet," Cutter had said.

"Man, you don't got that flash, you got nothin'. Nobody knows you're *there!*"

"Right now," Cutter had said, "I need cover more than I need flash."

They drove down the streets, avoiding Buckingham Boulevard, with the GTO doing conservative speed and Cutter still wearing his prison suit. The only thing he had changed was the shirt. It was now a black turtleneck.

"Sorry I blew on you," said Willie.

"Sure."

"Maybe, once you talk more, I understand more. Know what I mean?"

"We talk," said Cutter. "We work good together."

"What do I know about plans you got! Like nothing!"

"I got no ready plans you don't know about."

"Like for instance, why Shimmy's house? Meanwhile, Perrini wants to know—"

"Don't start that shit again."

Shimmy's house was a bungalow like the one Cutter was using, except this one was split with plywood partitions, so that two families could cram into it. Willie stayed in the car and Cutter stood on the porch.

The woman who answered the bell had a large body which was beginning to hang in useless ways. With all that softness, the impression of flint came as a surprise to Cutter. It came out of her face. Only the hard planes of her face seemed to hold her hostility, because her eyes let all of it out. Cutter stiffened under the look, even though he understood it. This was the strong mother who had to deliver her black child into the world that was waiting out there to chew him up. There was nothing she could do about the white evil that ruled her world, nothing to do but raise her son toward doom. The useless knowledge left her with a lot of hate. But why for him?

"Is Shimmy in?"

"I know you," she said. It came out like an accusation.

"Good. Would you ask Shimmy—"

"You're Cutter. The one that went wrong."

Cutter was getting impatient. And since when was a stretch in the Man's slammer like a fall from grace?

"You're worse than the dirtiest nigger selling his sister for sin money or killing his body with sin dope! Because you know better. Or knew better, when you did your good work!"

"Hold off—"

"And now that you're robbing your brothers, doing sin work for the Man, you ain't even of the blood no more! And I'm for sure not going to let that happen to my boy. Now you git, you black white man!", and she slammed the door.

When Cutter felt something again, it was a very fast and ugly rush of feelings. The worst of it was, they were all about himself and so fast that in no time only the anger was left.

That woman knew more than a harridan like that would be apt to know. Even the words weren't her own—Cutter got back into the car and slammed the door.

"Dock Street."

"School's out, Cutter. Past three now."

"Move it."

When the car rolled to a stop by the storefront school with the three R's on the glass, Cutter was much calmer. He got out of the car, he did not slam the door, and he could see by the light they had turned on inside that school was in fact out. They had moved all the kiddie chairs to one side of the room because the students were too big for them. They were about Shimmy's age, night-school types, though Shimmy was not there. Asikari stood behind a lectern and the listeners sat in a loosely-formed half moon on the floor. Asikari could see through the glass but he kept right on talking. Cutter pushed through the door."

"… not a one of us here who has not wondered, what's the point? Why suffer, with no hope for the white man's favors, when we can suffer and play his game, which at least offers a chance for his favors? And there are some, or at least one of us in this room, who have played it both ways."

Cutter slammed the door shut.

It was very quiet in the room now. Asikari pushed his hands into his sleeves and turned his eyes just enough to keep Cutter in sight. Otherwise, he did not move. Cutter stopped very close to the lectern.

"Send them out," he said quite softly.

"They are students. Perhaps they will learn something." Cutter had his hands in his pockets, his fists feeling like stones in there. It was a way of holding on to himself, or else the shaking might show.

"In fact," said Asikari, "perhaps the demonstration has more power than my abstract talk." He turned to the young men on the floor. "The topic, students. What is our topic?"

"Working for the man—"

"Charley fever—"

"Playing the game—"

"Kiss ass—"

"We are talking about you," said Asikari with a nod at Cutter.

"Why don't you leave me alone," said Cutter. He took hands out of his pockets and let them hang.

"Because you set a bad, a misleading example."

"Get off my case, Jackson, because I'm doing my thing, my way. And I'll make it."

"I know, Cutter. That's why you're a misleading example."

"You been recruiting my men away. And you said you had no more organization."

"I don't. I only teach. You incite."

"You jammed on converts, Jackson? Because I haven't interfered with you."

"But I with you? Cutter, there's a difference between you and me at this juncture. You are dangerous, I am not. You set a bad example, I do not."

"You sold me out twice and that's two times more than any other man ever done to me. First, when I went up, and second, when I came back. You can stuff that good example, and I mean right up your ass!"

There was a snicker from the group on the floor and Asikari snapped his head around at the sound. He does look like a schoolmaster, thought Cutter. The thought somehow changed things for him so that he could walk out. He no longer wanted a teacher, and everything was way past school.

"Cutter!"

He stopped and looked back.

"I was not quite through," said Asikari. "Your ludicrous accusation—"

He stopped when he saw Cutter smile and probably knew the same thing Cutter knew. They were done. Cutter was free of him. Cutter was even free of his own anger.

"Kisu," said Asikari. "The knife that got dull."

"Won't work," said Cutter. "You just teach. Don't try to incite."

Asikari pulled his face in that rare way, when his control was very thin. He moved with care, stepping a little closer.

"You're a loss," he said, "turning back into a punk nigger. In fact, a loser."

To Asikari's astonishment, even that did not stir Cutter. He saw the smile again which confused Asikari with its touch of thoughtfulness.

"Wrong," said Cutter. "I just cut free. Free of all the shit and stuff behind me, and including you." He changed his tone, adding a clearness to his speech, like something heard in a distance. "I'd rather feel this way and be doing your kind of thing. But that's all pissed away now. It's a loss. Meanwhile, I've come out of the hole."

"Again?" Asikari's laugh was like a pencil tapping the top of a desk.

"Yes, Watchman, again. And maybe again, every day."

"Wait!" said Asikari. In the haste of the moment he only knew that he must not lose something now. Nothing better than a cliché came up, the speaker losing his audience. When his eyes locked on Cutter's, he knew that it had already happened. Cutter shook his head.

"What's it like, Watchman, teacher lost a pupil? No. The Supreme Leader in search of—"

Asikari was extremely fast. He caught Cutter on the chest with the side of his foot but when he moved in there was not enough damage. The next two blows hit the bone of Cutter's forearms and the knuckle thrust for the throat ended up scraping across Cutter's skull. The worst thing was, Cutter never hit back. He stood with head lowered while Asikari gave distance so that he could recover. Only Cutter's eyes followed him.

"Rafer! None of that now, you hear!"

She was holding the curtain back where the passage went to the kitchen.

Asikari's chest was pumping and his hands hung dead. Cutter brushed his tie back into his jacket.

"Thank you, Ma Jackson," he said, and walked out the door.

The young men on the floor did not know whom to look at, the old woman by the curtain, the strong man by the wall, or the walking punk who had not made any sense at all—

CHAPTER 16

Perrini, who had been losing some weight, gauged his shrinkage by wrapping his windbreaker back and forth around his middle. When his phone blinked he did it one more time and then picked up the receiver.

"Yes, dear Becky."

"Your wife is on the phone, Mister Perrini."

"Ah. And you told her I'm here?"

"Yes, Mister Perrini. I did convey to her though, that—"

"Never mind. Plug her in."

He sighed with one hand over the mouthpiece and waited. He eyed his cognac bottle. When his wife came on, he closed his eyes and turned his face to the ceiling. He would wait for his medicinal until later.

"*Bella*," he said into the phone. "What is it?"

"Are you busy, Francisco?"

Of course he knew she would say that. Nevertheless, he had a reaction.

"Yes," he said. "I am busy. Just a moment."

He put the receiver on the desk with unnecessary impact, he arose from his chair and reached for his pillow, and then put the pillow on top of the telephone. Next, he poured some twelve-dollar cognac into the three-cent paper cup and swallowed without gargling the stuff, as he would usually. He took his pillow back and sat down.

"I'm not busy, Magdalena."

"Oh good. I just wanted to ask you one question."

"Oh good. Ask me one question."

She hesitated, because of his tone, and because she felt in a vague way that there was something irregular about the routine of their conversation.

"Well? What is the one question?" His voice made her jump at the other end of the line. "Of course! You would like me to bring home some ricotta."

"Is something the matter with you, Francisco?"

"There is nothing the matter with me, Magdalena. Now, about your question of the ricotta."

"No," she said, "I think you must be busy. Besides, when Rosanna left the house this morning—she left at nine in the morning, Francisco—"

He waited for the rest. When he got ready to shout something unusual, he heard his wife's voice again.

"She never gets up before eleven. Today, she leaves the house at nine."

"I know that, Magdalena."

"You do?"

"Goddamn it, you just *told* me!"

"Francisco, you are swearing again. I hope there is no one else in your office."

He breathed something at the ceiling. The anchor sound in the lengthy breath was the filthy word *minquia,* which was repeated several times.

"Before you interrupted," said his wife, "I meant to tell you that you don't have to get the ricotta because Rosanna, when she left—I mentioned that already—offered to bring some back for me."

"Yes, yes." He did not know what else to say. "A good girl," he added in a mumble.

"Francisco, do you realize where she offered to go at nine o'clock in the morning? To that awful neighborhood!"

"Whatsat?"

"Where those Poles live!"

"That's where Mister Rosetti sells the ricotta. He lives there too!"

"So I wish you would speak to her about the places in this town where she might and might not go. Father to daughter, Francisco."

He stared at his cognac bottle, imagining that the liquid was beginning to vaporize under the intensity of his eye. "I meant to ask you, Magdalena," he said as if from a distance, "there's something wrong with my cognac in the bedroom."

"I don't know anything about cognac."

"I know, *bella*. I think Rosanna has been drinking from that bottle, and then, like some kind of idiot who knows nothing about cognac, has added water afterward. *Your* own daughter!" and he banged down the phone.

"Campi!" he yelled.

His man stuck his head through the door that led to the extra office with the unlisted phone and to the stairs that were the back way out.

"Call the lookout by that Polish club. Rosanna is heading that way, left about half an hour ago."

"Sammy's been following her, like you said, Preach, but he hasn't called in about it."

"She doesn't get up till noon, so he naturally doesn't start tagging at nine o'clock in the morning! Get on that phone. I want to know, if she finds the *cretino*."

While Campi did as he was told, Perrini called the place where he could reach his button men. The call, the way he worded it, raised no eyebrows going through the Tri-State switchboard.

"A car for a meeting with the non-union people. At their address."

Campi came back.

"You just called out the troops?"

"Right."

"You heard from Cutter? It's starting to move?"

"No, I haven't heard from Cutter and no, nothing is moving."

"Then why ..."

"Because that dumb cluck daughter of mine is likely to find the *cretino!*"

"She's been hunting long enough. How'd she tumble on his place in that slum?"

"How the hell do I know? Get the car. I want to see this."

Campi ran down the back to bring the car around but without under-standing why. He misunderstood why Perrini had been having his daugh-ter shadowed. That retarded broad had silently lost her head over the house-guest Angelo, and once that snake in the grass had left Perrini's place, she had started hunting for him. Maybe the Preach was all wrong. Maybe his little one had been balling that Sicilian all along.

"This I gotta see," said Perrini when he got into the front seat next to Campi. He said it mostly to himself and just watched across the white hood of the Mercedes Benz. He did not worry about the high-level visibility of the car. It might even give the *cretino* a start.

"See what, Preach?"

"Stop calling me that."

"Okay. What?"

Perrini started to grin at the hood and then he turned it on Campi.

"Did you ever hear of a case where some *cretino* tries balling the daugh-ter of the *caporegime* and nothing happens?"

"You mean they have been? I been wondering about that."

"They have *not!*—Watch where you're driving!"

"You gimme such a start. Besides, I don't get any of this."

"They don't ball, right under the nose of Magdalena. Even I don't ball right under the nose of Magdalena. And since he's gone and she's been looking around for him, they ran into each other once, in the lobby of his hotel. That's it. Till now. You sure you gave the lookout the number of this car?" Perrini tapped the phone which hung under the dash.

"Yes." They drove without talking for a while. Then Campi said, "Preach, I don't like it."

"What?"

"You need the troops to keep that punk from balling your daughter?"

"The troops are for the Sidgies that could be there. And stop using that word."

Campi ignored the tone. His loyalty was not affected by Perrini's irritable little ways. He felt he had something important to say.

"I got to tell this, and I don't care if you get mad," he said straight at the windshield. "And if you want to start yelling, I'll pull over to the curb and we talk till we have this out."

Perrini turned silent and alert. He nodded his head and waited.

"I'm not talking about how you feel about your daughter. That's not my point. I'm talking about you letting personal feelings run into the business."

"Don't stop there. Just finish." Perrini did not sound pleased.

"You're going to lean on Angelo for what he's done—I mean, wants to do with your daughter. That's one way of looking at it, Preach. Here's the other. It's like using your daughter for pushing around the son of a bitch who's muscling your territory. You got Cutter for that."

Campi slowed the car and entered the narrower streets that led to the Polish Club. Perrini nodded to himself and then he put his hand on Campi's leg.

"You're a friend, so I'll explain it to you. I don't know about Cutter. He hasn't called, he hasn't moved. Just those little tricks of his. Maybe I need him, maybe I don't, but I don't need him to think that he's the one who's saving my hide. So I move. I catch the *cretino* so it looks like he's—what's the word—compromising my daughter." Perrini started to raise his voice, though he did not use the preacher sounds on Campi. "I disgrace the Don's right hand! That's how I crack the Don!" Perrini breathed deeply a few times, rubbing the side of his chest. "That's how. I need that on him, the disgrace."

Campi looked sideways for a moment and saw the light sweat on Perrini's face. Then he looked front again, saying nothing. He nodded a few times, which could mean that he agreed or that he was thinking about it. He slowed the car, because they now had the Polish Club in sight down the street. The lookout still had not called.

"That's the greasy spoon where Barney's sitting?"

"I'm just trying to park there."

"Make a slow pass. You see him?"

"Not there."

"Some lookout," said Perrini. "Stop right here and go inside."

As soon as the Mercedes had come to a stop and before Campi was out of the car, somebody tapped on Perrini's window.

"Christ, what's he doing here?" said Campi.

"Hello, Mister Perrini," said Cutter.

Perrini rolled down his window. In spite of his heavy overcoat, the wet outside air made Perrini shiver, and before he could open his mouth, Cutter started talking. He sounded curt and far from Perrini's idea of a hired hand.

"Your carload of muscle almost loused things up. If you're going to take a hand while you don't know which end is up, I wish you'd let me know first."

"What in hell—"

"Those *are* your men with their stomachs hanging out and their brains tucked away, aren't they?"

Perrini followed the gesture and saw three of his button men standing around on the street like pilings exposed when the tide runs off.

"Fortunately, they were too late. The club's empty."

Perrini grabbed his own nose and pulled on it a few times, as if there were a terrible itch.

"Maybe I'm losing my mind," he said to himself.

"You seen Barney?" Campi asked past Perrini's face. "If you know who Barney is."

"I know who Barney is. I sent him off."

"*You*—sent him *off!*"

"For some reason, your daughter was hanging around the street. After she'd gone into the club, she came out again and drove off. I don't know what it's all about, but I thought it best to have Barney follow her. I told him I'd wait for you."

"I think I need a drink," said Perrini. "I get this certain dizziness in the head and a drink helps. Get in the car, Cutter."

One of the men from the carload Perrini had ordered to cover the club came over with a slow shamble. He seemed in doubt whether to call attention to himself or to act as if he were not there.

"You can send them off," said Cutter. "The show's over."

"Just get in this goddamn car," said Perrini. The self-control seemed to drive the moisture out through his pores. He waved his hand at his man on the street and told him to get lost. Then he rolled his window up, sighed, and Campi put the car in gear.

"Where to, Preach?"

"Maybe we should ask the cousin?"

"Take the second left, cross the bridge, and go into the Belt. I'll direct you from there."

For a while Perrini simply held on to himself. He felt ridiculous, comic, and most of all, he was surprised at himself. He discovered that it was not so much surprise as worry, a very anxious concern over the lame-brained way he had acted this morning and over the persistent way in which his own body seemed to be tripping him up. The sweating, the sense that his ribs were too hard, and the jumpy operation of his brain. Maybe, the fact that he had not taken his leisure at the little round table in the hall this morning—ridiculous. Maybe those goddamn calls from Magdalena. Ditto ridiculous. I gotta get myself laid—He almost said it aloud, which made Perrini furious with himself.

"Turn on Twenty-second," Cutter said to Campi. Then he turned to Perrini. "Private place where you can have that drink, that okay?"

"What about your bungalow?"

"Lots of cats coming and going. This is more discreet."

"I'm looking for my daughter. You just happened by, Cutter. The reason I'm—"

"I told Barney to stay in touch with your phone in the car. Either when she stops or when he loses her."

This son of a bitch is running my life, thought Perrini, but he was in sufficient shape again to say nothing about that.

"Your way. You also know what I'm drinking?"

"Cognac," said Cutter.

Perrini was afraid to ask how he knew. Instead, he closed his mouth and breathed through his nose.

"That doesn't mean they got your brand," said Cutter. "Will Hennessy do?"

"I think it wise," said Perrini in imitation of culture tones, "that the entire matter should be left in your hands. Among the other things in your background, have you also been a butler?"

"No," said Cutter. "Only ghetto stuff."

"Because I was thinking, when you're done with this ghetto stuff you're doing for me ..."

"No. Pull up by that house with the porch, Campi."

Campi stayed in the car to watch the phone. Cutter and Perrini were let in by the woman in the suit and shown through the parlor with the plum-colored couch and into a small study. There was a bay window with a seat in it, an old iron coal grate inside a small fireplace, and one wall was draped in flesh-red velour. The furniture was a card table and a few straight chairs. The light from the outside came through a tall hedge by the window and seemed mostly green.

"Nice house," said Perrini and sat down in the window seat. "Cat house?"

"Yes."

"Looks like a home and smells like Lysol. What's the take in a night?"

"The house runs three regulars, plus three rooms for walk-ins. That's on a rental basis and varies a lot."

Dottie came through the door, carrying the tray with the bottle of cognac and two glasses. She had the face of a child who needed sleep. Her tell-tale body did not show because she was wearing the bathrobe again. She put the tray down, smiled, and left with her bare heels clomping along like a boy's.

"What's she doing here? She ought to be in school."

"She's tired," said Cutter. "Ten tricks a night and she takes her work seriously."

Perrini poured cognac, tossed it down, but in spite of the pleasure he felt he also missed his paper cup. He sighed and had some thoughts about that little one doing ten tricks a night and taking them seriously.

"How long's she been doing this?"

"She doesn't remember and I don't think you'd want to know."

Perrini, in spite of Cutter's tone, did not allow himself to get upset. He attended to the effect of the clean alcohol. It was good for him.

"What about your daughter?" Cutter went on. "What's her mess?"

"Why, you goddamn filthy—"

"Sit down, Mister Perrini."

It was the sound of "mister" more than anything else that hit like a stiff finger under the heart, but Perrini sat down.—Or else he'll see the cock-eyed shape I'm in, and what in hell kind of shape is it?

"My daughter has a thing for that Forza person. All in her head, but she keeps hunting for him. I heard she went to that club and I came down. I mean, as a father."

"That why you had a carload of apes at the corner? Mister Perrini, you're either not thinking straight or you're not telling it straight. Don't matter," Cutter, with a wave, stopped Perrini's reaction. "What does matter is your hanging around there, or your men hanging around there, while Forza is moving out."

"Where?"

"1020 Buckingham Boulevard, where his new horse-parlor's going to be."

Perrini got up from the window seat and came over to the table where Cutter was. He sat down and put his arms on the table. Cutter could see that Perrini was back in some kind of shape. Whatever that queer flight-iness of the man had been that morning, now he was *capo* again. As far as Cutter was concerned, that was all right. It would not change his own work.

"I'll tell you why I let him," said Cutter.

"Yeah. Please do. And in the same breath, please, all about that tricky business of harassing their customers, cutting their phones, pulling the pants off their runners in public, all that shit, to use your expression. Because, what I see instead of moving on anything, you've just been *shufflin'*."

"It's the shufflin', Mister Perrini, which drove him into the Belt. It was a gamble, but now he has put his operation and his base into the same area. If he had not, we would have."

"You talk like a goddamn jungle fighter or something."

"Or ghetto, yes. The alternative plan—"

"Cut out the briefing session."

"You called it. The customers he does have are going to see the break-age with the naked eye. In addition, here in the Belt, I can make a corpse disappear more easily than out there in Whiteyville."

"*Porco,*" said Perrini. "You're one cold-nosed bastard."

"I'm getting paid for it."

"You know what I think, cousin? I think you like it."

"Mister Perrini, you don't know anything about me, and as long as you keep riding me, you never will."

"Don't you take that tone with me, sweetheart. I saw what you were like when you went in that hole in the toolshed."

"It doesn't matter much how I go in. It matters how I come out."

Perrini knew well enough what his own sparring was all about. It had to do with his fear of where the underling might be moving with him, and for that reason it was necessary to keep the top and the bottom relationship fully known. In this case, it was first a matter of establishing such a relationship, to bend it where it ought to be. But Cutter did not bend. He would not be stroked and he would not be whipped. He heard none of the power sounds Perrini was making, and perhaps all this establishing of proper places was just a fart in the wind.

Perrini smiled. In spite of his preacher tag, it was Perrini's special excel-lence that he could give up on pretensions when they did not pretend so well anymore.

"Agreed," he said, as if there had been a lengthy discussion. "Now tell me what happens next, Cutter."

The door opened and Campi came in.

"Barney called. Rosanna just stopped here in the Belt."

"Where?"

"Ten-twenty Buckingham Boulevard."

CHAPTER 17

Cutter looked at Perrini and waited. This was clearly a double-edged thing of father and daughter on one hand, and of Perrini and Forza on the other, not the kind of mess that he, Cutter, had been hired to handle. Perrini looked at Cutter and said, "What do you think?" and while he asked it he was thinking a swirl of things, which contained a search of the house, a gun in the belly, a chase through the cellars.... He was thinking that same upsetting nonsense that had started him off in the morning.

"I think," said Cutter, "that you should pull up in the front with your man at the wheel, you should go inside, and ask to see your daughter. And then you take her home."

Blessed sanity—Perrini felt so grateful that he quickly poured cognac so that his feelings should not show too much. He did not drink from the glass but just put the bottle down.

"That would be best," he said, and smiled at Cutter.

"And in case you want somebody along, take me. If nothing else, I'd like a look at the layout in there."

Perrini got up and slapped his belly with both hands. But then he had second thoughts.

"Do they know you?"

"I just look black to them. Not even hard enough to be carrying iron for you."

The winter sun, yellowed by the fumes of the city, gave its last light from a low angle that avoided the clouds. This was a mid-afternoon in the winter time and the warm light seemed to quiet the air. There was not much movement on Buckingham.

Ten-twenty on the boulevard was a concrete building that had housed a beauty parlor and a shoemaker's shop. Upstairs there had been a dentist's office with a lab attached. The gold lettering on the upstairs windows still said so, even though the dentist and his lab had moved out some time ago. The beauty parlor had been closed by the sanitation department, and the shoemaker was all deaf and mostly blind. There was a cardboard sign on the glass door leading into the hallway of the building, which said: *Closed for Alterations. Shop By Phone, open soon.* The whole thing was handwritten, with a script resembling something from an exercise book.

"That's cute," said Perrini. "Shop by phone."

"Plus, they mean it," said Campi.

Cutter said nothing. He did not like the mixing of jobs that was coming up. The mixture included the personal, and that would make everything trickier. He got out of the car, turned his head down into his overcoat collar, and waited for Perrini in the entrance arch. Then they went through the door with the sign. They went toward the stairs, because they figured it would be on the second floor. The hall smelled of wet dust.

"Just a minute!"

The voice had a heavy accent, the shoes were pointed like a kayak, and the face was like all the others, as far as Cutter was concerned. Perrini took charge.

"Who are you?"

"I am the watchman of the new company. The mail-order company is not open."

"You don't know who I am," said Perrini.

"I don't care who you am. Out."

Perrini got smooth as silk. He could have talked in Sicilian, but he did not want to get that familiar.

"I'm Francisco Perrini. To see Angelo Forza. Since I'm expected, you just stay where you are."

Perrini was up the first step when the watchman remembered his instructions, which were, no matter who—

He came forward with the simplest intent, which was to step up quickly and grab the old man by the coat. As for the Negro, hands in pocket and shoulders humped, they were all alike, they were easy-going—in spite of recent events—they were fun-loving—which explained their tricks— they—

Cutter lashed out while turned half away, which gave his backhanding fist a lot of travel. The Sicilian flew backward until the wall stopped him with the sharp sound of stone on stone. When he folded to the floor, his eyes were crossing and his jaw was no longer in place.

"What in hell'd you do that for?"

"For demonstration," said Cutter. "Just in case the father-daughter act doesn't go over."

The noise had not alerted anybody, and Perrini went up the stairs. Cutter followed in the same posture that had fooled the unconscious man in the hall.

They were clearly not expected when they came into the long, bare room that had been the dental laboratory. There were some tables standing around, some phones on the floor, and a lot of cartons with manufacturer's labels. The cartons seemed to hold junk items like vibrating eggbeaters and fluids for improving engine performance up to 81 per cent.

There was one man who was moving a mattress into another room and two others were wrestling with a stove. Rosanna sat on one of the 81 per cent boxes. She looked up when Cutter shut the door.

He thought she was one fine-looking chick, built like a recurrent dream you might have in a cell, the face gentle, except maybe either dumb or confused. There was no question that she was confused when she saw her father. For one beat, Cutter thought that she was also glad.

"Rosanna!" said Perrini, and held out his arms to her.

She flicked a smile but hesitated a moment too long. Perrini let his arms down again.

"Just heard you were here," he said, not quite knowing where to position his voice in the throat, "so I came up to get you."

"Hi, Father," was what she managed.

"So? You got a coat or something you want to get?"

"I've got it on," she said.

"So, let's go."

But it was not that simple for her. Cutter could tell that she was glad to see her father but that she also did not know what to do with the feeling. She moved her arm in a gesture that tried to say something casual but never managed to say anything.

"I was driving around," she said, "and then I saw Angelo here. Did you know Angelo is here?"

Perrini had walked up to his daughter and now he just nodded his head. He put his arm around her shoulder.

"I know, *bambola*. Let's just go."

There was a shift in the background, some men moving out of the way, others grouping. Perrini looked up.

"Mister Forza," he said, mocking the man with his tone. "I thought you had left."

"Wrong. I'm moving in."

"And we're just moving out. Come, my dear."

"She came to see me," said Angelo.

He looked tense. There was too much explosiveness in his voice. One of the men with him moved close to his side, brushing his arm gently. It did not gentle Angelo. Cutter saw all this and took his hands out of his pockets.

"Angelo is going to open a business here," said Rosanna. It sounded like a bright ping on the piano after the low chords had already finished the piece. "He's going to sell things by phone. You see these things here?", and she waved at the boxes.

"Yes," said Perrini. "I see things here." He took his arm off Rosanna's shoulder and stepped out of her way, so that she could head for the door. "I want you to come now, Rosanna."

"Maybe she wants to stay," said Angelo.

The man who had brushed Angelo's arm stepped forward and made a very sudden, engaging smile.

"My name is Tratto, Mister Perrini. We did not expect you of course," he made a little laugh, "*pero, meno male, negli affari ...*"

"Talk English," said Perrini. "And I'm not here to talk business." He was starting to sound rough.

"You haven't got any business here," said Angelo. "So get her out of here. Or did you think I *asked* her to follow me around?"

Tratto said something rapid to Angelo but it did not seem to work. Angelo moved a step forward, as if shaking off interference.

"Let me tell you something about that broad." Angelo's voice was getting higher, and when he saw that Perrini's face was turning red, he laughed. "That broad, such a nice, quiet daughter, first time she laid eyes on me, up at your house that was ..."

"Angelo!" Rosanna almost screamed it.

Cutter was next to the girl and took her by the arm.

"If you have to talk to him," he said to Perrini, "finish talking. I'll take her downstairs." He led the girl rapidly to the door.

Behind him he could hear Perrini breathe heavily and he could hear Angelo laugh.

"Hey, Perrini! Who's the shine? You now got to hire shines to keep that broad in line?"

When Cutter turned back at the door he saw Perrini leaning on one of the boxes. His face was the color of clay and sweat dripped from his nose. One of his hands was plucking a button in front. Cutter yanked the girl his way and talked into her face.

"Go down the stairs, out the door, and into the white car. Campi is at the wheel. Now git!"

"My father—"

Cutter yanked her away from the room and pushed her out of the door. Then he went back to Perrini.

The color was back in his face. He was standing up straight, sucking air with, a sound like a kitchen drain. He blinked his eyes and showed his teeth.

"Let's go," he said. "I can walk. Where's Rosanna?"

"With Campi."

"I can walk."

He walked with the stiffness of someone who had joints missing in his legs, but he walked, head up, and there was even a dignity about it.

Cutter held the door for him. When Perrini was through and starting to go down the stairs, Cutter looked back. He had not seen as much as might be useful. Just this room, the two doors leading elsewhere, the hall window showing a fire escape. That was good to know. He had seen five of the Sidgies, plus Angelo and that Tratto. That was good to know. Maybe the thing to do now, with just a few words sounding like banter—Cutter did not get any further. He saw Angelo's furious gesture, and he heard rapid words.

Cutter had to stay in the room and shut the door behind him, just in case they meant to go after Perrini. This way they would not.

They were not very clever, but there were a lot of them. Cutter, who was the much better disciplined fighter, confined himself to the strenuous job of blocking the worst of it while making it look like ultimate damage. But tricky blocks and tricky groans paid off just so far. His mouth bled, his stomach was cramping up, and one ear burned like an electric fire and felt the size of a bursting balloon. The worst was the errant blow near the neck because then everything drained out of Cutter's arms.

When he sank in a heap, he could hear their greedy breathing and some of the shouts. Sounds of pleasure. Don't go to sleep. They're done. Like a turtle now—face in chest, arms on stomach, heels on groin, don't sleep! He slitted one eye and saw the feet move away. Then he gasped. They had made room for the leader. Angelo had delivered his ceremonial kick.

Because of Cutter's arranged position the damage was not as intended. The kick had deflected from the scrotum, sliding on Cutter's two heels, but had driven into the sphincter with an inside tidal effect which ended up by driving the bile into his mouth and the saltwater into his eyes. And again—

"Enough," said Tratto.

Angelo laughed and said, "*Solamente por dimostratione,*" which was no end of a gas, as far as Cutter was concerned, because he understood the word demonstration, having used it himself, one year ago, downstairs in the hall, where he had crumpled up and thrown away that white thing.

"Get out of here," said Tratto.

"Good-bye," said Angelo. "And when you see Bonafacio in the hall downstairs, tell him I said it's all right for you to walk out, if you can walk out."

Now Cutter was afraid. He used the push of fear for the strength he did not have, but even though he could move now and get up, the fear did not go away. One of the men went with him and followed him down the stairs.

There was a limit of anguish beyond which the wisdom of the body would not follow the brain along. Cutter had met that point before, and he met it again. He walked down the stairs with the help of the bannister and no longer cared. He felt he walked rather well. He wished he could see better and he wished there were a different taste in his mouth.

Somebody stood in the hall, waved, and came forward. The man behind Cutter went back up the stairs.

"Can you walk?"

"I'm walking."

"Sez you."

Campi took Cutter's arm.

"There's a man, a man here," Cutter heard himself saying.

"Forget it. I hauled him out half an hour ago."

"I see."

"Sez you. Watch the door."

"And the kid and the old man?"

"Sent her off with Barney. Perrini's in the car."

"*Madre*—" said Perrini when Cutter sat down next to him.

Cutter began to feel himself again. He rolled down the window next to him because the heat in the car would put him asleep. Campi drove and the cold air was like life on Cutter's face.

"Thanks," said Cutter.

"For what, for heaven's sake?"

"For waiting."

"Don't talk crap. I wouldn't be waiting, if you hadn't stayed. Where do you want to go?"

"Steambath. I'm starting to stiffen up." He gave Campi the address.

They did not talk for a while and Cutter could hear Perrini's breathing. When he looked over, Perrini shook his head.

"Nothing. Forgot to take my pill. How long you going to be out of action?"

"Give me a few hours, is all."

"Call me at Tri-State," said Perrini. His voice had changed.

"You can tell me now."

"Kill him," said Perrini.

CHAPTER 18

Cutter sat on the top shelf in the steam room and noticed how he became gradually limp. It was what he wanted. The softer he became, the more of himself would seep back into his shape. He did not worry about the oddness of the thought because he knew it was right for him. But he did worry about the bum play at Angelo's place. He had ended up not as some kind of shuffiin' house nigger who held the door open, brushed the coat, or maybe drove the car. What the Sidgies would learn was that there had been this unexplained black who had very swiftly smashed the jaw of their lookout and who had let himself be beaten and mauled to protect his master. Maybe Angelo's peasants and Mister Angelo Big himself would not bother to put that together, but one of them might: the one who had said his name was Tratto. Maybe he should be the mark.

For the time being he let himself go limp and attended only to breathing. His belly went slowly in and out, the way a baby's might. He looked like something dark that hibernates up near the ceiling in a cocoon of vague steam.

But all the action had now come to depend on him. The lines, even unbeknownst to some, reached out from his dormant shape to the ones he had touched in some way. They were all waiting.

Perrini could do nothing until Cutter moved.

Willie, who had once borrowed Cutter's name, had to wait for Cutter to give him direction.

Tratto tried to explain it to Angelo in several ways that this must have been more than a father fetching his daughter, and that the black they had beaten up had done more than some houseboy would.

Even Asikari felt the dependence on Cutter's next move. Too many ideals were at stake, and Cutter had broken too many rules.

And Don Santino waited, knowing that he must hear from Angelo soon. He did not know how soon.

Cutter stayed in the steam room for one hour. After that he had a twenty-minute deep massage on the large muscles but skipped the skin-toning work. Some of the places where bone came close to the skin were too sore. He swam in the pool for twenty minutes to stretch and flex everything back into place, took a cold shower, and then slept in one of the restrooms for two hours. When he woke up he was new.

He stayed in the small room, wearing a towel around his middle, and ordered a meal: a small glass of red port, for quick heat, a rare plank steak for the lasting effect, and a big tossed salad with lemon juice, to keep the insides moving well. While he waited for that he made a few calls.

"Where you been, you mother?! I been hearing all kinds of things!" Willie yelled over the wire.

"We move," said Cutter.

"That's boss with me, but what do I do?"

Cutter told him how Willie would start it off, and he told him very little about the ways in which he himself would finish it.

"And get me Benjamin."

"Big Benjamin? You jiving me, man?"

"It's the superfly finish." He also asked for a change of clothes and a man to drive for him. "I want Drury," he said. "In half an hour."

"Why Drury? That Bahamas high hat is like as not gonna drive you up the wrong side of the street."

"I want him. And he should wear gloves the way he once told me. He'll know what I mean."

"What *is* all this shit?"

"Willie," Cutter sounded patient, "maybe you came in too late, that time with Asikari, but you should know about the rules of a cell. What you don't know you can't spill, and what you do know, nobody else is wise to it. Can save your life."

Cutter felt that was good enough and would give Willie direction. Willie thought that Kisu-Cutter did not trust him any further than he could spit. They both hung up at the same time.

The glass of wine came. Cutter sipped carefully from the top, waiting to feel it go down. He took one more sip before calling Perrini.

When the phone rang Perrini was not allowed to pick it up. He sat within arm's reach but the arm was swaddled in the inflated belt of a sphygmomanometer. The man who was pumping the tube was old and rough.

"Hold still or I'll make your hand turn blue," he said. "Bad enough I got to do my work in some filthy trucking office."

"Come on, Jerry, I got *business!*"

"Which is why you're a mess and why I am here. All right, two minutes, or the patient may die."

"Goddamn it, don't talk that way." Perrini picked up the phone. "Yeah," he said and then, "Look, give me five minutes, and call me back on this other number." He gave the number and hung up. "You see?" he said to the doctor. "Two minutes."

"You see?" said the doctor and pointed to the mercury column of his apparatus. "Two hundred." Then he took the arm band off and folded his gadget away.

"You're done?" said Perrini.

"No. Just beginning. Your blood pressure could boil an egg, and your heart sounds like there's a cylinder missing. You've reduced the medicine, and you've probably increased the liquor dosage. Lemme see that bottle."

"What?"

The doctor did not answer. He pulled the drawer open, took the bottle out, and held it up to the light. "When'd you open this?"

"I don't know. Maybe yesterday?"

"Maybe this morning?"

"Come on, Jerry, stop riding me. I got scared and called you over, that's all."

"I'm going to scare you some more, Francis. If I were a second-hand-car salesman, I'd be ashamed to have you on my lot. If I were sentimental, I'd send you to a museum, and if I were mercenary, I'd melt you down. Now, in spite of my professional jargon, did you follow the diagnosis?"

"Can I button my shirt now?"

"For God's sake, please do."

"I know what you mean: Take it easy. Right?"

The doctor snapped his bag shut. He had already given up. He sighed and took his overcoat from a chair.

"Francis," he said, "I don't give a damn."

"What in hell is that supposed to mean?"

"It means you either show up at the hospital, like I said, or I'll show up at the chapel, to view the corpse. Good-bye."

They parted on a note of mutual misunderstanding. The doctor thought he might have scared Perrini sufficiently, and Perrini thought that the doctor was kidding. He looked at the cognac bottle but suddenly did not like the thought of its taste. It was something that rose into his nose like brown smog and then settled on his tongue like the silt of the flats.

I could retire, he thought. God knows, he could have retired some years ago and moved to a village he did not remember, sat in a cafe that did not need to be faked in the entrance hall of a cold house on Lake Erie, he could have had the tobacco store that was closed all during siesta.

"Preach, Cutter's on the phone."

"Don't call me that!" he yelled at Campi. *Calma, calma,* he said to himself. I'm having thoughts like a dying man and the kind of temper like I'm scared.

Then he got up. He took his tie from the back of the seat and dropped it again and walked to the back room.

"What do you want?" he said into the phone.

"I've been thinking," said Cutter. "I think that man Tratto is more important than the other one."

"What in hell's that supposed to mean?"

"About your instructions, is what I mean. I think Tratto should go instead."

Cutter did not have to explain it. In spite of a brain that was now full of subterranean thoughts, Perrini understood clearly enough that Tratto might take over and delay everything that much longer.

"Okay with you?" said Cutter. "We skip the kid with the glasses and take the other one instead?"

"No!"

Cutter waited until the sound died down in his ear and until he felt that Perrini was ready.

"I don't think you can afford to send him back to his uncle in a box."

Perrini cleared his throat and changed his voice. He now felt more like his usual self, even though it was fake. "Glad you brought that up, Cutter. I was out of my head when I said that in the car."

"I can understand that."

"Good. Let's forget it. Now, go ahead like you said. I'll think of another way for the one with the glasses."

"Want me to think about it too, or let it go for right now?"

"You got thoughts?"

"That's why you hired me, Mister Perrini."

"And the uncle doesn't get it in a box."

"That's my thought, Mister Perrini."

"Let me know when you got it worked out."

"Right. I'm moving tonight."

They hung up and Cutter smiled at the little table top in front of him. That had been easy. The steak had not even come in yet. And what Perrini thought he had just now decided was already set up. When the steak came, Cutter was still smiling.

CHAPTER 19

Cutter had solved his manpower problem in a simple way. He did not build a gang, an organization, or even cells. He paid for specific jobs. In that way, the man never knew the significance of his sector and Cutter had no important loyalty problems. To a degree, this was even true in the case of Willie, whom Cutter had only picked because Willie knew everyone and had no loyalties of his own. The other exception to the policy—again in a limited way—was Drury.

They had met in prison, both on a similar charge. There were no political overtones to Drury's confinement. He was a professional second-story man and had beautiful, useful hands. Bethelport was not his beat. He had a circuit that covered Buffalo, Pittsburgh, and Miami. Bethelport was only a place to hide out, something about enmity with a robbery ring. Though it was not easy for Drury to hide, even in the Belt. He was tall, moved with commanding composure, he had a symmetrical ebony face, and was unusually silent. In Bethelport, his British accent embarrassed him.

"Your coat, suh," he said, and held it out for Cutter. It was a joke between them, the butler act and the stupid shine.

"Hotdawg, ifn it ain't. Now what, boy?"

"We just pop into it, suh."

"Shonuff? But Ah done popped mah pop a long ways back, boy, ifn Ah don't disremember."

Cutter did not have anybody else to joke with, and even so, they were not that comfortable about it. They dropped the act, nodded at each other, and went out to the street. They left the car behind and walked. The night air seemed touchable after the thaw, and it felt like rain.

"Eight o'clock," said Cutter. "If he's on time, Willie's going in now. If it works, they'll come out after we take our places. Think you better put the glove thing on?"

"Matter of fact, been wearing them for an hour. Takes time, you know."

Drury turned the cuff of one leather glove back and snapped the rim of the surgical glove underneath.

"Must be sweaty," said Cutter.

"Which is the point. Articulation and so forth becomes quite remarkable." Drury flexed his fingers.

When they came close to 1020 Buckingham, they saw the lights on the second floor. They separated to take their positions. Willie, all alone, had just gone up the stairs.

Only the side where the dental lab had been showed light under the door. Willie could smell tomato sauce cooking. He knocked on the door and waited.

The man who opened had a towel stuck into his collar and one side of his mouth was full of food.

"Excuse me, sir, could I see the boss?"

The man had to swallow first before he could talk. It did not diminish the bulge in his cheek. He looked toward one end of the room and said something that took a while to get out. Willie did not understand it, and he did not understand the answer. Then the man turned back toward Willie and said, "No."

"Thank you, sir," said Willie, and walked into the room.

Three of them sat at a table, eating out of a common bowl. One of them was shifting a box, which he dropped when he saw Willie come in. Another, beyond an open door, seemed to be standing at a stove.

"Ah," said Willie. "How good it smells," and to the man with the towel in his collar, "and you don't smell too bad either." Then Willie took off his hat with the feather and waited, just as the others were doing. He recognized Angelo by the glasses.

He came from the back, putting his white windbreaker on, walking like somebody who was not really leaving but was taking charge.

"What do you want?"

"I dunno—I just come by, like, to apologize." Willie's street clothes—the leather coat, the white shoes with black heels, the electric shirt and the pink suede vest—all looked suddenly out of place on his frame because he was grinning and scraping like a shy picaninny.

"For what?"

"Uh—maybe I better go. You all go on and eat. I'm sorry."

"You stay right there." Angelo put his hands on his hips and flared his windbreaker. He wished it were as big as that leather coat. "How come you knew we were up here?"

"My brother told me. The one you beat up on." Someone in the back was translating for the rest, and there was a stir around the table and men moving slowly to form an arc.

"I didn't mean no trouble, sir."

"You're goddamn right you're not, because any—"

"Let him talk," said Tratto. He came from the back, wiping his hands on a rag, and when he was done he tossed it at one of the men.

"Thank you, sir," said Willie. "Like I came to tell you, we knew you were coming here."

"Who's we?" Tratto wanted to know.

"Us, you know, the neighborhood."

"So?"

"So it's superfly—I mean, we're glad you come."

"You haven't said who you are yet."

"Willie, Willie the Kisser. I'm around, you know, in the neighborhood."

"Doing what?"

"This and that, you know. Gotta pay the rent."

In a way, thought Willie, this is the pitch he would give in the grilling room, same evasions, same endearments, same invulnerable stupidity about everything. Except, in this case, he had them buffaloed. He almost giggled with delight, but turned it into a shy cough.

"You're not saying much," said Tratto.

"I'm trying to tell it," said Willie. "All us cats who's doing this and that, you know, in the neighborhood, we come to make friends, lay on some cheer—except that fucker come up here with a bad scene. And I come to apologize,"

"Lemme get this straight," said Angelo who had not understood anything. "Your brother wasn't bringing a neighborhood greeting. He was with some bastard by the name of Perrini."

"What I'm trying to *say!* That fucker's a Tom, a real—"

"What?" said Tratto.

Angelo translated by saying that a Tom was a black person who sells himself to a white person, and when that explanation went astray, he said that such a black person was not a whore, literally, but in a general way.

"Right," said Willie. "He shines up to that Perrini who wants to rob the neighborhood blind. I mean, the Preach is no good. Man, he don't even *live* here, like you cats, right in the neighborhood!"

Angelo looked around and started to smile.

"That's okay," he said to Willie. "We don't think all you black people are bad. Very glad you came up. Very good of you to come and explain about your brother."

"The no good fucker," Willie corrected.

"Fine," said Angelo, not knowing which way to head next.

"So I come to make it up to you, like I said, specially since I was going to come anyways, show you around, spread the cheer, maybe give you a hand with the neighborhood."

Since Willie had offered a favor, which always means that some advantage is sought, Angelo was now convinced that here was the genuine article, the man who could be bought. It was time to sweeten the cup, to be generous.

"Come in and have a glass of something, uh, Willie. Maybe some food?"

"Cheez, I mean, that's why I come! To ask you the same thing. Treat you to a spread, we got some fine places right here on the boulevard, I mean food and stuff, maybe tip a few, meet some cats from the neighborhood."

"Where?" asked Tratto.

"Like one block down, man, out in public. And if that don't fill the bill, there's a couple of other things I can lay on you. I mean, you name it, any color or shape. Fact is," and he did his modesty act, "I got some action in the snatch trade myself."

Angelo explained that Willie was a pimp. Tratto explained that they should not leave the place at night. Angelo reminded the other that fraternization was the bedrock of success. And after a certain amount of further discussion that did not include Willie, Willie won. They went to the place one block down, out in public. They left only two men behind.

The reason Cutter knew this was because Willie, when he led his sheep out of the building, was capering, laughing, waving his arms, and holding two fingers up like a victory sign. Cutter watched them go. Then he crossed the street and went to the back of the building.

"How's it look?" He could hardly see Drury.

"Looks like a hall window. Are their lights still on?"

"There's two of 'em left behind."

Drury continued to look up, considering.

"The dark window to the right of the hall, that would be in back of the lab?"

"Looks it."

"And dark as it is, there must be a door between that room and the lit front."

"You can't get from that fire escape to that window, Drury."

"You impugn my professionalism, sir."

"Drury, it's too risky. We can skip this part, I mean it man. It was just a thought, in case all of 'em left."

"You impugn—"

"Shit, man, I don't even know what that means."

"It means, let me do it."

Cutter thought for a moment, and then, "In that case, I'll decoy them, the way I said. That too much of a slight on your professionalism?"

"Yes. However, it does seem to be safer. Come along, I'll unlock the front for you."

The slight rain had turned into a steady drizzle that had cleared the foot traffic off the boulevard. Cars hissed by, their headlights like impersonal eyes that looked at nothing. Drury spent two minutes on the lock of the entrance door, and then he pushed it open. Cutter followed him in.

"Now unlock the beauty parlor door," he whispered. "I draw 'em down, hide in here, and when they run outside I lock the front door behind them."

"And the one who stayed at the top of the stairs unlocks it for the one out on the street. After shooting you."

"Okay," said Cutter. "Your way."

"Five minutes," said Drury.

Cutter waited in the dark hall while Drury went around to the back where he carefully pulled down the fire escape. It squeaked a little. This was not the noise that worried him. The men on the second floor were much more likely to hear the sound when Drury had to open their back window.

He stood on the iron landing and looked through the window that showed him the upstairs hall. There was one dim light. He could see Cutter come up the stairs. Drury waited until he saw Cutter knock on the door. After that, he went his own way. Whatever happened next in the hall, the men in the lab would not be listening to their back window making sounds. After that, there would be no sound, just sleek, unimpugned professionalism. Drury chuckled to himself and moved into his work.

And if Drury would have smashed his way into the window, the two men in the lab still would not have heard. They were talking too loud. Nothing like a knock at the door was expected at this time of night. The event bore discussion. Cutter could hear them while he got ready and waited. Then silence.

They were being cautious about it. Cutter could hear the creak of their shoes. When the door flew open, he stood out of the way in case they had decided to come out shooting at the space. They did not come out, which meant they stayed in the light and could see that much less of the darker hall. But that did not improve Cutter's sense of safety. They both held guns. They held them low and away from their bodies, as if they were afraid that the guns might blow up in their hands. Cutter was worried about the same kind of thing. He was certain that they would be much better with knives.

When nothing moved, which made too much silence, Cutter decided to go into his act. He slipped and rolled down the first few stairs. In the process he dropped a half pint of cheap whiskey. Drunken nigger with cloudy notions of revenge in the night. That was the image.

He started to blubber properly and scrambled to pull himself up by the bannister.

"It's the same one."

"No. This one looks darker."

"Idiot. It *is* darker. Go throw him out."

"Beat him up first?"

"And then throw him out."

Cutter slipped again and made a wet burp, to firm up his image.

"Maybe we should keep him till the others come back. Maybe Angelo wants to talk to him."

One man gave his gun to the other and came toward the steps. But the way things stood, it was still too risky to run, thought Cutter. The longer they stayed out in the hall, the better for Drury. He went limp, but let himself be picked up. He helped enough so that the Sicilian and he would not fall down the stairs. All that time he made a din in their ears with his foreign talk.

Once on the landing, everything changed. The man who was holding Cutter knew it first, feeling the change in his hands. There was muscle and there was movement of its own. Then Cutter's skull came up and snapped the man's chin up and his head back and some sudden twist broke the grip. All of this never became totally clear, because the next impact was of three separate stair-risers into the back of the head, the shoulder blades, and the small of the back.

Cutter was already into the Sicilian, who was holding two guns. One of those dropped immediately. The other one was forgotten as soon as Cutter's foot snapped one of the man's kneecaps out of place. He let the man fall and saw to it that the two guns got kicked out of reach. Then he slid the man down the stairs. What with the knee, the man would probably pass out from the bumping. But Cutter worried about them flat on their backs and not moving much. It was very important to play more games, to be seen in flight, to give Drury his chance....

The window had made an ungodly squeal. Drury did not close it again until he had rubbed both channels with soap. Then he closed the window again, on account of the draft. He found three rooms in the dark, not counting the big room in front, the kitchen part, and the toilet. The sounds in the hall were confusing, except for the thump. Then nothing again.

The one who had hit his head and back was watching Cutter all the time. He had checked himself and found that he could move in spite of the pain.

He felt for his knife.

Drury had found nothing. The dark did not bother him. He saw with his fingertips, with his nose, with his ears. What bothered him was the mess of everything. This way, no probabilities of search worked. Maxim: Never hit a place where somebody had just moved in.

Cutter was dragging the man with the broken kneecap back on the landing where he laid him down. That one was out. Next he looked for the two guns he had kicked away. They were in the dark, outside the shaft of light from the open door. Between breaths he listened for sounds behind the wall. Nothing.

Drury had tripped over a box and fallen like a cat. It was nothing.

Cutter, in the dark, broke the cylinders open and pushed out the shells. He could see the man on the stairs and how he shifted in a cautious way. Odd thing was, with that much caution, why no sound of groan or stifled breathing? Then Cutter smiled.

Drury, very reluctant on account of the silence in the hall which he could not see, moved into the lit part of the room arrangement. Kitchen place? Nothing. It would have to be bigger than a coffee can, bag of flour, packet of beans, olive-oil can. Drury noted that for the vegetable end of the spectrum there was only tomato paste and garlic. Now, front room? Can't risk it. But what if it was in that infinite number of boxes?

Cutter got back into the light and down one step of the stairs. Very suspicious now, like a drunk on the brink of the abyss of soberness. His gun hand wobbled, steadied, and jerked.

"*Paisano!*"

The back-injury case looked up with the baffled innocence of Judas Iscariot accused.

"See the gun? Hey, *paisano*. Lookit. *Boom-boom.*" Some more of that and some vigorous pointing with the finger of the other hand and, aha! The knife hand moved out very slowly, palm up, knife lying loose, and then the knife clattered down the steps. A very clever bastard indeed, thought Cutter. If I pass him and stoop to get the knife, he falls on top of me. If I leave it behind, he'll pick it up when I'm down the stairs. It was very good, and useless. Cutter, gun out like an anxious flashlight looking for something in the dark, snuck past the frightened man on the stairs.

Drury, still puzzling now and then about the inadequate diet that lacked all fresh vegetables, went over the three dark rooms once again. Once again litter of clothes and cardboard suitcases. Once again, mattresses on the floor and the refrigerator that stood in the dark passage, without hum, without light going on when the door was opened. Of course.

He opened the bottom panel and found no coils, no motor, no drip pan, but there was the little safe. Drury closed his eyes and let his fingertips illuminate the small dial and sense the faint differences in motion and pressure.

While Cutter reached the bottom of the stairs without having bothered to pick up the knife.

When he heard the painful scramble on the stairs he jerked around and watched the man drop the knife, raise his hands. Cutter's swivel seemed to take over all on its own. The arms flayed, the gun clattered across the floor, and he slid helplessly towards the street door. The man on the stairs was down in the hall like a slithering snake and got to the gun. Cutter weaved his way out of the door and into the street.

He was able to draw his pursuer into the rain, almost half way down the block, until Cutter disappeared into an alley and the Sicilian pumped a shot into the murk, a shot that was nothing but a click. A few more useless clicks, and the Sicilian ran painfully back to the shelter of his building.

Cutter had no idea whether his play had given Drury the time he needed. The rain drifted in sheets. Cutter's ear felt as if it might glow in the dark. He walked back to the boulevard, to the building, and what he could see, at the top of the stairs in the shaft of light, were two feet walking backward slowly and an awkward body dragging across the floor. When the door closed on the light from the lab, Cutter knew that two hurt Sicilians and one black second-story man were in the same place. Maybe a telephone call for a doctor, for sure some running back and forth to get aspirin, wet rags, a pillow, a blanket, and Drury plastered to the other side of the window, which was three feet away from the fire escape.

When Cutter was in the rear of the building again he could see well enough that there was nobody by the window, on the fire escape, or anyplace against the wall. He stood in the whispering dark for half an hour, as wet as if he were naked.

He was shivering. He came to the point where he had no idea why he was doing any of this. The only desperate comparison to something worse was the flash of recollection that placed him in the hole, the green walls stinking of his own filth, and the difference was that then he had not been able to get out, except by going crazy, while at this moment he could turn his back and walk away....

"I say—"

The shape was already this side of the window, lumped against the impossible smoothness of the wet wall.

"Catch this, be a sport."

Cutter ran closer to the building and caught the bundle, which turned out to be Drury's overcoat, heavier than any overcoat Cutter had ever known. Drury came swinging down the fire escape without bothering to lower the weighted end which hung away from the ground. Drury landed next to Cutter.

"You got out clean?"

"I wouldn't be here. Let's get cracking, shall we?"

When Cutter got to the car, Drury was already inside. The motor was running and the heater was on. Cutter threw the gross weight of overcoat into the back seat, and Drury put the headlights on and drove away from the curb. This was two hours after they had left together, only ten o'clock in the evening, and they needed time to dry out. Drury took the on-ramp to the turnpike going west along the lake and drove for half an hour at permissible speed while the heater was blasting.

"What happened?" said Cutter.

"They hadn't a notion I was there. Busy tending wounds, I'd say. There was a safe, case you're wondering."

"I was." Cutter was remembering an eternity of rain.

"Do take a look. The pockets are staggered, where you'd normally expect the lining."

Twenty minutes later, and with Bethelport way behind, Cutter had counted the bundles of bills, which were old and new and held by rubber bands.

One hundred and eighty thousand dollars, plus some.

"I guess we got their working capital," said Cutter.

"Gratifying."

"Thank you, Drury."

They swung off the turnpike, an hour out of Bethelport, and stopped at a place that said *Eat*. Cutter had something that was advertised as steak, and Drury had something that was advertised as a salad. They ate half of their orders, drank some coffee, and got back into the car. At the dark end of the parking lot, with the heater going and steam on the glass, Cutter held his hands close to the map light and counted notes in hundreds and fifties onto the console next to the gear shift. He stopped at twenty thousand, which was about 10 per cent for a job well done.

"I'm gratified," he said, pushing the rest of the bundles under his seat.

Drury got out of the car, put his moist overcoat on, and walked around the car while Cutter worked his way across and behind the wheel. When Drury was seated on the right, he picked up his bills and made them disappear into various pockets.

"If you could make the airport within forty-five minutes," he said.

Cutter was already guiding the car back up on the ramp and onto the turnpike toward Bethelport. At a conservative sixty, Drury would make his flight with half an hour to spare. The rain had become very thin and then stopped. The temperature seemed to be dropping.

"You wouldn't stay, would you?" Cutter did not put much hope into it.

"No," said Drury.

They sat without talking for a while. Cutter watched the road, and Drury watched his windshield wiper.

"Would you tell me why, Drury?"

"I don't like the town." Then he shrugged. "It's more than that, actually. Though I don't know how to say it."

"I don't know what you're talking about."

"I do, but I don't know how to say it. I'd best skip it."

But the quality of seriousness in Drury moved something in Cutter and would not let him go, as if Drury, too, were concerned with the imminence of everything Cutter was doing.

"If it's lousy feelings about Bethelport," said Cutter, "tell me." He slowed to take the off-ramp that would channel him toward the airport. Perhaps the rain and such would cancel Drury's flight? Unlikely.

"As I said, it's not the town, really." Drury peered at the airport signs that shunted to the traffic to different parts of the complex. "United is reached by the middle lane, did you notice?"

"I noticed."

"I knew a man once, in the islands," said Drury as if he had forgotten the previous conversation. "Fact, used to fish with the man. And this man had something about him. You might fish with him and catch as much as he, but back on the dock you might tip your bucket and lose most of your catch."

Cutter slowed for the access curve. The airport entrances showed in lights.

"He lived with a woman once and she caught dysentery. He did not. Another time, he had a perfectly simple business reversal, he and a friend. A bit of smuggling, and they got caught. The man I am thinking about got two years and one off for good behavior. His friend, in gaol at the same time, was stabbed to death in a fight. So it goes with that man. He had an effect."

Cutter rolled to a stop by the curb where it said United. "It's that kind of thing? That's why you're leaving?" asked Cutter.

"One catches a feeling for such a thing," Drury sounded vague but quite serious. Then he opened his door and got out.

"Who is it?" asked Cutter. "Who's like that here?" Cutter could only see Drury from the waist up. "Me? Or Perrini?"

Drury bent down to look into the car and Cutter half expected or possibly hoped that Drury would be smiling. He might smile about the Cutter-Perrini choice as if it were a joke. But Drury's symmetrical face was earnest.

"I don't know, Cutter. I just catch the effect. It might not be either of you."

Then he said good-bye and walked away.

CHAPTER 20

The rain had started again. It animated the halo of light around the carriage lamp below her window. Rosanna looked at the undulant space made by the lamp, and had the impression that the space was shrinking. It was an amoebic light which never expanded, always contracted itself, but would not disappear. She held herself with her arms, crossing them under her breasts. When she became conscious of the rounded weight, she dropped her arms to her sides, feeling disgust. She had shrunk and shrunk steadily but, like the light, was still there. It was an eerie, uncomfortable feeling, like a spell she sought some way to break.

Rosanna left the window and sat down at her desk. For a while she fingered a letter-opener that was shaped like a sword, with ruby and emerald chips in the handle. Then she picked up the phone. The operator connected her with the new number of Shop by Phone.

"I would like to speak to Mr. Forza."

"Who's this?"

"I am Miss Perrini."

"Ah," said Tratto. "He's not here, Miss Perrini."

"Don't give me that. I've got to talk to him. It's really important."

"I'm sorry about what happened this afternoon. I'm Tratto. You remember me."

"If you don't get him on the line right this minute, you're going to be sorry about something else that's going to happen!"

"And what could that be, Miss Perrini?"

"I mean it. Cutter is really after you people now!"

"Who?"

"That black man, for heaven's sake. Now you let me talk to Angelo right away."

Tratto looked toward the end of the long, unfriendly room with the boxes, where two more of his men lay stretched out, waiting for the doctor. So, the whole evening had been arranged. And, of course, the elaborate dinner, the introductions, the nightclubs, none of that had been designed solely so that the black man could beat up two of Tratto's men.

"Forget about Angelo," he said and hung up the phone.

He had no idea where Angelo and some of the others might be. That did not matter. Something else was more important. Tratto remembered that the cap of the broken whiskey bottle on the landing had its seal intact. That man Cutter had probably not been drunk at all. And Tratto remembered that he himself had pushed shut the back window upon his return because rain was blowing in by the bottom crack. Why a crack?

Tratto went to the refrigerator, opened the bottom, opened the safe. No question now. Forget about Angelo. Time to leave while he could and report to Buffalo in person.

Tratto packed a small canvas bag. It was a sign of his leadership quality that he could cut his losses by forgetting about those who had to be left behind.

After climbing the stairs, Perrini was aware of a shortness of breath. He stopped outside of Rosanna's room, to catch his breath and to gather himself for his speech. He did not have a ready role to fall back upon. On the other side of the door he heard a telephone being dropped in its cradle. There was silence, and Perrini walked into the room.

Rosanna did not look up. Perrini stood for a while, then sat down on a small, fluffy chair by the door, all the while holding a smile on his face. Rosanna did not turn around, and he dropped the smile. He felt that the least she could do was to inquire about his well-being after the scene she had witnessed in Black Belt.

"Are you all right, Rosie?"

Rosanna sat up a little but did not answer. She just shrugged.

"You look lonely, *bella*," Perrini said.

She turned his way, and for a moment Perrini thought that she was going to get up and come toward him. He immediately let the smile set on his face again, and then their moment, their almost-moment, was gone. Rosanna closed her eyes and bit into her lip. When she opened her eyes again she looked at her father from a distance.

"What do you want?"

"*Bella*, I want ..."

"Don't call me that. I'm not your wife."

"Rosanna! I've come to talk. I've been meaning to talk to you for a long time."

Rosanna turned to lean her arms on the desk. One finger made nervous taps on the miniature sword.

"But you've been very busy," she said to the wall. She turned her head to look at her father. "There's something you want, isn't there?"

"Ah, Rosie, Rosie," he said like a sigh. He got off the silly chair and started to walk around. "I want you to be all right. You are my daughter and what I want ..."

"Of course, Father."

"Hear me out. When I see my daughter get foolish thoughts about a man, a type like that Angelo—Well, *bella,* let me put it this way."

"Let me. You want to know what went on between me and that type.

Correct?"

"I'm sure there is nothing to tell."

"But you want me to stay away from him."

"That's right."

"No. I won't."

"Rosanna, your voice. Er, why won't you?"

This time Rosanna got up too.

"Because at least he was around!"

"That's no reason, Rosanna, no reason to keep company with a very bad man!" Perrini began to think more about Angelo now than about his daughter. He hit his stride with, "A conniving, underhanded piece of filth, who pretends one thing and then uses you for something else. And that's bad!"

Perrini listened to his heart pound in his skull. In a moment he could see his daughter again. She stood straddle-legged nearby, her eyes flat as glass, and with a smile on her mouth that connected to none of the rest of her face.

"A bad man! Listen to the good preacher-man tell about good and bad! That bad Angelo gave me his time, looked at me, wanted me, and stayed with pleasure! And thank you very much, father priest, it was worth the pleasure! And when it comes to that ..."

"Do you know whom you're talking to?!" roared Perrini.

"Oh yes I do! I'm talking to a conniving, underhanded, spoiled priest, I am, who pretends one thing at home and then uses his front ..."

Perrini's hand slapped the rest of the words out of existence.

"Prostituta! You're not my daughter!"

"I know that, Preach!"

When he swung at her face again she raised her arm so that his hand slammed across the miniature sword in her hand. When he felt the pain he also saw her face—not his daughter's face, but the young female with wild life in her eyes and a loud, free laugh beating at him, full of derision.

He hit her with his fist.

He could see her bounce when she flew into the desk and he could hear the *crack* when she hit the wall.

All the time it took Perrini to understand and to forget what had happened to him, Rosanna lay on the floor and did not move. Then he went to her and saw her looking at him. One eye was crossed over and her neck was already visibly swollen. She made scrabbling motions with her fingers and she breathed, but she could not move her legs anymore. That was all the doctor said later.

What was going to happen to Angelo had been in the making for some time when Cutter reached the house on Twenty-second Street.

Cutter had changed his clothes in the meantime, and the bundles of bills were no longer in his car. He stopped the motor and sat for a while. His body had returned to complaining. No steam bath could take the place of a rest for very long. He sat and heard the rain whisper on his dark car and then, from a wavering distance, the sounds from the house. Motown sounds reeling off a tape. Cutter felt as if he heard more the distance than the sound, an unpleasant experience, a reminder of his desert, which was no longer supposed to be there. Cutter felt strangely reluctant to get up and to go into the house. Motown sounds servicing the white son of a bitch in there, and the black, usable women servicing the white son of a bitch in there, until the setup became his fall....

Cutter touched the pack of cigarettes Drury had left on the front seat. Careful Drury had left something behind. He had left cigarettes behind and a comment about somebody's evil effect. Cutter lit a cigarette and smoked it like a novice. He discovered that he sat behind the wheel, sat inside his clothes, sat, as a matter of fact, on his own ass like a novice who did not feel he belonged on top of his own ass. And he was going to get the young son of a bitch and later the old son of a bitch as sure as man could make plans, feeling all the while that perhaps none of this mattered. There had been a lot more fire, until five years ago. Or if he had Asikari's hate, that, too, would make everything clearer. If I make it, it's the Charley fever; and if I don't make it, I'm a jive punk.

The desert stretched again, with rain falling, but the rain made nothing grow.

Or maybe just take the money, cut clear of everything, and live on it. And where could a black nothing-man live on a lot of cash money before Charley with the pasty nose and with the waxy fingers came messing him over? Since I didn't give you this, nigger, you ain't got no right to it. Back in the hole.

Cutter threw the cigarette out the window. When it plopped he watched it hiss before turning the window up again. The fact was, the only place safe for a nothing-man was where the great white thing did not care to go: the ghetto. Cutter could walk there, eat there, kill there, love there, and rip off his brothers there, while the Man kept his cautious distance. So, the trick was ... Cutter did not find Asikari's hate but something vaguer in sound, though more solid in the bone: he would insist to survive.

He got out of the car and slammed the door and looked up and down the street for a moment. Bleak as the view was, Cutter felt a touch of good humor. True, it had a thin, black edge to it, an edge like a knife.

Motown gave him a blast in the face when he opened the door to the house. There were people in the parlor, and there were more on the other side of the hall where the sliding glass doors had been pushed back to open the dining room. The parlor smelled of smoke, spilled whiskey, and incense. The dining room smelled of ham, sugared yams, and incense. None of what could be heard, smelled, tasted, or touched upstairs or downstairs was free. Even the laughing and squealing had the kind of jacked-up intensity that tried to squeeze the last drop out of everything because it all cost money.

Cutter knew some of the faces, but most of them not. Somebody tried to buy him a drink, somebody wanted to dance. It was not his party.

"Hey, Cutter," said a man who used to run errands for Tiffany. "You been asking around for Lillie?"

"Right." Cutter hesitated, not knowing whether to stop.

"She off and went to college."

"You know where?"

"Where? College! I just said."

It was possible that Lillie had gone to college. It was also possible that she had married a white man, which was another story Cutter had heard. He saw Willie wave at him from the other side of the buffet in the dining room. Willie was hatless and coatless, a rare sight. His pink suede vest gave him a chicken-chested look, and the puffed sleeves of his electric shirt made his shoulders look one yard wide.

"Where you been, man?"

"Took Drury to his plane."

"Drury split?"

"That was the arrangement."

"Shit. How many you got left to count on?"

Cutter did not answer. The anatomy of cell organization meant that only the head knew how large the body was.

"How's the Angelo thing?" asked Cutter.

"No sweat. But I'm telling you, man, that cat's an athlete. Listen, you put Dalton across the street from Ten Twenty?"

"I did."

"He called in. He says Tratto split."

"What do you mean, split?"

"Went upstairs and I guess saw the mess you left and *zowee*."

"How did Dalton say it?"

"Comes back alone, like real leader type who don't cut up with the troops on their night out, silent type, like you."

"What did *Dalton* say, damn it."

"Is up there twenty minutes, comes back down with his bitty canvas bag and an extra set of vines over one arm, gets into his car. Hey, there's a cat here says Lillie went off to college."

"Did Dalton tag him?"

"Right. That's next. Tratto stops to gas up—Dalton checked with the man at the station, Arnie, one of your men in the new cell, right?"

"And?"

"And Dalton checks him far as the intersection where the turnpike lets you off to get to Route 90."

"Heading for the city, looks like."

Willie was more sober now.

"What's it mean, Cutter?"

Cutter took Willie to the back of the hall where the door went to the kitchen. The door was closed to customers.

"It means," he said, "we're just about in. It means the Sidgie has no confidence in Angelo, and it means he's after reinforcement from the Don. It means we start swinging!"

Cutter would not say any more. He only said that if all went well upstairs, they would all meet in the bungalow tomorrow and have a meeting. Then he gave Willie a pat on the arm and turned to call after Jerutha.

She stopped on the stairs and leaned over the bannister. She had a customer with her.

"Ten minutes," she whispered. Her customer was already weaving ahead, up the stairs.

"How's the Angelo thing doing?"

"Jeesis God," she said. "He run through five of us. That joe is a machine!"

"Got a reputation to build, maybe."

"Not by me. You know, I don't think he feels a damn thing."

Her hard little lemon breasts showed in the vee of the working outfit she was wearing, and when Jerutha saw Cutter looking that way she made a small, practiced motion to hold the material together in front.

"Ten minutes?"

"I'll be busy. Take you home later."

She shrugged and went up the stairs, and in a moment Cutter went up too.

The original ground plan of the two-story house had not been altered except in one respect. What at one time had been the master bedroom, the largest room upstairs, had been made even larger by including in its space the far end of the hall. The room was an arena. The bathroom that had been across the hall adjoined the arena now with a blind wall. The bathroom had been converted to a place with a row of seats and the blind wall had a large oil painting on it. Seen from the bathroom, the oil painting was a one-way window.

Cutter sat down in one of the chairs and looked at the other man there who was holding up a tripod with a camera on top.

"When's it going to be?"

"Big Ben says the chump isn't drunk enough."

"Hard to believe," said Cutter while looking at the table in the arena room, covered with full, half-full, and empty bottles.

"He keeps working it off," said the photographer. "He's a machine."

Angelo was weaving around the room, doing some kind of marginal dance. A tape was doing one kind of beat and Angelo was singing another. He may not have been drunk enough according to Big Benjamin, but he was drunk enough to be naked with all the others in the room. There was Marge, the woman in the suit, wearing her suit. There was Big Ben, naked, and deserving the name, and there was Dottie with nothing on and standing by the wall next to the giant bed. She was just standing there with her legs crossed and her arms folded behind her. Her child's face, her thin arms and slim ankles made a strange contrast with the fruit-ripeness of the rest of her body. For some men the combination produced an inordinate thrill. She watched Angelo with a stubborn look. It did not change when he stopped in front of her.

"So do it," he said, continuing something that had started before Cutter had come.

"I plain won't!"

"For the last time!" The menace in Angelo's voice was slurred and ineffectual.

"Now you listen here," said Dottie the way she might talk to a younger brother, "I don't stand on my head for nobody. Just what do you take me for?"

Big Ben got up from the bed. He was twice as large as Angelo, heavy with muscle, and with a face full of brutal bones. His walk was oddly precise.

"Come on dear," he said to Dottie. "You sit yourself and take a rest. Sit by Marge."

Marge got up from the couch at one end of the room but Dottie did not get very far.

"I'm paying for this," said Angelo. He grabbed the girl by one arm and spun her around so she landed on the bed. Then he grabbed her ankles and hoisted her so her head would hang down. Dottie screamed and Big Ben smiled. He reached between Angelo's legs, gave a simple squeeze, and Angelo collapsed.

"Oh, dear," said Big Ben. "Don't know my own strength." He tossed Angelo on the bed, face down, and nodded at Marge. "You two ladies go on now," he said.

In the room with the row of chairs, the photographer got up and shifted his equipment around.

"Finally," he said and hit a switch on the wall.

Five spots flared up in the ceiling, making a bright, unnatural scene of the room. Angelo was on the bed with his legs hanging down to the ground. Big Ben was patting the white behind. He turned his head and looked at the window.

"Take your time, sweety," he said to the photographer. "Let's not rush a good thing—"

Cutter did not stay long. The final prints, completed by morning, captured seven different arrangements. Angelo was clearly awake in five of them.

CHAPTER 21

The frost dried out the air and made a week of brisk, bright weather over Bethelport. The air now had turned to an almost Alpine purity, and the sky was a still blue over the tired water of the lake. People experienced an onslaught of unusual vigor, though most of them did not know what to do with it.

Cutter kept the place on 1020 Buckingham Boulevard. The boxes were stacked in the back, and the beds, suitcases, clothes, and personal trivia were thrown out or given to neighborhood agencies. The physical plant was cleaned out and tightened up. Cutter kept the name Shop-by-Mail, changing the handwritten sign to a professional printing job.

The real tightening up was not as clearly visible as a swept floor, phones in a neat row, records in black ink and red ink. The real thing happened with the men.

There was no more recruiting problem. On the one hand, there was money in the Cutter camp; on the other, nobody was sure how Cutter had made it. The jobs Cutter gave out were specific, and the pay was clear-cut. Anybody who ran a line on the side was cut off and thrown out. And since nobody knew what Cutter knew about his total organization, his men were very much dependent on him.

There was no more drop-out problem. Cutter saw to it that the drifting kind either did not get in or that the man on the fence got fired. Meanwhile, the unit of the working body remained the cell. Asikari, from his distance, understood all that.

At the same time, Perrini received regular messages but had no opportunity to meet with Cutter. The messages detailed weekly take on numbers (Tiffany's operation was being absorbed), on book-making (Perrini had been persuaded to keep his wire available), and there even was money on a dream-book concession.

So far, Perrini had not seen any cash. The take, in the form of an accountant's statement, was already one-third higher per week than the most that Perrini had ever taken out of the Belt. But, as part of the accountant's statement, the money was held in reserve for distribution at the end of the month.

Menotti did not think there was anything wrong with that, at least not in the beginning, because if worst came to worst, the Perrini influence could always cut off protection.

While Perrini got very little consultation from Cutter, he was getting a great deal from Buffalo.

—What are you doing to control the uprising in the Belt!

—Where are four of the surviving Sicilians?

—Do you have a percentage arrangement?

—Where is Angelo Forza?

—Who is using our wire service?

—Do you need outside help?

—Do you think Angelo Forza has absconded with money?

—Tratto's analysis suggests that the Belt is in fact not a profit area. Do you concur?

—Why did you think it was in the first place?

—Where is Angelo?

—Where is the income?

—Specifics urgent.

Perrini lost a further ten pounds. He worried about Rosanna. He allowed his wife to continue her cognac-diluting, because he felt it might be beneficial to his health. Under the cover of emergency business meetings, he spent one night of the week away from home. The emergency meetings took place at a syndicate-owned resort hotel that was closed for the season. What he met came one at a time, was invariably less than twenty-five years old, and did a professional job. Perrini's business met with fluctuating success. His health stayed about the same. So did his fantasies.

At the end of the month, Cutter sent his apologies for the delay but announced that he had sorted things out well enough to make his report, because he now felt that his assignment had been successfully completed. And he would bring the money himself, since—at this stage of the game—no routine channels for transfer had as yet been established.

With report in pocket and belt pulled tight, Perrini had Campi drive him to the Porter House, which was a better restaurant than the trick name would imply. Way back in the velour darkness and the smoked walnut. Menotti had sat down to eat. Perrini took his overcoat off and sat down.

"What's that?"

"*Coq au vin.* And over here, Brussels sprouts with a lemony sauce that—"

"Never mind."

"It's good."

Perrini ordered a large glass of burgundy and told the waiter not to bother him with the name. Then he unfolded Cutter's latest message, typed on plain bond, and laid it on the table so that Menotti could see it while he ate. After the wine had come and Perrini had drunk a good deal of it, he said, "The last sentence. What's that sound like, Menotti?"

"Sounds routine to me. He must have picked up somebody who took a typing course where they learn about phrases used in correspondence and so forth. Kind of makes a good impression all around, the way he's been handling ..."

"Handling what?"

"Well, handling correspondence. Sounds straight enough."

"Straight? You know what that punk is saying to me?"

"Francisco." Menotti gave up trying to eat, put his fork down, and dabbed his mouth with the napkin. "Not punk. If you continue to think of him as a punk, you're at a disadvantage."

Perrini drank the rest of the wine. Menotti looked at the correspondence again.

"Yes. I see it."

"'As yet no routine channels of transfer'—you see that?"

Menotti sat back and held the bridge of his nose for a moment, closing his eyes. Then he put his arms on the table.

"Francisco, did you really think you had hired somebody to knock some Sidgies around, or is it not true that you in fact engaged someone willing and knowledgeable enough to establish a permanent link between you and a heretofore inaccessible territory? Honestly now, Francisco."

"Yeah, yeah." Perrini was mumbling. "Rub it in."

"Of course you knew. And of course he now expects to discuss details of a continuing association."

"You're right, you're right." Perrini sighed and looked at velour drapes, seeing nothing. "I get rattled so easy, you know, these last few weeks."

"I know. How's Rosanna?"

"The same. We're taking her to a new doctor. Let's eat."

He waved at the waiter. After ordering, he asked for another glass of wine. Menotti's undemanding face and quiet mind gentled Perrini.

"First let's eat and then talk Cutter afterwards."

"Sure, Francisco."

"Anything come in at your end? Are you holding Buffalo off well enough?"

"I think so."

"So. Nothing new then."

"Except one thing. Angelo showed up in Buffalo."

Perrini waited. This could mean any number of things.

"I first heard it from Longstreet, who's talking for Santino now. Angelo did not *try* to show up in New York. Actually, he was trying to leave the country."

"*Cornuto!* So he *did* steal the money!"

"He says not. Matter of fact, he doesn't say much at all."

"First you heard it from Longstreet. Who else?"

"Santino Forza himself."

"Ouch."

"He said he could not reach you."

"Yeah. I was in conference most of the night."

"Quite all right. He then called me and he talked readily enough."

Perrini patted his vest and took out a pill. He swallowed it, dreading the thought of more mystery. He said, "He wants to send the nephew back and have him try it differently."

"Matter of fact, he would like to. But Angelo, as the Don put it, is not ready to commit himself."

"What in hell does that mean?"

"I'll summarize my conversation and my impression. I gather this: Don Santino, whose eventual level-headedness I would never fault, would indeed like to send Angelo back, under a more cooperative arrangement with you—he was quite generous in his thinking—except, as I read it between the lines, Angelo refuses."

Perrini grinned.

"For a minute there I thought we had a problem."

"We do, Francisco."

Perrini's first course arrived, a bowl of fragrant soup, which stayed untouched on the table.

"I'll add this," said Menotti. "I called two of my Buffalo sources, and their description of Angelo's 'not ready to commit himself' is something else."

"Oh? He'll come back only if he can replace me?"

"I wouldn't go that far," Menotti started, but when he saw Perrini's face, he switched his approach. "The description of the young man is quite odd," he said. "Stays locked in his room, no association with former friends, male or female, sleeps with the lights on—matter of fact, seems to sleep sitting up in a chair. And there seem to be a number of medical problems."

"Like what? A loss of guts?"

"Matter of fact, something in that area, in the medical sense, of course. He sees an internist who specializes in intestinal problems, whatever they are, spastic colon, for example."

"Get back to the other thing. What did Santino really want?"

"He has a problem. There is no question he wants Angelo to come back, insists, as a matter of fact, that he complete his assignment. The problem is the conditions Angelo sets: Guns, terrorize the Belt, autonomy from you, plus a slice of your established territory. Don Santino wishes to know for what remuneration you will conform to these conditions, and how you might—I'll give you his words—guide the nephew by lending your wisdom."

Perrini gagged.

"He's insane—"

Before Perrini could work himself into something monumental and useless, Menotti took over for him. His voice was quite stern.

"Don Santino's qualifications are neither here nor there. But his purpose and the weight with which he can invest it, that is our concern. He is obviously willing to pay a great deal to—er, continue the traditional bloodline. What does he care whether that purpose renders one territory temporarily unproductive? He has ten more! But *you* care, Francisco, because you only have *one*."

"—work of a life time—"

Menotti felt a slight edge of disgust.

"I advise you," he said, "to view this as a matter of business, as a matter of necessary manipulations. Francisco, you have done it before. And remember also, please, that I am here to help you."

"Sure. Just gimme a minute."

"Of course. We'll work it out. Let me call Cutter for a conference tomorrow evening. That gives us almost two days to prepare an approach."

Perrini, in spite of temporary lapses due to age and health, was a trained athlete in his own right. He began to recover visibly. He looked at the soup and got up.

"Let's eat. I know a place with wonderful *cannelloni*."

Menotti went along, though he had, sometime earlier, lost his appetite.

CHAPTER 22

The girl who had typed the memorandum to Perrini had been given the empty beauty parlor downstairs. The place now held a mimeograph machine, desk, electric calculator, typewriter stand with machine, and file cabinets that were mostly empty. On the store window it said, Secretarial Service. Cutter had equipped and painted the place, and the girl received her salary from him. Outside work, which came her way sometimes, was her own.

Walking in and out through the hall he would stick his head through her open door and if she happened to be looking up, he might wave to her. Most of the time she smiled back.

She was much darker than Cutter, including her hair. She wore it neither straight nor Afro but kept it quite short. This gave her face the sort of prominence that made it impossible to overlook her moods. Her eyes, long as Cutter's, showed calmness most of the time, but her mouth, which had a sculpted quality, added the touch of calmly amused, calmly cold, or sometimes not so calmly upset. Her smile changed everything.

She did not have Jerutha's shape, which would look best in a leopard skin, and she was far from the Rosanna type, a basket of big fruit. For Cutter there was no comparison needed. She was her own thing; her own thoughts, her own feelings, her own body.

He leaned in the doorframe and waited till she turned around.

"When you going to be done this eve, Kate?"

"Closing time."

"I got something coming up but should be done, say, ten o'clock. Want to come over for sounds and a drink?"

She swiveled her typist's chair his way, crossed her legs and crossed her arms. She cocked her head.

"You can stop hitting on me, Constable."

"Don't call me that. Doesn't suit me."

"I know that," she said. "The way you keep hitting on me doesn't suit me. Don't you know that?"

"What's right by you, Katy? Dinner no good, drinks no good, let's make it no good, weekend no good."

"All I said was no. That means no. And yes means yes."

"When?"

"When you stop looking at me like you're picking another one of your house kittens, that's when."

Cutter groaned, half meaning it.

"I been *trying*."

"Cutter, when you make it, I'll tell you. Promise."

"Don't say 'make it.' I don't know what that means anymore."

"You will, Cutter, you will." She gave him one more smile which pulled at his roots and then swiveled her chair away and started to type.

He saw what she was working on. The fat index of colleges, listed state by state, lay open to one side. The stack of envelopes she was addressing lay on the other. She was preparing the same letter, over and over, asking whether Lillie was at that school. When somebody had mentioned that Lillie had joined VISTA, he had sent a letter to their Washington address, too. They had never heard of her.

He left the building and walked. Cutter had three hours. The sun was slipping fast. Three hours nothing-time until Perrini-time and no use going over everything in the head, he had it all together, he had it by the balls, he had time. Shoot pool at Tiffany's—go visit the house—take in a movie—have a quarrel with Willie—spit on the sidewalk—call up Gottlieb for a gut-level talk—call the weather number for the word on the winds on the lake—walk.

He did not do any of those things, but then it was time anyway. He stood in the living room of his bungalow and felt ready. Turtleneck white, suit dark. Attaché case black and full of stuff. The black Lincoln Continental Mark IV glistening by the curb. White smoke-tendrils burbling from the exhaust, Dalton to drive him. The Yarby brothers for bodyguards. One a deserter and ex-Marine, the other a health freak who had flunked out of the police academy. They were called Ham and Eggs, but not in front of them.

The silent drive took forty-five minutes. Where the hill country started on the way south they took a cut-off down a blacktop that said 5 Miles to Summer Lane Resort and Hotel. They passed into the grounds through a gate that said Summer Lane once again and through a stand of beech and maple, frost dry and black in the night. To one side there was a black lake, and to the other there rose a spectral assemblage of verandas, porticos, curlicues, bay windows like bubbles, and rows of other windows like teeth. Though the building was a massive three-story structure, it was made to look like filigree with Swiss-chalet dormers and gingerbread towers. One long window was lit under the swoop of the veranda in front and two oval glass-panes showed where the main entrance was. When Dalton eased to a stop under the porte cochere to one side of the building, they could hear the lonely creak of wood. The sound came either from the building or from the stiff trees.

Cutter left Dalton behind the wheel, motor and heater running, and he made the Yarby brothers disappear in the dark by the drive. He walked to the front of the building, past Perrini's empty Mercedes, and into a dim front hall. There was furniture under sheets and there were oil paintings of shadowy hunting scenes. Mostly, there was cold space. Only one double door had light coming through at the sill.

"Good evening, Mister Cutter," said Menotti.

Perrini nodded and Campi did nothing. Two electric heaters glowed at an arrangement of coffee table, couch, standing lamp, and some easy chairs. The rest of the room was a deserted dining hall. Everybody was wearing an overcoat.

"Have a brandy," said Perrini. "Campi, pour him one."

Cutter sat down, unbuttoned his overcoat, and put the attaché case on his knees.

"No, thank you," said Cutter. "I can't handle it."

"You an ex-drunk?"

"No, Mister Perrini."

Menotti was getting nervous about the tone that was developing.

"I refused one before you," he said to Cutter. "With similar results." He made a meek, laughing sound.

"You nervous, Menotti?" Perrini sounded like a teenaged tough.

"We are all a little bit nervous, it would seem. You will learn to appreciate the signs, Mister Cutter. When Francisco here talks like—like that, it usually means he feels, er, he is in some sort of bind."

"Don't patronize me, Menotti."

The menace in the tone did not work. Menotti turned cold.

"I am unable to negotiate in a climate of gross incivility. The subject matter does not deserve it, Mister Cutter does not deserve it, and neither do you. Or would you like me to leave, Francisco?"

Perrini groaned. Cutter could not tell whether it was theatrics or the straight thing. He was used to Perrini's rudeness, but not to his switches in mood.

"I'm sorry, for godsake. Cutter, listen, I'm in a hell of a shape. Let's start over, okay?"

"Fine," said Cutter. "Maybe this will be a good start."

He opened his attaché case and started unpacking.

"Eighty-six thousand, one hundred and twenty-five." He piled six bundled stacks in front of Perrini. A folder of type sheets went to Menotti. "The month's breakdown of income and expenditure. It's in more detail than the memos I've sent you, but the final total comes out the same."

Unexpectedly, Perrini said nothing. He shot a quick grin at Cutter and then looked at Menotti, who had his face down over the sheets.

"Thank you, Mister Cutter," said Menotti. "Beautifully done." Silence. Menotti looked up. "Isn't the total quite high?"

"Yes," said Cutter. "Except for running expenses, I'm turning in the whole take."

"But we had discussed a percentage that ..."

"I reasoned that through afterwards," said Cutter, "and thought it would be neater, or just plain straight, if I kept two things apart. One, the job I got hired to do, which was to clean out the Sidgies. I did that. You paid me twenty thousand for that, which I took off that total. While this was going on, because of hassling and picking up and all that, the busted operations got put back together, at least sort of. Income from those operations is right there in front of you, Mr. Perrini. We have no contract for that part. It's yours."

"Part one, next part two," said Perrini. He looked at Cutter with genuine admiration. Then he turned to Menotti. "Did you get it, *consigliere?*"

Menotti nodded.

"Beautifully done, Mister Cutter."

"And if I want any more of that stuff," Perrini waved at the stacks of money, "I'll know where to get it. One month, and you put the operation together. One month, and you can deliver more gross than I've ever managed in all those years."

Perrini started to laugh. First, he laughed like a grandfather, just chuckling away because the baby had done something funny. Pretty soon it turned into a locker room laugh. It did not end there, because Perrini started to sound like a screeching woman. Cutter looked at Menotti but got no help. Campi came out of the shadows and his jaw hung a little bit open. In a moment, Perrini stopped. He gasped a while, but he was not laughing anymore.

"Pour me one, Campi." He watched the cognac go into the dining room glass. "Give one to Cutter." He looked up and said, "And this time, Cutter, better take it. Or at least keep it handy."

"Let me handle this part," said Menotti.

"Shut up." Perrini drank the stuff down in one toss. Then he leaned on his knees and peered over at Cutter. "You want to tell me about your cut for future deliveries?"

"Here are the figures."

Cutter took the sheet with the contract proposal from his case and handed it to Menotti. Perrini snapped it up, never looked at it, punched the paper into a ball, and tossed it over his shoulder.

"*Now I'm going to tell you about the future!*"

Perrini was screaming. He half rose and kept yelling in Italian. In a while, he sank back down on the couch. He kept talking with a hoarse voice, rapidly.

"Translated into English, cousin, you get no cut. From now on I pay the rent, I pay the men, I set the percentages, and of course I pay the protection. And you, cousin, can go on a salary—or you can go period and out!"

Cutter felt blank for a while.

"I don't get it," he said, looking at Menotti. He had the impression that Menotti did not get it either.

"You don't get it? Then get this, Cutter. This is my way of talking to a crook."

"*What?*"

"What happened to the ten thousand you didn't account for?"

"On deposit for salary. It's right on that sheet."

"What salary? Where's it say *what* salary, cousin?"

"I hired my own actuary. I wasn't sure I could rely on getting odds in time while everything—"

"*You* hired your *own?* You were taking over my end of the operation! Next, maybe, you're going to buy your own wire service?"

"Keep this up, Perrini, and maybe I will."

For just one instant Perrini caught the change in tone, a tone he had not heard from Cutter before, just as Cutter had never before omitted the "mister." But Perrini had too much momentum to change his direction. If this bulldozing maneuver was going to work at all, it better happen—it must happen.

"And while I'm at this, cousin Cutter, talking about your funny ways of trying to do business with me, it says right here in that column," and Perrini tapped one of the sheets on the table, "it says right here, while I'm looking at it, that you put out more in expenses than I ever paid out to you!"

That was sharp, thought Cutter. That piece of information was fairly well hidden. Careless. Overdoing it, while trying to make an impression.

"You're right," he said. "So what?"

"So what, he says. You hear when he said so what, Campi? Now, cousin. All that means to me, you're being tricky! And when you're tricky with me, you son of a bitch, I don't come back handing out cuts of my business! *Where'd you get the money?*"

"Sharking," said Cutter.

That stopped Perrini for a moment.

"Sharking," he repeated. He talked in a low voice, but getting fast again fairly soon. "He goes into loans. What percentage, Cutter? Five a week? Twenty a week?"

"Five per cent."

It did not stop Perrini.

"Five per a week and you make enough to handle that kind of difference?" He tapped on the paper again. "And all that, on five per, in less than a month? You know how much money you'd have to put into circulation to—" Perrini just breathed for a while. A few times he breathed "*minquia.*" Then he smiled a very unfriendly smile, right at Cutter.

"You made even more, didn't you? You opened a full-scale sharking operation and never let it show on that shiny business report. Why should you? Wasn't it my money you were putting into circulation, eh?" He leaned forward again and acted confidential. "How much did you take out of that safe, eh, cousin?"

"Fuck off," said Cutter.

This time Perrini did not ignore the tone. He now got very ugly himself.

"I'll shut you down. Not another cent in protection."

"Won't work, Perrini. I'll have to retrench, but nothing's going to come apart. That's what you're after, isn't it? Can't figure why, but don't matter. I got the organization and it's built so you can never touch it. I got the business going to a swinging start, and I got cash in reserve. Even if you did bust me up, man don't you know yet you can't ever make it in the Belt on your own? Get with it, man. You can crowd me all you want, but you can't do without me!"

"You threatening me, you black son of a bitch? The last time one of your brothers started bothering me with his high and mighty organization—"

"You—" said Cutter. He half rose, then sat down again. "You pushed the pigs and the politicians to bust Asikari's thing!"

"And so help me God, if I didn't send you to jail that time by intention, I'll damn well do it now!"

Cutter felt the trembling start inside, the shivering which would empty him out, make a hole, make him flat like a desert. But that did not happen now. The trembling became heat, and the heat turned to hate. He sucked it down into himself and saw that he could move with surprising precision. He started to gather the papers up. He never touched the money. He put the papers into his case, snapped it shut. Then he looked at Perrini as if he did not know him. He sounded dead calm.

"You just busted us up." He thought of saying more, that no honkie could ever bust him up anymore, could not even find him in the middle of his safety anymore, but he let it go, because he did not quite know how to say it. He shrugged and looked at the old stranger again. "Why'd you do it?"

Perrini did not look good. His breathing came badly and his color was wrong. Menotti touched his nose, then took over.

"May I tell him, Francisco?"

"Doesn't matter. I got my way." He looked as if his way had cost him a few years of his life.

"In an effort to salvage—let me begin differently, Mister Cutter. The unique pressure that produced—er, this destructive maneuver—Let me start over, Mister Cutter. Don Santino is sending Angelo back."

To Menotti's shock, Cutter started to laugh. It was a sound like metal on metal, hurting the bones and the nerves. When it stopped, Menotti picked up as quickly as he could.

"We have no way of preventing the move. I won't go into its sources, but it is a development that is bound to be extremely costly to all of us." Menotti sighed a sigh of loyalty, no matter what his personal judgment. "Mister Perrini, in his extremity, decided to make the, uh, return maneuver very much less attractive. You follow me, I believe."

"Wreck the Belt. Then what's to come back for?"

"On that order. Frankly, Mister Cutter, I would have handled it differently. I would have invited your cooperation, please don't ask me how at this very moment, I would ...."

"You stupid son of a bitch," said Cutter. He said it very calmly, looking straight at Perrini. "No different from that lame fossil who thinks sending his family name into the jungle is all it takes to tame the animals. And if you can't have it your way, like every brainless honk in the world, you smash it to shit." He looked at Menotti now. "You follow me, I believe."

"Er, yes. I wouldn't put it quite the same way."

"Forget it," said Cutter. He opened his attaché case again and kept talking, this time to Perrini. "You said to me, kill him, and I said I had a better way. But you don't listen. You thought maybe using your daughter, how the Don's right hand made a fallen woman of her, you thought that might bring pressure. Couldn't do it, could you? Couldn't kill him either, could you? Instead—"

"Campi!" But there was not enough force behind it to make Campi do anything dramatic. Campi just moved a little closer, until Cutter waved at him and Campi stopped.

"You could have saved yourself the expense of using me like you did. Here," and he tossed the manila envelope on the table. "Show that to the Don. Tell him to scrap Angelo. Or else the Forza name is going to be nothing but a shithouse joke wherever that name used to mean anything."

There were seven 10x12 in. high-gloss reproductions of Angelo loving it with the biggest black rough-trade buck the world had ever seen. In two of the arrangements, Angelo seemed to have swooned with it. In the others he was clearly conscious, his face stretched in a terror of passion.

"I ask you," said Cutter. "Who's going to send that little white queen out into the black jungle?"

Menotti was wiping his glasses, at first with the end of his tie, and then by mistake with his fingers. Campi let out an involuntary giggle. Perrini had sweat on his face, thinking—while he still could—of the useless, the treacherous muck in his head, where he had believed he had brains. The spittle ran out of his mouth, the pain ran like acid up the inside of his arm and went searing into his chest. His eyes saw mustard, then milk, then nothing at all.

Campi drove the Mercedes with Perrini lying in back. He drove at a violent speed, while the sounds of breathing came and went as unpredictably as the winter gusts on Lake Erie. Menotti accepted the invitation to join Cutter for the ride back to town. They had a discussion that made much more sense than anything Perrini had been able to offer.

CHAPTER 23

On the next day, it started to snow. It was the cold, tiny kind that came and went and blew around in flurries, making the whole day look the same. Cutter watched the snow from an upstairs window. Occasionally a gust of wind struck the pane with a whoomp.

"It looks like it will never let up."

Kate looked up at him but did not answer. She turned back to her work and flicked a few pages around. Cutter walked to her desk and looked over her shoulder. She was doing the Lillie letters.

"Take a ride with me?" he asked.

She looked up, then put her head down again. "What about these?"

"What about these," he said to the window. "Let's forget about these."

While Kate got her coat from the hanger, Cutter took the sheet out of the machine and dropped it into the basket on the floor by the typing table.

They took his car, and he worked it through the streets and the snow up on the turnpike. He took the first off-ramp to the lake. There was a lot of flat land and a few houses, shut for the winter.

"You pick empty places," she said.

He nodded, and when they came to the lake and could drive no further, he stopped and looked at the water disappear in the sky or the sky melting into the water. The snow was blowing.

"Rough and clean," he said. "Like before the people came."

"Not the friendliest place to be."

He smiled straight ahead and jerked his thumb over his shoulder.

"Not back there, either."

She watched his profile and touched it.

"You're not rough and you're not clean, Cutter, but I'll go back there with you and make it the friendliest place."

They spent that long afternoon in the bungalow with the front door locked and all the shades drawn on the windows, except for the one in the bedroom upstairs. When they lay the right way on the bed they could see the blowing in the sky, no horizon, and the light which could be anytime.

When it was dark, he got ready. He dressed in that formal way he had adopted, but for this trip he took no attaché case along. Menotti had all that was needed, and Menotti would do most of the talking.

Kate had his bathrobe on, big and loose, and when she lifted her arms to put them over his shoulders, the whole thing opened up in front in the most casual way. Cutter was reminded of the phrase she had used, about making this the friendliest place to be, but he said nothing about it. He felt shy and secretive with the thought. She kissed him on the chin.

"Worried?"

"Not worried. Little spaced out, but not worried."

"You're a success," she said. "You've made it."

He grinned, rumpled her short, strong hair.

"I said that once and the answer it got me was: That makes you a bad example."

"Depends on the user," she said. "Last kiss?"

"Last kiss."

When he walked out of the house, the night was immobile with cold and the snow had stopped falling. Cutter's parade sat by the curb with all the motors humming. His black Lincoln was in the middle, with Dalton at the wheel and the two brothers in the back seat. Cutter looked in and nodded at them. The lead car held four men. Willie sat in the front, next to the driver, and the two others sat in the rear. One of them flicked on the dome light and grinned. Cutter nodded back at him. Willie made a fist and raised his thumb, which was a species of salute he had learned five years ago. He winked at Cutter and Cutter winked back. The tail car held another four men. Cutter checked them through the window and they nodded at him. One of them even waggled his gun in the air, he was so excited about everything. Then Cutter got in next to Dalton and the caravan moved away from the curb. If Cutter had looked, he would have seen Kate by a window, looking after him.

The lead car set a conservative pace, which meant it took the caravan over two hours to reach the deserted hotel.

The winter access and the deserted house looked much the same to Cutter, except that all of the downstairs windows, all of the long veranda, and a wide sweep of the lawn in front were lit up. Somebody had even turned on the lights on the dock. The visible part of the lake shone like onyx.

Four cars that Cutter had not seen before were spaced along the curve of the drive. There was a basic Chevrolet which probably belonged to Menotti. The other three cars were limousines, at least one of which was custom-built. It sat closest to the steps leading into the house. The roof was high, an aerodynamic offense but a convenience to the passenger on the inside. The right rear door swept into the shape of the roof, so that there need be no stooping on entering or leaving the upholstery of the rear compartment. However, there were no seats in the rear, except for a single, small folding variety. Cutter remembered that Don Santino Forza came packaged in a wheel chair.

When his own cars had spaced themselves in the same pattern as the limousines, Cutter and his two bodyguards walked around the Forza machine and went up on the veranda. The two men at the entrance door nodded. Cutter had seen no one else outside. He saw two more at the door to the dining room, same nod, same manner of passage, and next the dining hall.

It had not been lit the last time. The room was cold and immense. There was an odd contrast in the festiveness of the chandeliers shining under the ceiling and the warehouse effect of stacked tables along one of the walls. A row of French windows looked out at nothing. There were a few dead flies on the floor.

Five anonymous men stood spaced about the room. One of them sat on the couch that Cutter remembered. No one else was there.

The man in the couch got up and walked over. "Mister Cutter?"

"Right."

"My name's Longstreet. I'd like to ask you to have your men wait outside."

Cutter did not know how to handle that. He could feel the two brothers tense up, moving away from him slightly in order to get a better field.

"What about them?" asked Cutter. He nodded at the anonymous men standing around. The question sounded stupid in his own ears.

"They're only here in case you didn't come in alone. You carry a weapon?"

"Just my men do."

"Then why don't you ask your men to wait outside and I'll send ours out at the same time. Reasonable?"

With or without bodyguards, if anybody wanted to wipe Cutter out, they could do it. And if he did not want Santino Forza to leave alive—whatever good that would do him—there were two carloads of his own very sharp button men waiting outside.

The whole thing was ridiculous, a stage-setting for a fossil who could trace a bloodline but could not read a balance sheet.

Cutter nodded his head and stepped back against the wall. Forza's men and his bodyguards walked out of the dining room. Cutter stayed by the wall, and Longstreet went back to his couch. It was quiet and barren now. No theatrics. Cutter felt danger.

He watched Longstreet light a cigarette, which made a tiny sound. Out in front, near the cars, somebody seemed to be laughing. There was another sound, from one of the doors that led to the kitchen or the serving pantry perhaps. Cutter was not even sure there had been a sound. "Where's Mister Forza?" he asked finally.

"In conference, I guess."

Longstreet, who was about the same age as Cutter, watched the smoke of his cigarette. When he saw Cutter looking at him he smiled casually.

Then he smoked casually. Cutter envied the man his ease.

"In conference with Menotti?"

"Yes. They came shortly before you did. Together with Angelo."

"He's here?"

"Of course. Right-hand man, and so forth. You knew that, didn't you?"

Cutter looked away. He did not want to answer. His answers depended, once again, on something that somebody else was doing.

Now that he knew what to listen for he could hear the sounds from the door in back and make it out as a conversation. He could not understand a word, but he knew that three people were talking.

Actually, he heard only two. The first was an even sound, a monotone, a Menotti sound. The second always ended on an unfinished high note, like a climb that had nowhere to go. The third was distinguishable by its silence. Two voices holding still, and a third that held them. Cutter could not tell how the third one did it.

In a while, Cutter said, "How's Angelo?"

"I can't say. I'm not one of the family." Longstreet was filing his nails.

At that point the sounds on the other side of the door changed their co-ordination. There was an overlap, there was even the added sound of a third voice, and then one of them took over while the others, by and by, dropped away. One now. A ranting, clawing, spiraling sound that became purely screech. After hanging up there for a painful length of time, the voice started to slip and tumble, as if something were collapsing under its own weight. Even Longstreet turned around with some interest.

The door in back flew open and hit the wall. Angelo came out.

He was going fast until he was in the large, empty room. He slowed in an awkward way and took a few more steps.

"Longstreet?" he said.

"Yes, sir." It sounded attentive enough, but Longstreet stayed in his seat.

"Where are my men?"

"Your men, sir?"

"Where are the men that were supposed to be here?"

"I sent them out, sir."

It was hard to tell what was going on inside Angelo, because he stood very still and he was wearing the glasses.

That dead stillness, thought Cutter, I know that stillness. He saw the other man in a desert of his own.

Angelo started to walk across the room. He moved as if all his joints were new to him, as if his body were not really his own. He made very little noise and he did not say a word. When he closed the door to the hall behind him there was just the tiniest snap of the latch.

The door in back stayed open and then the Don came in. He whispered across the floor in his chair with the smoothness of a mechanical thing, a shrunken man.

Cutter saw mostly the head. It was large, with a hard face, and an impressive mane of white hair. Where the eyes should have been, Cutter looked at a set of small black glasses.

Don Santino Forza stopped. The chair stopped. The man himself did not seem to have moved at all. Menotti arrived near the chair a moment later. He smiled across at Cutter and put his hands into his overcoat pockets.

Cutter moved across the floor and stopped near the chair. The old man made a motion with his mouth, as if he were sucking his plates into place. The black glasses were looking at Cutter.

"He's not *very* black."

Cutter held his upper lip in his teeth. He thought he had never heard such an ugly voice. It was rich and calm but had said something very cheap.

The manila envelope was in Santino Forza's lap. He picked it up and waggled it toward Longstreet.

"In the fireplace," said Forza. "Burn it."

Nothing else was said while Longstreet did as he was told. When Longstreet was done, Forza said,

"What's it look like, Cutter?"

A thousand answers, a thousand dangers—

"I'm in," said Cutter.

Of all the possible answers, no matter what happened next, it was the only one that made Cutter feel he had done his best.

"Let me put it this way," said Menotti. He sounded the way he always did, searching for the precise statement and quite certain that he would eventually find it. "Essentially, your operation in the Belt will remain the same. We can discuss the details of percentages and outside participation at another time—what it boils down to is that we control the wire, the protection, and the limits of your territory—"

"What about Angelo Forza, Don Santino?" said Cutter.

"There is no Angelo Forza."

I'm in!

Cutter heard Menotti talking, the qualifying phrases and the matters of clarification, a lawyer's talk droning on while he, Cutter, tried to absorb the event of his success.

"… Perrini due to retire at any rate, which means, in effect, you will report to me," Menotti was saying. "There is no change, otherwise."

No change. What in hell do they know about change?

"You listening?" The old man sounded harsh.

"Yes. Right."

"You're a success, you heard that part?"

"I know it."

"On probation. Maybe you didn't hear that part," said Santino Forza.

If this had been the warden, Cutter would have had a struggle to keep from buckling under, but this legendary monster in a wheelchair was not his warden. If Cutter needed all the Forzas, then all the Forzas needed him.

"Anything else?" said Cutter.

They seemed a little surprised and did not say anything. Cutter nodded and turned to go.

"The negatives," said Forza.

Cutter did not walk back towards the chair but just turned around.

"Shit, man," he said. "You know damn well they don't make one fucking difference."

Santino Forza did not move or say anything, except for one flick of his mouth which might have been something like a smile. Cutter walked out.

He walked through the hall, across the veranda, down the drive, and to his car. The Forza men stood the way they had stood before, except they looked a little bit more like human beings who were bored or cold in the winter night and were waiting for the word that they could go home. Cutter's three cars were burbling white smoke from their exhausts, and all the men were back in their seats. Cutter waved at them and they could all see him grinning. He slammed the car door after himself, and Dalton put the car into gear.

"Didn't take long," he said.

"I had it before I walked in," said Cutter. "Any trouble out here?"

"Naw. The others drove around some, but none of the Forza guns moved a muscle."

Cutter's three cars made a procession through the woods and swung down the five-mile stretch of road that led back to the turnpike. Cutter checked the lead car and the one that was trailing. He sighed and pushed back into his seat.

"They'll peel off in the Belt," he said. "You take me straight on down to the bungalow. What I saying is, right on up to the friendliest place."

Dalton nodded and the two brothers in back laughed.

The Lincoln bucked on a hump of snow and kept going. The lead car, because of the Lincoln's motion, blared its tail lights for a moment and then kept going too.

"They sure treats you like the precious thing you become this night," said Dalton. "You speed up, they do. You go in the ditch, they do. How's that feel, Cutter?"

The Lincoln bucked again. This time the road was smooth. Dalton stepped on the gas but nothing happened.

"A lemon," said Dalton, while one of the brothers in back leaned over to see the front.

"How come that dial says this mother's outa gas?"

"I filled this tank—" Dalton started to say but at that point the big car started to hang on its gears. The whole long mass of it seemed to hump, then it dragged itself to a stop.

The brake lights of the lead car flared red and the headlights of the tag first grew big, then bounced, and became immobile.

For one moment, Cutter was immobile too. Before he had the chance to get his door open, his button men from the front and the rear had bounced out of their cars and came milling around the Lincoln. One of them opened Cutter's door.

"Lemme give you a hand," he said.

Cutter was out of the car, and then he looked at the man. He had never seen him before. He did not bother to check the others but went with the bright burst of fright or anger that blew up inside his muscles. He leaped toward the empty stretch of snow to the side of the road. When he knew that he was running on solid ground he heard the three shots by the Lincoln. He would keep running as long as he could. Three shots. Dalton. They got him and Ham and Eggs in back of the car.

There was an unreal sense of being out of it, making it out of the light and into the nothing-snow up ahead. The impact was so bad that for one long moment Cutter did not know he was no longer running.

He lifted his face out of the snow, turned on his back, had a beginning notion to test his joints and see if he might have broken an ankle. The shape over him was black and featureless in front of the glare on the road. How ugly, he thought, and his voice said, "Fuckin' honkie trick!"

"Naw, Kisu. You were a success."

Cutter saw the way Willie held the gun out, holding the gun wrist with the other hand.

"You made it," said Willie. "But it's a bad example."

"Asikari said that!"

"All of us, Cutter. It's either you, or all of us."

There was no time for the black pit to open or the desert to spread, but maybe those terrible places would not have come back to him anyway. Because he thought of a wild, clean place without people, and his head blew apart.

THE END